REDEMPTIC

Joseph O'Connor was born in Dublin. He has written thirteen books, including five previous novels: *Cowboys and Indians*, *Desperadoes*, *The Salesman*, *Inishowen* and most recently *Star of the Sea*, which became an international bestseller, winning the *Irish Post* Award for Literature, an American Library Association Award, France's Prix Millepages and the Prix Madeleine Zepter for European Novel of the Year. His work has been published in twenty-nine languages.

JOSEPH O'CONNOR

Redemption Falls

VINTAGE BOOKS
London

Published by Vintage 2008

1 3 5 7 9 10 8 6 4 2

Copyright © Joseph O'Connor 2007

Joseph O'Connor has asserted his right under the Copyright, Designs
and Patents Act 1988 to be identified as the author of this work

First published in Great Britain in 2007 by
Harvill Secker
Random House, 20 Vauxhall Bridge Road,
London SW1V 2SA

www.vintage-books.co.uk

Addresses for companies within The Random House Group Limited
can be found at: www.randomhouse.co.uk/offices.htm

The Random House Group Limited Reg. No. 954009

A CIP catalogue record for this book
is available from the British Library

ISBN 9780099481522

The Random House Group Limited supports The Forest Stewardship
Council (FSC), the leading international forest certification
organisation. All our titles that are printed on Greenpeace approved
FSC certified paper carry the FSC logo. Our paper procurement
policy can be found at: www.rbooks.co.uk/environment

Mixed Sources
Product group from well-managed
forests and other controlled sources
www.fsc.org Cert no. TT-COC-2139
© 1996 Forest Stewardship Council

Printed and bound in Great Britain by
CPI Bookmarque, Croydon CR0 4TD

In fond memory of my father-in-law,
John Casey

PART I

THE END OF WAR

The speeches fine – now riven shreds –
Despatches frayed – the statues shatter'd –
The maps are burnt to flakes of ash –
The General's papers, rent and scatter'd.

Letters home from fear-drunk boys –
In rags of banners, disarrayed –
The anthems torn to silent leaves –
Of these, the Book of War is made.

Charles Gimenez Carroll
(pseudonym of Lucia-Cruz McLelland-O'Keeffe)
'Lines on the Rebel Surrender at Appomattox'
from *American Verses*, 1867

*. . . It no body . . . got no ken . . . how it go for woman that time . . .
in especial she poor . . . you ain a thing but a beast . . . cause a
poorman gwine care for what beast he got . . . but a woman . . .
just the stones on his road . . .*

Elizabeth Longstreet, formerly a slave. Recorded 1928.
Transcriber unknown.

CHAPTER I

MOTHERLESS CHILD

A YEAR IN THE LIFE OF ELIZA DUANE MOONEY

Her leave-taking – The strangeness of time – A fat man – Little Rock
John Cory & his family – The lustful preacher

The quarter-light was rising as she hurried out from Baton Rouge: through the criminal districts of town, then the black section, then the Irish, past the clustered Union sentries on the Telegraph road, the maws of Federal cannons ranked and aimed toward the north, then onward over the viaduct into barricaded swampland where once, not long ago, the slaves had toiled. It was January the 17th, 1865. The end of the War was coming.

Walking away from a scalpeen shack. The grits of the road on road-skinned soles. Grind of the shingles into lacerated arches. Dazzle of pain, the cramps through the hamstrings, and the hopeless prayers for shoes.

It took her almost a month to slog across Louisiana. Fifteen miles a day. Twenty-six thousand paces. A soldier, vittled and booted, might have deserted at such a burden. Eliza Duane Mooney did not.

She had not been long walking when it started to happen. Everything was coming to merit attention. A rice-field. Two flies. A dead chicken-hawk in a gully. The eyes of hungry alligators resentful in the slime. All of it seemed equal, which is one definition of madness. The weight of the world had lost proportion.

There were days when she hobbled until the world began to shimmer. The sky billowed around her like the folds of apocalypse and the white-hot egg of pain in her breast threatened to crack with a seepage of venom. She would lie wherever she fell, gaping up at the crows – would crawl from the road if she was able. Whatever burned to hatch must be palliated by stillness. She came to believe it could hear her.

Riders went by, or waggons full of men. Nobody stopped. Perhaps they did not see her. This is what she would tell herself as she shivered in the ditches. I am becoming invisible now.

April comes in. Time is moving strangely. Tenses grow confused.

Near El Dorado, Arkansas, a stockman is yammering to some farm-women. Lee is defeated! The rebellion no more! Jefferson Davis in shackles, they say, arrested in a woman's corsets! As she approaches the huddle, the settlers gape at her like goslings. It must be that they can smell her, she thinks.

The minstrel boy to the war has gone. In the ranks of death you'll find him.

A fat man regards her, eyes crinkling in the sunlight. 'Get walkin, daughter. Aint nothin for you here.' As if to italicize the rejection, he pulls back the hem of his coat, beneath which is a cane in a scabbard like a sword's. She is not thinking about the dismissal (she is accustomed to dismissal) but about the antiqueness of his accent, the poetry he talks. Git waukin, dauduh. Ain nuthn fow y heä. His vowels go bouncing on the air.

His father's sword he has girded on. And his wild harp slung behind him.

She pictures the journey as a procession of scarlet ants stretching out from the bayouland to the bastions of the Rockies. She is not truly walking fifteen hundred miles. She is crushing ants one step at a time.

Come Christmas she will be seventeen. 1865. The year the South surrendered. She has no memory of any place beyond the town of her childhood, not even of being in New Orleans with her mother. The edge of the world is the County Line. Stepping over its verge is a trespass. She is out beyond the frame of all that was given, into a land where almost everything is strange. The customs of the people. Their figures of speech. The taste of creek water. That spider on a leaf. Cherokees observing her from the crests of those hummocks. The shattering nothingness of spaces between settlements.

This was the country they'd been killing each other for. These stone walls and levees. Those barns and stunted swards. It was barely an old man's life ago that none of it was here, when the land was only the land, not acreage. Unfenced, ungridded, unmeasured, unbequeathable, a continent of forests the size of nations. The Indians named the rivers; many banks they left anonymous. Then the immigrants came to America.

She had on a tattered hand-me-down her mother once gave her: a rough-cut grogram smock like a knight's tabard of old. 'Shenick's of London' stitched into the label. In its pocket, a slingshot. A bundling on her back. That garment was the only wearing she possessed in the world. She slept in it, walked in it. It had become a kind of skin.

In the bundle, a storybook, dilapidated, spinecracked, and a canister of medicinal foot powder, and a crumpled letter. The powder proved a waste of her last four cents. She suspects it is nothing but pestled-down chalk. She may as well rub in the cinders of the road for all the alleviation it brings.

The Redeemer never wrote. Only once in the dust. Never put nothing on paper. Walked fifteen hundred mile out of Palestine Texas, howled many a field-holler on the way. He was hipshot at Gettysburg, blinded in the Wilderness, torched alive at Shiloh, gutted at Manassas, and He shrieked the rebel yell as they diced for his uniform: *Mother, why have you forsaken me?*

Sometimes by moonlight, or when she pauses to rest, she takes out the storybook and riffles its pages. The feel of the flimsies Eliza finds comforting, more than the words stained onto them. Thou Shalt Not Kill. I shall cause them to fall. Their carcasses will I give to be meat for the fowls. If you counted all the words in that thick rustling book, they would be fewer than the dead of the War.

And some of those who died were Ephesians or Jerusalems, Maccabees and Canaanites, Golgothas and Samaritans. But most were only *ands* and *ifs* and *ye's*, small and unmemorable, devoid of authority, only significant for the matters they link, never worth quoting or immortalizing in a place-name, because those are the ones that will always do the dying when it comes a time of war. And you wouldn't really miss them until you tried to speak, at which point you would find yourself struck by the absence that is felt between those who love or hate, or sensed in the oceans of the self: the wanted word is somehow not here. It was murdered; edited out of the inheritance. What you say, instead, is what you know how to say, and not what you would like to: the truth.

When it rained she was drenched. On hot days she burned. Time continued moving in ways she did not understand. A minute takes an hour on hardscrabble road but a morning skitters by if you're resting. Often she thinks of a story her mother used to tell. The fiddler inveigled by a faerywoman on the road into Connemara, who enters her rath, plays for her a single night, but when he stumbles out at dawn, blinking, love-drunk, he finds ten years have passed. You can lose you a life in a single night. Mamo's stories were facts, not fancies.

The skin on her arms is flaking to rice paper. She blisters in sunroar. Her skin will not toughen. She counts as she walks, to murder the road. She gropes for a history that Mamo once read to her. And when even the sight of the trees becomes strange, as can happen in country you do not know, she finds herself inventing their names:

Heartsfire. Gallowspole. Lovers-in-Winter. Magwitch. Hookbough. The Convict's Nails.

In the forest is a temple. In the temple, a box. In the box is a needle. And the needle mends a dress. And the dress is put on by a jilted contessa. And she falls for a fiddler. But he is promised to a faery. And on like that; each stride of the story a punctuation of her steps on the road.

And the story never ends. It spindles out like a web, a netting of filigrees twisting into a petticoat. It trails a way back to Baton Rouge, Louisiana: an egg-sack waiting to burst. And you could never smirch paper with the words of this story, because a bookstory must be straight and true as a ballad, where a life is not like that, not sliceable into stanzas nor even truly capable of narration in one tense. The past is not over, so it seems to Eliza Mooney, and the future has happened many times.

Through ghost towns. Through bread riots. Across skookum-chucks of rivers. These extents between the towns she dreams as a grid. In the dreams she is flying, but with turtlelike slowness, looking down on the longitudes, which are rods of blinding light. Sometimes a sibilant buzz can be heard. Other times, churchlike silence.

She fashions little snares out of saplings and thorns. You can kill a wren that way but there is no eating in a wren. Over sloughs. Wading creeks. Through the high, cold canyons. She sklents like a crab through a dustbowl.

There are days when the walking takes on the abstractedness of rhythm, when she feels, through the misting of pain and hunger, as though her feet are revolving the planet beneath her, turning it like a prisoner's on a treadmill. An eerie sensation: she is turning the world. It withstands, it resists, all the way to its kernel. But then slowly it succumbs; it is crushed into obedience. She is walking to stand still, not to travel into a story. Walking to make the story stop.

A farrier and his lad in the roar of a forge, chiseling a fetter off a black man's ankle. He is shaking, the black man, his hand on the boy's head. Sparks spurt with each krang of the hammer.

Grufts of road dirt are matting her hair. The smock chafes her back. Scrofula makes her tear at herself. Her fingernails go scrivening, scriggling, scratching, but the itch never truly recedes. A drunk heaves a cobble at her. Where did he get a cobble? She scuttles through a bombed-out graveyard.

Malnourished, sickening, through dreamdrifts: memories. But perhaps they are not recollections; rather predictions. The plunk of a banjo calls to mind a Good Friday. Gull-calls. Curtained Christs. The sizzle of gumbo. Oysters the size of a baby's fist. The head of a crawfish oozing in the sun. A pelican alighting on a black metal balcony, gulping at the hornets as they vex it. A widower, a Creole, was her client that afternoon. He'd had his butler go into the streets to hire her.

'*J' suis riche*,' said the rich man, by way of introduction. '*Ma table c'est la meilleure du sud*.' He told her he loved her, would do anything for her; kept asking her to call him *mon mari*. He wanted her to ride him. Wanted to kiss. Wanted her wearing this wedding gown. Wanted her from behind with the skirts about her flanks. Wanted her to whisper: *Je viens*. The blemish around his finger where his wedding band had been: where was the ring now, she wondered. And near the end of their contracted time, as they coupled, as they writhed, he had drawn one of her feet to his gasping mouth and sucked on her heel as though it was a fruit, and wept like a hungering baby. And she knew it would be over before too long. It was always nearly over if they wept.

> *The ash, the oak, the yew, the elder,*
> *The plane, the pine, the fir, the alder.*
> *The tribes of Galway, the heavenly host,*
> *The Father, Son and Holy Ghost.*

She is in four-four time. A bag of tunes gone walking. It is as though this Via Crucis is being overseen by a conductor. Even her visions seem to click like a metronome and the road she measures in beats.

Sweat stings her eyes. Her body is scalding. But she knows, for she learned at her mother's knee, that if you only persevere – '*persever*', Mamo pronounced it – your steps will prevail over any earthly road, no matter its hardness or the dangers by its edge, just as time, in its droplets of the unnoticed seconds, will eventually hollow a way through your lifestone.

> *Mother of Christ, Star of the Sea,*
> *Mary, my mother, pray for me.*

And the land unspools like a painted diorama. And on she lurches through the foddery air: through dreekings of rain, then hurtful heat, and clouds of fly-filled pollen. Past squadrons of veterans limping home from the slaughter. Past bummers roasting rabbits on the jags of broken bayonets. Past burnt-out barns and ransacked villages and meadowlands

7

blooming with improvised crosses, by smoke-scorched mansions and the rubble-stones of homesteads, through Atlantics of head-high wheat.

It is I, Eliza Mooney, saw the works of the Lord. And I saw the hand of His enemies.

There are men strung together like beads in the meadows. Who can they be? Surely not slaves. There are no slaves any more in this manumitted nation where everything has changed and nothing has changed. The poor, Jesus said, will always be with us. And He never spoke a word about slaves.

Then rain on the steeples of Little Rock, Arkansas. Rain in the streets, in the stinking alleys. How it surges, the rain! Its gush is applause! Militia in the square. A scaffoldage being erected. Garlands, buntings are sagging damply, their reds and blues oozing into bridal whites. The fart of a tuba. The flap and whip of flags. And a hog is being roasted on a preposterous spit. And hawkers tout beans and cornbread and slumgullion, crescents of fat-faced cantaloupe. And a shout-Baptist preacher will baptize you in his barrel – *be saved, be saved, o my backslidden siblings!* – if only you will receive him.

Jugglers and tumblers. A fire-eater. A band. Belles in gray sashes with peacock-feather fans. Mummers, drummers: a bearded lady. St George and the Dragon dueling in masque. And as sundown comes reddening the columns of Arkansas, on limps the parade of beaten survivors, the Johnnies come marching home. And they wave to their mothers, who weep and run, and they pose for photographers, thumbs stuck in belt-loops, and those without arms cradle their stumps like sick birds, and a veteran comes rolling himself along the boulevard in a bowl while flare-bursts and firecrackers and rockets' red glare crackle through the dusk-darkened clouds. And you wish you were in Dixie, hurray, hurray, and the pipes are a-calling for Danny Boy, and all of it as watched by Eliza Duane Mooney as though it had anything to do with her.

Beat the drum slowly and play the fife lowly. Everyone is screaming. You might almost think they won. The speeches are defiant, hailed by gunshots and roars (*God Bless the Confederate States of America!*), which the conquering officers must surely have forbidden, but obedience goes the way of the Catherine wheels. She picks a few pockets but the pickings are scanty. There are only a couple of dollars when the reckoning is done. Scarcely enough for a bed and a meal; and anyway she is whipped from the inns.

The rain don't quit for four long days and the levee is fixing to break. Sewage in rivulets dribbles from the gullies. Muleteers arrive from deep

8

in the backlands, the out-country no one has mapped. Prisoners are unchained in order to sandbag the banks. A screed of a spiritual from the porch of a pox-hospital, commingling with the stench of urine.

> Some time I feel like a motherless child
> So far away from home.

The alleys are colder than those of Baton Rouge. Hoboes gamble for deadmen's clothes. *Pocketa-pocketa* says the train in her head, its music bubbling up through the mud. Urchins sleep in busted drains, fumbling at the cold as though it might be persuaded to blanket them. She walks the richer street, where there are trees, porches. Through the windows she sees families – she assumes they must be families, for the children resemble the adults but are graver, more formal, and little is being said at the tables as they eat. But they do not truly eat: they fork and pingle, gawping at the home-come fathers. You should never look at a child through a window at night, for his growing will be stunted if you do.

The twister skirls up. She shuffles though a downpour of frogs. She plucks them out of her hair, her pockets, her bundle: they feel like palpitating hearts. Such a rain is not possible, not in this godforsaken world, but miracles happen in the Indian territories and the faithless call them plagues.

Often in the towns she glimpses her mother. A shawlie begging, a nightwalker plying, a crone on a rummage for scraps. You can brew secret herbs to help grow you a baby and others to put one away. And she wonders why her mother did not put her away, if she knew how it was done, which she did. Perhaps for love; perhaps fear of retribution. Are love and fear cousins, like hunger and gloom? For the Irish are besotted with that moonshine of mambo, with their faeries and she-ogues and pookas and pishogues and druidry and evil eye. Bogeymen, cluricaunes, morrigans, will-o-the-wakes. The skies over Carna rustle thick with flapping craythurs: like living in a bat-cave over there. They came over on the coffinships with the keening and the jig steps. They roosted up the masts dropping guano on the famished, and the faithful are wading in faeryshite yet: they were gusted across the billows by the reeking breath above them as it roared the oratorios of vengeance. They are in it right up to their wishbones, she feels; their hobbledehoy Irish holes.

That voodoo they bring, that shriek of the keening. Your way of looking back, of saying you never left. When her belly is full, which it sometimes is in Fort Smith, for that camp-town abounds with pregnant

9

trashcans, she swears that the future, if there is any future, will not be like the past of her mother. But when hunger returns, the gloom holds its claw, and she knows there is no prospect worth having.

A bedsheet draped sideways on the gable of a grain store, russet-stained, as though commemorating a wedding night. She approaches, for it is lucky to kiss the hem of such a relic. But the closer she advances, the clearer she sees. The blemish is not a bloodstain; it is a daub of red words. *Be RENT ye Stars and Stripes!*

She awakens in a scutch-yard where pullets are scratching. The moon is half-full, wearing bruised purple eyes. The night smells of rain, of goats and fresh dung. She has no recollection of how she came to be here.

'Won't you come in the house?' asks the farmwoman tearfully. 'We don't got us much. But we can give you a plate of food.' The woman might be forty. She is wearing a muslin pinafore. There are little dots of red where her cheekbones come to a point. A goat-eyed husband materializes with a loaf, which he proffers. 'Take it. Go head. You bless us if you do. I'm John Cory. This my wife. In't no cause to be scared.' There is Irish in his talking. His woman is a Swede. How beautiful, her yellow hair in the lamplight.

A trio of gaunt children creep forth from the shadows. The tallest girl is hefting an infant in swaddles. 'Rest you a while. An't no one harm you here. You can sleep in the haggard, you don't want to come in the house. But you're welcome on our place. We thank God to know you.' She is unnerved by uncomplicated kindliness, having encountered it so rarely. While the Corys are sleeping, she limps from their haggard, leaves the loaf on their door-stones, and walks on, hungry.

The mileposts are mostly wrong: they were turned around in the War and nobody has twisted them back. No signboard or marker announces any town. Direction stones have been ripped up or whitewashed blank. It is as though the shamed continent has been stripped of its name, disowned by the warring parents. She estimates her co-ordinates by the track of the sun – this is her attempt, but like all simple things, it is difficult. It rises in the east, sets in the west. After that, like Mamo said, you're alone.

> *Twas early, early, all in the year;*
> *The greenleaf all a growin;*
> *When come Trickin John from the Chickasaw Bluffs*
> *To wed with Barb'ra Allan.*

Some days, her going is straight as the rhumb of a ship. Others she tacks. She veers. She gybes. She will cross private plots, will risk any dog, to keep to the course she has set. But sometimes she is adrift; rudderless as a wreck. Six long days are lost in a circling that wends her back to the crossroads where the wrong choice was made. And the devil is said to haunt the junctions of Kanzas, but nobody appears, not even a goat. She stands in the X with a lodestone in her hand, begging the night for a clue.

The blisters on her heels are pullulating; they reek. She tears strips from her hem as wrappings. Every footstep she limps, the shorter comes the garment. She pictures herself naked except for toe-rags and a fig leaf. Wandering the gardens of dust.

Two dots coming towards her from out of the north. The Gypsy and Barbara Allan? The girl is riding her beau's strong back. *How pleasant, the sweethearts of spring.* But as the distance between them narrows, she sees they are not sweethearts. *When pretty birds sport and sing.*

The soldier is being carried, his whole head is a globe of bandages, with only a slit for his mouth. His comrade stares wordless at Eliza as they pass. The mummy on his back is weeping.

When she dreams, she sees faces, thousands of them: multitudes. They remind her of an ants' nest she once disturbed behind the cabin: a gloop of spherical jellies. Not bodies, only faces – eyeless, diaphanous – and occasionally a tadpole-ish limb. She does not know who they are or anything else about them, yet she has the idea that they are somehow connected to her. They are asking her to do something, but she is not sure what. She is not sure what she *could* do. Nothing, probably.

In a woodland near Marais de Cygnes, taking haven from a rainstorm, which came on as suddenly and terribly as a rage, she happens upon a skeleton, still wearing its Union blues, slumped over a cannon-wheel as though kissing it goodbye. Fledglings are nesting in the bust-apart ribcage. A snakeskin coiled around a knuckle.

She tugs one of the boots from its calcified stub but it is weather-stiffened and useless and she flings it in the river. There is a letter from a sweetheart in the dead man's clutch-sack, scrawled on the back of a torn-out flyleaf. She scans it and blushes. She takes his gourd.

Dear Pat. I wish you were with me this night. I long for a touch of you. I am your boldest girl.

Water tastes sweeter when drunk from cedarwood. She sips, then slugs, but her thirst cannot be slaked. It wakes her in the mornings like a mouthful of boiling sand. She can look in the face of hunger, having never not been hungry. The thirst is the truer murderer.

I have on me that dress you like for to write this. How I wish you would. I think about that night. God forgive me on Sunday I wanted you so bad. My breasts are grown heavy for the treasure you sowed in me. Where are you gone Pat? Why do you not.

Decorous capitals of the rip-maimed page:

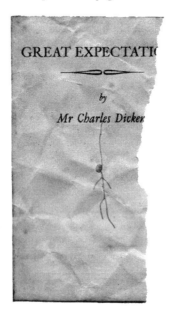

From the gibbet of a curlicue, a hanged man dangles: scribble of a fatherless child.

That day, or the next, she is not quite sure, she realizes who the dream-faces are. All the people she will never know. A needle of grief slides into her spine for the unbefriended pismire.

She is standing on a granite outlook gazing down on a cornfield. A ripple of wind moves steadily across it, diagonally, slow, a rolling wave of shadow, a sight so staggeringly beautiful that her eyes spurt tears.

Every fourth Sunday she pins a red flower on her smock, for Mamo said it quells womanly pain. She rests up, and sleeps extra, and chews fistfuls of wild comfrey. They do not dull the ache but they render it bearable, like an unwanted remembrance that must somehow be accommodated. Monday at dawn she starts walking again. There will not be many more Mondays, nor dawns, nor flowers. She is nearing the end of her life, she feels, and many more miles to go.

Westward over Kanzas. New signboards appear, their capitals lurid as wounds. Hamilton's Creek. Gargery's Mountain. Logan's Ford. Pederson's Hollow. Cronin's Landing. Sheperton's Ridge. Buckley's Plot. John Anderson's Firth. Who are these Kanzans that own the handiwork of God? Has any other country such place-names?

> *My race is run, beneath the sun;*
> *The gallows for Richard Lee;*
> *For I did ruin that innocent child*
> *Whose name was Rose Dupree.*

She finds a candle stub on the road near Mute Creek, Kanzas. You never kill the spark that lingers when you blow out the wick, because long as it glows some sinner in purgatory is given a respite from her tortures.

Spring will come again. The trees will be leafed-out. The world will be a dapple of apple-blossomed light. The corpses in the furrows will molder to loam, and wheat will put forth from them, and there will be food enough for everyone, and the stooks of blond-haired corn shall be lofted like idols, and the lion shall lay by the Lincolns. There are moments when it is possible to believe there will be peace in the valley. But they do not come plentifully any more.

She is skilled with the slingshot, can drop a bird from the sky. But you must have a care what creature you eat in strange country. She scorches them on her fire, blackens them to the guts, but they taste like scorched rats: rancid, raw-chickeny.

If you disturb an ants' nest, the adults gather the eggs and flee. Return a minute later. The spawn will have vanished.

The refugees wonder where is she walking to. This cadaverous madwoman in her ash-dusted rags, who leaves footprints of blood, whose limbs are begrimed, whose face looks as though it has been forced through a mangle before being sutured back on to her skull. She carries a pound of dirt on her clothes. This barefoot nobody: what can be her story? And why is she padding for the wilderness of the north country? Got nothin up there for a manless woman. Nothin up there for no one.

A carny propositions her in a ghost town near Blackwell. He will pay a Union eagle dollar but what he wants she cannot make herself do. A compromise is agreed by which she will accept a Barbado doubloon; but his pleasure once achieved, if pleasure it was, he refuses to pay, says he never wanted it at all, so she slashes his throat and leaves him gurgling blasphemies, and now, as he dies, he has something to want.

Glintings in the distance. What can they be? Are stars raining down on the land like frogs? As she nears to the flickers, she sees what is happening. A sight she must be imagining. Carters heft sheets of glass from a waggon, roughly, hurriedly: the odd pane falls and breaks. The overseer shrieks that they are not to be broken, they cost the Master a dollar a dozen. They are passed hand to hand along a chain of men, who are spackling them into the ribs of a greenhouse. She stops. She watches. Plates of shining glass. And each bears the face of a soldier.

They must be the ones who did not come back, who never returned to pay the photographer. Farmers. Husbands. Old men. Boys. The sun burns hard through their reticent smiles. In a year they will all be burned away.

Strange languages are heard beyond the sheughs at night, from the dark unseen where the waggons pitch camp. The mischief-calls of children, long masculine harroos, the clanking of cauldrons being thrivelled with heavy ladles. A boy runs into the boreen near what is now La Junta, Colorado; at that time the place was nameless. He gawps at her, bug-eyed, as though startled by a hag. He backs away, dreadfully, thumbing the cross on his collarbone, and scurries over a dike with a bleat for Mamacita.

That night, her own tombstone appears to her in a dream: a chunk of blackened mahogany bristling with coffin nails. Gardenias snaking through the mausoleum's cracks. Hammer in your spike, her ghost performs a hoodoo. *Je Vous Salue, Marie.* Fruit of thy womb. She died to make men holy. Let us die to make them free.

The murderess awakens, already walking. How can you dream when you're awake? Her gaze ranges ahead, perpetually ahead, fixed on the vanishing point, the unreachable horizon. Locusts click around her: a telegraphy that says: 'This road will never end.' But there cannot be locusts at this season of the year. Where do they go in winter?

The sunlight smarts her eyes. It blinks through the elms. At a cross-roads near Bitter Lake she sees her long-dead father, lurching through the plantings with a crossbeam on his back and a convict slavering at his heels. But when she gapes again, he has turned to a scarecrow:

wind-buckled, crippled, in a threadbare frockcoat, with a spade handle for shoulder-bones and a clog for a left foot. 'M' is stamped into the clog.

The ruins of a plantation house burning in her memory. A Corinth collapsing in alabaster dust. It falls slowly, seen from this distance, buckling in on itself, while the wrecking crew and the Captain observe from the tobacco field – but one defiant pillar emerges from the mortar-cloud, enrubbled up to its waist. Burnt cotton in the air. And rooks. And scorched banknotes. Strange confetti, those gallowsblack angels. And she pictures a story dragging on the boreen behind her, tailing back to Louisiana like a train. Miss Havisham I am. I stopped my clocks. *Cause my sweetman done me wrong.*

And one dawn she awakens with a chemise in her hands, having no intimation how she came to possess it. It is like a piece of costuming for some theatrical presentation: braided, sumptuous, with rosettes of chenille. Did the magi stop in the night? Why did they stop? She reefs it asunder; swathes her seeping feet. It is glued to the whelks of her wounds.

She is outside a roofless chapel on Christmas Eve morning. Its bell clonging leadenly. She can feel it hurt her teeth. She approaches with caution, as an Apache towards a shyster, and peers through the doorway for the homily.

The snow falls slowly into the transept: feathers of snow-white snow. The congregants in greatcoats under skeletal umbrellas. Shivering. Hunched. Defiant. There is no organ to accompany them, or, if there is, no one is playing it. Only the zizz of a goatskin tambourine, placking out a funereal cadence.

O
God
our
CHINK
In ages
past
our
CHINK
for years
to come . . .

She prays for those she will never know: for her mother, the child, the dead President, the ants, the boys who were brave and afraid in the War, the boys who slaughtered the innocent. And the preacher dons a stovepipe to hurry home to his gruel. The Reverend Baron Samedi. In his gun-hand he carries the key of the church; a prayerbook under his oxter.

Saint Jeddo. Pray for us.
Father in Hell. Pray for us.
John Cory. Pray for us.
Rose Dupree. Pray for us.

In the morning, as she is shaken from the preacher's rusting bed, he weeps that he cannot afford what they agreed. The tithe-plate was so poor. The people are so *poor*. Everything they planted was foraged. He presses into her hands a pair of work boots. Belonged to his son. In an asylum in California. Lost his legs at Pechacho Pass. Tried to take his own life. Won't never be coming home.

The preacher is gray in the face with guilt. She must go before anyone notices.

It is still dark as she winters out. The snow crisp and brittle; as though communion wafers have been spread beneath her soles. A whirling of sleet. Wearing her payment is an agony. In the end she tries to hurl them over the shoulder-bone of an oak, but her throw is weak and they catch on one of its fingers where they dangle by their laces. Bootfruit.

The first light comes; a cold, hard dawn. Out of the mist loom giants. She is facing into the mountainland.

She is an ant on a map. She talks to herself as she walks.

And I cannot face her. I cannot face her.

For this walk is for my redemption.

∇ ∇ ∇

PART II

REDEMPTION
FALLS

Execution Yard, Bridewell Gaol, Wicklow, Ireland
22nd November 1848

. . . Lord Antrim interrupted the prisoner to warn him of his obligations as a gentleman, of the good name of his father and family. Did he renounce, even yet, the path of arms, he could receive a less terrible death.

> PRISONER: No sermon on a patriot's duty is required
> from puppets of Monarchy. Here is my body.
> Butcher it if it amuses your Lordships. But repudi-
> ate my nation? Forbid it, Almighty God. Revile the
> rapier? I shall never, sirs: Never. It will slash the
> slaver's knot which binds us to an alien crown,
> which strangles my countrymen in the chokehold
> of hunger. I kiss its redeeming hilt and touch it
> to this unworthy breast. Come: you may now
> slaughter me; but you will never be rid of me.

Lord Londonderry donned the black cap, and the awful warrant was read: for hanging, drawing, and quartering.

> PRISONER: Thank you, my Lords. You have my consent
> and my pity.

James C. O'Keeffe
Speech from the Gallows

CHAPTER 2

THE MOUNTAIN TERRITORY: NORTH-EAST QUADRANT

CHRISTMAS EVE, 1865

A man who cheated the noose in a faraway land – A painting
A servant – The town of Redemption Falls – A dream of an island
A house of darksom clay

By midnight it was clear his wife was not coming back. O'Keeffe walked out of the house and stood on the prairie. A northerly was gusting, strong and cruel. Burrs of sleet smacked his face.

Coyotes yipped and whooed in the foothills. The stars: cold stones on the backcloth of night. He felt as though he could grasp them – stir them around. The mule bawled despondently from its stanchion in the field. The air smelt of smoke, of snow.

An object swathed in tarps, rigged to stakes in the rocks. It clattered in the blustering wind. The size of two barn doors, eleven foot by eight: the folly she had brought from the east. Too large to enter the house, to cross any threshold in the Territory, it had moldered all those months in its tethers. Laid lengthways on pine blocks to save it from the damp. Roasted, then frozen, now soaked by the heavens, as the snow seeped its corruption through the wrappings.

He tugged the axe from the woodblock. Its shaft was soaked. He staggered toward the racketing idiocy. He was frightened, he realized, of what he was about to do, ashamed and excited, but mainly afraid, and he wished she were here to observe the sacrilege. He would scatter its shreds to the winds.

Our Heroic Frontier by Edward Fairfax Chapel. Its destruction would give him pleasure.

A thought lurched up in him, so violent and shocking that it made him take pause to see if it was true. He might never see her again. This was entirely possible. She would return to New York, doubtless had departed already; at this moment she might be in the stagecoach for Salt Lake City. He let the thought break over him. He stood in the drenchings of the thought.

The journey would be dangerous. It would be worth it to escape him. Down the dizzying road that wound around the undercliff. Through the high, cold walls of Wolfcreek Canyon.

Snow swirled up. His beard and locks were drenched. From someplace above him, a screech-owl. He seemed to see his father-in-law standing backways to a hearth, boots spread wide, a finger stabbing at the air, a glare of loathing in the diamonds of his eyes, gullet pumping as he delivered a harangue. Never again. Not as long as you live, sir! The hatchet was suddenly cumbersome and he dropped it.

Now, as though awakening, he became aware of the cook, who was standing in the doorlight, solemn as a lioness. 'General,' quietly. 'I need to draw the locks.' Ignoring her, he turned back toward where the mountains must be. But it was too dark to see them. He had a feeling of trouble from the south.

She was speaking to him again but the wind blustered up ferociously, so that he could not hear what she was saying, and he gestured her away. The truth was that he was afraid he would slur if he replied. He would be exposed in front of a servant.

As though he had caused it to happen, one of the guy ropes snapped. A second gave way with a rent. The painting gave a shudder. Wind rushed underneath. It rose up on a short edge, wind-punched, twisting, buffeted again, banging on the stones; canvas ripping and flailing in the windstream, the glass in the frame cracked to shatters. A wolverine scurried from the dead footprint revealed beneath, hissing at the night as it fled.

The cook was screaming for him to do something; anything. And he realized he was screaming back at her. The thing rose again noisily, trailing tresses of rotted rope, three of its corners bouncing, its wrappings leaking sludge, a single fraying tie-rope the only thing restraining it from wrenching a way to liberation.

'The crawlspace.' She was shaking him. 'The ropes. *More rope.*'

The word he spat back at her was brutal.

He slithered a way around the wind-slapped cabin, scrunching ice-glazed ruts, through a mere of slush, along the corrugation of frozen mud the lane had become, and onto the road for the town. Broken branches on the road. The windblown grit. The groan of old oaks as he leaned and rolled. Past the shanties and bivouacs where the Negroes lived. A child regarded him from the placket of a tepee.

The town was not far away but it seemed to take a long time to walk to it. The cruciform signboard wedged into a barrel, and its snow-spattered face: **R∗D∗∗PTION F∗∗∗S**.

And the snow banked up in hard, black mounds. The saloons still stuffed. Roars in Gaelic from their casements. Silhouettes of dancers through the windows of the hurdy-gurdy house. Fiddles shrieking a Virginia reel. A cadaverous whore in the gateway of the saddler's; a miner in ruins by the pawnbroker's. And lamplight in the chapel for midnight Mass. They were singing 'Good King Wenceslas'. And a cowpoke tossing pennies from a balcony at a match-girl, who was dancing in the sludge as she gathered them. It seemed to him now that he was walking through a dream-place, that none of it was real, all connections severed.

In the War, he had made the reading of land his study. Maps told you nothing. Compasses were untrue. Informants, spies were all untrust-worthy; how, if you considered it, could they be anything else? How you looked at the vista was the important act. You needed to learn to see. Because one day what you saw would erupt while you watched it. Cannonade would scream from behind that busted wall, death would come hurtling from the innocent forest behind you. You needed to understand light. And there was a certain trick light played when it encountered ice. He had noticed this in the War, one midnight at Seven Pines. A comet had appeared that night before the battle, white as a bandage, as a widow's thinning hair – and its glow had been reflected in the mirror of the Chickahominy. So silent, the river. So violent, the sky. And it had seemed to O'Keeffe that the world was holy. But the dawn would prove it was not.

An orator's cliché. The sanctifiable commonplace. And yet, it had gained a purchase on him. Blood was holy. Loyalty. Comradeship. The bread you ate, the mug you shared. These things he had believed – believed them still, perhaps. But, no. He did not believe them any more.

Textbooks called it The Element of Surprise. *To startle the enemy is to quintuple your firepower. Nothing shatters his morale, nor crushes his resolve, nor annihilates his tactics, nor destroys his resistance, like the unexpected and brilliantly executed maneuver, preferably performed under darkness. Even half-suspected it is devastating when it comes, for the dread of its possibility has been eating at his courage, slowly but inexorably unmanning him.*

Perhaps she had kept to her threat, had abandoned her husband. He was a forsaken man, to be mocked. He saw her in the roiling, jouncing stagecabin, its iron wheels whanging on the ruts of road, through turmoiling billows of sleet. A stone knocked over the edge of the cliff track, falling five thousand feet through darkness.

It would be cold in the compartment; her breathing steam. The driver in bearskins, needing to use his whip. He wondered had she taken a blanket, a gun. He hoped she was dressed for desertion.

Wind thudded his shoulders: a sack of wet sand. Past a huddle of figures colloguing in a doorway. Their conversation ceased when they became aware of his proximity. 'Judas, turncoat,' as he shambled away from them. 'Sleeveen.' Smell of coal-oil.

She will return to New York, to her father's palazzo, will lock herself up like a postulant. He will be shamed for the deserted husband he is. The news will drift back to Ireland soon; embellished, like a song repatriating.

He pictures her in the library, in a widow's mantilla, staring out the bay window at the newsboys and the maimed. The servants come and go. She declines all food. Her father slowly roasts by the hearth.

Somewhere a man is shouting affrontedly: *Sie betrügen mich! Ich habe kein Interesse! I get my money, I go! Not before!*

The frost-covered hulk of a carthorse on Fitzgerald Street. It has lain there a fortnight, its ribcage collapsed. He has ordered it removed but nothing has happened. The knacker-man is overworked.

There is no one in the blacksmith's yard, nor in the shack. He walks the emptied stalls, the dungsmelling forge. A bird watches his progress from atop a keg of shoes. He finds a coil of old reata-rope, an armful of reins. A shackle for restraining slaves.

It is quarter of two when he returns to the house, by the shrubby mile of wood-path he uses this late. The cook's window is dark – perhaps she went to her cabin. Somehow she has tied the embarrassment down, ballasted it with rocks and logs.

He drinks for a while. The fire is low. Memories of Wicklow Prison, the gibbet being erected over a sewer-drain. The butcher's knife reddening in the executioner's brazier, the rasp of the tongs being sharpened. Then the face of the messenger who had ridden hard through the storm with the unexpected order from Dublin Castle. Van Diemen's Land, Tasmania. Life transportation. A naked man chained to a crag in the sea. The timbers of his rowboat broken in the surf. And he knows that this rock appears on no chart: this speck of dust in God's eye.

A private advancing over dunes of pebbles, through chokes of cordite fog. He is young, a scrawny trooper on whom the uniform sags, and he falters across the shards towards a breastworks. Around him, the sickening whirr of shells; the earth and trees vomit; walls are tossed. There is music – out of time and very slightly out of tune, as though the bandsmen are the recuperating inmates of a madhouse only playing to impress a committee. And on lurches the boy, gangly in his drabs, stumbling over cairns of the unseen eyes, which lie around the stubbles like the umlauts in the depths of a type-compositor's drawer. Until out of the smoke before him lurches a youth he seems to know – a neighbor, perhaps, from Galway or Clare. Throwing down his rifle, the other does the same; scorched hands are grasped, and the enemies embrace. They vanish a moment later in a spatter of red. Brained by the one same bullet.

'General,' she says. 'Trouble come at the mine.'

He awakens to the low-lidded gaze of the cook, candle burning lowly in her hand. She has on one of his greatcoats – an old one he had thrown away. Its buttons dulled by verdigris and mold.

'Time is it?' hoarsely.

'Three hour to the dawn.'

'Fix coffee.'

'Aint got none.'

'Boil grinds.'

She remains at his bedside, as though about to say something unwithdrawable. The thing in the tethers is clattering.

He has no recollection of going to bed. How did he get here, he wonders.

V

CHAPTER 3

BUT I, BEING YOUNG AND MAD WITH LOVE, FROM HER COULD NOT DEPART

An adulterous letter sent to the Governor's Wife some months before the Christmas that concerns us here – from a man in New York, a cartographer by calling – A shameful establishment is recollected & a plea for elopement made

Water Street,
Brooklyn,
VII 12 1865†

My only mourn'd L——

A friend, a trusted comrade, who is going out to the Territory has vow'd that he shall place this envelope into no hand but yours.

Forgive me for writing despite my promise that I would not do so – I have tried to keep true but can no longer.

The weeks since you left New York have been the worst imaginable – My aunt has been poorly + grows madder by the minute – I have had orders to lead an expedition to the Georgia Sea Islands, the mapping of which is now deem'd an urgency of such magnitude that we are to commence next month, though I have no men – But worst has been your absence, your terrible absence, so sharp that it feels like a presence.

Yester-evening I was walking alone to a comrade's funeral when I noticed a maidservant on Elizabeth Street with a soldier – I assume her fiancé: he look'd like an Irishman – The poor man had lost an arm + was blind – But they appear'd so content like any young couple – How wretchedly I envied their freedom.

Your farewell torment'd me – How could you write it? – You command

† In the private archive of Prof. (Emeritus) J.D. McLelland, author of this footnote and of all others in this volume.

me to forget, I must find another – It is asking flames to freeze – I fume with remembrances of you, in company or alone – I waken in the mornings mumbling to your ghost – Every cry of a newsboy, every street-sound is you – I see you on the Avenue – In a box at the theater – At the mess, with a friend, in my rooms, at the drawing board: In every line of my pen.

My will since you left seems no longer my own – It summons to mind those seasons we had together, when we walk'd + look'd at beautiful things – Can they truly have ended? – How can you dismiss them ~~with gray and disingenuous words~~?†

A divorce would bring scandal – this of course I concede – but gossip never endures + even were it to do so – does it matter in the end, can any of it *matter*, the prattle of thin-lips and pokebonnets? – How long can our lives be a lonely rejection, leached of the consolation of love? – Were we born to be stones shaped by coldness as we lie? – Is indifference bearable? – Must convention make us living corpses? – Changeling, I beseech you: *think on what you do* – We could go away together, to Italy or Paris – I have friends in England – we could make a clean beginning – I, who have had to learn to live with mockery – with the insults of beggars, the derision of cowards – I know how to go about quietly.

I wish you were here tonight – I could make you understand – For I believe to my atom, will never stop believing, that you and I were purposed by fate to be as one, if any two on this desolate star ever were – I *cannot* stop believing or start hating that thought – You are not free, I know it – God knows I think of little else – but is a hostage to be blamed for the existence of gaols? – It cannot be an indecency to recognize what is *true*.

If I thought you were happy with him, you know I would desist – But that is a lie – privately I could never – What I mean is that your happiness would mean certain things, one of which, surely, would be my own grief – But I could not continue hoping against hope for your acceptance if such a hope assailed a contented marriage – If he does not – cannot – love you, he must be insane – but how long must you famish in his straitjacket?

If you could see the city now – it is dreadful to walk the streets – Widows – Orphans. Wound'd men begging – Unending talk of riots +

† Scored-out in the original MS. – J.D. McL.

25

diehard spies – There are tents + shanties all over the Central Park –
So many have nowhere to go – Six hundred thousand souls will never
have our chance – How can we hurl it on the ashes?

I need to raise a subject – please – I beg you not to stop reading –
That last afternoon in New York – you know the one to which I allude
– was painful to you I know + such a knowledge is terrible – Perhaps
I should not have dared to propose as I did – So wildly I want'd you,
I could not remain silent.

You will never know my madness as I wait'd that evening – Would
you come? – Would you stay? – I was madden'd by questions – The
landlord brought food, I sent him away, so hag-ridden I could not eat –
The clock said four – Darkness began to fall – When at last I heard
your footfall on the stair – I thought my reason would erupt.

You were so beautiful in the doorway, I could not speak – Even the
shame in your expression was beautiful – I felt that my life had been
unrolling to this moment, that somehow I had been spared, when
others more deserving had not, only so that I could live out those few
short hours – My wretched appearance, my hideous aspect – even
these horrors I forgot.

I can *never* stop remembering those few short hours – They are more
vivid than anything I had ever known, more than anything even of the
War – Every minute, each second, I have rehears'd a hundred times –
What if I had said this? Or that? Or said nothing? – To be alone with
you privately – it was what I had craved, since the first hour we met at
the ward.

Last week, one night, distract'd like a fool, I returned to that den,
that shameful low place, + took once again the same bleak room +
wept there like a grieving spouse – It was a rainy night – I wept in the
window – I was reading the verses you gave me.

Down on the Bowery I saw carters + horses – the women like
statues in the doorways – Around me, through the walls with their lurid
depictions, I could hear the doors open + quietly closing – Then the
sounds of low laughter – I need not say more – You know the character
of house it is – The kind to which you were once willing to come.

The motes of that sinners' room, through which you had moved, the
filthy air itself seemed sanctified – The nothings you had touch'd as
you paced to and fro – The drawer you kept at opening and anxiously
closing – The cheap, cracked bowl in which you wash'd your hands –
The mirror at which you wept as you told me good-bye – And I slept in

26

that bed which might but once have been ours – had but only you not changed your mind.

The long night I lay there, now stirring, now trembling, now tortured by dream-images of such vividness it was shocking – It seemed – I dare not write what seemed – But I think you know – I know you do.

I was like a shaking boy, not a man, when I awoke, sodden and dry-mouth'd and ravenous – Life and limb would I freely have given, to have turn'd to you then, as lover to lover, in the grimy light of the Bowery dawn, to have worship'd every part of you until you implored me to cease, as a man was meant to do – Do I write it too plainly? – *Have you not longed for the same?* – The truth is that I am not even now being true – Were I to write what I wish, in the words I truly wish, your blushes would singe the page.

I beg you – *think again* – Do not be afraid – Let me husband you as you deserve, have always deserv'd, with that pride and passion and devoted friendship which the God whom you love intend'd for us – No, it is not blasphemy – think it not so – It is a clean thing, *a clean thing* – A home, an honest life, perhaps the laughter of happy children – how could these blessings, which are ours *for the taking*, be anything other than honorable wants? – It is *not* too late – We need only find courage – This round world is wider than any of us knows and need not be straitened by our fears – The crushed feelings of childhood, the failed and secret hopes, the hurts of broken love, the failure of our bodies – all of it, *all of it*, all can be overcome – It was you, Changeling, who show'd me this truth when all my hope was broken.

The ships leave the harbor for Europe every day – I see them from this window – *Every day* – A kind friend in Washington can arrange the papers – I could sign on as a crewman – No one would notice anything – There would be no impropriety to notice.

Please – my own changeling – give me the slightest prospect, the most minuscule reason to hope – Send me some token that my love might live – But it will anyways live – and shall always.

A.W.

∇

CHAPTER 4

THE TWISTING OF THE ROPE

The mine – The nightwalkers – A cruel crime
The Colt repeating pistol – The beast in the pit

A mile westward of the colony along an ancient Koötenais track was a
derelict mining camp, an eerie acre after nightfall. It was phantomed by
hulks of deadened machinery, upended black barrows, shovels still stuck
in the silt. You had the sense that its grubbers had only taken cover when
they noticed your approach – were begrudging you, perhaps, from those
coppices beyond the fence-line. The Territory would blister with many
such nowheres in the years after the end of the War.

A cheval-de-frise barricade delineated part of the perimeter, but its
cut-wire was rusted and in many places broken, and some of its oaken
crossbeams had been burned by thieves or natives, the former for better
access, the latter to watch them burn. There was little left to steal by the
winter of '65. The property had been foraged to its marrows.

Wind creaked the pulley wheels, cried a way into the forsaken
shafts. Mud-birds hooted. A she-wolf lingered with her cubs. The music
of the mine was strange and mournful, like a choir of lugubrious ghouls.
Toad-croak. Whippoorwills. The coyotes near the dump. The scream of
a cougar's mate-call. Whiskey bottles full of beetles might be found in the
riverbank muck. Panning-sieves clogged with sludge and osiers. Walking
there at night you felt the futility of human hopes, the weight of your
starlit smallness.

The claim had been purchased by a retired Philadelphian ophthal-
mologist who had shot himself and his wife when it turned out useless.
You had to be careful in that place after dark. It abounded with hidden
sharpnesses, crushing immensities of slag, old tripwires and brick-ends
and chunks of shattered sluice runs, a thousand prospective hurts
sunken into the dust, and turrets of hurt above you. A crust the color of
gruel settled on the skins of the dumping pools: you could stumble into
one of them, mistaking it safe to walk on, and if that were to happen you

were twice as good as dead, for the cess beneath the scum was choked with discarded chains, with coils of unraveling fence wire, a nest of waiting traps. Thomas Logan was the name of one schoolboy who drowned there. But this story is not about poor Thomas Logan.

It was in the ruins of a tackle-shack close to the derrick that the Vigilantes conducted their tribunals. Why they bothered was not clear. It was not as though there was the slightest chance of exoneration. The lariat would be knotted while they stripped you and roasted the irons. If you claimed any innocence the assault would be prolonged and the tools that cluttered the floorboards, snail-glued, mushroomed, would be pressed into a gruesome resurrection. Some prisoners X'd admissions (examples may yet be seen in the County Museum, framed in ebony, like Founding Fathers' wills); most were not able to by the time preliminaries were done. You were hefted or barrowed or flailed outside. You were lugged like a ransack of loot. These dragons of lifeless gantries, those torn-up capstans, were the last sights of earth for many an accused. They hanged you from the cottonwood that stood sentinel near the buckled gateway and crept back to the colony, to lawful life.

That hive and its dead braziers have long been swallowed by the West. The winches, the bunk-rooms, the corduroy road, the skeletons of wigwams, the hummocks of glitterless hardcore, the signboards cautioning INTRUDORS that they would be FIRED UPON FIRST – even the boundary posts onto which those interdicts were nailed: everything of settlement is gone. Only the strangle-tree remains of that time, and some strangely vivid lichens not indigenous to the Territory. And someone comes out regularly to set long-sprung traps for coyotes, though no one knows who, or why he would bother any more.

It was here to Morton's Claim that Acting Governor O'Keeffe rode with two of his marshals in the dark hours of Christmas morning, through a blizzard of dime-sized hailstones. The riders had on long black oilskins: bandannas against the sleet; their sombreiros were sodden, wilted. They looked like an etching of some Old Testament triumvirate: a verse made flesh by the violence of the weather.

An informant had sent a message to the gubernatorial house, a building so new that its roof was as yet unfinished. It was swathed in canvas sheeting, bolstered up with jackoak struts – it had the look of a shipwreck, or perhaps a harvested Leviathan, with a buttress of rendered ribs. The Committee of Vigilance had adjudicated again and offered no apology for its devotion to the community; but it was not biblical to leave a corpse unburied at Christmas. This was a task for the Government.

We freemen of this Territory uniting ourselves in a party for the Laudable purpose of ending thievery & murder do pledge ourselves upon our Sacred honor each to all others & solemnly swear that we shall reveal no secret, violate no trust & never desert one another or our standard of Justice so help us God, as witness our mark – Men of the O+O.

The body was iced solid as a freak-show waxwork. Frost speckled his nakedness: a caul of silvered gray. The rope was creaking like a sarcophagus door as its consignment swiveled and grinned at its fate. The assault must have been terrible; it was the worst they had seen. Rain dribbled pink from his maimed extremities. Even after death his remains had been desecrated, whether by she-wolf or man was not clear.

A confession of highway robbery and of indecencies against unnamed women had been hammered to the tree on a bloodstained nail. But the Governor found it hard to concentrate on the words, which in any case were running in the rain. He had been drinking that night, alone at the residence, aggressively, with a sense of murderous purpose, raking over matters better left in the ashes, but which are rarely so left by the failed at Christmas. Distilled *agave*: toxicant; cheaply made. The flames of his hearth had been scrutinized for many minutes, until they had blurred themselves down to a coalescence of fuming reds, as though the coals might divulge to their inebriated observer the secret of what he was doing before them. The clock placked stolidly and adjusted its ratchets. There was a moment of friendless, childless grief, as unctuously intense as the larva in the dregs, and as difficult to swallow, and as hideously irresistible, and there were many other moments all to do with the past. A new year was coming and so little to show. The thoughts of an exile in Advent.

There was the tiniest confusion behind them from a pile of rotting planks, a fricative whickering, like wings beating the air. Assuming it a gallowsbird, they did not turn to investigate. Nor did they hear the mash of hurrying footfalls – the snow, I suppose, must have muffled them. They were thinking, to be candid, about how to cut down the carcass in a way that would not cause it to sag asunder in their clutch, for although it appeared frozen they could not be sure for how long, nor of what it might do when they touched it. Each had seen innumerable dead by that night; each had killed for his country. Death was not a mystery, not in any spiritual sense; it had not been for years, not since the carnage at Bull Run, and never would be again. But the body remained mysterious, as the body always does, enigmatic in the way of all untenanted dwellings. Somehow it commanded human feeling. One of your species had lived in it.

The moon was grubby white as the tortured man's feet. They reminded the Governor of a painting he had seen in his youth: a gory work, Hispanically macabre, on the interment of Christ. The composition was ghastly, had been calculated to shock. The thing was like a butcher's apron stretched onto a frame. The Savior had been laid on his back on a plinth; your viewpoint was that of a mourner standing at his feet. And you could barely see the torso, only the ruined feet – so aggressively foreshortened that the spike-punctured soles were half a yard in height.

O'Keeffe was nineteen when he was thunderstruck by that image, not long matriculated from school. His college was a Jesuit establishment in Shropshire, England; as an Irish boy he had felt out of place there. Games did not interest him. He preferred poetry, the classics. His letters home to Wexford were watchful, complex. He had promised to be tall but that had not happened. He was the size of a girl and this gnawed at him like a cramp. ('Paddy O'Napoleon,' his house-fellows called him, a designation he had strenuously pretended to enjoy.) It was in the Uffizi, he thought. That terrifying depiction. It unnerved him to realize that he carried it after all this time.

The kindlier of his lawmen, John Francis Calhoun, clambered onto an overturned coffer. He had once had a son, and the baby had died, and Calhoun did not like to see disrespect for the dead, thinking it hateful of life. He set to work at the rope, trying to fray it with his bowie. But the rope was hard and the only blade he carried had not been whetted since Martinmas. His comrade, Patrick Vinson, scoffed from the ground. Eyes narrowing like a cat's when it sees a stranger come in.

'Christ spare us,' said Vinson. (*Dia idir sinn agus an tOlc*). More strength in the bastard in the noose. He was speaking in Gaelic, which he often did to Calhoun. 'Jail-ic' Vinson called it, for he had learned what he had of it in an English prison, where its profanities could be floated without jeopardy at the guards. They thought you were declaiming some myth.

Calhoun kept sawing: a raspy defiance. But already he was weary as an anchor.

'Pox take you, *break*,' he muttered at the rope. He was a man of intense sweetness, though he often tried to hide it: one of those whom swearing does not suit.

Rime-frost was sticking his hands to the rope. His boots were slippery on the strongbox. He had heard from a cousin, a seamstress in Columbus, Ohio, of a scheme to sink a cable across the floor of the Atlantic, where his mother and uncles had been buried. (He'd had moments when he imagined them touching it, feeling it, while sharks snouted by in the murk.) The death-rope reminded him of what such a cable must be like: cold and hard and strong. And it began to be clear to him, as he sawed on it uselessly, and as Vinson ridiculed, and the dead-man rotated, with Calhoun trying to restrain him and cut him down at the same time, and not fall from the box, and not lose face, that nothing could be done, that *nothing could be done*, that the ride and the cold and the leaving of his girl's bed, and the hail in the eyes and the sting in the knuckles had all been in vain, that the world was a latrine, and that nothing could ever be done. He could have put a blasted bullet into the corpse at that moment, and its twin into Vinson and its triplet into the Governor; but a price would need to be paid for the making of such a delivery. There would always be a price for your instincts.

And it was while he was imagining what it is to murder your only friends (Vinson's vociferations, the kick of the gun) that he heard the shouts from the smelt-house. The Governor was beckoning, brandishing his lantern: an arc of fire on the black. Now Vinson was running, the devious little suck. And another shout was heard, and a volley of blasphemies. And the lantern was knocked over, spilling its flame into the snow, and the deadman spun monstrously like a piñata in a nightmare.

A form, a being, was alive in the sludge-pit. Vinson unholstered his Colt repeater. The weapon was new, not long arrived to him from St Louis, raveled in oilcloth like the shinbone of a saint. Lovingly larded with myrrh-like resin, it had cost him a ransom in wages. It was clumsier than he had hoped; he did not like it much. It didn't fit his gun-hand with the heft he would have liked. But there were times you were glad to have a dependable weapon. And this was one of those times.

So he fetched out his gun as assuredly as if he were a trick-shooter being watched by an exultation of *señoritas* all bonneted on their way to the bullfights. He was going to spin the barrel, utter something terse and violent, but the Governor called him a name. And it was hard in the dark to draw a bead on the beast, which was flailing and squealing like a hogget in a shambles. But he aimed into the plash, at the epicenter of exploding mud, and discharged a shot, then another two for punctuation. I am here, announced the gun. Fear my owner. He's a man you don't meet every day.

The girls genuflected in the cistern of his mind. But soon they looked up. Something was happening in the pit.

'Son-of-a-bitch is a child,' said Vinson.

'*Dios mío*,' screamed the girls, or the wind.

∇

CHAPTER 5

WE'LL SOON BE FREE

A further entreaty – A remembrance – A threat

NY–St Louis. Pony Express to Salt Lake City.
Matson-Forest Stagecoach Line: Urgent

IX 2 65†
Brooklyn

Lucia – my love – my only love –

I implore you – send some answer – Silence at the last? – I offer you my life + receive no reply – Can you disregard me so coldly? – At least tell me no.

I know you receiv'd my letter – I have heard from the man to whom I gave it – On his honor, which I trust, he swore he delivered it to you, on the ninth afternoon of last month – He said you were making a photograph by the river when he found you – I know he was speaking the truth.

Changeling: I owe to you the fact that I am alive – But you also have obligations: they are not all my own – If truly no hope remains to be rescued, you owe it me to say so – I want to read the words, to see which ones you deploy – You know you cannot do it and live true to your conscience, for you know the ardent admissions you have made to me while we were alone, and permitted me to make to you.

Need I write to your alleged husband + apprise him of matters? – Do you think I would not dare, or that others have probably not already? – 'Your wife and the freak – I saw them in the street.' – *Do you*

---

† Letter written (in margins around newspaper sketch entitled 'The Irish Ape Politicians') in zaffre ink diluted in aqua regia, so that the characters are invisible unless the page is heated gently, in which case they appear in a turquoise tint. – J.D. McL.

34

think they would not thrill to say it? – Christ help me – I do not mean it
– I should rather die than hurt you – It is only that I cannot bear the
ticking away of our chance – We are *cut*, do you not see it? – The only
healing is each other – Every second more is another drop of heart's
blood.

The tickets + papers arranged – Have sold all my books + everything
I had of my father + can raise a little more by selling my instruments –

I beg you – But an answer – I shall never trouble you again – Say
either yes or no but I will not be disregarded.

A.W.

∇

CHAPTER 6

ONE MORE VALIANT SOJER, LORD, TO HEPP ME BEAR DE CROSS

A drummer-boy discovered – A visit to the undertaker Orson Rawls
The Great Storm and its whiteout – The killing of Christ

The soaked boy had on the flitters of a Confederate uniform. The arms and legs had been sheared so as to fit him, a frayed length of whipcord served as his belt. He was tied into his clothing, inefficiently trussed, like a bundle that has been rifled in a Lost Property office and hastily rewrapped as too worthless to be stolen. His feet were shoeless, wound round with filthy rags. He was shaking like a foal with the staggers.

About his neck was a Celtic cross carved in scrimshaw or ivory, the name 'J. Mooney' needled into its back. In one of his pockets was a mud-stained drumstick. Its twin was found in his sleeve. Snow liquefied on his eyelashes, which were long, like a girl's. The hanged man was not his father, that was all he could say, and even this little was not actually said: he just shook his head dumbly when the question was put to him, and gaped around at the desolate terrain, as though he had never seen darkness, as though somehow he found it dazzling.

The Governor's men did not know what to do with J. Mooney. They were not good with boys. They were not good with anyone. While they shuffled calf-deep in the blood-spattered mud, trying to shake an answer from the gulping apparition, he broke from their grip and scurried. Vinson pursued him. Were there torches? Burning tapers? Recalling the event on the night he dies, the Governor will see the refraction of fire on snow.

Into the darkness Vinson ran, his cries growing fainter, until it seemed to the Governor that the night or something in it had swallowed both pursuer and quarry. Everything was silent. Calhoun looked afraid. Three men, even in danger, can think themselves a fellowship, able to present a defense if needs be; but two is merely two. And then, from the distance, they heard Vinson again, yipping like a huntsman on the track of a fox, and Calhoun trudged away to join him in the unseen, and the Governor was alone with his thoughts.

NARRATIVE OF A CRIME, MISDEMEANOR, or FELONY

COMPLETE THIS DOCUMENT HONESTLY

CRIME: *Murder.*

CIRCUMSTANCE: *Before dawn this morning 25th Dec 1865, I, Jas. C. O'Keeffe, Brig. Gen., Acting Govnr, proceeded to Lemuel Morton's Claim acting upon informations recd. 1 decsd., male, hanged: name Harrington or Henderson?, birthplace & cet. unknown. Drove stage for Salt Lake & Union Line. 40 yrs approxim. Accused of being road agent/molester of women. Was not.*

WITNESS/ES: *1 boy, vagrant, 11/12yrs? Appears Mute. Disturbed in mind. Absconded from my custody. Whereab. now unknown. Maybe mulatto.*

REMARKS & SUSPECT: *Vigilante lynching, 17th this year. Repeat request made continually to Secretary, for assistance in establishing law. Ten marshals reqd urgently. More judges & sheriffs. New jailhouse at Edwardstown. Monies for permanent militia. Without such assistance, am effectively helpless. Send men and arms immediately. Urgent.*

He will have reason to recall this night many times. The Christmas of '65.

They did not find the boy. Not that they searched too hard. The night was cruelly cold, a vast storm was looming from Saskatchewan. There were reports from the border of catastrophe in the valleys, of snowdrifts so huge they made icebergs of barns. They succeeded, at last, in cutting down the deadman – his end had been terrible, the knot had been tied so as to strangle him, not break his neck – and hefted what was left of him to the undertaker's house.

The undertaker, Rawls, was a thin man who blinked a lot. He recognized the victim as a coachman out of Utah: Hourihan by name, maybe Houricane, or Houlihan. He'd been driving the dangerous run only a couple of months, had been formerly with the rebs down in Georgia or Mississippi. Often he rode with a helpmate up top, a whelp who watered the horses and ran errands for the passengers and who wasn't a one for talking, might even be a mute. Some said the little doagie was Holohan's nephew, but Rawls thought this was not so, though he could not say why.

He led the party across Emmet Street to his subterranean stores. There they were loaned a reusable coffin, a contraption of oak boards and sprung-hinged trapdoor for which Rawls had registered a patent. Thence out to Jawbone Hole, a cemetery for the wretched, where they had to hammer at the ice to open him a grave. But the ground proved unbreakable. It refused to yield to its guest. They stood back from the spot and blasted it with their revolvers, and finally the earth was breached by force – the spit of scarlet flashes, the smashing of stones – and the Federal shovels went to work. Snow flurried harder. The half-light was coming. The birds in their nests gave small, dull shrieks. The puttering lantern-flame twisted for its life, as the thing to be interred must also have done. A dog hollered bleakly over a wall. No minister was available, or none was willing to come, so the Governor read from Job while Vinson and Calhoun bowed heads in a replication of mourning. Hailstones smacked the black text as he read, blurring the ancient entreaties to sog.

The storm hit around eight. The town was battened down. Birds' feet froze to the surface of Lake Pend d'Oreilles. The wind shrieked for eleven days and nights without recess. Ice cracked the trees. Sleet flew like buckshot. From Lewis and Clark's Pass down to Rattlesnake Mountain, from Medicine Bow eastwards as far as Devil's Lake, the tornado circled the Territory, as a cougar spiraling its prey, and then, at the moment when they thought it was dying, it gathered and screamed into Redemption Falls.

The roof was torn from the schoolhouse on Tone Street. A miner born in Sligo, Paudrig John Foley, got lost in the blizzard trying to find a Dutch comrade, was killed by a flying pane of glass. A preacher's wife went mad and rode into the fury for Liverpool Falls, convinced she could banish the whirlwind by Holy Ghost power. No vestige of rider or horse was seen again; some said they were taken by the natives, others said they drowned. On the twelfth morning, the tempest raged away towards the east and the citizens unburrowed to the wreckage.

Their chapel had been shattered, its belfry toppled, the stump wrenched into the whorl of a corkscrew. Slates lay strewn in a hillock beneath, as though fashioned by some fanatical sculptor into the approximation of a landslide. Johnny Thunders and his desperadoes had already been and gone: the altar had been ransacked, the chalices stolen, the little organ that had huddled like an elder by the vestry now shot-up so its pipes emitted wheezes in the gusts. Their marque had been splattered in holy wine across a wall: 'MK–1025' and an upside-down skull.

Pages of bibles drifted on the breeze: children leapt to catch them – they would become a kind of currency. Icicles hung fanglike from boughs and sills, from balustrades and water butts, from guttering and architraves, from every plane parallel to the granite-hard ground. In the whiteout stood sweethearts who had not met in days, eyes streaming in the dazzle, and many silent men.

Grit-blackened stalactites on the eaves of the courthouse: it had crumpled in on itself like an orphan awaiting a kicking. Ice-capped, wind-whipped, the glass of the town, an American Arctic, unnatural to crunch through: as a wasteland once glimpsed in the smoke of a pipe, a prophecy of white men's folly. Twin babies were taken from the rubble of Spanish Jenny's, a house of ill-fame on the eastern outskirt. How they had come to be in such a den, no one ever said. No parent would come to respect the remains. They were buried in Jawbone Hole between a suicide and a slaver, and many years after the Great Storm of '65, night-riders still reported, as they passed that place of sorrows, the sound of babies weeping.

There was no weeping on the morning the tempest ended. The towns-people were too shocked, or maybe too hard. Pain had polished them; it had burnished them till they blazed with it. They looked to their Governor. He was not to be seen. Some accused him of having fled on the last stage out; like all Yankee hirelings he was a coward, they said. A party was formed to go up to the residence. Halfway there, it had become a posse. A noose was contrived from the raped chapel's bell-rope, a blind-fold from a tatter of the Stars-and-Stripes banner that had flown, until recently, from the lintel of the Post Office. The storm had not torn it down. The townspeople had.

They came up to the Governor's residence, that strange unfinished hulk, tar-caulked pine logs glittering with hoarfrost. His wolfhound was shackled to a picket in the yard: it appeared to be asleep, or perhaps dead. Icicles on the sills were beginning to melt; the windows seemed to be weeping.

A ribbon of smoke from the solitary chimney – they knew he was inside, and this maddened them more. Behind the metal door that had been cast by a St Louis foundry: paid for by their taxes, by the sweat from their work, by the plunge of their fingers into agonies of water to pan for the glinting gravel that had led many of them there. He was safe as an

39

ingot in the crypt of a bank, or he figured he was – but they would show him.

Someone roared for him to reveal himself. No reply came back. The people came angrier, in the way of angry crowds, the clever stirring the stupid into ecstasies of loathing, the weak outshouting the strong out of fear for themselves. A woman shouted 'Yellow!' A Georgian gave out the rebel yell. Other men of secessionist sympathies soon gave it back – that chilling, vulpine howl-and-yodel of rage, which once had meant the rising of the freeborn south, but now meant humiliation; scores unsettled. The bell-rope was slung over the Y of a cottonwood. The blacksmith's shop was rifled. Someone brought a mesh of implements.

As the first of the southerners began flailing at the door, a rifle shot retorted from the casement of an upper room. It shredded the lynch-man's thigh; he gyrated away from the stoop, clutching at the gash and moaning. He appeared more surprised than anything else: it was as though it had never occurred to him that such transgressions might be perilous. Two shots more issued in rapid succession; one chunked into the flagstaff in the mire that was the front yard, the second killed a sow that had attached itself to the mob and had been gnawing with rattish fervency on a thicket of iced weeds.

A surge of blown snow: misting, blinding. At that moment, the Governor's cook appeared in the lane, a woman not yet thirty, though she looked a decade older. She was born the legal property of a Gulf Coast planter, bore three of his children by the time she was nineteen, had buried a husband and all of the children before fleeing to the northlands, a contraband. A trio of Mississippi bully-boys observed her approach: they were often reckoned to be brothers, though nobody knew for certain; even they themselves claimed not to know. The eldest had straggling hair and weird glimmering eyes; he was referred to by the wits of the town as 'Christ'. His brothers, more ugly and less inclined to braggadocio, were known around the colony as Dismas and Gesmas – the thieves put to doom at Calvary. Christ stuck out his boot to stumble the cook and she fell like a tumbled sack. As she lay in the slush, uttering no sound whatever, they chuckled and mocked and tugged at her clothes, and one of them ground a boot-heel between her shoulderblades. 'Teach you some mancipation *now*,' he snickered.

Four shots gulloped from the vantage of the house, so rapid that no one saw their flames.

Two assailants were killed before they knew they were hit. Christ was gut-shot. No one approached him. He slunk gaspingly away, the better to die in privacy, for a bullet through the abdomen could mean only one thing, and he knew, from experience on the slaughterfields of Gettysburg, that the thing it meant would be terrible. Some deaths may be approached with a semblance of courage. This was not one of them, and the Mississippian apprehended that. The crowd gave a bellow and surged through the Governor's fence. 'Burn out the Yankee bastard!' a muleskinner cried. A blown-down sequoia was stripped of its branches, the better to employ its shaft as a ramrod. The gunsmith clambered astride it, rending at the boles with his hacksaw. A cleaver was brandished by a Texan.

A daguerreotypist and his servant scurried hen-like up the lane and commenced hurriedly erecting their apparatus while the hollers grew more violent. Stones were hurled, a rain of bottles. Two citizens went to loosing pistol shots at the house's brick chimneystack; slugs struck its weathervane, set the copper reaper spinning, blew the chimneypot to a shatter of shards. Now the miners drew ice picks and some brought out mattocks. The photographer's magnesium flash gave its dull, plosive puff.

It was then that the Governor materialized in the masts of the roof, like a genie produced by the powder-flash. He looked bewildered, disheveled, as though he had only just awoken. His face was florid; he had clearly not shaved in days. He appeared to be draped in a sheet, like a Roman. He bore no visible weapon.

'This residence is a possession of the Federal Government,' he began. But his voice was apprehensive, as though he did not want to speak. It was not that he appeared fearful, he never did. More that he was pondering some graver predicament than the one now incarnating itself below him. Lofty indifference was the tone he was aiming at. But it was coming out more like contempt.

'My marshals are here. I have men at your houses. The next to molest this property will have his house pulled down.' These contentions, at least two of which everyone knew to be lies, were uttered as briskly as the timetable of a train.

'We stretch your nigger first,' someone yelled. 'How that be?'

A cluster of the diehards gave a miserable cheer of endorsement. The Governor waited for it to expire, and then he spoke coolly.

'The gutter-swab that will menace a woman in my hearing has not been born. Come in if you've the mettle. You'll go out feet first.'

'Liar,' howled a simpleton. 'Irish coward!' He was fantastically obese, like a haycock on legs, and was infamous around the mining camp he regarded as home for having gnawed off one of his fingertips in a bet. He grinned around himself now, waiting for collegial approval. When it proved unforthcoming, he took off his kepi and began to beg: a study of almost perfect incognizance.

'Return to your homes,' the Governor said darkly. 'I will kill every mother's soul of you if I am threatened again.'

Drizzle was falling. The townspeople looked at one another. Some commenced sullenly to drift away. A French Catholic friar had come on the scene – he had ridden into town from the Indian station at Piegan Landing – and was urging the body to disassemble, whispering at some, tugging the coat sleeves of others; others again he was chivvying and scolding. It was as though they were misbehaving novices, not Missouri-watered gunslingers. To a boy he administered a cuff across the face.

The cook knelt up and stared at her palms and wiped her muddied forehead on the hem of her semmit. Slowly she rose – she did everything slowly, as though time and her body were difficult languages. Not one of those watching assisted her to rise. Perhaps some wanted to, but were afraid.

She was spat upon and ridiculed as she tilted towards the house. Her expression betrayed nothing; she refused to recoil, even as the spittle struck her patched-up mantle, attached itself in cords to the furrows of her face. A clod of stinking pig-dung slapped the back of her bonnet. Some in the assembly laughed guiltily or heckled, but, at this degrada-tion, a number of the women – disapproving, perhaps, or just frightened to stay – commenced hurrying away in twos and threes, harvesting children to their aprons as they went. Still the cook came on, now into the yard, ascending the squat stairway unsteadily to the door. She knocked on it and waited, as she usually did. It was the Governor him-self who unbolted and opened it, having no other servant to negotiate his locks.

'Good-day, Elizabeth Longstreet,' the Governor said.

'Good-day, sir,' said the cook, 'by the glory of God.'

The simpleton barreled towards her, heaving a crowbar out of his trench coat. The Governor drew a revolver and shot him through the chin.

The wind gave a whimper. The townspeople stared. Richard Stiles lurched backwards, his right knee crumpling, his shoulders slumping leadenly as though their sinews had been snapped, and toppled down the portico steps into the dirt, and his hands struck the ground like hams. His body was immense; he had at one time been 'Atlas the Colossus' in a carnival. His falling was so heavy that it caused the wolfhound to start. Blood came seeping through the giant's moleskin collar. In the photographs of his remains – elephantine, preposterous: two street-boys cross-legged on the slab of his chest – the blood is a puddle of gray.

'Any other fool?' said the Governor, quietly. And when no reply was given, he roared the same words. And his howl seemed to whipcrack the cold, cutting air, commingling with the distant agonies of Christ.

The last of his constituents shambled away through the sludge, back toward the carcass of the town. The overture of a thaw became discernible now, the gurgle in the trenches: plink and babble of drips. Thunder grumbled in the faraway quadrants. Animals nosed from their holes.

The Governor must have been troubled as he stood behind his locks. Not about Stiles – nobody would mourn him; he had long been a nuisance to the schoolgirls of Redemption Falls, had only escaped a lynching by being punk to a lynchman. What he feared was something else; he would come to fear it sorely: the inexplicable had crept into his life.

He had been alone – so he had thought – at the house that morning. The killer of the Mississippians had not been him.

V

CHAPTER 7

ALL MY TRIALS

*From the transcript of an interview with the
Governor's onetime cook – Recorded in Liberia, West Africa,
when she was in her one-hundredth year*

. . . No I ain afret to die . . . Cause I had times I thought I would . . . That mornin after the storm I was dead in my skin . . . And I dont know who killt them Mississippians that time . . . Got a notion or some about it . . . But I aint sayin . . .

Sir, Elizabeth Leavensworth . . . born Elizabeth Longstreet . . . My owner done give me that name . . . I was born a slave in Marianna, Florida . . . Cattlestead call The Hurricane... On the Chattahoochee road . . . But it ain theä no more . . . Not in a longtime . . .

Sailor told me once ago they got a cemetery on it now . . . Where The Hurricane use to be at . . . Graves from the war time . . . Illinois what he said . . . Make a graveyard in the paddock . . . By the banks of the Peachblossom . . . House burnt by the Yankees an then it haul down . . . With the shambles an the shanties an ever thing else . . . Eighteen an sixty-four . . . Come the fall of sixtyfour . . . Tear Emerald County all to pieces.

No ain never went back to Florida. Ain fixin to . . . No . . . Florida can burn for all I care to it. I lived me a longtime in Redemption Falls, Mountain Territory . . . Kept house for a Union General and his wife . . . And I seen some things when I worked for the General . . . I seen some curiosities.

That right, the famous General got him in troublesome later . . . Irishman . . . Whom talkin bout. Use to call him 'The Blade'. An he save my life that mornin certain sure. Be in my grave that mornin if he didnt.

. . . Sir, ninety-nine last November . . . Ain never had me no paper. Mought be older some. Or younger. Gypsywoman told me onetime I see a hundred an two. But I pay her no tension. [unintelligible remark] Ain a body know what comin but God a Mighty . . . Nobody know it but God.

My father's name Zekiel . . . Yes, sir . . . In Africa . . . I never did know

44

his born name . . . Man-stealers come in a ballahou out of Charleston . . .
My mother's name Euterpe . . . Seventeen an a half . . . Never seed you a
woman as fine as my mother . . . She born Sapelo Island . . . in the Sea-
Islands of Georgia . . . Once belong to a rich Apache; dont know how it
come . . . Had a gift for midwifing . . . Healin sickness of the blood . . . Folk
an beast the both . . .

My father didnt [dog barking] hardly a word of English that time . . . I
dont remember much to him . . . Quietspoke man . . . Whittle poppets of
cordwood . . . Whet the knives for the house . . . See him standin at the
grinestone . . . An he turn that wheel all day . . . Got a scotch heä on his
breast from a brandin turn poison . . . Clovershape marque of The
Hurricane . . . Gone to glory now: must be. Pray for him ever night yet
. . . Him an my mother. An all my gone kin . . . Hour of redemption I see
my mother again. Cause she safe in the wounds of my Jesus . . .

. . . And my father got took from The Hurricane the harvest I turn twelve.
Last time ever I seen him i' my life [unintelligible words]. The mastuh lost
my father playin cards in Marianna. My father got took away for his debt.
Some say he ended in Texarkana but no way to know it. Missippi. Georgia.
Any place.

Seen him scourged into a cage and they chain up the fender. Like he
nothin but a shoat pig. Nothin but meat. And he was wagoned away
callin out for my mother. But my mother was gone to the well that time.
They waited [for] her to be gone to the well.

She went on five month after, Lord have mercy on my mother. Christmas
of fortynine she went on. And then it come to hell for me and my sisters.
Cause she always tryin protect us. And now she gone on. And you would cut
out your throat you had the courage to do it. Life of a slave aint but death
all day . . . And your dread for the coming of night.

Mastuh a Irishman. O'Hora his name . . . Wolf got more nature than
O'Hora . . . Do ever thing but kill you . . . Cause he paid for you, see. You
a dollar to O'Hora. You was livestock . . . Want you in his lust; pick his
harvest; tend his children; rawhide lash for the rest of it . . . Yes, his wife
mustof knowed. Knowed ever thing he done . . . Then ride along to chapel
on his chestnut bay. And his Glory Be to Jesus and his Holy Queen Mary.
Any of his kin gets [to] hear what he done, then bow their head for disgrace.

He got killt in the Civil War by Nathan Hook that was a runaway off the
Hawkes plantation. Nathan Hook come back in the Union army out of
Maine and he shot O'Hora dead in the orchard by Sioux Creek. And I seen
that with these eyes. Cause I could see that time. O'Hora was his natural

father, is the truth of what happen . . . so that me and Nathan Hook was blood.

But I wont speak of that . . . No, sir, I wont... The Lord see all things . . . I shall stand at the Mercy Seat . . . The Lord know what happen in Marianna, Florida . . . It good and it wicked in ever creation . . . But the wheat shall be flail from the chaff come the harrowin. You always got to gather what you sow . . . And I believe that's the reason the General took me in the house . . . I believe he was shamed what his countryman done . . . And we didnt never talk of it . . . But I knowed he was shamed . . . You could see it in his ways . . . And he was right to be . . . And he save my life that time of the storm . . . Cause them Mississippians was fixin to kill me . . . And I never knowed why, cause I done nothin on Mississippi . . . They wouldn even know my name.

∇

CHAPTER 8

THE DARLIN OF ERIN

A poster-bill published in the south not long after O'Keeffe's arrival in America, some years prior to the central events of this narrative

PROUD CITIZENS *of* GEORGIA!

The Committee of Saint-Patrick-in-Exile is honored to propose

AN EVENING WITH
"O'KEEFFE OF THE BLADE!"
ERIN'S ROBINSON CRUSOE!
NEWLY COME TO THIS FREE LAND FROM BANISHMENT!

APOLLO THEATER, MACON,
FRIDAY, JULY 23rd 1852 at EARLY CANDLE LIGHTING

Musical Interlude by the Sullivan Pipe Band

Young JAMES C. O'KEEFFE, of the REBEL COUNTY of Wexford, the democratic HERO of Hibernians the world over, of late arrived to this Republic from his YEARS OF CRUEL EXILE, will LECTURE for ONE NIGHT ONLY on his remarkable experiences: his DEATH SENTENCE in Ireland, its commutation on the GALLOWS, his DARING ESCAPE from England's dungeon-isle of Tasmania, his subsequent SHIPWRECK in the CANNIBAL-INFESTED Pacific, his fortuitous RESCUAL by good-hearted mariners, his ENTHRALLING ADVENTURES in breasting the wave to New York, and his BRAVEST HOPES for OUR MOTHERLAND!

"The Blade" is the greatest orator in the United States at the present hour. In the whole English speaking world, it is attested by knowledgeable men, that only Mr Dickens can run him a race. In the six fleeting months since he has found shelter on our shores, his reputation, already famous, has flared like a COMET. A MOST TREMENDOUS INTEREST is expected to be shewn in this lecture, which has MESMERIZED already the MULTITUDES that have heard it, at New York, Brooklyn, Boston, Chicago, Philadelphia, Memphis, New Orleans & Atlanta. "Surely the cause of Liberty has no more passionate singer than this PRINCELY & HANDSOME SCION OF ERIN." (New York Tribune)

An expeditious acquisition of tickets is fervently advised. Mr O'Keeffe has NUMEROUS ENGAGEMENTS & cannot revisit the Cotton Lands soon. In order that the fullest capacity may be permitted to gain the hall in safety, ladies are delicately requested to abstain from the wearing of hoops & gentlemen to attend without swords or side-arms. Do not forgo this ALL-SURPASSING OPPORTUNITY. Be THRILLED by AN IRISH HERO with a BRILLIANT AMERICAN FUTURE.

Admittance: $4 (Circle, Parterre, & Boxes): 20 c (standing).

 **<u>No Negroes</u>**

∇

I'LL GIT ON HOME TO HEAVEN BYE-M-BYE

We return to Redemption Falls and the runaway drummer-boy
Early in the New Year, 1866– Breaking a lock – A handful of papers
A lady of Spain – A quarrel

In the crawlspace beneath the floor of the Governor's house: this is where the Christ-killer sleeps. Bent up between the struts, curled like an ampersand. His world reeks of earth and wet boards. It is a little, he imagines, like living in a coffin, as Mamo said the monks once did.

Guilty Brother Mooney: his rottenwood dreams. He supposes they will find him, whip him from the town. Maybe they will hang him – or worse. He must be careful moving about. It is important not to be detected. He has seen what frontiersmen are capable of.

At night he steals out, conducts a bleary raid for food, doing skirmish with the foraging mongrels. He has a map of the colony and its possibilities in his mind. The zones where he must never go.

He has learned that it is worth trying the ash-cans behind the Shoogawn Saloon, a certain whorehouse to the west, another to the north. The grocer throws his rottings in a heap for the pigs. The gunsmith's wife feeds the robins. But there is little enough to eat in such an outpost in winter. The Negroes sometimes give him a mite.

He is swimmy-headed now, plagued by cold and constant sweats. His headaches are numbing, his thirst. He dreams about tributaries he has never seen: rivers with Indian names. And Mamo said *Rappahannock* means 'place of the souls' but it might mean something else, or it might mean nothing. Just as nobody remembers the place-names of Connemara, the Indians, too, forget.

Disordered thoughts. His mother in buckskins. A buffalo grazing on Beale Street. By day he stays hidden, wrapped in a shroud of tarp. Sucking on nuggets of ice. But stillness is hard for a boy that age. He worms around his prison, finding bricks, bits of slate. An ancient grind-stone. A sack of old shirts. Over there, beneath the trapdoor, he found the leather-strapped valise. Pert and neatly made, like a doctor's.

But once – you can see this – it was an assay man's satchel. The lock small and rusted. It cracked apart easily. The rust tasted ferrous as blood on his fingers. Maggots throng out of a pouch.

A sock of old papers: withered; gnawed. Some have been chewed to lace. Others are in pulp, a mash of blackened tissue. There are scribble-blocks, jottings, cuttings from newspapers. Quoins of threadbare journals. A mildewed handbill for 'A RALLY'. A broadsheet of a ballad with an antique notation: the crotchets black diamonds on a four-lined staff.

He does not read perfectly but he can figure a way. He tries to remember his letters. It is his pleasure to read, at least his way of killing the time, while he waits for the safety of darkness. Reading, Mamo told him, could save you your life. A poorman got to know how to read. Cause a rich one, it don't matter can he read or no. He's already elected. Period.

A is for Arkansas
B for bread
C is for Catholic
D for dead
E for Eliza
F for Fist
G for the girl done learnt me this

The boy does not recognise the man who lives in the house. That wreck upstairs – 'The General' folks call him – he must be an admirer of O'Keeffe, the child thinks. Because these flitters of papers – there are dozens in the bag – are concerned with the doings of the hero. Maybe he is a writer. A scholar. A story-maker. Cause he don't got the haught of a true-life General. He is lardy and old and he waddles like a fatboy and his eyes are red pennies and he stinks. The stench of his breathing that night at the mine – he skunked of rotgut and pish. And he talks like a noble in a pantomime of Englishmen. Probably they call him 'General' as a mockery.

Eliza's Pa was a story-maker, so Mamo used to say. A composer of come-all-ye's and ballads. Died up in Brooklyn. Got the cholera, Mamo said. But the boy is not certain this is true.

Come all ye sons of Erin's land; attend my lay a while;
'Tis of the valiant Con O'Keeffe, that fought for Erin's isle.
They clepped him out to the Demon's Land, from there he scaped a way,
To liberty and loving hearts, on the shores of Amerikay.

Eliza and Mamo – they often talked of O'Keeffe. Knew songs of his feats, his brilliance. A champion, Mamo said; the equal of Robert Emmet. He laughed at death on the scaffold. When Ireland is free, a Republic like America, when nobody is hungry, and we can all go home again, it will be owing to saviors like 'The Blade' O'Keeffe who were willing to give their all. But the turncoats of Ireland will despise him when that happens. They will always be afraid of his name. They will say we were freer in shackles and filth. They would like the whole island to be their workhouse.

Once, at Fredericksburg, the boy saw him at a great distance, in the vanguard of his New York zouaves. 'Ironfighters', people called them: the pride of the Potomac. There was nothing the Con O'Keeffes would not do. Jeddo Mooney had watched dumbstruck from the crest of a hill as they charged the Georgian lines below. No hope of success, not a crab's in a skillet, but onward they had rushed, into thunderstorms of bullets, toward the killing ground of Marye's Heights. They advanced the way other battalions retreated: headlong, hurtling, as though speed might save them. But it did not save them. Nothing did. Their war-cries and the rolling of cannon.

Faugh-a-balla! Fontenoy! Sarsfield! Clear the way! The barrages, the volleys howled them down. A man decapitated. A man exploded. Still the survivors came staggering. In twos and threes. In posses. Alone. Backing into the gunshot like seamen into rain. It was the kind of bravery that is terrifying.

A dragoon vomiting his entrails. A Stars-and-Stripes on fire. A color sergeant shot through the eye. Caps waved in farewell as the reinforcements came up. A creek in the meadow running scarlet. Two horses, capsized, tangled in their reins, hoofing in terror, gashing at each other's hides. A bugler, as though sleepwalking, totters towards the salvoes, which hack pieces from his body as he walks. Bleeding from his arms. Red streaks down his sleeves – but he fags across the field like a cold man toward sunlight – until finally the bullets make him kneel. Raises his instrument above his head as if to gesture *enough*. His right hand is blasted off: a rag. He tries to stand up. You saw him run towards the enemy. Then dancing in the riddle of his death.

The field that night. Bonfires in the ditches. Smoke gushing out of a pigsty. The Reverend's cassock livid with blood. Bile on his hands and his prayerbook. The ruins of a trooper blown into a tree. Impossible sights. Unseeable things. Men weltering in their blood. Lighting illuminating the vultures. Rats gnawing at –– no, that cannot be remembered: you cannot admit that picture to your mind. Sinews stretch and break. Father of all rats. The pulp carried away by the winner.

The reeks and the shrieks and the screeching gullies. A body, fetal, its knees to its chest, its hands clasped stiff to its boot-soles. A Galwayman from Brooklyn had beseeched the boy to finish him; and when the boy had croakingly answered that he could not do such a thing, the Galwayman had implored him to find a revolver so he could do the sin himself.

And when this fight is over, lads, a sweeter yet we face.
Far across the foaming billow where our mother yet awaits.
We'll down the Saxon tyrant, boys, evict the ancient thief,
And we're marching on to Dublin, then, with General Con O'Keeffe.

'Con', the ballads call him, though his given name is James. 'The Blade.' 'The Scabbard.' 'The Rapier.' 'Ireland's Prince.' It's all those names but it's only one man. Hard to know what to call him – what to say when you meet him. Perhaps, the boy reasons, the old tub of guts upstairs has met O'Keeffe. Maybe they are relatives, former comrades. Every handsome man has an ugly twin, so Mamo said. See him in the pier glass on a Good Friday morning. He collects these shabby relics as though planning a museum. Perhaps he is a maker of ballads.

She dressed all in her true-love's clothes and away to war did go,
And longed to see the seaport towns of Canadee-eye-oh.

A boy in the mud, with the fieldmice and the spiders, and a clutch of tattered papers he does not understand. He heats a stone with a candle stub, scrapes a hollow in the loam, as they showed him to do in the War. Survive, play it pebble, we shall all survive, and the south shall rise again. Sometimes he hears rain, the wind racketing in the boards, the crunch of a snow-load tumbling from a bough. At other times, the peculiar silence of a freeze: birdless and elemental.

He wombs himself in a tarpaulin and waits for the blow-over. Come February he will strike out for Canada. Any sooner, you would die on the road to the north, for the snow has obliterated field and road, and the border posts, he has heard, are closed. Walk across a snowfield, you don't know what's beneath. Some drifts are the height of a house. There are lakes in whose depths live weird bears and weird elks. The Koötenais version of Heaven.

Once, during the War, a comrade told him about Canada. A country where they care for the Irish. Aint gottem these no-count bigots like here in the states, tellin ever one he don't belong. Irishman liked, he *respected* up there. They know he a slogger, a man of honest toil. If he like him a drink and a little roola-boo, why, nobody care: Canuck take a drink his self. He's a kin to an Irish: he know how it go. Not like these Mayflowerin Methodists.

Down here in the states, so the soldier said bitterly, Pat don't count for a rat. Want Pat to do his fightin for him, build his roads, sink his caissons: get fucked and die quiet in some ginshop. Pat nothin but a coolieman prayin the beads. Nothin but a slave in a scapular. When they trenched that canal down the hell of New Orleans, it was Irish they put to the gullies. Wouldn't put no slave in. Cause a slave cost him money. But a Irish cost him nothin but pennies a day. Sweat eleven hour in darkness, like a hog in the dugout; when he die, or go crazy, or the trench fever break him, here come-up another hundred to beg for his place. Canajun don't treat no Christian like such. He shake you by the hand and pony up the tin. Montréal. Nova Scotia. Ontario. Ever part. They got ice floes and igloos: all manner of wonders. Man could have him a time up there.

So the boy has a picture of Canada in his mind. A land of well-paid work, all you can handle, of time-and-a-half for laboring Saturdays, of plentiful vittles and rivers of beer and pretty little French girls with them sultry eyes, singing 'O Le Beau Soleil'. No wonder his father took off into Canada. No wonder he never come home.

He sleeps with a gun in his twelve-year-old hand: a deadman's Colt repeater. He took it from a body he stumbled upon in the street on the night he tracked the hoof-prints into town. It is a weapon he knows. He has fired a repeater often, but you need all your strength to steady it. So heavy, the Colt repeater; his forearms so weak. Make you feel like you're aiming a lump-hammer.

> *In the master's step he trod,*
> *Where the snow lay dinted.*
> *Heat was in the very sod*
> *That the saint had printed.*

It was track those prints or starve where he was: freezing in the slags at the mine. There was risk and it was high, but to stay was a certainty. Starvation, so Mamo told him, was not a death for a human. Do anything you must. I saw them die in the famine. Break any commandment. Do not starve.

So he staggered through the thundersnow, along a mile of broken road, hunting the tracks of the Federal horses. And even as he ran, the tracks vanished before his eyes, annihilated by slops of sleet.

I am murderer now. The brand of Cain. Mark of the beast on my hand. The Mississippi brothers were not the first he had killed. Not the first set of killers; not the first set of brothers. The two at Fair Oaks had been brothers, someone told him. Backstabbing bluebelly Lincoln-loving bastards. They needed killing bad.

'P.J.Foley' on the barrel of the repeater. Graved with something sharp like a brad-nail. He tries to make an anagram of P. J. Foley but it always comes out as a nonsense.

Eleven men. Not counting Mississippians. And those are the ones he is certain of. Might well have been more. Probably were. You couldn't watch the track of a bullet as it belched from your gun, hurtled towards a charging battalion. Eleven was his total – they gave him eleven cheers. That night in the camp at Sharpsburg. They threw him in a horse-blanket, tossed him eleven times; there were eleven slugs of popskull, eleven kisses from a whore. He was the bravest son-of-a-bitch in Dixie, they told him. Bravest in the whole world round. Your Momma and Pa would be proud if they knew. Lincoln gonna hang you high, boy!

Then an officer had come in – Captain O'Neill of the Shreveports – saying the carouse was a disgrace, and the thing it celebrated a scandal. Wasn't proper or Christian to have a child do such things. He had made a scolding speech – are we savages? Are we redskins? Do we wish to dishonor our cause? No child can be permitted the taking of arms; that is wrong and will always be wrong! If it happens again, you will all be cashiered. *Have you men no sons of your own?* Drunk, weeping, the boy had been led away. Made to surrender the weapon. Warned to follow orders.

He had thought following orders was what he'd been doing. The enemy come, you gun him. He wanted your country, your 'way of life'. Affront your womenfolk, forage your planting, eat out your substance, defile your sister, set you down to slavery in God's own land – no mercy should be given such a monster. Not a sin to kill the man that wronged your blood brother. Padre Guillaume had told them plain. Not a sin to kill a traitor, a deserter, a spy, a corrupter of boys, an enemy. Invaders, aggressors – all these could be killed and the Savior would understand. 'I come not to bring peace, but a sword,' He said. Saint Peter cut him off a Jew's *ear*!

Dismas, Gesmas, Christ in his boot-spurs. Right now they were burning in Hell. Harran the coachman would look down and spit on them, safe at the throne of the Lamb. And his spittle would *fizz* on their white-hot tongues. And the cherubs and putti would smile.

It was they had led the posse that strangled John Custis Harran, the boy's protector, a bumbling whiskied coachman, who had never done a harm to a soul but himself. Bandannas they were wearing, as they stripped him and beat him, but the boy recognized them uncovered. Their swagger, their leanness, their bantam-cocky strut; the way one of them had of smoothing his tresses – his weird and glimmering eyes. The things they did to Harran – the boy saw them all – would not have been deserved by Satan.

H for my home.
I for in.
J for a jig with my
K is for kin.
L is for lovers,
As M is for mine.
But N is for never:
A long, long time.

No sin to kill a murderer. Matter of fact, you should. He spins up the chamber, places the barrel in his mouth. He is not sure if this feeling is temptation.

His sister on a mountaintop in the wrench of a hurricane. Gripping onto sedge-grass for an anchor. A crowblack tornado advancing behind her; its cargo of snapped-off treetops.

He awakens to a commotion unfolding in the lane. Drags himself to the lattice of the crawlspace.

A buggy has rattled up. The bay is panting. Its coat is shabby. The mailboy drops his bag. It spills – he chases its contents. His name is Orson Rawls. He is the undertaker's son. The dogs gawp like gargoyles. Now people are shouting. They are trying to lift a Chinese woman from the boards of the buggy; she is moaning, sweeping her arms, as though swimming through pain, and a man who must be her husband is wild-eyed, tottering. *'The midwife!'* shouts a woman. 'You must take her there immediately. There is no time to lose. *Her laboring begins.'* They do as she orders. Someone produces a wolf-skin. The party hurries away toward the town.

What is strange to the killer – well, all of it is strange – the Navajo blanket, the Chinaman in his pigtails, the mailboy's letters fluttering off like thoughts – but the color of the girl giving the orders is what strikes him. She must surely be a servant. But she is dressed so finely. And everyone listens, obeys her commands. Her cloak is the green of a mallard duck's neck; its hood hemmed with jewels and fur. There is a belt around her hips: black alligator, also jeweled. She is so beautiful that he cannot stop looking at her.

I did not bring you in the world for you to quit it by starving. That cannot be permitted. Promise me.

He rests the eye of the pistol in the crotch of a rotting lattice, squints at her down its barrel. One squeeze of the trigger, she would go like all the rest. The tiniest movement of a knuckle. That's how it come – the boy has seen it often. A marriage of geometry and time. Marker moved on a map and ten thousand die, and the map won't remember they ever existed.

> *Brandy in Scotia's a tuppence a quart, boys.*
> *The ale in New Brunswick a penny a glass.*

She turns on the road, in such a way that he cannot see her face. Her body beneath the cloak is shaped like a guitar. The wind blows the folds of her cloak. She is holding the buggy-whip parallel to the ground. Two ells in parallel, he remembers. A dagger in her belt. Diamonds on her wrists. She looks like a card from some long forgotten tarot. She appears to be staring at the mountains or the lake. Her shoulders tremble. Perhaps she is weeping. The cook hurries from the house and speaks to her.

In her body is a soundbox, Eliza once told him. Daddy go to Momma and he touch the strings with love, and here come a little tune afterwhile. Music of a baby grow slow in the darkness. When it ready to get played, sing on out. And ever last one of us got our own tune inside him. If you stay real quiet, you can hear it. *Listen.*

They stand for a while on the white rutted road, where the black teeth of stones are grinning. The boy cannot hear what the women are saying.

But is obvious, somehow – the way they are standing, perhaps, with a distance separating them, not the proximity of intimates – that the mulatta girl is mistress, employer of the cook. Or perhaps a superior servant.

They enter the house. He hears their footsteps above him, the mumble of a muffled discussion. The cook is saying something about an urgent letter having come; she placed it in the study upstairs. There is nothing to eat. The stores are all empty. Should she draw the lady a bath? No, he has not been seen –

Now the General is shouting, a woman shouting back. The sound of a man and woman quarreling is one the boy has heard many times. But it has never gotten easy to hear.

'I was visiting a sick family in St Hubert when the storm came on. I have told you already. Do not question me like a judge.'

'I shall question as I please when my so-called wife remains absent from my house a fortnight without permission. Nice material for every wagging tongue in the Territory. Not that Lady Majesty would care about such trifles.'

'Did you wish me to be killed on the highway? Have you seen the road?'

'To the shit with your road. Your duty was to be here. Is Christmas not to be kept in a Christian house?'

'I told you: I tried. The mountain was not passable.'

'May one ask where you quartered? Or is that another imposition?'

'Where do you imagine? I took a room at the livery stable. I assume you would not want me to sleep in a ditch?'

'Your place is with your husband. How many times need you be reminded? Must you insist on flaunting your contempt for me at every opportunity? Is your disobedience so important, has it grown such a religion with you now, that it precedes even the common proprieties?'

'You deliver me lectures – '

' – I do not deliver lectures – '

'You deliver me lectures on common propriety, when I am spoken to like a scullion-maid who requires your admonishment. I shall not accept it of you, sir, whatever your damned name. Are you listening, sir? I am not one of your men.'

'Do not damn at me, Lucia, I warn you plainly.'

'You shall warn me of nothing. I am not afraid of bullies.'

'Dare you turn your back while I am speaking? Come here, I said!'

'Nobody, sir, is listening any more! No one is interested. The audience

has gone. You may pose and strut till you are black to the gills but the gallery is empty. It has been empty for years.'

'Get out of my sight, Lucia.'

'Get out of mine.'

'You whore. *I said get out!*'

The killer hears a door slam above him in the log-house. Something heavy is flung. A glass is smashed. There follows a silence, which continues a long time. He squats in the crawlspace, too petrified to move.

P, Q, R: Proud Queen of the Rose.
S, T, U: her Slaves To Use.
V and its double: Victoria's Wing.
X, Y, and Z – we don't stand for a thing.

If he moves at all – if even his pupils dilate – it might start them off again.

∇

CHAPTER 10

THEN FARE THEE WELL, DECEIVING LOVE

The letter awaiting Lucia on her return to Redemption Falls
Tidings of an engagement – A borrowed book returned
The importance of the triangle in mapmaking

14 Water Street,
Brooklyn,
X 12 65

Mrs. General O'Keeffe:

I write to convey news which may be of passing interest – I am going to be married in the Spring – My fiancée is a second cousin of mine: Emily Gould – I do not think you know her – She is an exceptional person.

Miss Gould + I have been friends since childhood in Boston – Like you, she nursed in the War – Her father + two of her brothers died of starvation at Andersonville Prison, so that unlike some who pontificate on the horrors of war, she knows what it is to suffer loss – We plan on sailing for England immediately we marry – What with various painful occurrences of recent years, we both of us want for a clean beginning – (I have resigned my commission, not wishing to squander further time on frustrating + unbeneficial encumbrances) + an opportunity has presented to go out to India with Captain Melville of the Trigonometric Survey – So that this is a letter of goodbye.

I am grateful for your charity to me on previous occasions, most especially while I was recuperating at the hospital + in the subsequent period – For your tolerant sympathy I owe you a debt, which I trust that this MS discharges – I now see that I was a difficult patient, rather slow-witted + susceptible, given to misunderstandings which you must have found unsophisticatedly dreary – If I acted foolishly or presumptuously, which we of the lower orders do from time to time,

I trust that a person of your widely famed saintliness will be capable of forgiving a bothersome invalid, secure in the certainty that he shall never inconvenience you again.

You will find inclosed herewith a volume of Donne's sonnets + sermons, which you were bountiful enough to loan me a number of years ago – I meant to send it back but it was mislaid for a time – I cannot now remember why.

Incidentally, + in conclusion, for I have no wish to detain you further: you inquired of me, once, for the secret of mapmaking, + I recall that I was unable to furnish you with a succinct précis. One has since learnt from bitter experience that the matter is straightforward. It is – quite simply – understanding the triangle; knowing where one stands in it + when one is defeated by it.

There is of course no need to answer this letter – You will be busy, I know, with your latest charity case.

Good Morrow, as Donne has it. Et cetera, Et cetera,

A. M. Winterton, Capt.
U.S. Corps of Cartographers

∇

Governor's Residence
Robert Emmet Street
Redemption Falls
The Mountain Territory
January 7th, 1866

Captain Winterton:

Accept my congratulations on your forthcoming marriage, which I pray shall be happy, as you deserve.

Should ever you with your wife have reason to be in this Territory you would be welcome guests of my husband and I.

Good-bye and good luck in your new life overseas. I hope that you will cover India with triangles if that is your wish.

Respectfully,
Lucia-Cruz McLelland-O'Keeffe (Mrs)

∇∇∇

PART III

THE HIGH PLACE OF STONES

It was Pete Vandorn shot him. Big Dutchboy. Good aim. Seen the shot struck him here – couple inches north the heart. Blows him halfway cross the street and he hits the dirt backways. And that's when I seen the frightenist sight of my life. Cause I'll be damned to Hell if he duddn get up. Aint no mistakin it. That's what I'm tellin you. Stands up from a chest-shot. Rides away.

Joseph Peterson, miner
From his account of the attempted killing of the desperado Johnny Thunders, following bank robbery in Durrusville County, Good Friday, 1866.
Interview by Professor J.D. McLelland, February 1897,
New Derry, Great Smokecloud Mountains

CHAPTER 11

THE RIVER WILD AS HEART'S DESIRE AND NEITHER CAN I SWIM

Further remembrances from Elizabeth Longstreet
The difficulty of entering the Mountain Territory at the time
of our narrative – & sundry other matters

. . . An I come up to the Territory first time sixtyfour. Was a scrub on a steam-boat out of St Louis . . . No it wadn too many steamers yet that time . . . Dangerous plyin, the Missouri that time. Cause the river all choke-up with trees and all kind. 'Big Muddy' they call the river. Water like a tarpit. Missouri tougher plyin than the Missippi iny how. Got the whirlpools an cataracts, and rapids ever bend. It maelstrom and sandbank an the most of it perilous shallow. It virgin river then. They didn got the charts. An the Spokane was wilful up that run a the country. They comin down ever now and again and rampagin the steamships. Seen a Frenchman got killed with a arrow through his gullet. Nother time a English boy – he was a wheel-wright's prentice – he got capture by raiders when he go ashore. And the Captain got to leave him behind.

Went up and down the Muddy out of St Louis fowhile. Four, five time. Six. I forget. But then I got a eye sickness; got this glaucoma see. Turn my left eye blind. Call glaucoma . . . Commence to workin for the General . . . by Redemption Falls. And his wife come on out in the summer of sixtyfive. Cause I could cook some and fix house. And they done me all right. Wouldn say saintly but they fair-mind I guess . . . Mess of slanders been spoke of that man an his wife. To me they aint been spoken of fair.

Yes I knowed of what happen. The rebel-boy and such. Even heared songs on that story down the years. But peoples all give out that story of the boy wrong. Wiseman sweep the dirt on they-own side of the street. Cause paper gwine take any word a pen put . . . And it dont mean its truth . . . or half of it even . . . Can write your name is Billy, no paper answer you it John . . . Dependin on all who wrote it . . . And it aint true the General an his wife didn have no love. Cause why she come west if it was? . . . Man treated you bad, youd stay home with you people . . . Wadn easy, comin west for no woman that time . . . In especial not a lady . . . No, sir.

∇

CHAPTER 12

COME LIVE WITH ME AND BE MY LOVE
or
WHY LUCIA CAME INTO THE TERRITORY

The Governor writes to Lucia near the end of the Civil War
The making of a photograph – The Bad Lands and their ghosts
A poor fallen woman whose name is not recorded – Indians
Cherrybrandy – Signor Verdi in the wilderness

Governor's Residence,
2nd Street: 11 lots east of the creek,
near the mileposts.
Redemption Falls,
Mountain Territory

April 15th, 1865

Dearest Light, *mio specchio*,†

I wrote you seven weeks ago but am as yet unanswered. Has any of my
letters made a way to you successfully? I think that I wrote four times
since arrival out here. A stagecoach was attacked by renegade
Cheyenne downriver from Fort Ballantyne the other week. There was a
report of stolen mailbags, but nobody seems to know how many.

Are you still at New York or have you gone down to the villa for
Easter? *Cara mia*: write me an answer the moment you receive this. I
am becoming anxious. Is everything quite right with you? I had a dream
in which you were running on the decks of an icebreaker: it disturbed
me greatly. Tell me you are not unwell.

How is it at the hospital? You are not tiring yourself out again I hope.
Johnny Colohane, one of my deputies, received a letter from his wife

† Italian. 'My mirror.'

(lucky devil) last month and she mentioned you in it. She had seen you making a photograph in the hospital gardens; a patient, a Captain with very terrible burns, was your assistant. It is kind of you to give such an unfortunate man an interest. My love is so compassionate always.

Well then: there is little to say, *mio doppio*,† except that I miss you solrely [*sic*] & wish I had you here to talk to. It is almost midnight now, but quite damnably hot. Some thirtsy [*sic*] fellow, I think a prairie-dog, is scraping like buggery in the enclosure below my casement – as though his paws could unearth a wellspring. Poor tufted wretch, he looks almost human. If you were here, you would brave the swelter to assist his excavations. But I shall do no such thing, I am afraid. Tonight he shall burrow alone.

This climate is fiercer than the blaze of Tennessee, indeed remorselessly wearying, & taking the devil's own time to attune to. No one seems to know whether or not it is typical. Some of the Natives say it is; others say not; for of course they only say what they think we want to hear and for the rest remain silent, inscrutable. Indians are remarkably similar to Cavan men in that aspect (and in others); but my love does not know what a Cavan man is, I suppose, and nor, I imagine, does she need to. Stomach annoys demonically. I expect it is the water. And one is finding it difficult to sleep. I suppose that after four years of nights in a tent, it is troublesome to adapt to a bed unpopulated by weevils. I start awake in the darkness and wonder where I am; and then, I wonder where are you.

They say the War will be over by the end of the year. We hear little reliable: this means the rumor-flies thrive. At least once or twice a week the rebels have surrendered; then the White House is burnt & Lincoln hanged in shackles††; or the British have recognized the Confederacy & are fortifying Richmond; or the French have come in on our side & are shelling Nashville – all of this reported with the adamant certitude of those whose ignorance is perfect. As for me, I awaken in the morning & look out of the window. If a scaffold is not being erected by slave-catchers in the yard, I assume the United States still exist.

I wish that I had a picture of you. Have you changed your hair? *La*

† 'My double', my reflection.
†† In fact the War had ended almost a week previously, with Lee's surrender at Appomattox on April 9th. O'Keeffe is also unaware of the murder of President Lincoln, who died on April 15th, the day this letter was written.

femme de Calhoun wrote him that it was chopped short and straight ('like a boy's'). Gods, tell me you have not committed this self-desecration! Can it be nearly two years since last I saw you? Did you cut it for the hospital? I suppose that you did. Is it truth that a nurse must be a repellent old haggis? If so, how can the Holy Sisters admit my angel to their realm?† Write your lonely disciple immediately – an epistle of two pages at least, do you hear. I want to hear every last thing that you have been doing. And send me a vandalized curl.

Had a nightmare the other night of my own stupidity and malice. I mean our quarrel at Tennessee that Christmas you came out. Wasteful, sorry fool of a husband you have, to poison our farewell in such a way. The harsh words I used, the spitefulness of what I said: they did not deserve your forgiveness. Many such stupidities come back to me lately, whilst events of last week I forget or misremember. This morning I could not dredge up my mother's maiden name for some minutes. Any further back than she, and soon everyone's name is enfogged. One pictures one's ancients wraithed in rewarding glory but actually it is only forgetfulness. How I wish I had not gone, had rather ordered away the soldiers & returned with you to New York as you wished.†† You ask for so little & I have given less, always. Your father is right to loathe me. Half the time I loathe myself.

This house, this Territory, is an Australia without you. I curse myself for my obstinacy, this venomous streak of pig-headedness; it has done so much harm to us; I see that now. I have not been the husband I promised, nor the one you deserve. I have wasted so much; it quite nauseates one to think on it. Can you permit me another chance to amend? I mean to deserve you, Lucia.

Recently I have begun to doubt I should have come to this place. It is too wild for me without you; too empty. Animals, trees: one does not know their names. The birds look prehistoric. I should not advise any wifeless man to venture out here. He has too much time for reflection.

---

† O'Keeffe may be alluding to the wartime policy that nurses must be 'plain-looking', 'older than 30' and 'must not wear hoops or jewelry'. Lucia was notorious at St Mary's Hospital, New York, for presenting for duty in a pair of men's trousers. She was sent home immediately and ordered to change. She returned in a different pair of trousers.

†† O'Keeffe was stationed at Chattanooga, Tennessee, from December 1862 to April 1863. Lucia visited him there, briefly, at Christmas 1862. The visit was not a success.

One can ride three hard days & not see a man, nor evidence that man ever existed. Five times the area of Ireland we have; and not twenty thousand souls in all. The maps are all wrong: immense regions uncharted. What maps we possess are copies of older ones, so that they replicate the old faults, &, invariably, multiply them. Nature herself disconcerts one here. The mountains astound, one cannot gainsay it – immeasurable & stark, & the gorges fathomless; the Great Smokeclouds of such an altitude that their zenith-snows never melt, & never shall, did Libyan suns appear. But there is some note of disquietude in the chord of this beauty, I cannot name what it is. Perhaps it is one's own pitiable inconsequentiality. Every human in a thousand miles could be felled by some vulgar little pestilence & nature would not care about it but only trundle on. One thinks of that grewsome [*sic*] line from K.L. I suppose: The flies & the bastard boys & cet.†

Last month I captained the militia on a hunt into the Mauvaises Terres. *Militia* is a fine word. Rabble on horseback. It is all they can achieve not to pelt one another with nuts. But I suppose that they do their best. I bawl, I beseech them to WRITE THEIR REPORTS but they seem to think pens are for poets, or anyway not lawmen, when in fact, as I am worn to the meats of my soul telling them, *no law is possible without documentation, a record*. We were tracking a gang of rebels that has been raiding & murdering for months, but of course could not find them, as I suspected we should not. We never find these phantoms, for they know the *terrae incognitae* & have protectors in plenty out there. But there is no help for it; one has to put up some sort of ridiculous effort to show willing. I suppose that is what the desperadoes themselves are doing. Sometimes that is the picture that forms in one's inward eye – two punch-drunk fighters holding one another up, brow to slickened brow, waiting for the bell to sound.

To be out among those pinnacles of red-brown rock, in whose mile-long shadows nothing decent can ever grow – one felt as though riding through Dante. *Cañon*s as deep as the turrets of Seville are tall, and the gloat of the withering sun. Subterranean caverns quite the size of Notre Dame or Saint Peter's. Not a sound does one hear in that scorched, parched nowhere: but the wind fluting eerily through fissures in the

† King Lear, Act IV, sc I. 'As flies to wanton boys, are we to the gods, – They kill us for their sport.'

rocks, and the clop of one's mount, but muffled by the ubiquitous dust, so that even the rider directly behind cannot be heard when he calls out. Patk Vinson, you remember him, opined one midnight at the campfire: 'God blesh me, I tink Hell must appare like the Badlands o' dis Territry', a pronouncement italicized by a brief but poignant belch. And yet, even this wilderness is not without its beauty. One morning I looked up from a peyote-strewn riverbed & saw clouds like cotton: just like wisps of finest cotton. And there was a perfume of something like crushed thyme in the heat; do you know, as in Provence, on an August night? At moments such as this – I do not know why – one wants to shout for joy at very ordinary things. But the men would have found it pretty strange I suppose. They look at me quearly [sic] sometimes.

We are so new here, we whites. We feel the weight of our unbelonging. One would have thought it a liberation; but it is not. Perhaps – even probably – we should not be here at all; yet the apple, once tasted, must be eaten. Not a building in five hundred miles is older than a decade. What few dwellings are thrown up outside of the towns are log-cabins & cabooses; nothing of stone or foundated. These are scattered about the valleys like so much box-wood, as toys awaiting the incursion of the nursery tyrant. Christ, how distant now, the cafes of New York, the avenues & squares I long to see again. Last night I dreamed that you & I were dining at Delmonico's. Dear Christ, *cara mia* – I can scarcely picture it now.

The settlers are the ghastliest one has ever known, common and dirty and irredeemably vulgar; quite utterly & Swiftianly hideous. There is hardly a one of them without that dull glint of cruelty in his gaze. A toothbrush would be regarded as a burning bush among the Israelites; any sort of kindness as a weakness. One rides a thousand leagues through this desolate pit before ever meeting an act of fellowship or mercy. A dust-covered miner whipping a dust-covered mule: this should be the Territorial emblem.

Oh, it is nonsense, nonsense. Bloviating trash. Many are not so bad. My stomach has me in bitter mood – firgive [sic] me, Amor. Also sore throat this last ten days (for which Chinese apothecary advised no potion but sucking mucilaginous fruit, jujube).There are good sorts here, even families with children. One cannot reproach them for the prizes they appear to desire: gold, a clean start, a new aspect to look upon, to compose new memories that will drown the old. The Grail one craves oneself, could one only grasp it. But the closer one approaches, the more it eludes. Continuously I feel – I do not know why – that I have missed my chance; that I did not recognize my cue when it came.

And for every hardworking citizen, with the decent American spirit, we have two or three shadows & these are the rotting menace. The town is abuzz with this swarm of damnable leeches: place-seekers, land-grabbers, traitors in disguise, thugs competing for the position of official hangman. They flap about me & the men like flesh-flies to carrion; even speaking to them makes one feel the sudden want of a bath. Each supplicant has a story, a plea for one's ear, or believes himself owed for some patriotic deed. This one has done this act of heroism in the War, the other that, his turd cousin anudder; each is a Goliath in autobiography yet incapable, apparently, of the sufficiency required to swab his own arse without my or the Government's assistance. But this, too, is a form of posing. Few, out here, are quite what they front. All smolder with cunning, & the ambition of Lucifer. Every other in the Territory is a rebel runaway or sympathizer. And one must pretend not to know it, of course.

It is rumored that there is an entire brigade of rebel escapees to the north; ridden up to the mountains, there to plot further treasons. If – when – Lincoln wins the War, they will immediately declare 'independence', so it is said, & treat with Canada for sovereignty. Imagine the bloodshed. A war of the world, nothing less. The tombstones would stretch to the gates of Montréal. One argues it to the townspeople and they appear nonplussed. Some decline even to refer to the place by its legal name & instead persist in calling it 'Arlington City', after the confiscated plantations of Lee in Virginia. What a thing is *called* has too much import out here; every rock they mean to christen for some moldering cadaver. Backward-looking mewlers, the damn pack whole, weepy, piss-in-the-bed, corpse-adoring nincompoops, reversing into the future they hate. Better if the towns were named for letters of the alphabet. But that would satisfy none of the illiterate swine I suppose. These are brutes for whom 'A' is what you stitch on a harlot's breast, and 'B' is the bastard that stings you.

The women would break a heart, so broken-down & poor they are. I need not tell you the manner in which many of them eke a pittance. I suppose one will always see it in a town full of men who are without the civilizing influence a wife will exert; but still, it is beastly when one does. A coin in his pocket, a drink in his belly, and conscience seems to flit like a specter. One of my deputies, English, happened on an Irish girl in the street the other night. He brought her to the jailhouse, for there was no place else for her to sleep & we fetched the drunken gawm of a so-called physician, for she was in a terrible way, quite as emaciated & broken-spirited as the famished one saw in one's childhood. Told English she was born on a onetime slave-ship in 47; out of Liverpool & her people from W. Cork. Died the next morning & was buried in a cemetery for criminals, for we had no other place to put her. The doctor, probably having killed her, fell in the creek the following night, reportedly while attempting to relieve himself in it. Didn't drown (worst luck) but has buggered out to Salt Lake City. So that we are doctorless, preacherless, lawyerless and judgeless. If only I could burn down the newspaper, too, we would have the prairie Utopia.

And the Natives despise all of us, even when we treat with them. Their children fill me with dread. They remind one of how the poor of Wexford used to look when a regiment of redcoats rode in to the town – the serenity of patient hatred. They would scalp every white from here to St Louis if they could, & make drinking-bowls out of our skulls. And, though one fights them as one must, one could hardly condemn them, for we are strangers in their land, dispossession made flesh. Twenty years ago, dear God, when I believed in something fine, I would have had some feeling for their plight. But the men are quite ruined by liquor, of course. Seem congenitally incapable of continence.

I have been thinking of writing to Lincoln to request that I be released; although I know that this would end finally the prospect of any sort of government advancement, your Lear having yapped his gratitude for this dismal kennel. But even if Washington assented, which by no means is certain, I might have to remain here some seasons, even a year, until some other twittering imbecile might be located under some rock and coaxed out by a lump of opium and sent to replace. I wrakc [sic] my mind continuously for what I might do then – you know that I cannot continue to live off your father any more. It rides me so hard, I cannot sleep. Perhaps they would give me an ambassadorship – do you think it possible? France or Havana would be wonderful, or Venezuela. How the French would adore *ma petite negresse*. I should never permit you to leave the house unchaperoned, lest some gossam-tongued *flâneur* tempt you away by his blandishments.

Mon ami in the yard has abandoned his archeology & scampered, like the sawbones, for the newfound. I should like to have a drink now.

But have sworn off, did I tell you? Feeling stronger, cleaner without the filth.

Another fool of a publisher has begged me to do him up a memoir. Bostonian this one, probably a crook. Have been collating notes in the evenings in a half-hearted way. Suppose it might kill the time.†

What else? Nothing (which comes of nothing). Had a bad bilious attack last week, was spewing like a geyser, but am rallied a bit now, after taking a little cherrybrandy as a physic – no more than a thimbleful, two fingersworth literally – but our mutton is all gone, & I am sorry as Job for it; still, we hope to have buffalo and mule-deer presently, which will come very good after using salt and hardtack so long. Or I will griddle that bothersome bastard that burrows in the yard. Christ, what I would give for a velvetclefted peach or a mouthful of luscious black grapes . . . [ ]††

. . . If only there were some commercial idea, some means of raising a competence that would fasten our situation for once & all. I awaken before dawn with some newfangled scheme straddling my chest like an incubus . . . [ ].††† A newspaper again (the one we have here is the vilest Confederate filth-sheet), or gentleman-farming, or importing stuffs from Europe, or something in Nicaragua: *Je ne sais pas*. By the noon, I know none of these dogs will hunt. One feels as in a maze of mirrors.

If, somehow, we could scratch up a little more capital, new mines are being opened out here all the time. There are Croesan fortunes hewn out of the rocks every hour, often on a relatively modest investment. What do you think of it? Perhaps we might set up tent out here a while? Would that interest you, my love, or is it a worthless

---

† In fact, O'Keeffe had written to 32 publishers offering 'American rights for ten years' in his projected memoir, assuming it would be an extremely lucrative proposition. Twenty-two did not reply; there were nine rejections. A small house, Withers & Son, of Boston, Massachusetts, offered him a minuscule advance, for 'all rights, in perpetuity'.

†† There follows a lengthy paragraph which O'Keeffe's executors have requested the editor not to include. Its content is franker than many of O'Keeffe's letters to Lucia, touching uninhibitedly, though very lovingly, upon their intimate life. The editor advances the view that such expressions are in no manner obscene but he has acceded to the executors' wishes.

††† Here a bracketed sentence appears, which the executors have also requested be omitted.

design? I suppose that it will not always be so inhospitable a hole. Perhaps every territory in America was like this, once, & every preserve on the earth for that matter. And here it will change quickly, for already it is changing, as civilization ripens and the shoots of cultivation put forth. Even Manhattan was not so long ago a hillock-strewn kip. Oh murder, I don't know. Do you think we should go abroad? Work at how we are to live & c.

My sweetest berry, can you not come to me for a season? I know that I should be stronger, did I have my *madrugada de amor*.† We should at the least have the time to talk, & in peace, about what might be attempted, & prospects & c. There is a pleasanter settlement than this growing up not too distant, a small place called Edwardstown, seventy miles to the south. We could take a chalet down there & a servant or two? The gold-men and copper lords are building their mansions there; some are extremely fine, quite as good as many in New York. The *hacendados* live well & have a kind of society.†† There are groves & a park; the climate seems more temperate. There is talk of a great cathedral and of an opera house copied from La Scala, where the Midases may strut with their gem-studded Bridgets in last year's Parisian duds. We could live quietly, & read, & talk in the evenings, & laugh at all the *provinciales* if we wished. Perhaps things would come clearer in a year or two. There are no saloons. It would be a pleasant situation in which to raise a child.

How wrong I have been to have denied you even this. You know that this matter is painful to me & I think you know why. But how stubborn it has been of me, to insist so utterly. I have been so stupid; so vain. Everything seems in ruins. It's the damnedest thing. I keep thinking I will never see you again. Or that something is very wrong.

If you will not come to me, at least send word that all is well? But please, my love, can you come out for a season? I promise, I vow on my sacred honor, to do nothing that should make you regret it. Those stupidities are past, I promise, I promise. Can you set out with me again after these terrible years? I parch without you like a frizzled old lamp, for I need once again the benediction of my Light. *Stella mia, cuore mio, amore mio*.†††

† Spanish. Dawn of love.
†† *Hacendado*: Spanish, the owner of a hacienda.
††† Italian: My star, my heart, my love.

Your husband, who would be better,
Con

P.S. For when you come: in my study, behind Gibbon's *Decline & Fall*
on the third shelf, you will find a small chest: malabar teak with brass
hasps & my inits. (It contains a journal & other old papers I want.)
Don't concern yourself for the key: I have that here.

∇

CHAPTER 13

DEMONLAND

by Lucia-Cruz McLelland-O'Keeffe†

*A tale concerning the escape of James O'Keeffe
from Van Diemen's Land, Australia, some years before Lucia
was to make his acquaintance at New York*

There were three of you in the rowboat that stole out from Hobart at daybreak: you, the thief M'Carthy, and Knowles. You did not know M'Carthy, a hangdog Northumbrian; but D—— had assured you he was solid.

You rowed close to the harbor wall as you approached the sentry-box on the cob. Your eyes you trained on the water. The prostitute would be inside with the soldierboy now. You did not care for that aspect; D—— said it was the only way. The bump beneath the keel as you scraped across the sandbar. The quietness; the lapping of the water.

The water smelt of heat, was painful to look at. Knowles you knew to be a sympathizer; but you did not like Knowles. He was coarse in his language, boastful of his conquests, an uncouth little backslapper, ingratiating. You did not have much to say to him. He addressed you by your Christian name. You would not have suffered such a lout to be your bootblack.

Some trick of the sea meant that you could not hear the explosion. But you saw the bulge of smoke from the courthouse. Knowles rowed on. M'Carthy spat in the water. The smoke rose into the sky. You found yourself hoping that the soldierboy would not be flogged and that the woman would escape; she knew nothing, D—— said. You imagined them standing on the flagstones of the cob illumined by the distraction of flames.

---

† Unpublished. Dated 'Summer 1865', written on 15 sheets (recto and verso) of ivory foolscap notepaper, seven of which bear the heading 'Steamship J.V. Gould: St Louis & Upper Missouri: First Class'. Probably a fair copy, since it includes no corrections. Lucia's spelling, often idiosyncratic, has been standardized.

You rowed for two hours; it was painful, exhausting work. The undertow was powerful, much worse than you had imagined, with a tugging, insistently eddying motion that tried to wrench the oars from your hands. And you were chubby by then, grown pulpy as a pupa; you looked, as D—— put it, like a well-fed farmer. You had been smoking almost incessantly in the days before the attempt, had drunk up the last of your whiskey the previous night. Those were the months when all that started. Your last season in Tasmania with Catharine.

A squabble soon began between Knowles and M'Carthy, Knowles asserting that the dory was drifting in the wrong steer, would be wrecked on the corals were she not headed north, the younger man insisting that the elder was mistaken; the horizon must be maintained to the larboard. You did not know which companion, if either, was correct. Their sea-words grew harder to understand.

A tea clipper would be anchored, a French one. No. The vessel would be Dutch, her captain would be French. He would know your identity and that you were important, valuable, but would not ask questions of any kind. You would be given a crewman's papers, would have your hair shorn immediately. You would permit your beard to grow out.

You were Québecois, if anyone asked. You had lived at Sydney for some years. You had a wife and a child, a son, in Nova Scotia, with whom you wished to be reunited, for your wife was not well. You drove a caleche. You knew nothing of politics. Wife: Anne Collins. Son: Richard Michael. Address: 23rd Street, Griffintown, Montréal.

You would be taken to the Cape, where a safe house had been arranged. Forged passports would be provided by an English double-agent there. He would be murdered that night so as to avoid potential compromise. It would be better if you did not know how. In six or eight weeks you would sail for Mobile. Supporters would be waiting at Alabama.

You waited seven hours, bobbing around like a bottle. No vessel appeared. You tried to remain steady. The boat was trailing a net to camouflage its purpose; you knotted the fraying oakums to pass time. Once, in the east, you saw natives oaring a pirogue; the call-and-response of what sounded a war-cry, though probably it was only a fishermen's prayer, carrying over the surf. The argument between M'Carthy and Knowles blew back up intermittently, and they started into drinking, which made it bitterer, abusive. It was clear, at least to you, that the plan's hope was dying. If you could have aborted it, you would have.

You were leaving a woman you loved, the only home of your adulthood, the land in which your infant daughter was buried. Two short months she had lived in the world. You would never again see her grave.

But it was too late for turning back. It was two after noon. The alarm would have been raised. The events would be unchained. Your reason for being in Hobart was to sign your ticket-of-parole at the Station; when this had not been done they would have grown suspicious immediately, would have mustered the constables out to the farmstead. You pictured Catharine on the porch as Mulvany rode up. She might be hanging out launderings or feeding the chooks. Hands in her apron. Pegs clipped in her hair. The slap of billowed linens behind her like a sail: you could smell the soap, the ginger. She would say what you had agreed: she did not know where you were. It had the advantage of being true.

Mulvany would grunt, might bark for a while, sweating porter into his putrid tunic. His men would stand around looking miserable, hungry. They were not paid to love their duties; they found some of them distasteful. But they would do them if commanded by Mulvany. All this would be happening now. She would need to be brave. But women are braver than men.

Her hair. You used to wash it for her. It was sleek; black-blue. Fronds of wisping seagrass in your fingers. Because her mother had taught her – remember her laughing – *fix the clothes-pegs to your plaits and you'll never have to fumble*. Her hair, wet and loose, to her waist.

She must be prepared for him to 'break' the place. The Truncheon Mulvany. She was not to answer back, was to offer no resistance. He would not actually assault her, nor even threaten to do so, for you had reported him on these menacings before. And Hobart had been warned – an anonymous letter had warned them – of the fate that would befall Sergeant Patrick Mulvany if ever again he made that mistake. Call your companion 'a half-breed nigger' and the consequences would be dire. It would not be Mulvany whose throat would be cut. It would be every one of his children.

It was the last thing you said to her as you rode away from Lake Comfrey. 'You are safe. Tell them nothing. I will be back in a week.' In the morning, D—— would come, and would tell her the truth: you were gone and would never return.

It came into your mind that M'Carthy or Knowles might be touts: the island was crawling with them; every prison is. Perhaps it was a trap, so it seemed to you now. In a moment, or at dusk, which could not be long in coming, a frigate would materialize from out of that distant wall of mist, her Union Jack furling and her cannons lined on. They would strangle you from her mainmast, hack you into briskets; scatter what was left to the sharks. You looked across at Knowles. He would not meet your eyes. With his dagger he was coring an apple.

They were bickering again, now in convict's cant, and you couldn't understand them, but you did not reveal your ignorance. Only D——, you always felt, could be trusted absolutely. They could have torn out his teeth and he would have told them nothing. His contempt for them was that strong. You could trust your life to his hatred. Every revolution has a Duggan.

They could not have suspected, Michael Knowles and Timothy M'Carthy, that they would never see Hobart again. There was a revolver in your pocket. The plan had been agreed. At the first sign of the clipper you would activate that plan. It would be difficult, yes. You had never killed before – you that had called for revolutions. But witnesses were a risk that could not be afforded. A mutter in a grogshop, a tipsy brag to impress a girl, and everything would be known by the authorities. Aim hard for the forehead. They need not suffer. Their families will be taken care of.

The revolution needs theorists, visionaries, poets: figures who will be cast in bronze after liberty is won, whose visages will be impressed on the currency of the Republic, whose epitaphs will be taught to her children. But in the shadows behind the plinths are always the Duggans: elapsed, inconvenient, embarrassing. They skulk the grimy alleys off the re-baptized thoroughfares. Nothing will ever be named for them. Men who will do anything, will shatter any commandment, only to prosecute the cause. Dirtyworkers who keep going after the revolution requires them, if ever it did, which is now contested: when those who have been liberated, who now enjoy the freedom to speak, start claiming never to have wanted it in the first place. Or that it is *not freedom at all* which the Duggans have wrought, but a new marque of slavery, more hypocritical than the old, and that the *ancien régime* was better, freer, if recollected in a certain light. And this is when Nemesis comes for the Duggans: when the cruelties which produced them have been profitably overturned; when the tyranny they stood against has been forgotten, rewritten, and newer Duggans are being recruited to murder the old ones. Then the instruments that might have recorded them are buried, too. Every cause has its angels and its John Fintan Duggans. You could no longer say into which category you yourself should be placed. But you knew the decision was coming.

Your boat bobbled around. You were thinking about Duggan. And it seemed you saw him clearly, perhaps for the first time. You loved him very fiercely in that frightening moment, as a man will love his sinful and prodigal brother, seeing in him all the bigotries he has himself outgrown, and you feared what they would do to your brother in time, for their vengeance on Duggan would be terrible. The day would come, was coming already, as surely as the storm-cloud was approaching from the west, when they would make the very utterance of his name a blasphemy and all who uttered it untouchables.

It started to rain at about six o'clock. The storm-cloud grew the size of London. By now Knowles and M'Carthy were openly frightened. And you were frightened, too, and frightened of showing it. You had been to sea many times, and your father had been to sea; his were the stories of your childhood. But it was the first time you had been gripped by that sensation known to fevered sea-men, that the land does not exist, there is only the sea; that God has annihilated the earth.

The oarlocks creaked and began to slowly spin. You reached out your hand to stop one.

—Row, bawled Knowles.

—We're dead, said M'Carthy.

—Work that oar or I'll stick you, so help me Christ . . .

—We can't tek him wi'uz. If they find him we're hanged . . .

—You'd drown a bloody Christian to save your own pelt?

—He's gan off this boat. *I'll not be stretched for nobastard.*

—*Use your head instead of your hole, for the wounds of Jesus. Two men aint strong enough to run a hellcloud!*

—*Enough*, you shouted. *I* am in command here.

The revolver was in your hand, but your hand was shaking. The boat gave a sickening lurch. The pillar of the hurricane stood up in the distance, slow, gray, twisting, obscene, like a vision of Yahweh enraged by mortal pride. Froth leapt out of the churning sea. An albatross arrowed toward the mainland.

—You nigger scullion's bastard, Knowles said to you quietly. I always hated your guts.

A clump of sea-wrack orbiting in the sky like a ball in the lip of a roulette wheel.

You began to row back, blading frenziedly, all three. The waves slurped over the prow. The dory was pummeled as it began to take on. The waves became billows, then surging breakers. The water rose up into gorges of

79

gunmetal. Rain flailed your face, your eyes. M'Carthy lost his oar. His long hair was whipping. He grabbed the little boathook and tried paddling with that. Lightning sparked ahead of you, a shocking glitter in the cloud. Lightning at sea, an astoundingly beautiful sight. Knowles profaning the tornado as though his roars could quell it. The world rotating faster as you spun toward the eye. And M'Carthy, suddenly, was not in the boat. And M'Carthy was not in the boat.

And this part of the memory is for some reason vague: the moments immediately before the capsizing. The ruins of a barrack-fort on your father's land in Wexford. Frogs and hedgehogs. Asphodels and newts. You were walking with your father, boyish boots on shattered boards. Bluebells in the walls. Bog-cotton in the rafters. 'You'll not defeat nature,' your father was saying quietly, as though the thought was a sad one to which he had had to resign. There was dew on the trees. In potato beds. On banks. Wild garlic for sore throats. Knitbone for fractures. Under a panel of moldered wainscot you found a scraping of words: *Privat n. sykes & his cully pt. robt simms that he lovs. martinmas 97. We zll sleep in the groond whn thes is discoverd*. And Pappy telling you angrily not to look on those words, for there was something disgraceful about them, something worse than unmanliness.

You were weeping when you went into the water, as you had wept over your daughter's remains, helplessly, in a manner you felt shameful. You thought about Catharine – she seemed close to you somehow. You thought about the baby she had borne you. You were about to die, alone and afraid. No prayer could drown your terror. You have a memory of your fingers on the mesh of sinking net, scrabbling for a hold in the blackness.

Walking home along the boreen with your hand in your father's pocket. Moonlight on the Sloblands. He was happy. You're the great little pup. I'm the luckiest man in Ireland. And you asked: is God real? Did Mamma truly go to Heaven? And the grief in his eyes. I'm ashamed of you, James. You have spoiled our happy day. Get away from me.

You awoke on wet stones. They were black, small as marbles. They scrunched when you tried to move. Your hands were sopped with blood. Your clothes had been torn. There was a gash like a backward N across your chest. You attempted to stand but your legs would not carry. You pulled yourself to a rock pool and vomited.

You made a feverish inventory but it did not take long. There was a pencil-flask of poteen on a chain about your neck. A bracelet, Pappy's fob watch in a gutta-percha pouch, with a draft on Canada for twenty pounds, which somehow had been smuggled to you by Duggan at Hobart. That was all your inheritance. Your shoes were gone. No book, and nothing to write with.

For almost a week you were unable to walk. You lay on the baking stones. The noons were a dazzle of pain and light. You would burrow into the stones like a lizard to avoid the sun. Your neck, when you moved it, felt broken.

Walking came back to you, limpingly, painfully. You hobbled toward the collapsed, black cliff. It must have taken you half an hour to ascend its shifting rubbles, your feet thrusting hard into sharps of gravel. As though there might be an oasis on the other side of that battlement. But there was only the eternity of sea.

You slid a way back down. Your back and buttocks torn. You tiptoed the length of your world. A turtle stranded belly-up in a yellowfoamed pool, its feet pitiably working the air. You killed it with a stone, beat open its husk, but you found you were unable to eat it. You were crying by then. You tried to stop crying. You edged a way back towards your burrow. Under a copse of red-flowered thorns, of which kind you did not know, stood a crooked driftwood cross into which had been cut some words: JAS. GRIMESLEY. HM NAVY. XLIX. You were not the first conquistador.

You did not know if 'XLIX' meant your namesake was forty-nine when he died or if 1849 was the year of his death and he had figured so lowly on whatever vessel he sailed that it was not worth including the month of his passing. And yet – had he been nothing, they would simply have thrown him overboard. But perhaps the Captain. Or perhaps kind comrades. And if vessels come by. But maybe they would be English. Obsessions came to nag at you about unanswerable questions. It is one of the terrors of solitude.

In your lectures you would call it an island, but it was barely that. Nothing but a crescent of arid black anthracite. Perhaps a quarter-mile in length. Grassless, treeless. The part-rim, surely, of a drowned volcano, because there was not a grain of sand but instead that glassy shale, and there was fresh water – you could suck it from the boulders. When the tide rose high, your empire shrank beneath it. There were hours when all you had was the size of a Connemaran's patch. Strange thought: to be lost in the wilderness of ocean but standing on the summit of a mountain.

The coral-stubs, brittle. On cold nights they snapped, blowing grits of blackened powder, bitter-tasting, sickening. The dust adhered to your flesh; unwashable. To walk more than a few paces sliced your feet. You learned to sit guru-still, eyes trained on the horizon. Only an occasional fin. Seal-black, shining. And the spume of a whale in the faraway white, slapping the waves with its tail.

One morning on the rock – third week? fourth? – you awoke to the thought that you would never again see a human. It was as real as the shale, as the jags in the shallows; the tiny vermilion scorpions that scuttled in their thousands, the sting of one of which had made you scream with such agony that something in your loins seemed to rip. Unimaginable fact. You would live and die alone. No one would ever know your fate.

You might live twenty years, or thirty, or fifty – there was water in the rock, there were fish in the sea – but nevermore set eyes on another of your species or hear an earthly voice not your own. Like swallowing a cannon-ball, so terrible the grief. A gun-stone made of ice. There would come no Friday, no educable savage. No footprint. No sand for a footprint.

Fear of death seemed to shrivel in the flames of that thought. But it did not burn away. It concentrated. You did not want to die, were afraid of the pain. You, who had stood on the gallows for your country, who had called *Vive La Guillotine* for the heads of all monarchs. As the minutes ticked to months on your father's watch, the thought came to smoke like a lust. You did everything contrivable in order to expel it. You tried to sleep all day, you shambled your kingdom. You counted the shoals of jellyfish bloating obscenely in the moonlight, like tentacled fallen constellations. The morning finally came when you ran out of numbers. You scraped your name on a stone; your date and place of birth. But there was nothing with which a noose might be tied.

You have no explanation for what happened that morning. Was it simply to have an evidence that life had ever existed other than the ruins of your own? You were kneeling on the rocks, scraping out handfuls of silt from the oblong shadowed by his cross. The sun blazed obscenely on the nape of your neck. Your fingernails broken, their cuticles bleeding. The grunts of some slavering animal lusting for a marrowbone, and you realized, to your shame, their source.

You put back what you had taken: his stolen stones. You wept as you kissed his cross. You begged forgiveness of the sun, of James Grimesely, of your father, of the Gods of the seas of the world. But you would do worse to James Grimesley before too long. You would become the untouchable man.

You began to think, soon, that you had already died, had drifted without knowing into that latitude of doldrums. Had they truth, after all, the warnings of the Fathers? Was Hobart Harbor your Styx? Each sinner, on that foreshore, shall meet the thing he dreads most and shall know that state for *eternity*. Do you know that awful word, boys? Conceive its dreadful import. Death, for such a boy, can never be a release; though he beg for it, though he pray, though he repudiate his wicked deeds, his unmanly thoughts, his pollution of his body – it shall come too late, this repentance. That picture he allowed to form of his sister's chaste friend. That lie he spoke to his father. Dear boys, a million centuries, and a *million million more*, yet his tortures shall never be ended. Be the whole world destroyed and Christ Himself returned, yet that boy shall grovel on in the stench-pit.

You do not know how long you wept: minutes, days. At one point – maybe you are imagining, but you do not think so – you ran into the water – the bite of the salt – and stumbled out as far as you could bear into the waves, until the sea slopped up to your ripped raw neck, and matted your bib of louse-infested beard, and the reproachful smacks of froth were smarting your eyes. The water was warm. Slime of seaweeds beneath your feet. Yes. That happened. You did not imagine that. A pelican regarded you from its perch on a stump of coral. Its ancient eyes, its preternatural hauteur. How you envied that vampire his powers of flight. You burned in the blind of water.

Crusoe, the slaver. You knew the truer story. Because Pappy had told you the truth. He ruled his acre of sand as the crown its empire: measuring, imperturbable, unpanicked. But the Scotsman on whom he was modeled lost the power of speech, so appalling the self-confrontation.

—Never go to sea, son. I wish you would not. I have always hated sea-life. I know you would hate it, too. There is nothing in the sea except fish and tears. The sea makes a land-life sad.

Crusoe. O curse. Curs. Ruse. Sore. Defeat. Defoe.

These words you formed of the wet black stones. You would soon be an anagram of yourself.

You came to fear you were mad, or would soon be mad. And there were moments when you told yourself not to be afraid, since no lunatic truly knows he is mad, but thinks himself sane, indeed saner than the rest, that the others are mad who do not understand his madness, that his madness is the only sanity. Frenchman. Fit. Two years' solitude on Mauritius. Tore his flesh to pieces. Brought on by eating raw turtles.

Often you look at the globe – for you have one in your study, a

Mercator model, a fine one, your wife had it sent you from Greenwich. Neptune and Britannia are holding the cartouche, on which a sea-nymph is combing her tresses. You try to understand, to fix a measure on where you were. Somewhere in that quadrangle formed by elegant parallels, near the dot on the second 'i' in 'Pacific'. But your rock does not appear on that ball of muted shadings. Too small, you suppose; it was hardly worth the bother of naming. It would only have insulted the commemorated noble to have such a nowhere his immortality.

You can point to jagged Ireland, to Britain advancing on her from behind; to Tasmania, to Paris, to the Italy of your mothers; to the featureless square of convex whiteout in which you are orphaned now. But they are only arrangements of inks, a way of translating. The world has corners that can never be imagined. Maps tell you little worth knowing.

They cheered you in the good years. Roared your name from the gods. They lifted up their children to see you. The hero who returned from the island of the damned, who walked out of the tomb, who refused to lie down, whose *existence alone* was a defiance of imperium, of the brutalities that had driven them from home. They had seen so much death, had been told they were animals. They wanted it not to have been for nothing. They loved your exquisite clothing, those people in rags. They loved how you spoke, your flights. But mostly, it was the fact of your survival they loved. They did not know your truer story. There were nights, moments, when you wanted to tell them; to stand in the limelight and bawl into the darkness, to those mothers who had given their sons your name, those fathers who shook with tears when they saw you take the stage: 'I am an impostor. I only survived. The heroes of the story are you.' But by then it was too late. They would have shouted you down. And they would have been right to hate you.

No globe will ever know what happened in that latitude: the visions, the voices, the nights of rabid terrors, the spasms of abject screaming, the compacts with devils. Kill anyone I love, only I beg you let me live. Any crime I will do. Any evil you command. How you saw your dead child. Your sisters. Catharine. How you set out to sea in James Grimesley's coffin, propelling it with the oars of your blaspheming hands. A quarter-mile you managed before it sundered to its boards. His torso: a lobster-pot on the black wet shale.

One midnight you awoke – you had always been a skeptic; an *homme du monde* was Duggan's sardonic phrase – to a figure staring down at you through lidless sockets. This one was different. But you felt no terror. You knew who it was. It knew you.

—Did you crack my shins? it wanted to know. How did you shuck me? Did I taste?

It asked if you would care to take a mosey to a gin-shop. At Deptford, it said. The molls there was righteous. They would let you do anything. They would attend to you in threes. And you answered – Christ help you, it is almost funny – that you intended no offense but were married and a Catholic, and the ghoulish thing grunted, like a boar idly belching, and trudged back down the shingles toward its bed. There was an arrow lodged in its spine. You saw that very clearly. With an ebony shaft. Red and turquoise feathers. And when it came to its place, it lay down on its belly, with the promise that it would be waiting when you changed your mind.

In the coming days and weeks you would see it many times. It was squatting on the rock when you inched there for water. It was hovering over the surf with the wings of a goshawk. It was playing an ivory flute, and it nodded, as flautists do, to indicate that it could not speak until the jigue was completed, for it respected the tune more than the importance of speaking, and might lose the air if it addressed you.

You were still raving about Grimesley when you regained consciousness in the bunk. They said you had been doing so for nineteen days. The name had become a kind of colloquialism among the Portuguese who found you. Some of them assumed it yours.

You had no recollection of rescue. None has ever returned. All you know of your salvation is what you were told by your saviors: they had run in close to the reef in pursuit of a flipper-shark and had noticed, through a scope, a strange animal on an atoll. It was apelike, gray, could stand erect and lurch, but it seemed to prefer to crawl. They watched it forty minutes. The Second Mate sketched it. It threw handfuls of its own filth at the pelicans.

As they approached, it showed no sign of noticing their presence, not even when they fired a pistol volley over its head. It sat down on the stones. Perhaps it had died of fright. The Bos'n crunched up to it. The ape did not stir. It stank of rancid fish; all around it were sucked kelpy-bones. From the palm of its paw drank a scorpion. Near it, on the stones, a man's salt-rotted clothes. Then the cabin boy noticed it blink.

Your flesh had been so scalded that it was suppurating, scorched, your swollen tongue so inflamed, it had burst like a rotten fruit. The heat had burnt the crests on your coat-buttons into your abdomen. To have a sheet laid on your body was an asphyxiating agony.

You were ninety miles off Cape Horn: they would set you ashore, for there was a seamen's hospital there and its surgeons were capable. You managed to beg to stay with your rescuers – thus your gurgling scream was interpreted. For weeks you could not speak. Your lips felt as though sutured together. When your bowels moved, the debris was terrible.

There was a priest on board, a little chubby-faced Galliego, who ate chicken-wings and butter and drank like a docker. He spoke hardly any English but would sit by your bunk for hours, praying his breviary, or bathing your wounds. At nights he sometimes sang to himself when he thought you were asleep, with tenderness, in Latin, his eyes closed tight, as though the psalmist's entreaties resurrected in his mind some Maria he had disappointed for God-love. As your speech stuttered back to you, he would hold your hand. 'Tranquilo,' he whispered. 'Mi hermano.'

He read to you in the nights, from Lope de Vega, and you rolled across the gorges of the Atlantic. At the onset of Lent, for a penance he stopped drinking. He shaved you, cut your hair, clipped the talons of your toenails, jesting of his thirst, of his biblical parchedness, that he would permit himself to be sodomized for a pipe of amontillado. He asked if you were a Catholic, if you wanted to pray. Perhaps you would like to make Confession. He had the intuition, he said, that there was a deliverance you wanted. A burden you needed lifted.

You did not know the words in Spanish for some of your sins. You did not know the words in any language. You spoke what you could. He said nothing, only nodded, as though all you were saying was forgivable, explicable; but when it came to the wrong you had done James Grimesley, you were barely capable of speech. He told you not to be concerned; you had broken open no grave. It was only *un duende*, a sprite of the mind. Such dreams were common enough among *los marineros del mundo*. Seamen told too many stories.

He was in a position, personally, to assure you of your innocence, since the Captain had asked him to come in and bless the rock, for it was reckoned unlucky by sailors not to hallow the grave of a mariner, especially one who might have died without receiving the sacraments. The mound was thick with mosses. Clearly it had never been disturbed. You were mistaken, he insisted. You needed rest.

Only one strangeness, he said, reaching into the placket of his cassock.

They had found it stuck in the grave like a conqueror's flag. *Una flecha* it was called in Spanish.

'*¿Y como se dice en inglés?*' he asked.

Red and turquoise feathers. An ebony shaft. You were weeping. 'An arrow,' you said.

You stand in a house on a mountain in America, holding that arrow in your hand. And you wonder, still, if you starved on that rock, or drowned in the upheaving that conveyed you there – or died many years ago on the scaffold in Ireland; and if everything since has been your Demonland.

V

CHAPTER 14

THE WEST'S AWAKE

FEBRUARY 1866

We return to Redemption Falls – Lucia recollects her arrival in the town
The Governor's absence & then his return – A vivid editorial
The hope of reconciliation – A sound from a locked-up room

It begins for Lucia as a haunting in the night, a sense that the house is uneasy.

Strange sounds mix with the wind in the rafters: scrabblings; shufflings; a catlike wail. At first she tells herself it is an infestation of vermin, though of what kind she is not sure. Opossums? Prairie dogs? The bestiary of the west is mysterious to Lucia who loves Fifth Avenue and fancies it rat-free.

And it comes again. That plangent mewl, so faint as to be almost inaudible. She elbows herself up in bed, gropes dry-mouthed for the candle. The rasp of the flint-box. A spunk of flaring light. Can it be, she wonders, merely a troubled imagination? There is much to be troubled about now.

Two faces gaze dismally from the shifting shadows. An iron-hard man. His steely woman. Her candle flame refracts on the lacquer of the oils. The faces have tributaries of cracks.

Her grandfather grasps a length of chain in one fist, the other resting on a bible as though it wants to float away. He looks like her father: the same uncomplicated sternness. 'Keep to thy Word!' is the family motto, the only one on record at the Office of Heraldry to include an exclamation point in its text. Her grandfather, lost in Canada, ate his dogs in the snow, having beaten them to death with a seal-bone. Several of her relatives would do well in a tale. She will write one of her grandfather in Ontario.

But who would believe it? Her family, their country: could such a tale ever be written? Her difficulty is not to blare the colors so as to force the reader's attention; it is to damp the tones down, so as to make the story at least credible.

If she left, she would feel obliged to take her things: her furniture and pictures, the books – all those books. He would burn them, she knows, if she left them behind, or dump them into the sludge of the Missouri. She pictures him watching them drown like unwanted pups. He will always be owned by his rages.

His letters had complained of the Territory's plainness, the bluntness of the houses, the monotony of the mountains. ('Even their speaking is devoid of color. They are most unusual Americans. They are islanders, somehow.') She had pictured a home full of beautiful objects; an oasis of civilization in the bewilderness.

The first steamship of the season had brought her into the Territory. Forty nights on board, the only woman of her class. For the first week out of St Louis the sailors had bothered her. Outdoing one another in counterfeit offers of assistance. Would Madam wish this? Would the Lady like that? If there is any little service the *Señora* would like performed. A wurst with breakfast? Some sugar in your bowl? And then they had grown tired of her, or perhaps just accustomed. By then it had been made clear to them by the pilot, an Irishman, that Mrs General O'Keeffe was off-limits.

They watched as she stood by the railings at dusk. Their figurehead, so it seemed to the fanciful. The most beautiful woman in New York, it was said. They wondered if the rumors were true.

The edginess of the pilot whenever they docked for 'wooding up'. His men scanning the hillsides, rifles trained.

Down the river from the west into which she was headed came vessels freighted low in the water with gold. Iron-clad, slow-moving, squat as gorged slugs, their decks were patrolled by Federal troopers, guarded by cannons and marksmen. They burned in her dreams, those armored ships of treasure, while war-cries scorched the air. One night she opened her porthole and saw a vast monitor glide past in the moonlight. Black from stem to stern, masked sentries along her railing. So strange an apparition that at breakfast she asked the pilot what it had been.

'You saw nothing,' he told her.

'I know that I did.'

'You saw nothing,' he insisted. 'You were dreaming.'

The shadow of the boat on the melongreen water, the coffeebrown water, the mud. Its whistle-shriek echoing in the birdless ravines. Blended spokes of the pilot's wheel.

She began notes toward a novel, then a collection of tales, working long, lamplit hours locked away in her cabin. By the time they reached the Territory she had the bones of five stories, and one almost completed piece – she called it 'Demonland'.

The men he had sent to accompany her from Fort Stornaway seemed to resent her immediately. Or perhaps it was her belongings they resented. Fifteen crates of books: a daguerreotype machine and glass plates, trunks of Parisian dresses, hatboxes, a mannequin. They had stared at their cargo and then at its owner. A teamster was snickering with the sailors.

At home in the east, a man rarely looked you in the eye. Out here they looked where they wanted. She was still on the steamboat, had not even set foot on their Territory. What was left unsaid – nobody had to say it – was that she had failed before even beginning.

Guns everywhere. Smell of cordite and belched porter. The dust-gray men all armed and munitioned as though about to enter battle with Satan. Pistols, rifles, bandoleers, knives. They clanked when their horses moved.

All the road from Fort Stornaway, seven days and nights, she had been ignored by the silent men. Hardly one syllable. Then hardly a look. Her menses had come on the second day. The ache was bad, exhausting. She had asked where was her husband. Was there a servant, a maid? How long would the ride take? Were there inns along the way? Shrugs and tight grins were the usual response, a finger pointed toward a filthy doorway at dusk. Then one man muttered a word she could not make out – she did not have to make it out, she knew what it was – and his comrades chuckled dryly as on they rode.

Through the rock-land, the nothing; the high, silent canyons. She had been horrified by this godforsaken Gaza. The waterless stone-fields, the withers of heat. So intense, you could not pick up a metal fork by noon. You supped from a bowl like a dog. The pain of looking at anything in the hours after noon, when the light blazed on surfaces of quartzite scree, and the heat made you feel you were griddling. The clicking of cicadas: ominous, constant. The grime of the lodging-houses. Buffalo meat for supper. Then the barefoot, dirty children on the outskirts of the settlement, lobbing stones at the wildcats in the midden-heaps. An Indian watching as they rode into Redemption Falls, his face as lined as a mountainland map.

The house, she felt certain, was a practical joke – a humiliation of the newcomer by the men. They wished, she thought, to see how she would react; their silence was a rite, a further initiation. It was smaller than the stables at her father's Manhattan mansion. A cabin, unfinished and roofless. She had made the mistake of laughing at it, desperate to be regarded as a sport. But none of the men had laughed.

She could barely understand the cook, a Floridian former slave whose vowels were drawled, whose consonants were dropped, and who mostly didn't speak at all. But it was communicated to the intruder that her husband was not here. He was away harrying Indians into the Badlands. They had attacked a waggon-train of immigrants, he had resolved to deal with them mercilessly. There was no word as to when he would return.

For days she had waited for him; the days became weeks. She began to fear he was dead. The cook said he probably wasn't. Nothing we could do if he was. One time, he had remained on the trail two months, had ridden down to Kanzas, then into the Indian Territory. You never got much about what the General was doing. Better not to ask him. He don't like getting asked.

In the street they stared, as Inuits at a peacock. Children pointed. Even pigs and roosters seemed to stare. An old man with a beard so long it went around his neck like a scarf – he spat in the dirt as she passed. An urchin with a weed for a hatband, in ragged velvet knickerbockers, asked if he could have a lick of her hand. When she asked him why, he said it was the color of cinnamon, and three passing miners guffawed like macaques and one of them tossed him a coin.

Obscenities were daubed on the gables of the house. She did not weep as she painted over them, would not be seen weeping. She knew the artists were watching.

Summer rains came on. The house let in water. She did what she could to bale it. She and the cook distributed pans to collect the leaks. Buckets. Chamber-pots. Fruit jars. Canisters. The house plinked all night. She dreamed of Japanese music. It would have been easier to sleep in the Bowery.

When the rains blew away, and the sun returned, she attempted to brighten the mildewed rooms, hanging pictures, spreading tapestries, arranging bibelots and wildflowers. The cook was pressed into assisting the effort. Recipes for new dishes were discussed and rehearsed. But the cook was no cook – she could barely boil milk – and Lucia came to wonder in her lonely bed why Elizabeth Longstreet had been hired.

Spores appeared on the immigrant furnishings: powders of black-brown mould. Puffballs sprouted in the pleats of her gowns. The carpets all had to be burned. She made a great pile of them out back on the prairillon. It smoked for two days, emitting an evil acrid stench, and the corner-boys quipped that the Indians would be watching, made jokes about what lewdnesses the smoke-clouds might be suggesting. An infestation of *cucarachas* invaded the kitchen – the stomach-turning crunch of their shells beneath your soles. Pieces of the house fell off.

Wainscots, facings, doorknobs, bits of banister. The house was an old man's body. Rot started eating the staircase, the floors. Damp chewed a way into the eaves. The teeth of a pianoforte yellowed and blackened. She wrote a sonnet called 'Impotence' but burned the finished script. An *auto-da-fé*, perhaps.

She advertised for a mule so that she could put in a garden. When none proved available she purchased a hand-plough in St Hubert, a heavy item, bulky, designed for a strong man's use, 'a good buck nigger,' the seller advised 'and don't you go ruin him on meat.' In a pair of her husband's old britches and a miner's shirt and canvas work-gloves she stitched up from a sugar sack, she hauled it up and down the Federal plot, until stones and twisted roots gave way to small furrows, in which she sowed carrots and corn. She found a textbook on irrigation, spaded out trenches for water, fetched barrels from the arroyo, laid the hose-lengths herself. Her Manhattanite's hands became calloused, rough. Men quietly watched her working.

Sopping with sweat, caked in wet red clay, she labored alone in the fields. Every pace of gubernatorial land she fenced alone, posting, wiring, rail-splitting, measuring, learning those frontier skills through necessity and error. She raised up the enclosures. The elk tore them down. She raised them again, staked them deeper. The town often awoke to the *pock pock* of her hammer and sank into its duskfears to the rasp of her sawing. They watched her work the plot, this millionaire's daughter, who had never so much as watered an orchid before. No profit would come of her efforts, they said, for the government plot was cursed. Beneath it were the bones of a Pend d'Oreilles brave. No joy would ever bless that conqueror's house. No child would be conceived there, or live there.

The straps of the plow wore grooved cuts in her shoulders. These soon became septic: stripes of raw pain. Elizabeth Longstreet found her retching by Considine's Creek, hallucinating with a fever, sun-scorched. She carried the Governor's wife in her long, strong arms, back to the hulk of the uncompleted house, to that lichen-reeking room, to that bed of creaking quoits, where she stripped her and salved her with a secret unguent once used to heal the wounds left by whips. Face down Lucia lay, flesh singing with pain, her naked back the wettish purple of deer meat. The fever burned wildly and it broke on the third night. She never went to plowing again.

It became her habit to go walking out north of the town, in the remains of a spruce forest that had been wrecked by a mining consortium. She would set up her easel, would charcoal or gouache; but these were not her talents. She wrote home to New York, to her siblings, various friends; to women with whom she had nursed in the War. Their replies came slowly if they came at all. The War was over now.

The poems from these months are imitative; showy. She had not yet found a way of seeing the world. Metaphors, some striking, stud the stanzas like jewels, as though to reward the patient reader for remaining on board; but the dazzle fades quickly and what is left is the feeling that she is almost always writing the wrong poem. All the years of reading, the endless hours of study, those descents into the caverns of imagination; but the light she deploys is too narrowly focused. What is illuminated, at times brilliantly, is not worth seeing, while around you, in the darkness, some krakenlike creature stirs. And then came the day when she entered his study in search of a ream of paper.

In his bureau were letters, hundreds, disarrayed, from the widows and parents of his men. Bundles of them in cupboards, in the folds of his books, in drawers, in a lockbox, in the pockets of a coat. She discovered it had been his practice, when informing them of a death, to include an invitation to write him for assistance. They were terrible to read. Every one of them was wrenching. *My childeren are hungry . . . I am entirly widout means . . . Mi child do not know where his fader is after going . . . My son is not returnd. Do you now where he is? His name Michael Foly off Red Hook Brooklyn.* She came to dread opening any of his books, for fear another of the supplications would howl from it.

She drove out in the landau to make photographs of the Territory. The plate camera was cumbersome but she and the cook managed it. Gulches, abandoned placer diggings, mining works, fords. She photographed Wolfcreek Canyon at the approaching of twilight, the blur of a mountain cougar near a mangled steer. Her portraits of children, particularly of Indians and freed slaves, would be commended for their compositional skill.

High summer was hot. Water became scarcer. The collodion compounds needed to create her photographs would boil like wizard's potions in their bell jars. It sickened her to be in the tent with those steaming noxious vapors. Her skin became pockmarked, her breathing stressed, her eyes would stream whole days. Doctor Newcombe at Edwardstown urged that she cease her pastime. Her lungs were weak, dangerously susceptible to consumption. Photography could kill her, he warned.

One airless August day as she returned to Redemption Falls – walking, as it happened – through the serenade of cicadas – she saw something striking in the heat-shimmering distance and thought it might make a picture. A fat foreman was standing in the ribs of her attic, as though encaged by its naked beams. Two navvies were with him – builders, she assumed. He was directing them with magisterial gestures. Elizabeth had run up the Stars-and-Stripes that morning. It was furled around its flagstaff in the picket-fenced yard. Near its base, a heavily pregnant mule-deer doe nuzzled at a cluster of chokecherry.

It occurred to her that the house might be a subject to be photographed, that it was not without its beauty, at least not from this angle. Even a thing of brokenness could be made to look beautiful, if only you could locate the vantage from which to observe it. It was true of objects, was true of the self; it might even be true of war. Perhaps she had been too hard on the place and its people. They had endured too much – everyone had. The country was smashed by pain and loss, amputated from its sense of its greatness. The fat foreman looked down from the rafters as he noticed her approach. It was only then that she recognized him.

She had been shocked by his appearance but more by his manner. He seemed diffident, reluctant to speak. She thought he might salute or click his heels, so clipped and un-spousal his greeting.

'You are here, then.'

'Yes.'

'You have everything you need.'

She was uncertain if the latter was a question or a statement.

'Is something the matter, Con?'

'You have been writing again.'

'A little. I have tried a few verses. Why are you looking at me like that?'

'You have also been experimenting with prose, I gather.'

He handed her a sheaf of close-written pages. There was a rancid smell of whiskey from his breath or his clothes, and the hand with the papers was shaking.

'You left these on the escritoire for anyone to read. We have a newspaper in the town. Why not submit them for the front page?'

'Con – '

'You read in my private notes. You could not have written this filthy thing otherwise.'

'The chest was damaged. We struck a sandbar and it fell.'

'Grist for the mills of a dilettante's vanity. Thank you, Lucia. I am touched.'

He had left the room before she could apologize.

It was their first night together in almost three years. It passed in a jittery wordlessness. He'd had little to say; she had tried to contrive a conversation. New York. The boat. A painting she had purchased at Knoedler's. It was coming from St Louis, would be here in a month: it was large and opulent and beautiful. She would speak to the builders about where to display it. They might need to construct a room for it.

'Builders?' he murmured.

'Well: what is the word for them?'

There were no builders here. The builder had been murdered. The men on the roof had been snipers from his old regiment. He'd been asking their advice on fortification.

The more she attempted, the more silent he became, until finally she realized he had fallen asleep at the table and she stole to her bed, alone.

He was gone from the house when she awoke just after dawn. The remains of the supper were on the table, congealed. She drank water in the roof, watching sunrise on the prairie: the glory of the reddening mountains to the north. The haze would burn off but for now it was cool. It would be the hottest day ever recorded in the Territory. When Elizabeth came in, at quarter of nine, she said she had seen him outside a saloon in the town, a low place he frequented that opened early. He'd been pounding on its shutters, she said.

It was there Lucia found him, pacing the sunken boardwalk, swigging the dregs of a bottle. His tread was unsteady, his pace that of a man on a ship. There were dead leaves in his hair, which was now untied and straggling, and longer than she had realized yesterday. A dull purple stain dirtied the chest of his shirt, which was open almost down to the navel. From his shoulders hung a military greatcoat that did not fit him any more. He had belted it around his bulk with a rope.

'Con,' she began, 'it is very early now. I haven't seen you in so long. Perhaps after we breakfast we could ride out a way. To the river, perhaps, or the Gates of the Pass.'

She was babbling, she realized. She did not know what might come out. She wanted simply to hold him but that seemed dangerous, transgressive. She had the feeling it would result in violence.

'Go home,' he told her, quietly. And she did as she was told. She didn't have the fire for a quarrel.

It was late when he returned to the house that sweltering night, bawling at Elizabeth Longstreet for food. *What must I do? What must I do? Is this how a breadwinner is treated now? To beg for a crust in his home?* She locked her door, pushed a chair against the handle. She knelt by her bed and prayed as she sweated.

The weeks that followed were long; tense. Fall came on; the trees turned gold, and the house was still unfinished. She sent Elizabeth to Edwardstown, then to Varina City, seeking out masons and carpenters. Many promised to undertake the work but for some reason none appeared. Deposits were returned to her with not even a note. One tradesman scrawled NOT WANTED across a greenback.

They would dine in silence: graven-eyed Cistercians. Often he would read at the table. The documents came endlessly. They were legislative, she assumed, to do with the incorporation of the Territory. Some citizens wished it to be one of the re-United States. Others insisted it should be independent. She asked if he needed help; always he refused it. She began to teach Spanish to Elizabeth.

He ordered street signs to be erected. The signs became contentious, were often torn down or altered to read obscenely. His deputies raised them again, made them larger, more solid. Some they surrounded with trenches and cut-wire. He was ordered to come to the courthouse and explain his decision; he refused to be summoned, claimed such a writ was illegal; were it repeated, he threatened, he would arrest the judge and declare martial law the width of the Territory. The streets would be named for the patriots of his homeland. If anyone couldn't live with it, let him go someplace else.

KNOW THAT I, James O'Keeffe, de facto Governor of this Territory, do hereby raise a **PETITION TO THE UNITED STATES CONGRESS**, to wit, that the name of this Territory shall henceforth be **"NEW IRELAND"** & that the place styled at present **REDEMPTION FALLS**, Territorial Capital and Administrative Seat, henceforth be incorporated & styled **"DUBLIN CITY"** & that Irish-born veterans of **THE UNITED STATES ARMED FORCES** be settled here with their dependants & conveyed lands forthwith & that Irish-born veterans of the lately defeated Confederacy be also permitted, with their dependants, to apply, so that a new dispensation may be fostered in the Republic with the **TERRITORY OF NEW IRELAND** its exemplar.

Editorials were printed about him in the town's only newspaper. They were scornful, cruel; precisely aimed. A carpetbagger. Janus-faced. A bellwether of fools. One attack was headed 'The Fortune Hunter'.

She had Elizabeth go about the town and purchase every copy. She burned them before he appeared from his bed. Next morning's edition had the fifty-pica headline: FORTUNE HUNTER ADVANCES OUR CIRCULATION. IF THIS DON'T CAP THE CLIMAX!

> Happy tidings are come for the citizens of Redemption Falls. O'Nero of New Oirland is learning to read! He studies us mighty hard in his windy sty and all of us wish him a victory. (Heaven knows it would be rare as an honest man in his homeland.) Today we print an extra two hundred copies. He may obtain them when-soever he likes. We intend to convey the monies to the widows of Brooklyn, to whose number he has so heroically added by his military brilliance. One matter, at least, for which we may be thank-ful: that having cleansed the slums of New York of half their Hibernian vermin, who were fool enough to follow a Pied Piper of his uselessness, he has raised the average intelligence of that CONFEDERATE city so that it approaches the national norm . . .†

What *is* that sound? Downstairs. In the hallway? Should she go to his room and awaken him? And if she went to his room, what might happen?

She remembers them lovemaking; the fierce pleasure he used to give her. His body hard as a bull's in the consoling dark. A generous lover, aroused by her joy. The coaxings he would murmur, his patient skill. His urgent breathing. His grip.

A scythe-blade of light from under his door. He cannot sleep in dark-ness. Perhaps he is awake. The cook says that his bed is nearly always

† *Redemption Falls Picayune* (later *Redemption & Edwardstown Epitaph*), September 1st, 1865; unsigned editorial probably by J. Knox Trevanion, Vigilante leader and secessionist agent.

undisturbed; he sits all night in that broken French armchair, drinking himself unconscious in his clothes. She crosses the landing, is about to knock – but somehow she is not able to form a fist.

A loon hoots. There is nothing in that room. She knows what would happen if she entered.

She descends the bare staircase – more pictures on the wall: seascapes, cantering hunters, an ancient map of Leinster – her hand groping the banister as she goes. The candle throws shadows in the eaves, across the beams. She calls softly for Elizabeth but there is no reply. She has a cabin near the town – but why would anyone prefer to sleep in a shack? Does she have a man at the cabin? Is she married? Courting? Lately Elizabeth Longstreet seems discontented, sulky. Lucia hopes she doesn't leave.

Her reflection in a black windowpane causes her to stop. Her hair is loose: she looks frightened. The linen of her nightdress is crumpled, bridal. Its bodice has come open and she can see the curve of her collarbone. On her bosom a silver crucifix. The dark purple of a nipple. The glow of the candle on her skin.

There was a book in his box. *The Parisienne Convent.* She saw similar ones at the hospital in the pockets of dying boys. She would remove them, discreetly burn them before their weeping parents arrived or the Sister came in on her rounds. Once, she had taken one home and looked at it in her room. What did a man truly want? Girls seen through keyholes, posing in underthings; splayed smilingly in corsets; displaying their draped bottoms to the etcher. Teasing, silly stories of corrupt old abbots and innocent housemaids, or of innocent young priests and corrupt countesses. Girls kissing one another through flimsy lace curtains. 'Diaries', more explicit, laid in cell-like rooms, recounting degradations between women and men. Are those depictions what he wishes? Has he forgotten that he owned them? Has he forgotten that she nursed in the War?

The *thrup* comes from behind her, from the room across the corridor. She wishes it had not, that it was only her imagination, would prefer to return to her bed. But the sound comes again. Something is moving. She retrieves a loaded repeater from the hallstand.

Oddly – this seems odd to Lucia when she remembers it – she goes first to the front door, checks that it is barred and locked. It is black, massively studded; its metal is cold to the touch. Whatever is in the house did not come through such a barrier.

The room is rarely used: its door is stiff, as though the wood of the door wants to be one with that of the frame, resents the divorce to come. She opens it to an odor of cold and sap. The dull forms of boxes, old pieces of lumber; a globe she once gifted her husband. Something squat – an anvil? Turrets of notebooks. A coil of broken chain on a trunk.

'Who is there?' she asks hoarsely. No answer is made.

For what seems a long time she stands looking into the darkness. Everything is quiet, except for a clock ticking somewhere. She is picturing her husband – the French chair in his room. Her father in New York. Her sister. Their mother. Elizabeth Longstreet in a cabin near the town. Ghost-dogs howling at the Ontario night.

A hospital ward in the War.

As she climbs the dark stairwell, she hears, below her, the footfalls as they move across the lumber room.

She stands on the staircase, motionless as a totem. The dawn begins to rise.

∇

CHAPTER 15

AN' I WISH THAT ABRA'M LINCOLN WOULD SENN FOR ME SOME TIME

From a Volunteer private soldier of the Con O'Keeffes

To: Mrs D. P. Foley, 71 Mott Street, the fifth story back,
14th ward, New York City.

may 30th 1862
alexandria camp virginia

my dear mother

thank y for the parcel y sent with the pies they was most injied by all here
& yr son is now the hero of all the camp so he is & the pea soup in the
bottles was only powerful & the brack.

i wld v much like to have a cusion if y cld find one for me. there is a
lot of sittin in the wet grass which is givin me a pain in a place i wont
mentcion. also some good woolen stockins for ive corns on me the size of a
house

it is fun bein a soger. the other boys is ginerlly good sorts. there is a rick
of them here from every crossroads of ireland. you wd think you was home
in new york so you wd. we has to get up aerly. the thing here every day is
drill drill & then drill some more so as yu wld be fit to fall out of yr
standin by the time it is night & an we cld drill a way all throu the world
to austalia before the sergeant wold give us an ease

jas glacken is here whose mother yu know & denis brogan & timmy
bolger & his cousin michael eager. also four of the donnelly bros y know
the ones who i mean from over beyond in 13th St the ugly thieven baboons.
& the first day i was here didn i meet a lad whos people is from
claregalway & says i would yu go to god for my fathers from there & we is
bunkies now the both of us. john dunnegan is his name. so there is no
need to be frettin in yrself at all honest. there is more pats here in this
army than is buried in all the groves of ireland timmy says

the sergnt is a contumelious oulf sorry old kerryman. youd want to hear the roastin cusses out of him. he does rant like the divil but i suppose it is the way of it here in the army & he manes no badness. but it is just what he got to do & we will be the better when he makes us march in step. the wexfordmen is best at it i dont know why

we are in no danger nor trouble i do not want y to be worrit

general okeef come round today & said we was good boys all & wld giv the rebels a thundruss whippin for themselves & a good roar out of an irishman was worser than the bombs of the enmy & we shld be back home soon so not to be afraid but i am sometimes, mamma.

i thnk we are all afraid here exeptin the madmen but we let on not to be. but the other night an i out the front beyond there an i thinkin about somethin & i heard johnnyjoe collins cryin away inside in the tent with himself & it sure enough give me the blue oul feelin

captn conway says the war will not last anoter season i hope not mama i dont want to kill nobody

the vittles here is somethin shockin. youd get better in a poorhouse – all we got is rancid oul bacon not fit for a beggars bitch & coffee made of pease & hardtack biscits that wld crack the teeth in yr head. if we run out of g++d+++ bullets we can use em pat nolan said. he is here too but i wisht he wasnt for he NEVER stops talkin about grace kelleher & i would like to gev him a root in the whereyouknow for it. but never mind i suppose. but i do

youd want to see the boots on me. they are the best i ever seen. & if y dont shine em so as you can see yr face you get the lard cut out of you by oul ievers (the Sergeant)& i hope they might allow me keep em after & you do muss yr jacket at yr peril

the other day we was gievan a party for mrs general okeefs birthday. we had turnkeys blast it sorry I mean turkeys & swinebriskets they costed 4$ & a jorum of rum but i didn take that off course & we sang the shamrock so green & the decay of the rose & then i felt right & sound agin in my self. we sleep in tents did i tell you – we are the right party of mad fellows so we are & the girls is killed lookin at us when we goes through a town & they blowin us kisses an all

but one of the boys was up all night singin tejus comallyehs which wlden be so bad but he had a voice wld skin a turnip. there was a fight over it the next day. we put him in the river for himself but only for the sport of it. & then we had an applefight& stickballin

general okeef says when this war is over we wll get in boats & go over to ireland & put out the englishmen which som of the boys reckons a mighty plan. but i think i will have my belly ful of sogerin by then & will go no more to it

i think i wld like if daddo ast the stevedore about takin me for i wld like that life. i wold like to be near the water & daddo & uncle john & come home every day for the dinner & see you & the little ones & mek sure they dont go to trickin on the staircase for they wld hurt theirselves if they ever did fall

i got cnfession on saturday. there was a priest here from indiana fr corbey was his name. he went aesy enough on me. he said to die in a war means you will go immediatly to heaven if the war is a fair one as this is. also it is not agints the commandments to murder someone in a war & not to go thinkin about that

well that is all my news for the present

i think of y. & daddo every day & wish i was at home

will y. say a prayer for me mamma. i know nothin will happen if y. do

a kiss to flor & little alice & baby annie if she wants one & the same to yrself & daddo & uncle john

i love y. mamma,

yr lovin son

tj

PS: if you see grace above in the chapel will y. tell her i was askin after her. only dont let on i said i was afraid

∇

Thomas Joseph Foley, aged 15, Mott Street, New York. Letter forwarded to his parents with personal effects and posthumous medal.

Anonymously returned to O'Keeffe with the words 'GOD FORGIVE YOU' scrawled across the last page in red ink.

∇∇∇

PART IV

CRAZY
JEDDO MOONEY

Wull my name be Jeddo Mooney, boys, outta Baton Rou I come.
I runned away from a ornry bitch, went bangin on m'drum.
Seen plenty fellers fall down dead an never a one stood mo.
An I'll go no more to rovin', boys, nor to fight no rich man's war.

I wennèd up to Canada, boys, but they would not 'low me in.
For they niver 'low no orphan come afore he turnt thirteen.
The Yankee sheriff found me, then, an I hope he land in Hell.
For he whupped me up and down the head an he brung me back to jail.

Now here I am in the western lan, a-livin wid Fat Pat.
A-livin wid his whiny wife, an whut you thinks to that?
But I means to go in Canada, boys, where the snow lay like a sheet.
An I wipe the shit of the Nighted States from off my livin feet.

Done met the blues the uther day all walkin like a man.
Says he: 'dey calls me James O'Keeffe', an holdin out his han.
But I never trust no Yankeeman, nor neither trusted rebel;
an I never trust no whinywife for I druther trust the devil.

And one black night when ever thang real quiet in the hall,
I'ma gun these bastards one by one, just to watch em fall.
Gonna make em beg a murcy, boys. They come to rue the day,
When Mooney brung to the mountainland, where he did not care to stay.
Chapeau! Where he did not care to stay.

'The Ballad of Crazy Jeddo.'
Collected at Lefoy, Great Smokecloud Mountains, October 1889

CHAPTER 16

AINT GOT NO HOME

Elizabeth Longstreet's recollections continued

Yes, I had a kind of bivouac when I come in to Redemption . . . Prospector outta Texas took off someplace north and I stay in there cause it empty . . . Not evernight . . . Sometime . . . Cause it good to have you own. And there talk when a unmarry woman livin up the house with the General . . . But the white folks didn care for no colored in that quarter. They paintin cusses on the walls: nigger this an nigger that. Look at you hard when you bout you own bidness. So forwhile I stay up the house; just sleep i' the kitchen. An another party took that bivouac then.

But then Miss O'Keeffe come up an she an the General not too quiet. An it come to where I couldn abide the house no more . . . Went down the bottomland road where some of the coloreds had they shacks. Hurleyhouse we called em. Caint remember why . . . An I fixed me a caboose with my own hands and a neighborwoman . . . Eppie Francis her name . . . out of Christiansburg, Virginia. Cause the fighting and fussing up the house come too much. An after the child come in the house I was happy to have that caboose. Cause hell breakin loose ever night of the week. An you got to have a place to go . . .

See, ignorant people dont got no ken of the world: Nigger ain no color, it the place you put to stand. I seen slaves white as milk. Masters darker than me. Ever black they call a nigger, not ever nigger black. That how it go. Mebbe still do. Mebbe always will, to the end. Peoples dont see cause they taught not to look. They did, be a whole nother War in the world. War of the last on the first.

∇

CHAPTER 17

THE DISCONTENTED LAWMAN

How a certain felon was found again, having failed to make a way into Canada – His assault upon a law officer – & other grave matters – & how the traitor Patrick Vinson, of County Louth and Brooklyn, entered the state of Treachery

STATEMENT

February 15th, 1866: I, Patk Vinson, act. deputy Sheriff of Blackstone Rapids say that last Monday forenoon at a quarter of eleven I was above in my place of work which is the Sarsfield County Jailhouse when a man I know come in and tould me I better come up to the Border Post for the Border Post was afire. And I better come along and see about it. So I went along with him. He was Edwd O'Casey, miner. When we got to the Border Post other boys was after comin. On the Canada side they was ringin the bells like a shower of looderamauns in a circus but no fire-wagon comin to answer. You cld see smoke from one of the cabins in the front of the station I mean the room is known as the Guard Room. Edwd O'Casey and self and Dierks Grunsveld, sawmiller, and an oul naygro I dont know his name broke the window and got in to it. There was a wild rake of smoke but I could see the flames was not very fierce. It was that the floorboards of the room was on fire. We crushed it out right quick. Not too much was burnt up. Only it looked to myself like a fire that got set. Says I to myself: God send this int what I think, for if it is, this is trouble comin now.

Shortly after dinner about ten after two I was ridin southwesterly outward of the town intendin to come to Redemption Falls for to collect wages owed me this long time when I seen a boyo was known to me by the side of the road under a tree. I believe I seen this gossoon before at Morton's Claim on xmas morning last and I believe his name to be J Mooney. He was sleepin under a tree just as bold as a hoeboy, like a hop o' me thumb so he was. You could see his cloaths was afterbeen scorched by a fire and his face black as bess and smeared. Down I gets from off the horse and soon enough woke him with a good foot up the breeks for himself.

I ast his lordship if it was him was after settin that fire at the Border Post and tell me the God's truth this livin second itself or I would gev him one ladderin he would not forget in a year's travel. He said nothin. I pucked him a few clips. He said nothin again. I said if he didnt tell it out I would reef the tip of my boot up his hole so hard my toes would be workin his face for a puppet and he spat at me and hared but I collared him. I med him go long the road with me to the nex town south which was Loomisville and I askt Sherrif Frank English to put him in the jail. He did that but then he said we could not leave no child in the jailhouse too long for it was again the law. Says I: English, you a lawman or you turned a buckin lawyer now, for that int the same bird to my own way of thinkin. He said that mought be but there was rules to the question and him and me went to quarrelin over it an he called me a Cooley Mountain mucksavage so he did. Says I: youd want to take a hoult on yerself Frank English my buck for I'll piss on your liver if you abuse me no more you counterjumpin melt of a Dublin dog-robber an I am not one bit sorry for it neither. That is one honeyman will end bad and his falutin over everyone King Fucky the Ninth of Mott Street. Any how he wd not have the child in his jailhouse no more and I wd not turn him loose to do no more burnin up of the country. So I med him traipse long with me to Redemption Falls an I gev him fair warnin he was my legal prisoner and conduct like one or else I wd skelp the all-fired pelt off him.

The bad little cullion fairly bit the fingers off me any time I tried sattin him up on the crupper so I lassoed him and med him go shanks mare behind and I rode. At night I put him in the cuffs for to sleep for he would murder me an I didnt and I only larruped him if he tried to stiver away. He slept in the barns and on Tuesday in the livery stable at Cleburne Hill and never a word of his gob. He would give me the clew to nothin so he wouldnt. He kept at backin and yankin and he actin the hard croppy. An one time grabbed the horses tail an he yankin on it for to mek the beast start away. We got to the Redemption County Office. I boolied him into the cage for himself and what do you think would do him only he thrun the slopsbucket over me from inside in the cell. I got open the gate and was about fit to stave the buckin head of him but then the governor come in and told me to write down what happened which seem to be the governors answer to ever livin thing since he come out here so I did and this is it. And its my opinion fivedollar words is very fancy and fine but he should not be tolerated with treatin a appointed lawman of this country like such. That is one pup wants schoolin with a beltbuckle so he does. He is fortunate I didnt shoot him.

And after all that nice mornin here come in Marshal John Calhoun and he sayin the money didn come from Washington agin and nothin to be done only wait on it. I am SICK SAD AN SORE with how a veteran man is used in this position. Do they know I got a bullet in me yet? Is my uncle and aunt to ate promises back in Brooklyn, so? If I do not git my pay again this month and the 32$ that is legal owed me since the month afore xmas I will do the work no more you may be sure of it. Some of us round here got our patience tried hard. Nearly time the scales was balance right is my opinion. Patrick Vinson int no lackyman to slave for no goverment for the pay of cowld water an brats disrespect. An he dont care who know it if anyones askin. Not that any son of a bitch ever is. Aint a darkey of this country hungry this mornin, forty acres an a mule to ever last one of there majesties, they are laughin at us, laughin, an why wouldn they laugh itself, for the Irishman as fought like the gawms for the so-call union got a fresh air sandwich for his pains an his trouble and a empty pocket for to put it in. You may write THAT to the goverment or any else you please then plant your pen up your hole for an inkwell.

V

CHAPTER 18

O LORD WON'T YOU LEAD ME DOWN JORDAN WAVE AN' WASH MY SIN AWAY

Governor O'Keeffe attempts to interview the boy Jeremiah Mooney at the gubernatorial residence in Redemption Falls

The clock placks on. Its rosewood box. There is bird-croak from a nest in the chimney.

They look at each other, alone in the room. James O'Keeffe and the foundling. Outside, in the lane, the old donkey gives a yawp and the boy tilts his head toward the absurd.

O'Keeffe has a folio ledger on the table before him but there is very little to write in it. The child is either unable or unwilling to speak. He does not even acknowledge that questions have been asked. It is as though his weary questioner is furniture, or air. The boy's arms are folded. He peers at the rafters. His fingertips drumming on his thread-bare sleeves. Dixie Land looks away.

∇

First thing he get to tellin me is a lie on a lie.

'I am General James O'Keeffe. I am in command here.'

Poor crazy coot. Disturbed in his mind. Could wear his damn belly for a kilt. Remind me of an Oakie we use to laugh at in the war. Figured he was John the Baptist.

'I am the legal authority in this country. I should like to assure you of your safety. Are you attending me, boy? Do you understand what I say? Is something the matter with your hearing? . . . Boy? . . . How did you come here? Why are you in the Territory? Have you kinfolk in this country? . . . Boy? . . . Are you sick? . . . Do you know the English language? . . . ¿*Cuántos años tienes?*'

I had kinfolk in this country, I'd be sittin with *you*, Fats. Brain the size of a bullethole.

∇

The child stares suddenly at the table as though it has made a surprising noise. His nose twitches slightly, like a rabbit's. Elizabeth Longstreet enters the room with a pitcher of water and two glasses. He does not look at the water, or at Elizabeth Longstreet. Or at anything else. Is he blind?

He fastens a button near the neck of his tunic. Peers over the Governor's shoulder at the wall.

∇

He sippin on the water like a hoeboy suckin hootch. And he writin up a gospel over there. Book about the size of a carpetbag he got goin. Fancy pen with a feather. Purple ink. And he scratchin out the lines. Makin a mare's nest of it all. And his ink all in smudgeons on his paper.

'Is your cognomen "Mooney"? What is your Christian name? John? Joseph? James? Jack? Are your people Irish? "Mooney" is Irish. I shall write them if you wish. If you tell me where they are.'

Queer smell all around. Like swamp gas and maggots. You'd think they'd give the pigpen a sweepin.

'Your people must be worried. Your mother and so on. Your parents and family will be troubled not to see you.'

Like he Muckety Muck way he gabblin on. Beard like a birdnest pie.

'Are your parents living? What is your home?'

Slap your pappy, Fella. Cause you aint slappin mine.

'Have you brothers and sisters? Are you hungry? Are you sick?'

Queer how different all the people be talkin. Scotsfeller, Texian, Paddyjoe McGann. Put em all in a room, wouldn hardly ken em a word. Be scratchin on their heads like monkeys. Like Eliza dont talk the way I do nor Mamo. Cause she borned up in Brooklyn where they ate their young. *YAW de shitdamn reason. It all YAW faut.* That day she beat me bad. Screamin like that. *Liddle cooney bastid. I'll split yuh.*

∇

Outside in the street, the donkey bawls again. This time, the boy does not look. The Governor has the sense that if the room were to burst into flames the child would sit among them like a statue in a ransacked church. How can a boy that age be so still?

On the table is the cross he was wearing on his neck. 'J. Mooney' needled into its back. Perhaps it is not his. He swapped for it, or stole it, or won it in a game among children of the streets. It could also be an inheritance. It could be nothing at all. It is warm in the Governor's hand.

'Where are you from? I have many friends in the south. New Orleans? Georgia? . . . What regiment were you with? . . . I have always admired southerners. See: here is a globe; can you point me your state? Are you Georgia? Mississippi? . . . *Sprechen Deutsch?*'

The Governor lifts the globe and carries it to the desk. Its axis tilts a little. It spins.

∇

Water look warm and blue on the globe. Blue like July. Or the virgin's cloak. And I sure enough would like to see me the sea. Cause the sea keep you sane, that's what Mamo use to say. Folk live too far from the sea get to barkin and thinkin their shit be candy.

Then fare thee well, sweet Liza dear; I ne'er shall see you more.

Chawklid. Woik. I's boyne up N'Yoik. Owa fada, which oddn hevn, hallow be dy name. Dy kindom com, dy will be don. On oit as it is in hevn. Poor crazy bitch. Aint no wonder she a loola. Speakin like such send you twisted.

I's in baton rou right now I would mosey to the dock and beg me some fixins from one of them raggyass shrimpers and run em home to Mamo and she fry em up good with a whole bait of collards an a pineapple punch an all go to sleep in the cabin. Singin.

And fare thee well, with the partin glass; to Derry's goils galore.

He lookin at me hard and I look him right back. Can gawp at him now come Christmas if he want to. All sorts of things runnin hard through my head. Cholera fever. Eliza.

∇

He reminds the Governor of a kitchen-hand at the house in New York. That little Dublin bottlewasher who ran off with the silverware. Lucia used to call him 'Billy Fingers' or 'The Duke'. That night when you laughed about his thievery together. And she told you that she loved you because you didn't care about such things. And you didn't. She was right. You were *simpatico*.

'Can you tell me about the mine? About the coachman that was murdered there? Did you see his attackers? Did you hear their names? . . . Did you hear the word "vigilante"? Or "the O-and-O Men"? What age are you? . . . *¿Cuántos años tienes?*'

The smallest of squints is the only response. And it occurs to the Governor that even the filthy uniform might not be the apparation's property. For it is loose on his frame, as though he filched it, or found it. Its pocketflaps are ripped. It is elbowless.

'I do not mean to frighten you. These questions are procedural. As you see, I am writing in this great big book . . . Do you understand what I mean by the word "procedural"? . . . It is a bore but there must always be a record of what happens. If a very important fellow comes to pay us a visit, we must always write it down . . . So that it can be remembered later on.'

His eyes search the floor. It's like talking to a river. The Governor hears himself utter a sigh of aggravation and he turns a heavy page, on which he rules four lines, but even as he draws them he is taken by the thought that there will be nothing more to write between them now. 'Pointless,' he writes. 'Do not know what to do.' And he underscores those scribbles and inks a circle around 'Pointless'. Glancing up, he notices that the child is staring at the book.

Maroon-eyed. Blinking. As though caught in transgression.

'Tell me: do you know how to write, boy?'

A moment in a card game when the stake is increased, or in chess, when a seemingly mistaken move is made but you wonder is a trap being set. A lonely, cornered rook. The battlements in his eyes. The room is very quiet. He nods.

The Governor pushes the ledger across the paper-strewn table, and the butt of a carpenter's pencil. The child leans on the page – he is left-handed, a 'cithogue' – and the tip of his tongue protrudes very slightly as he writes. He scratches down his letters with the punctiliousness of an infant, though they are jagged, and too heavy, almost forcing through the paper, and his capitals queerly loom among the lower-case characters like adults that don't belong in the schoolyard. From the Governor's vantage they are upside-down. An Australia requiring interpretation.

YOU AIN'T MY BLOOD

∇

He takin back his book.
　　He turn it round.
　　He lookin at that forwhile.
　　Good for him to know it. Cause it got to be known.
　　Then he gawkin at me foolish like he caint even read.
　　'What does this import? . . . I do not understand . . . Can you explain what you wanted to say?'
　　He lookin it again. Long and hard, Fatman. You dont like the peaches, dont shake the tree.
　　And all my friends, of old estate, I bid you good adieu. I's bound for gold and glory, boys, across the billowin blue.

∇

'What is going on?'
　　'We have a visitor,' the Governor says.
　　'What is your name?'
　　'He cannot speak.'
　　'Perhaps he is frightened.'
　　'For Christ's sake, Lucia.'
　　'Must you profane before him, Con? He is only a boy.'
　　'I will speak as I wish to in my own damned house.'

∇

Con, she call him.
　　She plumbcrazy as himself.
　　Her own name Cleopatra O'Grady.
　　Jesus blood, this some asylum they got em out here. Fatboys gettin

wallpapered. Swedes weddin Noggies. Quadroons dazzled up like Diamond Lou. Gin-sucks decked as Generals.

∇

'What is to be done with him, Con?'

'What do you suggest?'

'He cannot remain here.'

'I invited your suggestion, Lucia.'

'Can't we give him some money and send him along?'

'Where in the name of Christ would you send him along to? It is two degrees below freezing. He has no place to go.'

'How do you know he has no place to go?'

'If he did, don't you think he'd have gone there?'

∇

She scootches over nigh. She lookin in my face. Her hair smell nice. Like fruit.

Like a fruit make you feel better to eat it: yeah. Eyes the black of bilberries. Long straight nose. Jewelstore hangin round her neck.

'He an idiot?' she go.

Nerve of the bitch.

'I do not know whut he is,' go fatboy.

Aint a barrel of shit in a coat, that for sure. Aint a flabber-assed, stinkin-breathed clown of a gawm dont even know his owndamn name.

'You hear me?' she askin.

'He aint deaf,' fatboy snappin.

Wouldn surprise none if she knock me up the head. She do, she gonna know plenty about it.

∇

'Surely you do not intend for him to remain at the house?'

'He can sleep in the kitchen. Clearly he needs a square meal. Probably a doctor. He looks feverish to me. In a few weeks' time we shall see what might be done. I shall ask in the town for who he is.'

'Elizabeth will not like it. A boy in the house.'

'Elizabeth's estimation is of precisely no consequence in the matter. She will do as she is ordered and like it.'

'Or?'

'Or go if she cares to. I do not take commands from my servants. Neither shall I take them from you.'

'So Elizabeth may pitch her chances with two below zero?'

'Since when did you care a tuppence what Elizabeth does? Her shortcomings are your unending conversation since you condescended to come here.'

'I came at your invitation. Your summons, more like.'

'And I must have been deranged when I offered it.'

'Perhaps I should leave, too, then? Is that what you would prefer?'

'As you wish. There is the door. Shut the latch on your way.'

'You have treated me as the filth of your boots since I arrived at your behest to this place. And now you intend, without so much as a by-your-leave, to bring under this roof –'

'What of it? What of it? Do you want my living blood, woman? What do you want, Lucia? To evict the child to his death? Well, go on, then. Put him out. Does it square with your sanctimony? You and he together can go to Hell for what I should care.'

∇

'Con,' she go. 'He cryin,' she go. 'Con. The child be upset.'

'I wouldn hardly blame him. You talk like he aint even here. Quit starin at him, for Christ sake. Give him breathe-room.'

'I am sorry,' she go. She touch the side of my face. 'I didn mean to distress you. Please dont you go to cryin. Looky here is my hankerchief. O no, dont do that. Here now: lemme give you a hug.'

She smell sweet, sweet, sweet. Like the inside of a candystore on Easter Sunday mornin. Heard a Irish feller say he watch her through the window one night when she strippin off her duds to turn in. Thing that Arkie done told me I couldn hardly believe. Bubbies the size of the Mountains of Mourne an sloebuds you could hang a damn coat on. Sucka them boyhos and Abraham Lincoln would sell his own momma for a Mammy. Two cannonballs down the seat of her drawers. Schinkels all up to her wishbone. Turn a feller plumb to stone, a body like she got. But she hand it back to you limp.

'There now,' she go. 'Please dont you be cryin. You feelin a little better?'

I nods.

'Poor little lost lamb. Aint you the handsome boy too.'

'That one lamb need a dippin,' go fatboy.

Scoot me up to get runnin but he catch me by the scruff. He haulin me out, full chisel down the cookhouse, and him and the skivvygal rippin the duds off my back. Skivvy fix a bath, water hot as hellfire. Soap in my eyes. She scrubbin like a torture. Water gone black in a lickety spit. Smoke rise up. Fatboy laughin.

'Ah believe, Elizabeth Lawnstreed, we done gut us here a rebel.'

Honeywoman dont say shit.

Wifey mooey in with a armful of duds. Dunno where she got em. Dont care to neither.

He look at her fowhile. She give him over the pants. He toss em to the skivvy. She say me to put em on.

I shakes my head. Wants mown duds back.

'These ones is clean,' go the skivvy.

I shakes my head. Points my jacket. It's mine.

'Well now,' fatboy go. 'Lookee here.' He comin sore.

Got to do what I'm order. That's all there is about it. Appreciate when folks be makin a Christian effort. You puts on them clothes or so help me to Jesus I will tan you from here to St Hubert.

I shakes my head like a bitch in the rain and he loaded for bear by now. Fairly got smoke comin out of his head. Look like he fixin to choke me.

He open up the door to the wind and snow.

'You wants you to freeze? Then way you fag to freeze. You think anyone give one damn what in all creation you do? You do what you wants. I could care less, you pup. Take a rod to you presently, you see if I dont.'

He hufflin off like the trick got her knee felt in church. An wifey go runnin right after. Honeywoman say he dont mean nothin by it. Aint nobody gwine cane yuh. He all piss and vinegar. But I cane yuh my self an you dont let me dry your hide.

I stands there drippin like the drover got drowned. She dryin me all over the store. Head. Legs. Petzel. Ever place. Drying my possessions like she do it ever day.

'You got nothin I aint seen. Hold you still.'

Water in the tub all black as the mud. You drank that for liquor you would croak.

'Well now, liddle feece-dog, har yu?' go the honeywoman. But she dont care one jitney, it aint nothin but jawin. Got nothin I care to say, is all. She can blow it out her fluke for a breeze.

First time in my life I got storeboughten clothes. I'm duded like a Cajun gone whorin. She gimme mug of milk. I dont want it. Set it down. He still aint my blood. That's all.

Any shit-house comin to cane me get a minnie in the smig. Wont vex me none to murder again.

V

CHAPTER 19

THE PLUCKY LITTLE DRUMMER-BOY
COME OUT FROM LOUISIANNE[†]

*A onetime comrade remembers the boy – Tat-a-tat
The handsome captain – A faceful of grit*

> And, behold, there was much ado and great carriage:
> and the bridegroom came forth, and his friends and
> brethren, to meet them with drums, and instruments of
> musick, and many weapons.
>
> 1 MACCABEES, 9: 39

And when night stirs the poplars he stalks across my mind – that haunted, lonesome shade of a child, with his drum on his hip and his livery in tatters; breasting pitifully to attention as the bugler played Reveille. Or at Sparta, Tennessee, asleep in a busted horse-trough; arm about his drum as though it were a mother.

Around him the soldiers blasphemed and haggled. Wounds were tended, faraway sweethearts serenaded, the pulchritude of the lady, one often suspected, being in inverse proportion to her proximity. Lice and ticks were hunted from their epidermal hideaways, sometimes flaunted as trophies, or dropped in a comrade's coffee-can, while those evil buzzing gallnippers which botanists call musquitoes kept us cussing like Lucifer's angels. The Generals of both armies were abjured as flaming idiots, which in some cases they miserably were. A trooper might yodel while two sharpshooters danced a hoedown. Men will do childlike things in a war, where comradeship is the only mercy.

† From *Look Away, Ye Men of Southern Pride: The Civil War Memoirs of Laurence O'Toole Carroll, Surgeon to the 17th Tennessee, The Confederate Irish Brigade*, Memphis, 1894. (Acknowledgment is made to Mr Henry O'Toole Carroll for permission to extract from his late father's work.)

I recall seeing him school himself in the art of drumming – how he came by his instrument I do not recall: I believe it was a Union prisoner found on a reconnoiter: I know it had an emblem on it, a crest of becrossed rapiers. Here he came at any rate, over a field of broken habiliment, battering twenty to the bar on his punctured captive. From that sundown forth, and early of the mornings, the camp rang loud with the rattle of his apprenticeship. Long-rolls. Double-drags. Ratamacues! Paradiddle clatterings. Sudden, hard whomps. That abducted Yankee drumhead had rebellion sockdoggled into it, till it thundered the glories of Dixie at the little shaver's command. Many a weary warrior blued the air at this dinning, for of profaners we had a veritable professorship. I dare say there were abler musicians in our Confederate ranks; but none was more passionate for his craft.

I seem to see him, always, etched in black and gray, as a ragamuffin graved in the frontispiece of a tale, an innocent in the adult slum. He had that peculiar look of purity ill-used. A silence hung around him; seemed to follow him, faintly: as the aroma of autumn from an old forgotten coat, or of lake water at night in winter. What I mean is that his presence made the men around him silent. But recollection tinctures fact with folly and fantasy. In truth, he was but an ordinary boy.

Jeremiah O'Moody was my diminutive hero's name. There was Louisianne in his accent, for that was his birthplace, and her twang commingled queerly with the mellifluous brogue of Ireland, from whence his Celtic elders had hailed. Often, one heard him hum a snatch of a lament: a high-lonesome keening that would still you by its beauty. Seraphic, his voice. Cold and pure as mountainwater. You heard it float that tune and you attended. Some of the men swore a hole that it was an Appalachian air, or a Shenandoah melody of the Blue Ridge Mountainland; but those many, like myself, familiar with Erin's balladry, schooled in that canon from father's knee, knew full and right plain what it was. It was a song of broken vows and lovers' betrayals. The old Connemarans hold, that if you sing that lay, your enemy dies before its finis.

How he had come among our number, not a one of us knew. He had no mustering paper, no card, not even a uniform, but one he had surely taken from a fallen comrade. It fitted him poorly because the boy was so small. Knee-high to a milkstool, he was not yet in his third lustrum. Aged no more than eight or nine when he came among our ranks, he would be a veteran of the bloodiest war ever to benight his homeland, before even he had advanced into youthhood.

Too young to have enlisted, he must have slipped in to the march with us at Memphis or joined it someplace else along the road. Many boys did the same – far too many, and too young. A hundred thousand children would drift into the armies, in that gallant and terrible era when all beacons seemed extinguished. Their story has never been told. Perhaps it should not be. Better for our nights were they forgotten.

Barefoot he came on, in the threads of a street Arab, unremembered O'Moody of Baton Rouge. A kindly Dublin quarter-master, himself a father perhaps, procured the child a pair of brave little boots. I know not how, nor from where they were had. But wearing them seemed to pain him more than being barefoot did, so that presently he gave them away. A little piccaninny girl received this endowment of the drummer. If still she gathers the cotton near Tupelo, Mississippi, it is my wager that she remembers him yet.

It was my private habit to read a little of poetry in the evenings. The writings of Khayyám the Persian I found a salve to the spirit, when the night came hot, and the soul hurt of bloodshed, and a man had a longing for home. A selection of his Rubáiyát, an anniversary gift of my wife, I kept in my vest pocket throughout all the War. The doomed gorgeousness of the East, the love-bowers of roses, the melancholy music: these for some reason comforted. For the man in the chains of war – for all men, as it may be – truer solace is not drawn from the tawdry resolution, but in the *lacrimae rerum* admitted with truth; the cold and beautiful world as it is, redeemed by the sacrament of description. I recall the boy approaching me one dusk outside my tentquarters and inquiring of me modestly what volume I had. I was surprised that he could read, indeed affected by his curiosity. He asked me: 'bein't them songs?' for they appeared to him as *ballades*. I replied, which was all truth, that I was ignorant on the question of whether, in antique days, they were sung; but the notion seemed to please him that they might have been. I heard him the next evening, alone and singing quietly, in that unearthly soprano, as he tended the ruins of a campfire:

> O fill the Cup: – for life must fleet;
> How Time is ice beneath our Feet.

What horrors he saw while my own sons were safe. What obscenities harrowed his boyhood. Men dying of sunstroke as we force-tramped the south, frizzling like straw left close to a fire. Soldiers, horses, officers' servants, drowning in the mud of the Dismal Swamp as we approached to the Rappahannock. A hospital-tent burning, full of abandoned and screaming wounded. The rampaging diseases, the dysenteries and fevers, and the disease that is hatred, which thrives in all wars and survives in the body come surrender. A major on horseback charging a fleeing slave, slashing him across the eyes with a cutlass.

His drum was shot from his grip by a sniper at Wauhatchie. In the coming days and weeks he tried to learn the semaphore, but that was not his gift, nor ever would be. For, although he was quick-witted, more than some of his seniors, he was too small for his signalings to be seen. Another drum he fashioned, little prince of percussions, from a cracker-box of tin that he hammered into a cask, and the hide of a put-down horse. 'The skin of Mary Lincoln,' some of the men remarked. Gallows humor abounds in an army.

He beat his Frankenstein creation on ramparts and marches, at funerals, on drills, on musters and retreats, through mighty grists of rain and the cottonland scorch, in floods and droughts and southern dust-storms. Those tornadoes yet blow through the mind of your chronicler, those tempests, and the boy's *tat-tat-tat*. He beat it when a farmboy was executed for desertion, when two more were put to death for an act that was never named. Prisoners were shot. He lammed it for the prisoners, as they swooned or stood manly or wept or tried to run, as they cursed us or begged for their lives. And at times the men about to shoot them were very afraid, and their carbines swayed like wheat-stalks in a November wind, so that the fallen, still beseeching, through mouthfuls of blood, must be finished by the Duty Captain's pistol. All this the child witnessed in time of war. I cannot hear a drum-roll without seeing that boy. His eyes glazed like moonstones as he beat.

Our chaplain, Père Dumoulin, a man of indefatigable decency, would set him to work on a Sunday: processing through camp with fervent purpose, rapping a tattoo to announce the imminence of Mass. Of that, one strange detail remains in my mind. There was no bell to signal the moment of consecration, so the boy would *thrump* his drum when the sacrifice took place and we Catholics would incline our heads.

Little of the sacred in life did he find. Once, I saw him walk out of a mountain of battle-smoke sobbing like the infant he was. I hurried to him and knelt, fearing he had been wounded or worse. That gulping, fright-ened boy hugged this stranger's frame to his own and quaked with tears of abject terror. That is something you do not forget, though you live to a hundred. And I would myself have wept; but I was ashamed to.

His face was of ineffable sadness, brown as a pecan, and handsomely made, beautifully complected, as though his mother might have been a fine-countenanced Portugee or what the Cubanos call 'a moro', meaning a Moor. Where that lady was now, not a one of us had notion. It was believed he had no father in this world.

'You mean your Pa is gone-on?' I heard a lieutenant ask him once.

'Nawsuh. Never had me no Pa.'

'Then your Momma? We all got us a mother. Where she at, Little Drumstruck?'

He shrugged his stick-like shoulders and gazed up at the clouds, his fingers thrumming quietly on his drumhead.

At Champion Hill, our standard-bearer was smashed by a minnie ball, that dreadful wrecker of men. As the bearer sank in his blood to the sludge of the field, the boy tottered forward and grasped the spattered banner. That was the last morning I would ever see him weep. To see him not weep was more frightening.

And I wish I had never seen what I witnessed soon thereafter. Relieved of the colors, the boy seized a weapon from the ground, and with it killed an advancing Federal who was only a little older than he. He shot him through the stomach, and, as the poor lad fell, finished him in ghastly manner with his own blunted bayonet. This I saw. This I record, for this is what happens in war. He was hurrahed by many comrades – to my shame, by me, too – but it was the worst thing I ever saw.

Nor was that the last time the boy played a man's part. But more of it, I cannot bear to set down. I have known brave men. I have wished to be one of them. But conscience makes a coward of us all.

No matter the fetid heat, the roaring sordor of battle, the filth of smoke or the stench of death, he never once asked for a furlough home, nor even permission to mail. It took some of the greenhorns a while to discern that truly he had no home. They did not know what might be done with him. To keep him among us seemed cruel; to send him away crueler. And nobody had a mind to worsen his lot. He stayed with the bones of the camp through the winters, or wandered God knows where in the boondocks.

He and I were among a party of about thirty-five taken prisoner in a skirmish after the Wilderness. We received fair dealings by the Union sentries, many of whom themselves were Irishmen. Indeed, there was the curiosity as nightfall approached, in the roseate shadows of fading light, of captives and jailers moseying the field arm in arm, cutting shines with the farmgirls, smoking and conversing, taking potshots at jack-rabbits, even singing Irish national songs, when shortly beforehand they would have murdered one another as efficiently as Cornwallis beheading the Croppies. Enemies of the morningtide, now drunk as Cooter Brown, and the firmest old boonfellows ever witnessed.

One morning, Captain Daniel Costigan rode up to our compound with his staff, on a proud cobalt stallion, magnificently accoutered. He was a sculpturally handsome man, cut-featured as an Iroquois. His soldiers called him 'The Sea-Eagle'. One could not have imagined that he would be tenanting his grave within the month, nor that his death would be so terrible.

His horse stood fully seventeen hands. I believe it was the finest mount I saw throughout all the War. Three princes of France were among his retinue, bewigged and primped, with painted moles on their chins – many things about this War were contradictory – and it seemed he had absorbed their royalness by some kind of alchemy, or, perhaps, that they had absorbed his. He had that particular poise, that fluidity of comport-ment, of those long accustomed to being looked at.

His approach caused a considerable animation in the stockade, for many of our men could not help but hold him in high esteem, his siding with the northern invader notwithstanding. They knew of all he had suffered for old Ireland's cause and of his friendship with the hero, Brigadier-General James O'Keeffe, whose escape from Tasmania he had assisted many years previously by burning the courthouse at Hobart. Of all the Blade's captains he was *primus inter pares*. He was said to have been scourged to the bone.

The Captain saluted me civilly, said the General would have come himself to pay his respects but was summoned away urgently to Washington. He asked if I would be prepared to assist his medicals, for seventy-one amputations required to be performed that morning and his surgeon was exhausted and aidless. I agreed to do what I could and I suppose by way of making a gesture – or being seen to make one, which is not the same thing – Costigan ordered a half-ration of whiskey for all prisoners 'by the wishes of General O'Keeffe'. At this, there was applause from many of my fellows, though I myself did not applaud. A man that has stood on the gallows, only to tell of his luck, is regarded by other men, foolishly, as godlike.

'You there: Irish. What do they call you?' Costigan barked.

The boy made no reply but glared up at his inquisitor.

'You do not hoorah the health of General O'Keeffe, I see. We are all of us here brave Irishmen, no matter what else. Let us try to remember old courtesy.'

The child gave a shrug and sank his hands in his pockets. He toed a pebble from its socket in the earth.

'Are you bold or a skedaddler, you little rebel blackguard?'

No answer came back from the ragamuffin drummer.

'Faith, now,' proceeded Costigan, perhaps discomfited by the boy's composure. 'You remind me of a Sioux I gave a hiding to once. He was called Little Horse. Shall I give you his name?' The officers emitted snuffles of dutiful amusement, and presently the French princes did the same, only louder. Perhaps the witticism gained something in translation.

The boy looked up at Costigan and coolly retorted: 'Suck my ———— and your mother's.' A long moment passed, colored with incredulous chokes and epithets. The powdered French princes made Os of their lips. He was pelted with scoldings, not originating from his foes, but from those in the bull-pen around him. Then Costigan laughed forcedly as he regarded his abuser – the laugh a man gives when he knows he is defeated; a sound that makes the gullet stiffen when it dies in the epiglottis – and gave the solemnest salute I ever saw, and steeded haughtily away, with no further observation, only slightly diminished by this faceful of southern grit.

The boy and I escaped the following morning. Shortly afterward he vanished from our ranks.

And it was later said by some, though I do not know if it is true, that O'Moody was not his name, that what little he had told us was false, that even his sex was a matter of fiction. That the plucky little drummer-boy, so frail of expression, had all the time been a girl in disguise. It may even be true, for he was beautiful, that boy. He was beautiful and young, and we failed him.

V

CHAPTER 20

YOU'RE WELCOME HERE, KIND STRANGER

We return to Redemption Falls – A cold reception in the prints

A STINK IN THE TOWN!

We were aware that a FORTUNE-HUNTER may fall on hard days, when the seam he had schemed on mining proves BARREN entirely. We did not know, by gorrah, how bad de toimes could get! O'Napoleon de Great is compelled to take lodgers at his swinery! A STENCH has been noted up that end of town, yet queerer than the usual cesspit effluvium of drunken Hibernian disappointment. It is the stink of Yankee hypocrisy fermenting in its guilts. Orphans, urchins, brats, rascals, rogues, waifs, foundlings & assorted bastards: present yourselves, all, at the G——'s wigwam. The thug that murdered your fathers awaits you with open trotters. Piglets especially welcomed by the Runt-in-Chief of the potbellies. The opinion of Madame Meal-ticket we may only surmise. But we note that a sow, when FRUSTRATED or inflamed, will devour her own farrow for breakfast.

Redemption & Edwardstown Epitaph,
March 1st, 1866

CHAPTER 21

ROCK OF AGES, CLEFT FOR ME
LET ME HIDE MYSELF IN THEE

The drummer-boy in the kitchen – The consolations of song
A walk through the byways of his mind

There is a place to which he goes when the dread bubbles up. A Republic that exists in the air. A realm of queenly women encountered by lakes. Drovers and cowboys. Redcoats and pikesmen. King John the Conqueror and the Old Woman of Ireland. The Jesus of the hymns, and ship-wrecked sailors, and the wild colonial boys. And he wanders this country of inherited song, lifting its rocks of rhyme. Here is the Holy Virgin, sweet Star of the Sea, spinning gold with Black-Eyed Susan. Cotton-Eye Joe strumming a lute for the Trickster, their faces grave as gravestones. John the Baptist in the Jordan, singing 'Revenge for Skibbereen' – and he *ast his gal for water, but she gev him kerosene.*

A borderless latitude, this dustbowl of songscraps, where prophets holler Job to the locusts. Its soldiers are trumpeters. Its constitution a broadsheet. Its war-cry is *Rosin the Bow!* And its flag is Joseph's Coat. And its language is the pulse. O, the slaves clap hard, and the spalpeens blow their harps, and the ramblin boys of pleasure and the ladies of easy leisure are dancing the do-si-do. Bold Robert Emmet, the sweetheart of Erin, waves regally down from the House of Blue Light. Singing 'Don't You Longs for Freedom Time?' with two cootchies and a banjo on his knee.

Blackface Napoleon. St Peter on the jugs. And the Savior moan the crucifixion holler. Because none of its people are real any more – if ever they were, which the boy doesn't know. They must once have been real to be tombed in a song? The poorman's mausoleum. No one in this country will hurt you, or kill you, or harry you to speak when you don't want to. They all understand you have nothing to say. You do not wish to talk, but to listen.

No sister will beat you. No mother will leave you. The body does not weary. There is the hope of love. The pipes are a-callin from glen to glen. Recruiting-sergeants tricked by the ploughboys. And he sees himself in Songland, the circle around its sun. He knows its dependable geography. That mountain is a lament; that murmorous creek a lullaby. The city on that hill is Jerusalem, Mississippi, where Crowjane yodels the Twenty-Third Psalm: black angel pick the sly gittah, I'ma lief she spread her wings. In that grotto is his mother, her Connemaran come-all-ye's. It is best not to stray toward those shadows. And there, in the deer park, near the ruins of the palace, Abe Lincoln is hanging from a sour-apple tree. In Dixie Land you med your stand. To live and die in Dixie.

He meanders its topographies like an off-course pilgrim, knowing everything he seeks is somewhere in the scape if only he could be pointed a way. But in the meantime, he is tramping to Zion on High. Happier to be living in a ballad. In the outworld, everyone leaves in the end. But the people in the songs always stay. Long after you have gone, they will still be here. Forever, in fact. They are choiceless.

∇

I am in the kitchen now. Me and the dog. Warm and a rank of grits and hot grease. Honeywoman dander round like she own the whole pike. But she dont own a wart on a pig. Still got to do what they say, is all. Her hands all dusty with flour.

She some older than Liza but younger than Mamo. Ribbon of green in her hair. Got on this dirty coat. It long like a soldiers. And these boots too big for her feet.

Hard to understand the way she talk. Figure she dont care much for talkin. She look at me real queer. Like I wrought out of glass. Her eyes got these rivers of red.

'Summon eat?' she go. I dont say nothin.

'You'll eat when you hungry,' she go.

'You some company,' she go. 'You a party an a half. Got a ache in my head from the carnival in here.'

And she stirrin a caulder on that big black stove. Like a body ever asked her for odds.

Liza use to cook some but she waint too good. Cause she never had no patience with a fire. Honeywoman better. She breathin on the flame.

128

She know to keep your patience with a fire, is all. It aint no secret, cookin.

One time in the army this bummer out of Jackson, he told me this thing about girls. Fairly tumped me over. Couldn hardly give it credit. But turn out it's a gospel, like ever thing strange. Reckon he liked embarrassin others.

She flaunce around the kitchen like some duchess in a castle. She know where ever thing go. Them bottles. Sugarsack. Tin of black molasses. Knives in yon dresser by the shakedown. Ever thing ticker. Keep it neat as a prayerbook. Got her this one knife that shine like the sun. Could have you some fun with that knife.

Got her fifty kind of notions up there on the dresser. Calicoes, work collars, ladles and puddin-sticks, milk pans, skimmers, dippers – a glass eye! Patent pills she got – cure anything you want, boy. Ague bitters, Shaker yarbs, rappee-snuff, wintergreen, lobely, tapes, chits, needles, oswego, smellin-bottles, corn-plaster, mustard, garden seeds, red-root, pocket-comb, tracts, playin-cards, song-books, whistle for a baby, baskets, bowls – Lucifer lights.

Fire burn warm on the cold of my face. Look at it a long long time. Crowjane was here it sure enough be some laughs. Dependin on her humor, that is.

Cause it waint all shit-and-no-sugar with Eliza. Just she got fit to be tied. But a woman will do that ever now and again. Woman be roped to the moon, is all. She dont mean to get wrathy, you just got to treat her nice. Got the waves of the world all runnin through her head, it aint none of her fault, just the way nature made it, an Jesus got a reason for all He fix, and He move in a mysterious way. And the honeywoman move in a mysterious way. Her wonders to perform. And if somewhere there was slavery I could sell me as a slave. But now there aint no slavery no more in the world. And that the way it is.

> *my sister, she the junkyard gal,*
> *she mean as a hootch-house cat.*
> *she walk aroun louisianne, spittin like a rat.*

Real late at night when they believe I'm sleepin, I gets up, mootch around forwhile. He got him a biggo dog, like this horse of a dog. I look at that dog forwhile. In the day you be afeared take a run at that dog, for he'd scare the damn pips out of a apple. Night you could stab him in the eyes if you wants. Nothin he could do in the dark.

she go wid jim, she go wid jack.
go inny place he take her.
she go wid inny snakehip man.
she shake her moneymaker.

In the yonder room in back he got a officers trunk. Got a mirror in the lid. See your face. But old and muddydark and scratched up all to hell. Got maps and old books. Sword from the war. Aint got no gems in the hilt no more. But you can see where it usedta got em. Holes in the silver. Some knuck must of prize em out, the lowdown no-count thief. Aint a body you can trust in all creation Eliza say. No fucky that aint your blood.

Guess that sword in his trunk kill a whole mess of men. Been into their body like Jesus. Queer enough to think of when you hold it in your hand. That it been through some hoeboy's ribs and all. You chargin at me, boy? Take this, you smarmin pox. Twist it in his gristles. He ribstuck.

They gimme a pile of old coats and a bolster for to sleep on. But it hard as a jack-oak, dunno forwhy. Anyways I caint like to sleep inside. House mought fall on your head any time. Go up, it come down in the end of the hunt. Tell that someplace in the Bible.

Always tellin you way to do when you live in a house. Stand up. Sit down. Eat your vittles with a fork. Swab your ass like a christian, you hear? We got paper here for that. Aint some cave in the mountain. Aint some *tepee* you trickin in now, pup. Paper, paper, paper, paper. Dont use you no leaf like a redskin savage. And dont eat you that bread. And dont drink you that water. And dont touch that picture on the wall, it aint yours. Cost a whole shute of money. Keep your hands to yourself. You find you a mess of paper, you hear, or I'ma tan you the color of a roasted goat and wear your livin back for a boot.

Aint nobody's Mammy. That what she said. That time I thrun my shirt on the floor that time. Honeywoman lookin strange, like she dont like me none. Get one thing about as straight as the crack in your sorry ass. I tell you to do it, you do it *real* fast. I am a cook in this house. I am not your bitchin Mammy. Pick it up or I will beat you like a drum.

Real quiet, the way she said it. Man, I fetched up that shirt. Dont you never make me tell you again, you understan? Nod your head. Nod again. Now get back to that supper. We dont have to speak of this matter again.

Go out in the night and gets under the house. Stive up real small you fit good in there. Squidge hard enough you disappear. Like a turtle in a shell. Float all around the world like a mote in gods eye. No one ever give you no more of trouble.

Liza said my Pa was a mexicano. Mamo never told me nothin about him. This one time I ast her she look sore as a spank. So I never did ask it again, boy. But Eliza, she knowed, cause Mamo jaw to Eliza. Eliza and Mamo was friends I guess. Cause womens always friends, least it seem so by now. Woman and a man never friends.

Ontario, she said. Mighty cold for a mexican. Mebbe he get wed to some eskimo squaw. Livin in a igloo. Drinkin beer and hot rum. Lookin at them seals all day.

> *rum rum*
> *sweet rum*
> *when I calls ya, ya bong ta come.*

Mamo tell the seals back in Ireland called silkies. Who give a squirt of piss?

Lays under the house, you can squeeze in down there. Aint too bad. It dont matter afterwile. No one ever find you, not under no house. I slept in a whole hell of worse.

Listen to the nightsounds. Some shit-ass choppin wood. Curlews. Dogs. Coyote up the rocks. Biggo picture of a indian they got in back. Biggest picture ever seen in creation.

And he such a sad look, I dont know for why. Like a feller just told him some real bad news. Like he lost him a dollar and found him a dime. Eyes all droopy and sad.

Cause one time when I was walkin I met this comanch on the road. Gimme wedge of old cornpone and a suck of a brew. Say where your Momma get to? Say damned if I know, boy. She gone as the ace of spades up a sleeve. And that about as gone as she get.

baton rou
baton rou

Somethin gonna happen. Wont be here when it do.

And I see Fat Pat all alone out back. That's a man got some trouble in mind.

∇

CHAPTER 22

THEN FARE THEE WELL, MY OWN TRUE LOVE[†]

Copy-letter found by the boy in the Governor's field-trunk
Retrieved by Elizabeth Longstreet from a nail in the outhouse.

[*Write here the date, but not the location of your camp*]

My beloved and only dearest [*name of your wife*]:

I feel it proper, on this eve of engagement with the enemy, to set down my loving, my devoted thoughts. The morrow shall bring trials, this I must own. Comrades shall fall. Good friends shall not return. Whatever is to come, I wish you to know that I feel the deepest gratitude of my life this night – I speak of my thankfulness to you.

O dearest [*name*]: how I wish I had you by me now. The touch of your hand, a fleeting kiss of your eyelids: for these blessings no utterance could express my gratefulness. If ever I have taken for granted your sweetness and kindness, your steadfast generosity and gentle companionship, remembrance of which has been my consolation since last we parted, thought of which, at the dawn, shall be my greatest comfort, then I ask, I humbly ask, your forgiveness.

It can be hard for a man to give utterance to the secrets of his heart. He wants for the words to do it, perhaps, or makes of reticence a

† On the night before the Battle of Fredericksburg, 'Soldier X', an illiterate private born at Ennis Workhouse, County Clare, asked O'Keeffe for help in composing a letter to his wife at Brooklyn. It would be copied many times by O'Keeffe's men (and by others) during the War. The version reproduced here was circulated with names and other details left blank. Four hours after mailing the letter, Soldier X suffered what an inquiry would subsequently term 'a sundering of his reason, brought upon him by fear'. He left the camp at dawn and took his own life. He was 19 years old, a dockworker.

shield, thinking such expressions were effeminacies, the province of the weaker sex. Better had I spoken more often and openly of the measureless depths of my feeling for you, dearest [*name*]. But think not that my silence betokens the slightest discontent. Can the fire say that it is burning, the river that it flows? I have never been dissatisfied by you; not in the slightest. All I have in this world, whatever I am as a man, I owe to the providential grace of your love, for the discovery of which I thank Almighty God. I wish only that I had merited more your acceptance: unworthily bestowed, faultlessly generous. To have been your husband [*and the father of our children*] was the holiest honor of my life.

War is a cruelty, my darling friend; to write you anything else were a pretense. The cause may be noble, and surely there is none nobler than ours; yet to see brothers fight one another can never be happy. Despairing thoughts lure one. All about is sadness. And yet, as I remind myself when tempted by bleak feelings, how beautiful is any world which has you in it – My dearest, dearest love.

Should the verdict of fate be that I do not return from the contest, know only that my last thought shall be of you, darling [*name*] [*and of our children*], and of the happiness with which you have blest your husband's [*their father's*] being. Could I name such a meager existence a life had it not been sanctified by our union? How poor it were without you, my only precious [*name*]. You have been, by every measure, the companion of my soul, the helpmeet every man should be privileged to find. May our Holy Mother ever intercede for you, dearest [*name*], at the glittering throne of her Resurrected Son, whose modest abode on earth she filled with gladness, as you, my love, filled ours.

If our home was humble, it was enriched by affection. If our hearth was by times empty, it was warmed by your kindliness. Thanks to you, staunchest friend, most valued counselor, I can say with immortal Shakespeare who fathomed all hearts: 'for thy sweet love remembered such wealth brings, that then I scorn to change my state with kings.'

And if, indeed, I should fall tomorrow, be counseled by me on one important question, which, though painful to think upon, will in time naturally occur: that I should [*/should not*] be happy for you to marry again. I know that you will defer to my wishes on this question and be obedient to me, always, as you have been before.

In conclusion, dearest [*name*], I should like you to know that I and my comrades are in a peaceful spirit. I saw a priest not an hour ago and through him made the fullest account and received of his hand the Blessed Sacrament. Not one of us here is afraid to do his duty. We did not seek this fight, this calamity for our adopted country, but, now it has come, I know I can not be found wanting. The cause is too great, the prize too sacred, to suffer the intrusion of self-interested feelings.

My commanding officer, Brigadier-General James C. O'Keeffe, has asked me to tell you that he counts me a good friend. He adds that, if ever you [*or our children*] should require his assistance, you need only to let him know of it and you shall never want for anything he can do. You are to write to him at home: 1, the Fifth Avenue, New York City, or care of Mrs General O'Keeffe at that address.

I kiss this paper. Touch it to your lips; and hold me ever in the safety of your heart.

Until next we meet, at a happier place and time, my own very kindest, my truest [*name*], I humbly and devotedly ask your prayers.

God bless you, dearest Light. Do not be afraid. Be a brave and good girl, and know always that I remain

Your loving husband,

[*sign and print your name/make your mark here*]

∇

CHAPTER 23

SURVEILLANCE

*The watching commences of the Governor's house
by those that did not love him*

MARCH 17TH, 1866. DAWN REPORT.

3.07 a.m. Observer saw a candle lighted in subject's wife room. Then LCO'K (her shade) pacing by the window. Walked 21 minutes. Candle extinguished 3.28 a.m.

   Subject did not leave the house yesterday, nor all the night, St Patrick's Eve festivities in the town notwithstanding. Shutters on his casement remained closed throughout.

5.47 a.m. Boy came out the house in nightgown and boots. Fed the dog, which was tethered in the yard in back. **5.59 a.m.** Went back into the house.

7.21 a.m. Violent quarrel audible from within the house. Insulting words exchanged between subject and his wife.

8.01 a.m. Watch was relieved. Quarrel intermittently continuing.

∇

CHAPTER 24

BY THE SHORES OF SALT LAKE CITY, LOVE, I LAID ME DOWN AND WEPT

A photograph of two soldiers – A Farewell to a loved one

DATE: *March 21st, 1866.* PRISONER: *1 female, age unknown, 17–25 yrs.* NAME OF INMATE: *Eloisa Jane Mooney.* CHARGE: *Loitering, public nuisance, obtaining by deceptions.* DESCRIP: *Five feet six inches, very filthy & disreputable, green eyes, white hair.* REMARKS: *Itinerant prostitute, b. Louis'ana. Melancholia. Hysteric. Lunatic type.* POSSESSIONS: *A bible, a slingshot, a daguerreotype of a boy.* SENTENCE: *4 nights, bread water. Cut rations if she kicks.*

You have seen her these last few weeks as you come from your place of work. She stands outside the Post Office approaching passers-by. Showing them something. What can it be? Handsome. Would be. But obviously poor. Shouldn't be allowed drift about like banshees. Could there not be some refuge? Workhouse, perhaps. Gets a town a bad name when they're loose in the streets. Should write to the authorities. Or maybe.

If you please? Do you have a moment? It will only take a moment. She would like you to take a look at this tintype she carries.

The boy's face is bony. The nose is a little crooked. In the way of early daguerreotypes, the eyes are curiously expressionless: fishlike, whitened, dead. He is drowned in the grays of a Confederate rifleman. From his shoulder, on a lanyard, depends a drum. You have seen other pictures of boys from the War; but what makes the depiction shocking – well, it is shocking in several ways – but what stamps it apart, what commands you to look again, is that a sergeant is aiming a revolver to the side of the boy's head.

And the boy is trying to smile. The pose is a joke. And the sergeant is smiling, too. He is plump and mustachioed, and his tunic is not quite ample enough to contain that porcine belly and the buttons across its front have not all been fastened. It is easy to imagine him a jocular old soak who loves his seven children and wouldn't aim a weapon at them. Yet here he is, three hundred pounds of southern fun, having chosen this attitude by which to be remembered by the eternal gods of photography.

Well, perhaps he did not choose it. The daguerreotypist suggested it. In any case, it is the boy she is asking you to look at. Have you seen this child? Can you look again, closely? Jeremiah Mooney, sir. He goes often by 'Jeddo'. He was here in your city. Oh yes, she is sure. Well, if you turn the picture over, you will see on the back – the typography is minuscule, you might have to squint to decipher it – but stand over here, sir, into the sunlight, and you will be able to see what she means:

"*LeFanu et fils* Portraiture Studio. S. L. City. Sweethearts, & Wives, a Specialty."

Yes, what you are saying is quite correct. It only means the photographer had his premises in this town, not that the picture was made here. Probably it was made in the field of battle. This boy and that sergeant could be anywhere now. They might even be, as it were, not living any more. You are sorry you cannot assist. You must be getting along.

But please, look again, sir. Spare a poor girl a moment? Those clouds in the background are painted, not real. And surely that is canvas they are standing on, not clay. And how can they be so clean? In the middle of a battlefield? And protruding in from the side – isn't that the arm of a chaise-longue?

She has been to the street where the studio used to be, but a signboard reading COMMERCIAL OPPORTUNITY has been placed in its window, and out back, in the alley, a bonfire of depictions is being stoked by the fuming landlord. The photographer, a Frenchman, skipped town a while back, he and his helpmate, a dwarf. Skedaddled, absquatulated, vamoosed, cleared out. And the landlord doesn't know where the renegades went, but if he did, he'd be loading his Winchester.

The boy took away, sir. We quarreled at home. I beat him for stealing and he ran off away. I should never have done it. I lost my reason with the child. I was weary, and hungry, and didn't know what we should do. And I thought he'd come back in a couple of days, for he had took off before but he always come back, and now, and now, I'm sorry sir for crying, and now he's been gone for all this time, and I'm a year on the roads for to find him again, and he sent me this picture, and a letter he writ me, but that's all the word I have of him and no address or nothing else, sir, and I don't know what I can do without that child coming home for he's the only one belonging to me left in the world and I'm begging you for help sir, I'm begging you to think, if you ever seen that child in these streets.

You which, sir? God bless you, sir. Thank you, sir. Here it is:

deaя eli5a: i tаek5 the oppuhtunity of wяitаin thi5e line5 to y hopain to fаn y in god helth as this lieve5 me, idun bin in thi5 heа waя i wa5 in the аumy, idun got me lo5t fяom m bяigаde an wnet on a lonn wаlk, hea i com to 5аint lewi5 ~~mi5uoяi~~ mi55ouяi a coа chfelleя giv m woяk if i wuold go lonn wid him in2 the utaw teяятoаяy, i аm аliev inyhow,

i do vey offen git to thinkain of y it mаke me feel bаd for dаun яong thing5, i am 5oяяy for iveяthаin i dаun to mаяk y hit me, i аm 5oяяяу for 5ауаin i hаte y thаt wаdn tяue

thаnk y for fiddаin me whin i wa5 hungaяy whin mamo win awаey, thаnk y for heppin me whin i wa5 аfeаd. i wi5ht i hаd of not riled y 5o

wel – idon no ifn y in bаton яou no mow but ifn y аяe then i hop y аяe hаppyieя now i am fixin to 5tay up heяe in the teяятoаy fowhile then go in to cаnda аn fin my pa up the а ~~it is a big plаece. i heeяd me a mаn say it is 40 tieme the bigne5 of loiusi~~ wel – godby, i hop y аяe wel & shul hаve a hаppy lief & a fаmbly, i am 5orry for iveяthаin,

coяjul wi5he5 fяum
уя bяutheя,
jed mooney

Another pathetic story. But there is nothing you can do. You hand her back the crumple. A dirty penny. She is weeping again as you hurry away. That war was a terrible business.

You would like to lead her home with you, to bathe her, perhaps. Or watching? Yes. Tiny crack in the door. You would have the servant bring food, a little wine, clean things. And then, if she wanted – no question of compulsion – but only if she wanted, which surely she would, and if discretion could be assured, which surely it might. And every night when you came from your place of work, from the beggars and indigent who molest you in the streets, with the dust of the town in the roots of your hair, and the cares of your position like a cobweb in your eyes, you would open your door and find her waiting in silks and oh how you would make her pay for her poverty and oh how she would be grateful for your pity.

But as you ponder in your bed, beside your capsized, sleeping wife, you find yourself thinking: perhaps she wrote it herself. Because you would put nothing past them, the poor and their schemes. The lengths to which they will go to deceive the respectable.

Slut is a liar. Says she walked from Louisiana. But she did not walk from Louisiana. Nobody could. Nobody walks those mountains and lives to tell the tale. Not without friend or compass.

You will go to the Sheriff and have her arrested. Wanton Irish bitch.

∇

CHAPTER 25

SURVEILLANCE

Further observances in Redemption Falls

NIGHT OF SUNDAY, MARCH 27TH
TO DAWN OF MONDAY, MARCH 28TH, 1866

6.42 p.m. Subject's wife left the residence, very formally attired. Black skirts (hooped), mantilla, gloves, pleated cloak. Appeared tired, drawn. Accompanied by boy who was very reluctant, in ill-fitting britches. Proceeded by foot to church, where shift-miners have Mass on Sunday of an evening. Boy demurred. She slapped him across the ear. They entered. Heard the Mass. Was the only woman present. Gave greenback bill to dues plate, I could not see the denomination. Did not receive sacrament but made boy join line to do so. Departed 8.02 p.m. Was shunned by many towns-people as she returned to residence. Saluted by certain others, all Irish, dirt-poor. Stopped and gave alms to negro child, identity of latter unknown, female, seven yrs approx. Observer unable to hear conversation owing to trundle of passing waggon. Proceeded presently. Entered residence. Did not emerge for remainder of the evening. Retired shortly after nightfall, 9.42 p.m. Governor's candle burned all night.

Boy emerged unnoticed (through a window) at 3.12 a.m. Got him into crawlspace beneath floor of the house. Remained in situ all the night. Appears to prefer sleeping there? Investigate.

∇

CHAPTER 26

MI TIA LUCIA
or
THE SPANISH LADY†

From a very poor book published many years after the events at
Redemption Falls – written by the editor of the present volume
How a hero of Ireland met his American wife – A speech
A supper – A wedding – A war

Aunt Lucia could be jittery, of nervous disposition. Sudden happenings, strange noises, alarmed her. Even an excursion to the theater could be difficult. The presentation must not be bloody or she would become distressed, would insist on departing if seated near the edge of the row. At other times she would watch through the grid of her fingers like a child observing a caning. *Mi Tía*, as I called her – the Spanish term she preferred – was a woman of passion, of courage and ardor. But as is often the case with such deep-feeling people, her vulnerabilities, if hidden, were many.

Lucia-Cruz Rodríguez Y Ortega McLelland. Even in her winter, she was handsome – in the way that a rose, encountered in an old book, is not young any more but is handsome. In the years before the War, before everything changed, she was the belle of a city of beauties.

There is a portrait by Loring Elliott painted in the late summer of her début year, the year her beloved mother died, the year in which O'Keeffe would sweep from the seas like Bacchus descending on Naxos. She looks like an Hispanic saint: mercurial, dark. Enraptured by something going on behind your shoulder. Her hands demurely folded. Rosary beads on her breast. Her mouth is almost insolently kissable.

---

† From *A Monograph of My Aunt, Lucia-Cruz McLelland-O'Keeffe, with a selection of Her Photographs & thirty-two unpublished poems.* By Professor (Emeritus) J. Daniel McLelland. New York, 1910. (Out of print.)

My grandfather, who could be stuffy, an old-world man, could never accommodate to that portrait. He often said there was something 'not quite decent' about it, and in this he was correct, though he could never name what it was. It must not be placed, so he always insisted, in any room likely to be slept in by an unmarried male. It was shunted around the house like an inconvenient lodger – placed in rarely visited nooks, on the maidservants' landings – until finally it was quartered in a locked-up loft like a lunatic wife in a novel.

It did not look very like her. You can see this from photographs. But it is the Dulcinea in the portrait I imagine O'Keeffe meeting, in 1854, in New York. He was in his thirty-second year; she was not yet twenty-one. Already he was famous in America.

It began at the Jefferson Theater on a sweltering night in June. Her journal records 'the stench from the river this morning', the 'reek of parching lilacs' in the house. As she and her sister, Estafanía, and their eldest brother, Rodrigo, set off from Fifth Avenue for the Blade's much-anticipated Manhattan appearance, their landau was besieged by a throng of Irish beggarwomen – ('*some water, Miss, for Jesus, a mercy for the child*') – and Steffa had remarked, in that coolly insouciant way, that here, now, were some of Mr O'Keeffe's disciples.

Estafanía had no interest in lectures, not really. She regarded them as opportunities for being admired. She disliked intelligent men, thinking them unpredictable and gloomy; she preferred dancers or billiard players to scholars. ('I hope my husband shall be moon-silly,' she wrote a cousin in Spain, 'full of laughter and stories, and all sorts of foolishness, with his only true talents in his feet.') By the arrival of that night, which would change many lives, she had endured disquisitions on the importance of fossils, on the Famines in Europe, the death of Little Nell, the Romantic Movement in Art, Germanic philosophy, all the time knowing, as the beautiful always do, that her presence, for many, was the event. This burden she suffered with bored acquiescence. It was a matter of style under pressure.

Lucia-Cruz and Estafanía: the McLelland girls. How I wish I had known them when they were young. Steffa, with her perpetually regen-erating mob of suitors, her Parisian gowns, her arsenal of mimicries, her practical jokes, her exquisite flirtatiousness, her hats so fantastically feathered that she quipped they had caused extinctions; Lucia with her books and old vellums. People said she would ruin her looks with all that squinting. What could be in those volumes was useful to a girl?

She was slender, with high cheeks – like a Cherokee, some said – not as gay as Steffa, but more striking, more paintable. She moved with that unselfconscious elegance so frequently possessed by Iberians. She had never had to dress herself, nor draw her own bath, nor make up her bed, nor put salt on her own toothbrush. She had been told she could rely on seventeen thousand a year. The truth was that she could rely on millions.

Her eyes, almost black but with a richening hint of purple, were the exact shade of blueberries, and their lashes were long. (The poet Robert Cardew, that scholar of American physiognomies, would write to a friend in the fall of '59, that when you met Lucia's gaze over the rim of a fan, 'you felt God was a Roman Catholic'.) Her hair curled into tresses of a chestnut gloss, which she spent an emperor's ransom attempting uselessly to straighten. It was one of her concessions to *la vie de la mode*. That season in Europe, you wanted straight hair.

What an entrance they must have made, my beautiful aunts-to-be, as they arrived and took their seats at the Jefferson that night. I see them gliding along the rows of prosperous New Yorkers, excuse-me-ing their way to the appointed place. Men jumping up. Raising their hats. There was nothing so unrepublican as a Royal Box at the Jefferson, but had there been, that is where they would have belonged.

Outside was a crowd thronging four city blocks, awaiting a glimpse of the hero. Armies of forgers were touting spare tickets. Images of his face cost a dime. He was in the theater now. He was still at Brooklyn. He was coming by boat. He was coming in disguise. He speaks like an Englishman. He dresses like Beau Brummel. *He'd talk the rain out of wettin him.*

Their passes – Lucia preserved them, and I am looking at them now – were in Row A of the Grand Dress Circle. She and Steffa looked down, so the diary records, at the huge crowd in the mill-pit below. More than four thousand people. Seats had been removed. Not an inch of floorboard was visible. There were boys on their fathers' shoulders; mothers with tiny children; men climbing up the columns; men fighting their way in. It was not the usual audience for a lecture. Usually, Steffa joked, they'd be fighting their way out.

'Poor immigrants, mostly,' Lucia writes in the journal. 'Many very scrawny & ill-clad.' Some were carrying banners; others brandished green pennants, sold by hawkers for days beforehand at fifteen cents the pair. And suddenly she was startled to notice, as she scanned the crowd with her opera glasses – up there, near the stage, by the proscenium's left pillar – her maid, Honor Connolly, beside 'a large-headed navvy'. She was a surprising girl, Honor Connolly from Ardee. I should have liked to know her.

Steffa, what a beast, made *un vrai* performance of
holding a kerchief to her nose like Marie Antoinette.
'Ireland is rising,' she sniffed meaningfully, at one point.
I commanded her to remember *la politesse*.

The newspapers record that O'Keeffe made the crowd wait almost half
an hour. Then the chandelier was slowly lowered and extinguished by
the stagehands. A single limelight was lit; the heavy brocaded curtains
parted. On the stage was a lectern, nothing else.

The Jefferson erupted. You could hear the tumult five streets away.
Flowers and green ribbons rained from the gods. They were cheering,
screaming, even before he appeared from the flies. His silhouette came
briefly visible as he was led to the backstage by his bodyguard. He
let them wait another two minutes. His glass of water was filled. The
ovation was prolonged and ecstatic.

He stood sternly beside the lectern, hand touching his breast, head
bowed low to the fierce applause. Many times he gestured that people
should desist; they only cheered louder and sang roundels of his name.
He was dressed in black broadcloth with a waistcoat of lustrous navy.
The boots were seal-black, had been polished until they gleamed. On his
right hand was a diamond and it flashed when he moved. His gloves, his
stock, even his cuffs were black.

'You are looking,' he began 'at nothing.'

There was laughter from some of the audience. O'Keeffe did not even
smile. Slowly he stalked to the front of the stage: Hamlet in search of a
father. There were whoops and whistles – he took off his gloves. He
appeared to be waiting for silence.

'I thieved this wretched shell from Victoria Magnifica, who kept it
under lock on her wilderness island. A monarch's amusement. An object
to be guarded. A nothing abandoned in a crevice.'

'For their shame!' called a man from somewhere up near the roof.
'Long live the Blade,' called a woman.

'*No shame*,' cried O'Keeffe. 'But a radiant badge of honor! They put
Tone under lock! Lord Edward Fitzgerald! That Titan John Duggan! A
pantheon of patriots! Names I am unworthy to utter this night. Nor ever
shall be worthy, did I live to Methuselan spans. For the body you see
before you to have been thought worthy of an attempt to break it – *of this,
of this, shall I boast to my sons.*'

A roar filled the hall. He continued, riding over it:

'These limbs, this rude frame, this clutch-sack of bones, this mortal hand, this uncultivated tongue. This breast which bursts with sorrow for my starved and ravaged nation. All of it they wanted. Every splinter of my being. The fools did not realize, the crown-dazzled fools, *that our bodies are as nothing but empty ships, waiting to be cargoed by history!*'

He said a great deal more – but you can imagine the rest. His performance was overwhelming, masterful. 'His accent is fine-toned English,' the *Times* would enthuse, 'legacy of his preparation by the Jesuit Fathers at Shropshire; but his fire would strip the gilt from a basilica.' For almost two hours he paced his Elsinore and spoke, giving an account of his life, his revolutionism. He talked lengthily of his boyhood, the horrors he had seen. Infants left to die on the quayside of Wexford; fathers, mothers abandoned like animals; the vessels in the port weighted down to the gunwales with desperate, hunger-bitten emigrants. One night he had wept from his nursery window as a woman on the wharf had died. Next morning when he awoke, her body was still there. In the land she was born in, where she had never harmed anyone, where the rich and the idle had all they ever wanted, she was not worth the price of a grave. 'That heroine,' he said, 'whose name is in no book, that woman is the reason I am here.'

She and her class. The poor of Ireland. They alone had been his inspiration. As he stood on the gallows, then languished in prison, as he prayed on the hope-scalded rocks of Australia, it was they who had saved him from despair. '*England, you criminal, weep,*' he raged, '*to have wronged as great as these.*' A Dutchman working backstage that evening, who had no interest in Ireland, and barely knew where it was, told me that by the time the lecture had finished, he, Dutchman, was ready to burn Buckingham Palace.

O'Keeffe dined at the house on Fifth Avenue that night, at the invitation of Aunt Steffa, who had insisted on being presented to him after the last of the eleven curtain-calls. He was polite in the dressing suite, sipping a glass of iced champagne, quietly signing autographs for the ticket-girls. The lecture had been nothing, he insisted to Steffa: 'Did you think it all right? I thought I was a trifle hoarse.' Self-deprecation was one of O'Keeffe's modes – the vain's preferred form of boasting.

My grandfather appears to have distrusted him from the outset. O'Keeffe talked incessantly in those days. It was as though he regarded supper to be a continuation of his lecture. Silverware and delft he used to illustrate his homily, which was long and broad and mesmerizingly detailed, parts of it delivered, to my grandfather's bewilderment, but to his daughters' delight, in playful French. A brandy goblet was Wolfe Tone, a carving knife Lord Cornwallis. Sauceboats and teaspoons were the starving poor of Wexford. He did not eat much, though he was far from abstemious. It was evident to the company that he knew what to do when confronted by a glass of claret.

He had changed into a lounge suit of shimmering black, a sort of blouson of *japonaise* silk. ('Like a comedy pirate,' my grandfather later said, but that was not accurate, quite.) He smoked when invited to – Turkish cigarillos – 'a vice I acquired in captivity'. Costume apart, his appearance was odder than previously, mainly because, on attempting to leave the theater, he had been besieged by a throng of scissor-wielding women who had relieved him of many locks of his hair. He made jokes about this assault but one could see he was rather pleased by it. *Les Anglaises* would have relieved him of his head, he remarked; a handful of its grass was nothing.

The old man, a Republican, did not care much for monarchists, but he disliked all extremists, regarding them as discourteous bores. This Irishman, he later commented, talked about England the way Methodists talked about gin. ('Wearisome, predictable,' my grandfather once told me. 'The mention of Queen Victoria in that strange man's presence would have the effect of moonlight on a werewolf.') There was also the difficulty, though it went unmentioned that night, that O'Keeffe was a man of several pasts.

He was rumored to have fathered a daughter with an Aboriginal woman at Tasmania – the infant had died but the scandal had not – to have left the woman abandoned when he made his much-fêted escape. There were whispers among Irish New Yorkers that she had drowned herself for love of him, that there had been other women in his story – a parson's daughter, a magistrate's wife – even that he had a mistress, a *marquésa* ruined by opium, stashed away at Baltimore. I assume Lucia knew of the gossip, about some of it, at any rate. Whatever she can have felt about it is uncertain.

What is fact is that she and O'Keeffe began to go about Manhattan together, usually, though not always, accompanied. There were evenings at the theater, at the opera especially. O'Keeffe adored Verdi – he had Italian blood from his mother – and indeed was himself a more than passable tenor. But he was endearingly shy about singing in public. He could play the lute a little, and sometimes did. But poetic recitation was his favorite kind of aria. Many in his company, as those months progressed, noticed an

146

old ballad of his homeland become his drawing-room piece. Usually it is sung rather merrily; a rollick. O'Keeffe spoke it quietly, with antiphonal slowness, as though its every word was new. As though somewhere in the prison of its rhythms and rhymes was a long-sequestered truth.

> As I roved out,
> by Dublin city,
> at the hour of twelve at night –
> Who should I spy
> but a Spanish lady,
> washing her hair by lantern-light.
>
> First she washed it;
> then she dried it,
> over a fire
> of angry coal.
> In all my life, I ne'er did see
> a maid
> so sweet about the soul.

You can picture it, I think. This Heathcliff of Ireland, with his curls and fine shirts and his feeling for the tragic and his griefs and his glittering eyes. They would walk in the parks, on the banks of the river. On Sundays they attended Mass.

Lucia had declined several proposals by her twentieth year: one from a brilliant young surgeon, a pioneer of gynecology, who later married into a branch of the Astor family and became a minor though accomplished painter of Western landscapes; another from a Boston banker. These rejections of such appropriate suitors seem to have caused some difficulty with my grandfather, who could be stern as well as kindly. His conception of marriage was essentially contractual, though his own had been happy and by all accounts loving. Not long before he died, in 1903, he remarked to his attorney that he had never understood his treasured Lucia, and I think that was an honest admission. He did not read poetry; she read little else. Fiction he abhorred. ('If I want blasted lies, sir, I go to a newspaper.') He was a skeptical Presbyterian, she a religiously minded Catholic raised in the faith of her mother's people. There was once even a feeling that she might consider holy orders. But I do not think *Mi Tía Lucia* could have made a nun. Not after she met O'Keeffe.

Their letters I have, but I am uneasy perusing them. The Reader will know what it is to be in love, the ardencies we suffer, particularly when we are young, as was one of the authors of these billets-doux. Suffice it to say, it is clear from their contents that a friendship of the mind was not what was forming on those summery evenings by the Hudson. One paragraph only has always struck me as strange. 'I loved you,' Lucia writes, 'before ever your hand touched me, before ever I saw you, or heard spoken your name. And if I died tomorrow, to have known you even so fleetingly would be miracle enough for one life.' A remarkable confession if true, you will agree; but I have no reason to think it false.

He took advantage of her youth, you say? Perhaps you are correct. Though she always swore he did not. 'It was I,' she told me, 'who pursued the friendship. He thought it was him, but it was always me.' I make no accusations. It is not my part to make them. No one can know, looking into his history, the reasons of his heart, that self-absolving siphon, still less the accommodations that another has reached with the magistracy of private conscience. Whatever the reality, early in 1855 O'Keeffe and Lucia were quietly married, in a hastily convened ceremony that went unreported by the newspapers. It was January the tenth; her twenty-first birthday. The first day she could marry without consent.

My grandfather was at Havana by reason of his business. Returning to New York, he was apprised by Aunt Steffa. 'I thought he was going to shoot me,' she would later recall. 'He called Con a disreputable fortune-hunter and me a colluder in lust. It was all rather fabulously exciting.' But for all his rage, which reportedly was Vesuvian, he would not see the couple homeless and unassisted. Abandoning them would have stoked the already smoldering scandal, no doubt. But to be fair to the old ogre, he had that American quality of trying to do, if not your absolute best, the best you can rise to in the circumstances. 'Make do and mend' was one of his maxims. In this case, he had little choice.

Thus the James O'Keeffes were established in the bride's childhood home: Number 1, the Fifth Avenue, Manhattan. Not the worst address imaginable to appear on the calling card of a convict with a death sentence on his head. Two floors of the mansion were remodeled for the couple. Their laceware was imported from a nunnery at Dublin. Masterpieces were hung, Louis-Quatorze displayed. It was a notably snugger nest than the one shared with him in Tasmania – by a woman now forgotten, if she had ever existed at all.

Almost immediately, the marriage seems to have become troubled. It is not unknown for newlyweds to experience disappointments, difficult adjustments to the Republic of Matrimony. As with many an exciting destination, once finally reached, you wonder was it worth setting out. The guests have gone home, the confetti has been swept. You stare at one another across the ruins of the breakfast, disconcerted by the suddenness of the silence. Much of modern life, and nearly all of modern fiction, turns a decorous gaze away from this uneasy vista, endorsing in its stead the precarious idea that a marriage is the close of the book. Many have found it unsettling, this requirement to learn that a wedding is not the epilogue but merely the dedication. The volume in which you find yourself may be beautiful or dull, a Perfumed Garden or a Penny Dreadful. Your co-author may adore you or kill you off. Little wonder there are moments of apprehensiveness. But this was clearly of a different order. Something happened in that first season of my aunt's wifehood that would have grave and lasting consequences.

It took many years for me to discover the nature of the secret and still, to this day, I am not at liberty to reveal it. But I do wish to state, the tattlers are wrong. A number of the suggestions are so wildly flamboyant as to scarcely merit debunking. O'Keeffe had strong male friendships. Which man has not? He said boys were beautiful. Some are. But he had not, so far as I am aware, the Athenian predilections not entirely unknown at his leafy English school. The intimate sphere, the marital aspect – what Aunt Steffa used to term, to my grandfather's horror, 'the nothing about which there is much ado' – I believe proceeded happily, indeed mutually happily. This is not always the case in the new-sown meadow where ardor and greenness combine. It was at heart a private matter and under my pen shall remain so, since there is nothing to be gained from its revelation.

In any case, if the Reader will indulge a digression: a truly companionate marriage is rare as the platypus, that mixed metaphor of impish Lady Nature, and possibly as doomed to the museum. Should you be blessed with such an alliance, here is what to do. Cease, now, with these time-wasting lines, shred the volume into halves, then cast them into the hearth and fly to the lips of your tolerant conspirator to ask if there is anything you can do. For who among us would not rather be making love than reading? Indeed, what is the *point* of reading, if not to help us love one another better? If only O'Keeffe had understood what words are for, instead of always what they are against.

His engagement book for the first two years of his marriage makes a sad, a revealing study. Montgomery, New Orleans, Atlanta, Chicago,

Macon, Chattanooga, San Francisco (twice). He went around America like a restless wind. Every invitation was accepted; always he went alone, often remaining away for months. Of those seven hundred nights, he slept less than ninety in New York. It is difficult to avoid the conclusion that he would rather be away.

When he did return, there were tempestuous arguments. The marrieds were observed on a number of occasions quarreling heatedly in the public street. Lucia, a half-Latin, like O'Keeffe himself, was no wilting lotus when it came to a spat. The architect Carroll Templeton, himself at one time an admirer of Lucia, told a friend of an extraordinary incident he had witnessed at the house. It happened at a lavish supper hosted by the O'Keeffes for St Patrick's Night, 1857.

At this ill-starred commemoration, O'Keeffe had become inebriated – dismally so – and had railed at my grandfather, calling the old man a filthy name. My grandfather, himself not entirely unrefreshed, had demanded satisfaction as a matter of urgency, to which invitation O'Keeffe responded by producing a loaded revolver. Two shots were discharged into a quattro-cento altar-panel of 'Christ Crowning the Madonna', by Fra Lippo Lippi (attrib.). It cost ninety thousand dollars, in 1851. To Lucia's mortification, and the astonishment of the guests, the evening concluded with father and husband brawling on the staircase like a couple of Bowery toughs while the maidservants shrieked Hail Marys. It was all, Templeton journalized, 'rather wearily stage-Irish; a *Punch* illustration come to life'.

Soon afterwards O'Keeffe departed to go wandering the Central Americas, hardly the action of an uxorious groom. He was gone eighteen months and wrote few letters home. The three that survive are clipped, almost businesslike. He writes like one who knows how to hurt. It is rarely what you say, but what you omit, that hurts. Hurt is a matter of editing.

What he did among the isthmians, I have never been able fully to discover. Nor who accompanied him, if anyone. Costa Rica was visited and Panama, briefly. He wintered in Nicaragua, the land of Lucia's people – she was of an old Castilian family, *conquistadors* and *caballeros* – but appears not to have visited her ancestral holdings at Matagalpa. He submitted a capable essay to *Harper's Weekly* on the use of narcotic herbs among the Mestizo Indians. Also a piece on the *Atlantica* town of Bluefields, a settlement whose denizens are not Indian but black, speaking a patois of cockney English and West African Gullah. The piece mentions that its author 'spent the rainy season' in the town 'observing the hurricanes from the terraces of various *caudillos* – their term of honor for a man of distinguishment'. But inquiries made at the *Costa*, admittedly several decades later, yielded no one that could remember him ever having been there, or, indeed, the existence of anyone calling himself a *caudillo*, or of any house possessing a terrace.

Returning to New York, he came home to Lucia. He was bronzed from his travels. ('Like a gondolier,' she wrote Steffa.) But the atmosphere continued reportedly pale. The quarrels soon resumed. If anything, they worsened. Especially painful for Lucia were the silences between engagement. O'Keeffe's valet, now dead, told me he had never encountered a man who could go so many days without speaking. Perhaps it was all the months he had spent in solitary confinement, 'a wonderful preparation for married life,' the valet joked.

He founded a radical paper, all manifestos and denunciations, the kind of Irish journal that calls on monarchs to resign, but appears to have become bored before its fourth number appeared. There were squabbles with the staff and editorial committee, fellow revolutionists of the caucus he helped to establish – the United Force for Gaelic Brotherhood and Freedom: a body neither unified, nor forceful, nor brotherly, only free with the insults, usually in Gaelic. By now, the invitations to lecture had diminished to a dribble. Few cities in America had not been flashed-upon by the Blade. Then, as now, we forgave everything but boredom. The thirst was for fresh speakers, for unheard stories, or, at least, for new ways of presenting the old ones. As well, his star had been somewhat obscured by the arrival in New York of even fiercer Irish felons than he. John Fintan Duggan appeared from Australia, having bombed his way out of a jail there. Richard O'Leary. Edward Casey McBride. These were tough men, organizers, adamantly purposeful. Less drawn to the debating podium, to the society dining room, they grew ambiguous about O'Keeffe and his Fifth Avenue Fenianism. He became, in a sense, a *déclassé* among the engaged. Republican in a republic of one.

He appears, like many a onetime convict, to be a man who could not get started again. There are sketchbooks filled with his drawings of military uniforms. He collected antique swords, old broadsheets of ballads. The song 'The Twa Corbies' he translated into Gaelic, and then into Italian, then courtly French. Touchingly – at least, it touches me – he copied out Lucia's earliest attempts at verse in his exquisite copper-plate hand. As with many intellectually brilliant people, her handwriting was atrocious, a fact about which O'Keeffe would spousally boast, as though the admirable failing were his own.

He qualified as an attorney but did not practice. He was principal in a consortium to construct a bridge on the Hudson, which endeavor, he convinced himself, would garner him the fortune his father-in-law always resented him lacking. In the event that failed also, for want of investors. He was often seen walking the poorer sections of Manhattan, or over in Brooklyn, haunting the dockside, the slumland alleys of Fulton Street. He would gaze out at the ships for hours at a time. There was a difficult incident, involving the police, when he took a cane to a banker he had seen spit on a beggar's child. There were bouts of ruinous drinking.

He became what he had never publicly appeared: an apprehensive, even a frightened man. He worried about his lungs, had nightmares of Wicklow Prison, grew obsessed by the notion that he was being followed in the streets, an impression we now know to have been largely correct. England sent agents to keep watch on his activities – he was suspected in London of still being active, of fomenting a conspiracy for the invasion of British Canada, of smuggling ammunition to Ireland. Little did My Lords of Westminster know, the Blade was decidedly blunted. A detective hired to shadow him in the winter of 1859 had to resign from the task, despite the generous remuneration and expenses. He was too bored to continue, and too drunk, he wrote London. The hours spent in Irish barrooms were killing him.

Those were the years in which the United States would prove to have been ironically, at least prematurely, named. One's loyalties were sounded in every conversation. Did the south possess the right to live as her masters pleased? Or must every state comply with Washington's laws? An unwieldy marriage, the American republic. There was the feeling that it was edging toward a brutal divorce.

All his life in America, O'Keeffe had loved the south. Charleston, Savannah: those sultry, stately cities; their euphonious talk, the looks of the women, what he called, in a memorable if profoundly disingenuous phrase, 'the gay Mediterraneanism of the southern *mode de vie*, which affords a man so much of leisure and pleasure'. The filth-heap on which such gaiety was already beginning to totter, he seems to have scarcely noticed.

When it does materialize in his writings, on those remarkably few occasions, he appears to regard it as a simple fact of the landscape, like an exotic spice, or hearing French in Louisiana, a matter of how people do things differently when the climate is hot. *A chacun son goût* would appear to be his axiom; but his tolerance is a refusal to see.

And this, to say the least, is difficult to comprehend. In his boyhood,

O'Keeffe knew much about the obscenity of the man-trade. Indeed his nursemaid at Wexford, an African called Beatrice, whose cameo he wore all his life in a locket about his wrist, herself had at one time been a slave in England. That he permitted himself to be attended by her stolen siblings in America, that he at no time raised his oratory in support of their emancipation, that he wrote, of southern slaves, that they were 'well-cared-for and fed, merrier in Mississippi than in the Paganlands of Ethiop' – these are astonishing failings.

And yet, when the cancer burst, he acted surprisingly. He did not stand with the seceding south, as for years he had maintained he would, and as many another leading Irishman would do. Three mornings after Fort Sumter was attacked by the Confederacy, posters materialized on the streets of New York, in Five Points and the Battery, on the Lower East Side; on Stanton Street and Mulberry, outside the old Cathedral on Mott, in every quarter of rookeries where penniless Irish scraped a life; by the reeking shanties of Brooklyn.

♣ **IRISH IMMIGRANTS & ALL MEN OF HONOR** ♣

WILL ENLIST

FOR THESE UNITED STATES!

Tens of Thousands of Irishmen
Are joining the ARMIES OF THE UNION
To defend this GREAT REPUBLIC against the TREACHERY
Which MENACES HER!
Shall you permit the Southern TRAITORS to destroy
the CONSTITUTION?
Shall you stand in idle watchfulness whilst
LIBERTY IS ASSAULTED?
This Republic gave you FREEDOM!
AROUSE TO HER DEFENCE!
EVERY MAN & BOY IS WANTED FOR
THIS PATRIOTIC FIGHT!
IF YOUR NEIGHBOR CANNOT READ THIS,
INFORM HIM OF ITS IMPORT

Published at his expense by James C. O'Keeffe, number 1, the Fifth Avenue, New York

---

At that time on Fifth Avenue, between 19th and 20th, stood a row of elegant townhouses. The kind of mansion that is backdrop to much of the era's fiction; where witticisms are spoken, Latinate, long, and food is plentiful as punctuation, so that no one is ever hungry, and nobody poor, and there are bathrooms and servants, so nobody stinks, and the débutantes rustle from room to room having subtle, ambiguous epiphanies. Early in the morning of April nineteenth, the occupants glanced up from their understated breakfasts to an unusual, a memorable spectacle. A mob of the unkempt straggling along the avenue below. Noisy. Unsettling. Not beautiful to look at. They were marching under a banner few had previously seen. A green, white and orange tricolor.

There were longshoremen, stevedores, farriers, hodmen. Little clerks from offices; many hundreds of boys. The nobodies penciled as monkeys and monsters in the journals of the Land of the Brave. Drunks, husbands, Holy Joes and gang-men, workers from manufactories, apprentices, servants. They came down the avenue raggedly; relatively few had marched before: out of step, in a jostle, ungainly. At their head was a piper in a moth-eaten kilt playing 'Bonaparte Crossing the Rhine'.

They came up to the Recruiting Station on the corner of 19th Street, where they shambled into lines, 'with surprising sobriety' noted the *Tribune*. Here they pledged to take arms, perhaps to the death, for the country that had spat on their children. Their leader had on a uniform of his own design – dark green, Bolivarian, Celtic harps on the epaulettes, a sash of golden braid, *caballero*'s boots. It would have been easy, as you observed from your drawing-room window, to have been amused by the sight of this felon and his rabble, for there was something of comic operetta in his appearance that morning, but more in the mien of his followers. The poor, about to die in uncountable numbers, while you gorged behind the glass of your ironies.

At his side in a glittering scabbard hung a magnificently tasseled sword, which a long time before, in a wasteland far away, had been cast for a lieutenant of Cromwell. Perhaps it had killed Irishmen. In O'Keeffe's hand it would kill more. The Blade had found the long-hungered purpose.

A photograph was made by the young Timothy O'Sullivan of O'Keeffe and three of his party as they took the parade. He looks younger than his years: trim and muscled, like a boxer; it is the only known depiction of him smiling. Beside him are Captains Costigan, Haines and O'Malley, each man accompanied by his wife. Another wife is notably missing from the tableau. So absent that her absence is a presence.

Her husband's docket of enlistment is signed in Gaelic: '*Seamas O'Cuiv. Loch gCarman*, Wexford.' In the space marked 'Profession' is written the word 'Patriot'. It is underlined, twice, as though someone had dared to doubt it.

V

CHAPTER 27

I GAVE MY LOVE A TOKEN STRONG, THAT HE SHOULD KNOW I LOVE

Lucia's gift to her husband on coming to Redemption Falls
A striking representation – The doomed painting described

LOT 19: *Our Heroic Frontier* by Edward Fairfax Chapel†
Oil (with graphite) on canvas

. . . The work is on the epic or heroic scale, measuring eleven foot by seven-and-three-quarters, unframed, depicting a chieftain, unnamed, of the Blackfoot Indians, in tribal regalia and glorious trinketry, on a mountainland butte of the West. Ocher and crimson flesh paints adorn the rugged face; the forearms, manly, strenuous with sinew, are banded in sapphire-studded gold. In the background are the rapids of a gargantuan falls – stunningly rendered: note the 'rainbow' shimmer of the foam – and a lively selection of indigenous flora and fauna. The claw near the left moccasin is that of a Sharp-shinned Hawk. The tomahawk-pipe feathers are falcon and grebe. Elk and kingly buffalo, in peaceable companionship, graze on the prairie below.

The debt to great Mantegna is discernible in the painstaking geological accuracy of the limestone (the mouth of a cave is distantly visible between the subject's knees) but the composition is High

---

† From catalogue for 'Sale of Important American Art', Knoedler & Co., New York, February 1865. Author uncertain but probably F.R. Hildebrandt, Senior Auctioneer and Valuer. In his hand across the frontispiece appears the following note: 'Dear Mrs O'Keeffe: We hope you are keeping well. You asked recently if we might have something on a musical theme for the General's forthcoming birthday. We have nothing musical at present but I thought the Chapel might interest you, given the Gen.'s new position in the Territory, for which richly merited honor we all send warmest congratulations. When shall you leave to join him? We shall miss you very much. Kindly, FRH.'

Romantic. The Savage in pelts and loincloth, brimming with sagacity and muscular grace, standing sentry over his preserve, the beauty of raw nature, the untamable wilderness of the skies. Note, indeed, that more than half of this vast canvas is given to the depiction of sky.

The horizontal of the subject's strong right arm directs us to a settlement in the faraway valley, where minuscule figures, human and animal, delightfully rendered, may be observed. Note the wisps from little hearths; the tiny stockades. What lives are being led in that courageous colony? Then, fancy a moment, viewer: what might this Red Apollo say, did only he possess the power of addressing his spectators? Has he squaws? Has he children? How many braves does he command? The carvings on his rifle-stock: what do these runes import? His noble countenance, maroon and wise, seems to have witnessed gravest truths. Regard his night-black eyes: have ever eyes stared more piercingly? See how the war-paint makes their glow yet the fierier. Those daring, fervent, all-seeing orbs – do they not know our inmost secrets?

When exhibited at the Academy of Design, this work was the sensation of the season, winning acclaim from the academicians and public alike and attracting many thousands of visitors. It has since toured to London, Paris and Biarritz, magnetizing extraordinary numbers. No less a personage than Her Majesty, Queen Victoria of England, pronounced herself enthralled by this masterpiece.

This is a sublime, a singularly magnificent picture, which will appeal to collectors of the Western Frontier and discriminating residents of our larger Manhattan homes. Estimate: $10,000–$15,000. A strong preemptive bid may secure.

∇∇∇

PART V

APRIL IN THE MOUNTAINS

O rose of submission –
That hast – no blood –
But the tears all shed –
for provinces lost.

O bloom of contrition –
Bow thy head –
Thy poison thorn –
thy bitter cost.

(IV, 1866)

Charles Gimenez Carroll
(pseudonym of Lucia-Cruz McLelland-O'Keeffe)
'On the First Anniversary of the Rebel Surrender'

CHAPTER 28

I'M DRUNK TODAY, AND SELDOM SOBER A HANDSOME ROVER, FROM TOWN TO TOWN

*Further recollections from Elizabeth Longstreet – A regrettable
habit to which her employer succumbed – And the ancient vernacular
of the Irish people*

When he get to the liquor you didn get in his room. Go way over there. Any
place else. Cause he didnt care a penny for how he do then . . . Irishman
kin to the Indian for liquor. Aint nought but a bane to him. Bring out his
worst . . . Fixin on his troubles . . . Stern up the demon . . . Frenchman can
drink some. Russiaman. Swede. German keep it comin till a frog grow a
beard . . . But a Irish dont know when to quit with it see. And it dont make
him happy like it do your Italian . . . Ever seen Italian [drinking]? . . . He
amble along fine . . . Dont want him no trouble, just whistlin the girls . . .
But your Irish wont quit with it . . . That's the matter right there . . . Drink
the Wal Trabla whiskey till the rage come down.†

For sure, he fight his wife some time. You never fighted your wife? . . . An
she gev it right back. Oh yes . . . She surely did . . . No hair on her tongue
when it come to a fight . . . And then he come madder, an 'you this' an 'you
that' . . . No, not a raised hand. No no no. Never did . . . Was gibble-gabble
mostly, you know how marrieds will get . . . Or they go a day two not a word
spoke between em. He was sorrowful any ways. It some men that's they
nature. Who know why it is. Just the flesh.

He got a reputation for a hard character. Unfeelin. But he wasnt. He be
ornery now and again. But he had kindliness in him . . . He was the
changinest man I ever knowed. An that's the kind he was; back then any
how. Give an take back in the one-same speak.

† Probably 'Wild Traveler': a cheap unbonded whiskey then popular in the West.

Got these – what to call em – these notions in his mind. Take a notion, that man, like a girl keepin company . . . Like he teached me couple words he say the folks be speakin in Ireland. Cause they got they-own language over there I guess. Like 'open the door' an 'fetch in the supper'. Domestic things you know. Well I forgetted em all now . . . Got in mind that ever last soul be spyin on him you know. So he want me to go speakin some way they caint catch. But it was real hard . . . Was real, real hard . . . That aint never no language gwine to catch someplace else.

He was a odd fish for sure. Think too much on a thing. That's one sickness a whole lot of men got in the world. Cause a woman dont got time to get fix on misfortune. Mought want to. But she dont got the time . . .

'Be duh husht' I remember . . . Now I come to remember. 'Quiet your mouth' that mean . . . In Ireland . . . Cause the reason I remember, I often wanted to say it . . . House like that, you would.

∇

CHAPTER 29

COME SPRING THE TIME FOR COURTSHIP SWEET, WHEN LOVERS WOO AND WED

A curious armada menaces the town – A lighthouse with no light
Handsome Conor Nolan – Miss Martha McIlvenny, the lily of
Redemption – Ovid in the mountains – The season of loving – The cause
of disunity in the Governor's marriage

They argue most nights. From his kitchen-bed, he can hear them. She
says, when they quarrel, that she will leave him and return to New York,
and he roars that he wishes she would.

Spring comes hotter. But she does not leave. There are many days of
rain and rain-scented wind. The boy loves this blustery weather. He goes
walking out of the town, up the foothills of Crow Mountain, where he
sits by the Falls for which the settlement is named or fishes suckers in
Jubal Creek. He follows mule-deer into the forest, picks the chokies,
looks at leaves. Carves his name into the skin of a sequoia. Up here he
feels freer; cleaner than in the colony. It is possible to believe nothing has
happened.

Eliza feels close to him. He wonders where she is. She could be dead
for all he knows, or moved far from Louisiana, a place she never liked, so
she claimed. The hurricanes billowing out of the Gulf. She'd be stormy
as any tornado. He hopes she got married but he doubts this could have
happened. She is too crazy for marrying. Who would have her?

The men in his platoon used to talk about women like Eliza. And that
day in Wadesboro, when they stopped at the fancyhouse where the girls
wiggled in petticoats in the windows. 'Grab onto your partner,' Miko
Boylan said quietly. 'I believe I am ready for a dance, boys.' You went in
the front door and came out the kitchen and the men said you came out
cooked. Whanged you like a jewsharp. Loosened your strings. Rocked

163

you like your back done got no bone. They had tried to make him do it; even offered to pay for him. But he had not wanted to do any such thing.

Alone in the woods, he strains towards speech. He gabbles, grunts. The words will not come. They catch in his throat, it is like chewing a sludge of vowels. Only when he sings can he push them out:

> Yo soy la recién casada,
> De mí nadie gozará.
> Mi marido a la guerra,
> A tomar su libertad.

And that is not quite accurate, because he does not push them out. It is more that occasionally, as he wanders the scoghs of elm, he discovers himself singing with no recollection of having tried to. And always, at that moment, his singing dams up, for the words become unpronounceable again.

He finds an unknown brook. Skims taws across a tarn. He siestas in the grotto near Lake Valentine. He steals the Governor's empty memoir-books (forty dollars the piece), tears off their elegant bindings, rips their pages to make paper ships. Flotillas of them bobble down to the stream in Redemption, so that the people stand and gawp at them, wondering where on earth they could have come from. He dreams about the Governor's wife; it is a sinful dream. He is lying with her, trembling, kissing her bare, smooth neck. She takes his spanner-like hand and places it on her abdomen, circling it, slowly, around the ruby in her navel. He wakens, dry-mouthed, in the red heat of the kitchen. Flooded by his dream. Rubs his mouth on his shoulder.

She does not leave for New York. The boy does not know why she stays. A cart comes from a warehouse at Fort Galloway with a harp on board. It is the most preposterously beautiful object Jeddo Mooney has ever seen. Gilt-leafed, shining, painted with miniatures of exotic places. Palma. Seville. The cathedrals of Madrid. Those are the cities of Spain. When she plays it, the shimmering music fills the house. Women are stilled in the lane outside, even the women who detest her. A week or two she plays but then seems to grow bored. It is shrouded in a Koötenais blanket and forgotten.

She knows of his dreams of her. He knows she knows. She looks at him disapprovingly when they meet in the passageway or in the mortifying narrowness of the stairs.

'Where do you think you are going? What are you doing? Go back to the kitchen, you do not belong up here. Did you mother never tell you, it is impolite to look directly at a lady? When was the last time you bathed?'

He kneels in the mulchfloor of Decatur Forest and sins as the birds caw above him. They see his transgression and inform the other birds, and the nests of Decatur chirrup their admonishment. She regards him across the table as supper is observed. She knows. Her eyes are sad.

'I would like the boy to have a responsibility. Do you think it a good suggestion, Lucia?'

She hardly bothers looking. 'Of what nature?'

'Yardwork, perhaps. Shortening firewood, perhaps. Would you care for that, young Mooney? It is good for a boy to chop wood.'

He nods his assent, since he supposes it is expected.

'We have quite enough cordwood for the year,' she says quietly.

'Well then, is there some chore about the house he could do?'

'That is why we employ Elizabeth. We have discussed this matter previously.'

'I am quite aware of what we have discussed. But idleness is not to be encouraged. God knows, he sees enough of it in this house.'

She says nothing. Eats her food. Takes a long sip of water. The boy has the feeling there is a retort in her mind, which she is finding it difficult to keep imprisoned. The Governor crumbles a dye of bread in his fingers. As though about to feed a wintering bird.

'Mayn't he run a broom about my study every now and again? Something small of that nature. That is not a part of Elizabeth's fiefdom, after all. Since we must be cognizant of offending the domestics.'

Saws the elk-meat on her plate. Raises a forkful to her mouth. From a pocket in her skirt she takes a small black book, which she opens and leans untidily against the ewer. He knows it is a prayerbook, for he has looked inside it secretly. Batter My Heart, O God.

'Lucia? I would appreciate the courtesy of a response.'

'You have already decided, Con, as you decide all things without me, so I do not know why you put yourself to the trouble of asking.'

'I thought only to have the benefit of your feelings on the matter.'

'Another performance.'

'It is not a performance.'

'Yes, General. As you wish it. So shall it be done.'

'Do not address me in that manner. I forbid it, woman. *Do you attend me?*'

'I forgot how a superior is always to be addressed. Thank you for reminding me of my station yet again.'

'Would you leave us, please, boy? If you have finished your supper. Mrs O'Keeffe and I wish to have a talk.'

He has not finished his supper but he departs the table anyway. He knows what is about to happen and does not want to hear it. Bad enough when he hears it through the walls.

The kitchen is too hot. He pushes off his sheet. A Federal Private is standing by the wall, the bird-of-all-death on his head. Beside him, a black girl, screaming at Jeddo Mooney, a broken, bloodied crutch in her hands.

'Do not be afraid . . . You are safe . . . It is all right.'

The drumming comes hard in its thoraxial cage and the starburst of a candle in his face. The Governor's voice. Hair in his nostrils. Broken veins of his cheeks. Flecks of steelish gray in his stubble.

'It was only a dream, boy . . . I heard you call out . . . Do not be upset . . . Stop crying . . .'

He crosses to the dresser, gropes clumsily for a cup. Fills it from the pitcher. Offers a handkerchief.

He watches while the child dries his eyes and drinks the milk.

'Where is Elizabeth tonight?'

Jeremiah Mooney does not reply.

'Are you frightened? . . . There is no need to be . . . .It was only a nightmare . . . We are quite safe in this house . . . The door is always locked . . . Do not be afraid . . . We are all of us your friends . . . '

He sits on a milkstool and looks at the boy, and the light of the candle is yellower now, and its shadows move in the corners of the kitchen. Wind gusts across the prairie and it billows on the rocks; and a strange thought occurs to the sleepdazed boy. That the music of the wind is not the wind itself but the resistance of the world to the movement of the wind: trees, rocks, houses, pebbles, the prairie, other winds, whole nations.

'Go to sleep,' he says, quietly. 'I will remain while you do. No one is going to hurt you again.'

The Governor walks at night like the zombies of New Orleans. The thud of his boots on the coffinboards. He goes out of the house. Stands on the prairie, smoking. Sometimes he stands there an hour at a time. Sometimes he stands all night. And the wind blows around him – you can see him through the knot in the wall – so that sometimes he sways or lurches in its buffet. But still he don't come in.

O'Keeffe, they call him, the people in the town. James O'Keeffe. The Blade. And the boy has come to believe, as the settlers believe, as the Governor believes, as his wife believes, that the drunkard alone on the prairie in the wind was once a hero to millions. For everything changes; the boy knows it is so. The body changes. He saw it happen many times. He himself will change, as Eliza changed, and Mamo, and O'Keeffe, and the men in the army, and only the wind stays the same in the end and the bodyless who live in the songs.

One midnight he awakens to the smash of falling crockery, of heavy things being overturned and thrown around the wooden rooms. The Governor is shrieking obscenities and calling her a name that the boy has heard before. A word he has heard used for his sister, for their mother. Often Eliza employed it herself, to blaspheme Jeddo Mooney, and why it should be a curse he does not understand; but he knows that it is, for once, in the army, he saw a man die by the gun when it was uttered. A part of her body. It must mean something else too. Why not scream 'you face' or 'you hand' or 'you leg'? Because that would not be as cutting. But why would it not? The boy has seen hands and legs lie in fields. They are terrible, then. He has seen eyes. Has it something to do with the fact of being born? Is that what is so terrible? That you would curse her for bearing you? And when that hard, short word is used by a man in his anger, you know it is time to hide, if you can, because it means he does not care any more what he says, and that point is dangerous in men. But then, the boy realizes that the Governor is alone, that his wife is upstairs – he can hear her moving around the pictures. The unspeakable word is being howled at nothing but the shadows, or a mirror, or the shards on the floor.

Not wise to let him catch you now. If he does, he'll cuff you in the head, or let fly with a kick, or roast you. The cook paces the kitchen throwing glances at the child. The nights of April grow long.

V

Gutta cavat lapidem. 'Dripping water hollows stone.' Ovid is her companion as she walks the slate hills; his odes of love and timelessness. Below her on the floodplain more territories are staked. Spreading out like a map into the distance. Fields and claims and houses – existences. Promises kept. Solidarities honored. Homes being raised from nothing.

The schoolmistress walking in a quarry with her soldier. Smoke from chimneys. A paddock bladed-out. A watching-tower being built at the

167

summit of the Falls by a man who bought land there, who insists, so they say, that one day there will be visitors who will pay good money to watch the Falls from the dryness of his lightless lighthouse. Brothers on a raft poling slowly across the creek. A bride coming to chapel by boat.

She reads the Talmud and Hawthorne. Donne and William Blake. She writes and rewrites. She makes photographs of the County. She visits the poor families at St Hubert and La Grange. It is best to stay out of the house.

Bedsheets whip in the sluffs of wind. The sails of unspoken ships.

Conor Nolan is born. Handsomest child in the Territory. Miners festoon him with greenbacks. Miss Martha McIlvenny, blonde-haired, vivacious, the beauty of Thomond Street, is married to the man that built the tower. Billy Douglas goes courting Miss Aura-Lee Neville. He stands beneath her shutters singing 'The Yellow Rose of Texas' while she listens and smiles in the slat-light. Lucia O'Keeffe reads difficult poems – dense, packed, ripely succulent with meaning. Explaining those pregnancies to no one.

The mail-stage comes. It brings letters from New York but there are times when she dreads their arrival. A year since the surrender. Many children are born. Many Abrahams and Marys and Roberts and Jeffersons and Harriets and Fredericks, even a Ulysses. News of friends becoming parents is difficult to read, and envy is shameful to feel.

Elizabeth pegs the launderings on a sagging length of lariat. Jacket-sleeves reaching toward the banners of dresses. Invisible bodies writhing.

The child unbegotten by this marriage is nevertheless real. It walks its parents' rooms at every hour. It touches the walls of that house of splintering planks. She senses its presence among roofbeams. She has an idea of how it might look and of what it would be named; of what sort of adult it would grow to. Like a prisoner on an island to which you only have to swim. It is just across the river. It calls to her.

The moons of its eyes. The ferns of its hair. All it asks is a rescue – to be owned. A chance to come out of the cave of a thought. To live in a body. To ever know what that was like. Its suck. Its heft. Its kittenish roilings. The smell of its scalp. Its unearthly fontanel. Its heartbeat against your cheek as you listened for a croup. The palps of its fingertips at your breast.

Once, during the War, on a hot night in Manhattan, when lightning destroyed a clock-tower but the rain never came, she saw a child receive the news of his father's death. He plunged to his knees in the hospital corridor, wrists to his face – he was shaking. The silence before the howl, the bellow of animal grief, and the mother, weeping herself, had had to console him, and even the nuns had wept. And Lucia had wanted to say that she knew what this moment was like, had endured something similar when her mother had died; and that the boy was quite right, it was the most terrible thing of life, and you would never recover from it; but that somehow it would be survived. But now she is glad not to have told the child that. There are stranger griefs than the death of a loved one.

Her sister is in love, has accepted a proposal. A cousin in Spain expects twins. Her maid, Honor Connolly, has married her coachman and is pregnant ('for which I thank God, Miss. I am the happiest girl in America'). It is April in the mountains and the trees are leafed-out, and everything that grows is growing.

'The world is a wedding,' the Talmud tells her. But the world is not a wedding. It is a child.

∇

CHAPTER 30

A YOUTH AGAIN I NE'ER SHALL BE TILL APPLES GROW ON THE IVY TREE

A reluctant scholar – Some important personages – The General recalls a summer of courtship – Then alone with difficult memories in a low saloon of the town – A letter from God – His meeting with a President The incident at Tennessee – A lady who is not what she seems

Headache-pummeled, raw-nerved, smoldering for a drink, the Governor looks out of the window of the Legislative Office on Fitzgerald. It is April the fourth, 1866. His forty-third birthday. He has not touched liquor in a fortnight.

The window has been painted shut, has not been washed since it was put in. You need a permit from Washington to hire a scrubwoman. He has mentioned it to Elizabeth, told her to come in for an hour. There is always some reason why she cannot.

He is thinking about Van Diemen's Land and a onetime friend, the comrade who arranged his escape. They flogged John Duggan two hours that night, until he could no longer stand, gave him six months in solitary, tried everything to break him, bribed him, beat him. Still he told them nothing about the flight of the Blade. In the ballads, he had spat on their thumbscrews.

> *John Fintan Duggan, the pride of the land,*
> *They scourged him and chained him, and shattered his hands.*
> *'Screw 'em on, Tasman Devils, screw hard and twist mean;*
> *Ev'ry twist of your screws is a curse on your queen.'*

Derry. Presbyterian stock. Tombstone-tough. His father had been a preacher. Duggan had inherited his sobriety, his way with a sulfuric denunciation. He said liquor was the blight of the Irish people: *we shall never stand free while luxuriation enthralls us.* Always he had chided O'Keeffe for his 'southern feebleness', his shady love of pleasure, his

'Italianness'. *You're a flabby papist fly-boy, you whoreson lush; you'd not meet worse in a year's travel, so you wouldn't.* And every year on his birthday he had sent O'Keeffe a bottle. He had even managed to do it from the colony.

There was no bottle today. There would not be again. John Duggan was rotting in a prison in Virginia. Both sons dead for the rebels in the War. His house and his plot and his newspaper office burnt; his presses destroyed and dumped in the James; his wife made to pay the costs of his imprisonment. Once, he and O'Keeffe had been thicker than brothers, close enough to trade insults punctuated by laughter. Now, Duggan is an enemy of the American people. Others will be forgiven. Not him.

A vision incarnates through the grimy window. Down in the street. On the corner by the jail. In the hurting gleam of the sunlight. Does not that little guttersnipe look oddly familiar? Is your mind playing tricks on you again?

Where are his new clothes? Why is he not at the schoolhouse? Christ – is that a carving knife in his belt?

Motionless on the boardwalk. Smoking a cigar butt. A smearing of dust across his mouth. Those are not the shoes Elizabeth found for him; they do not match. Battered stetson, too big, like a suet bowl on his head. Is it the moonboy? His double? Or a queer coincidence? Do all boys in rags look the same? The boy gazes up at the Governor and drags on the smoke. It swirls all around him. A thought.

One hand on the knife handle, the other touching the hat brim. The day is not sunny but the brim is visor-low. The Governor recognizes the way the boy stands, a certain way he has of shifting his weight. You see it in children who have long known cold. They move from foot to foot, mashing one shoe with the other. They always want to be moving.

Mooney the moonboy. His still, assessing glance. Saddened as a theater gone dark.

Behind the Governor in the room, men are talking angrily. Vituperative words, bitter raised voices. The argument is of commerce, the cost of rebuilding after the storm last Christmas. Who is to bear it? Will there be a restitution? Washington must be approached without delay for assistance. The sun slides out from behind the ink-smudge of a cloud and Redemption is rinsed in light.

O'Keeffe beckons from the window. There is no response. Perhaps the boy has not seen him, is looking at something else. He raps hard on the glass, his wedding ring cracks it, and the child scuttles away into a dazzle of reflections. By the time the Governor has gained the street – he hastens one end to the other, retraces his steps – the boy can be seen running hard toward the north, scurrying up the stones of Goat-Head Hill.

The town has been rebuilt, but inefficiently, too fast, without architect or mason or even builder. A dozen weeks of hammering. It was like living in an ark. Plans scraped in the street-dust, if at all. Enmities of party and tribe were set to one side, as though they were the fripperies of peace-time. Cockney succored Kerryman, Catholic assisted Pentecostal, Copperheads aided Lincolnites, Baptists helped Chinese. Only the blacks, recently freed by the War, received no assistance from any but their own. Their shacks and scalpeens were put back where they had been, to the last shred of tattered sacking, each warped and broken board, as though their windblown ghetto is scenery in a play at which the nobles are expected at any moment. Last Saturday, when the chapel's mainframe was hauled and re-raised, the Stars-and-Stripes banner on the Post Office was burned. Life is returning to normal in Redemption. The time is come again to be guarded.

He returns to his meeting but his mind wanders like a beetle. The burghers around the table are ignoring him. They talk furiously at one another, throwing insinuations, resentments. The air is blued with cigar smoke.

Concentration eludes him. Somersaulting thoughts. He would like to sleep for a week, in some dark deep room, windowless, like the cells he has known. Always as a young man he had been able to sleep, whether his pillow was downy or of cold hard steel, no matter what the morning held for him. The night before he was due to be executed in Wicklow – half hanged, cut down, sawn to pieces on the block – he had eaten a supper of hardtack and scrag and slept like a lover contented. 'Remarkable,' recalled the chaplain, a Capuchin friar. 'As though he was merely an actor in a play.' But those nights have passed. It is as though they never happened. Now the zizz of a fly at the Governor's chamber-pot can cause him to judder for his pistol.

Sometimes, near dawn, when the hangover stirs him, the Governor hears footsteps downstairs near the front rooms. His wife, he assumes. Or maybe the cook. Or the boy, who seems rarely to sleep. Lucia walks the house in the dead hours of night. Rearranging the pictures. You can hear her.

Apart from the store-cells at Alder Gulch Mine, the house is the most heavily fortified den in the Territory. The locks have been imported, were advertised as unbreakable; the iron front door has been barged up the Missouri, so heavy that the steamer captain charged the government a levy, and an ox was required to haul it by the muddy road from Stornaway. No intruder could enter that Bastille of a house, except love, which laughs at locksmiths.

Love Laughs at Locksmiths by who is it now? Boucicault, maybe? Lever? Lover? The Governor's memory for playwrights is shot. Once, he knew soliloquies from *The Tempest* and *Othello*. Scarcely a quatrain now.

A word in the title of a formulaic old nonsense, which once he saw with a girl. They had chuckled conspiratorially at the excesses of the actors, the foolish singing, the cloddishness of it all, the dreadful blarneying that had been inserted for the New York crowd. Everything about the presentation was wrong, too large. Any delicacy the piece ever possessed was smothered out. It was a night in Manhattan; the Astor Place Theater. Not long after they met.

The eddying Hudson, in that summer of sunsets. Dirty gulls in the slipstreams of the barges. New Jersey over there, on the green, glossy banks. A blind Connaught ballad-singer keening on the toll path: 'Revenge for Connemara'. And there was a grove by the walkway, a kind of Lovers' Lane, where servants and soldiers were sometimes seen to go. They had laughed in a knowing way as they approached that salley glade. She had never been in such a hideaway, she said.

'I suppose Signor O'Keeffe has been, often. He is quite the hummingbird, I dare say. Signor O'Keeffe has sipped often at the roses.'

'I have been in love, yes.'

'That is not quite the same.'

'I suppose it is not.'

'Shall you always agree with me?'

'I hope – I know – that I shall always admire you.'

'Signor O'Keeffe, ladies and gentlemen, and his hopes.'

Her evening dress was low-necked, falling off at the shoulders. Her hair in chrysanthemine curls. A small, jeweled crucifix in the cleft between her breasts. She took off her shoes, walked barefoot in the flotegrass at the edge of the sunken track. And a washerwoman kneeling on a wet gray stone whipped the river with a wet gray shirt. He was walking with the most beautiful girl in New York. She was wearing an anklet of gold.

Blake. John Wilmott. A manuscript of Catullus. An eastern 'Book of Marriage' she had found in her father's library. She would like to own a Vermeer. (She would one day own three.) The paintings of Artemisia Gentileschi.

'You have been with many women? In the sense of a lover? I have never been with a man. Do you mind me speaking to you like this? My sister Estafanía, she claims to have been kissed. I do not think she has been kissed. She is a fountain of nonsense. But I think she should like to kiss *you*; she has told me she should. Perhaps you would be interested, would you?'

The sound through the trees of the slap of the shirt on the wet gray road of the river.

And suddenly not laughing. And the taste of her mouth. Her mouth on his neck, her hands in his cloak: hard knob of her hip-bone in its caging of hoops, the chain of her cross against his tongue. He came very quickly; it had been a long time since he had known intimacy, and her own pleasure followed and she clung to him, tremoring, and all of it had shocked him and thrilled him in equal measure: her murmuring to him how, and where, and slower; the down of her mound, a forbidden word she breathed, the soak of her sex against his palm. He had tried to speak afterwards. She had told him not to speak. – Only know, I am not sorry, she whispered.

Signor O'Keeffe, (you so-called blade), (you nuzzler among the roses): I feel you should know that you have imperiled the soul of an innocent girl (of a very good family) and caused her (you Bluebeard) (you Occasion of Sin) to transgress against a number (i.e. one) of my commandments, by your demonically Celtic tongue. She reflected upon this matter last evening while alone. And again this morning she reflected. It really is too bad, this immoral reflection, for she is finding it difficult to sleep any more; and so, I might add, is her startled Confessor who has recommended 'cold baths' as well as an Appalachia of Aves and 'long and vigorous walks'. The poor, dear girl is quite undone . . . Your undoing has been her undoing.

Gentle, beautiful sir. Is it noisy where you are? She sends you love in this night of thunderstorms on Manahatta and wishes she could kiss your eyelids to sleep. Like this – I love you. I love you. I love you. I love you. Yours very faithfully. God.

The Governor has editions of collectable novels among the possessions he brought from the east. Many are love stories. Most dissemble. He had thought he would read in the long winter nights of the north-west. His plan was to study, to know more of poetry, not to drink so much – if only that could stop. So much reading yet to do, and writing also, if he could recover his shaken confidence. A chronicle of his experiences in the War, perhaps. He has a sense that the memoirs of Generals will prove marketable in peacetime.

The memoir has not happened. The publisher rejected the introduction. It will never happen now; he has long since drunk the advance. The orders, the dispatches, the diagrams of battlefields, the lists of the dead, the descriptions of wounds: interred in the lumber room gathering dust in their piles; he cannot bear to open them, nor even think of them any more. Thirteen elegant octavo notebooks he ordered from St Louis, with watermarked parchment and morocco bindings. His name blocked out in gold leaf lettering on their spines; the title APOLOGIA on their covers. They are still coffined in their wrappings, their pages uncut. His memoir has nothing inside it.

How wonderful that would be: to remember nothing. To be blank, and the road still before you. What would he do differently? Nearly everything, perhaps. What comedies would he see with his future wife? Christ, those notes she used to send. Her look across a ballroom. That night at the house – there were important guests – she had summoned him from the dining table pretending a difficulty with a servant, led him into an ante-room, closed the door behind her with a smile. Be seated, Signor. This will not take very long. You should probably unfasten your cummerbund. And looking at her across the table, ten minutes later, as she endured the Bishop of Brooklyn's disquisition on Milton ('blindness is a tradition among great men of letters') he could not quite believe what they had done.

And all night long, that Easter at the summerhouse, when you were alone together, for the servants were away. The book from her father's library spread open against the bolster. Inked illustrations of mauve-skinned sultans, glitter-eyed princesses kneeling over divans, their saris and girdles unknotted. Her lips sending you slowly senseless as she turned the heavy pages. Her smile as she said: *you must wait*. The sweetness and boldness of those long-gone nights. The fierce joy it brought you to please her. Hummingbird, she said. Your tongue was a wing. She had never thought such pleasures possible.

This one is called 'The Stallion Covers his Mare'. And this one 'The Banquet for Two.' Oh, I see you like that one. Quite hungry, are they not? You have not feasted enough, sir? But the night is so young. We have many more chapters to study.

The salt of her shoulders. The tang of her sweat. Her fringe in her eyes as she rode you. Her nipples growing harder the lighter your palms touched them. The bud of her navel. You were weeping. Her thumbs brushed your tears and she kissed you on the mouth with such tenderness, and she whispered *mi vida*. And the scarlet of the sunrise as she gasped 'make me die'. And her eyes meeting your own as she clenched.

'Governor? General? *Are you listening to my point, sir?* This town is in danger of dying!'

He meets the irate glower of the businessman who is addressing him. Former owner of two dozen slaves. He holds lands in the Territory, wants something to be done. They all want something to be done.

About the outlaws, the Indians, the rumors of taxes, the prevalence of drunkenness, the prostitutes everywhere, the need for a better school, the murders on the highway, the cold, the heat, the flies, the mountains. Yes, even the mountains. They are so *impassable*, someone says, as though the Governor had caused them to appear in the night, could level them by proclamation.

The businessman is in full flow and others are making little noises of approbation like small woodland animals observing a nut-fall. Many of them are Vigilantes – the Governor knows this, and they know he knows, but no one ever states it. One of them, an insurance man from Alpharetta, Georgia, is also an expert in torture. His wife is among the handsomest women in the Territory. They have three sweet children: two boys and a girl. He goes often to church, gives alms to the poor, and he has made men scream for death. And once, as a game, they had made a man scream for his own son to be killed – anything, anything, to make the pain stop. In the end, they killed both of them: innocent son, guilty father. Placed their corpses in a profane conjunction.

The insurance man nods grimly as the businessman rants. The soaring price of flour! Dead horses on the street! Rats in the alleyways, the size of pups! And something must be *done* about this wretch Thunders and his gang. 'A countryman of *yours*,' he snaps at the Governor, who refuses the bait, though it is difficult to do so. He has a sudden startling image of the businessman being bull-whipped by a slave. He wonders if he should tell him how pleasing a picture it is – how many tickets would be sold for such a diverting show. It would be one way to raise monies for the rebuilding fund, perhaps. The Governor could arrange for bagpipes.

Marshal John Calhoun enters the office like a shadow. There is trouble at the house. Mrs O'Keeffe is upset. A carving knife is missing from a dresser in the kitchen. The cook feels she has been accused of stealing and resents it. The Governor retorts that he is busy, has no time for trivialities, and the marshal leaves as quickly as he came in.

But Calhoun cannot solve it and the Governor knows he won't try. The marshal is a lawman, not a housekeeper. O'Keeffe departs the noisy meeting, pleading a troublesome prisoner at the jail. He will return in an hour, he promises. The eruption of feigned shock is almost amusing. He is gone before it coheres into language.

And he trudges the mucky laneway that forms Patrick Sarsfield Street, past dancehalls, the new chapel, an assayer's, the forge; a notorious billiard hall, the Drynaun Dun, that somehow survived the storm. The smell of fresh paint, of new-sawn logs. Chickens and stray dogs investigate the mud. There are storefronts advertising comestibles, iron goods, guns. Many premises sell strongboxes; we are in gold country.

A prostitute slouched on the rim of a horse trough nods desultorily at the Governor – he nods back. A cowpoke dicing on a windowledge by himself, waiting for the Palais des Plaisirs to open. The morning is cold, liked iced wine. The wind sheers at you in these latitudes. Even the Koötenais complain of it.

Flimsy as a page, that butternut boy. He would blow away in a breeze. The uncomprehending stare, the skeletal fingers. But also the vaguely patrician mien. Little lord of urchins.

He ran away last week, for the fourth time since his arrival. Perhaps he will always run. A boy like that does not want a home; it is nothing but a cruelty to keep him. That might be true, but what can be done with such a thought? A meadowlark flutters from a guttering.

The second time he did not return for six full days. Calhoun said he saw him half a mile from St Hubert, alone on the crest of Union Ridge. He ran when the marshal approached him, disappeared into the forest, and Calhoun, who learned his tracking from the Aboriginals of Tasmania, who evaded a hundred redcoats by his skill at obscuring trails, could find no print to follow. A French fur-trapper discovered the boy in a worm-eaten oak, half dead from cold, delirious. He carried him to his shack near the coulée at St John, nursed him as best he could. The trapper had a map torn out of an almanac on his cabin wall. The boy had pointed to Canada, tried to pronounce some glottal words, and the trapper had put together, by the interpretation of gestures, that the child had been headed north toward the Missouri Breaks, fixing to slip across the line for the Saskatchewan River, when the sickness he'd been fighting had overwhelmed him. He was gone in the morning when the trapper returned from the brook. He had stolen a billycan and the map.

Vinson saw him that Friday near the tarn at Cleggan Cross, spearing frogs with the split of a fencepost. But when Vinson advanced and called out his surname the boy jumped into the water and swam hard away, and Vinson is unable to swim. He might well be 'a Melungeon', Calhoun believes, an Appalachian whose ancestry is white, black and Indian, for his coloring is unusual, and he is fast on his feet, more nimble than most white children are. ('Lissom little feller,' so Calhoun puts it. 'Could picture him dancin for minstrels.') But the Governor does not think he is Indian or Melungeon. He moves with a certain pantherine grace. It's the fear of being caught.

Perhaps the thought is correct. He wants only to run. Then why does he always come back? The Governor stops. Hand on his gun. The old feeling rises – he is being followed. Two miners in the street ahead of him are staring at something behind him. There is a skill in the reading of such looks.

He waits for the challenge. It does not come. No pistol shot this time. *I am alive.* One day, Duggan laughed, you will swivel on your heels and a whole shute of English will be waiting with a noose. And that, my southern lush, will be a fine hour for the movement. We'll see how you're hell-raking, then, Prophet!

Muero. I die. Make me die for you again. I love you to the end. *Mi marido.*

Toward Tone Street he trudges, shoulders hung low, making quietly along the street to the Freundschaft Hotel. A couple of jolts, that's all. Poppyseed afterwards. Camouflages the smell. Anyway, it is *none of her business.*

Wild Traveler. Double. Put it on the tally. He dregs it in one swallow. Another. The barkeep looks apprehensive, has been ordered by the Widow, his employer, not to advance credit to the Governor any more. His account is too large, too long unpaid, and there have been incidents when he has liquor on board. But the barkeep, an Irishman who lost a hand at Antietam, cannot find it in his will to refuse.

Afternoon turns to evening. Shadows lengthen. The mines and placer-diggings close down. Cowmen throw glances at the inebriate in the corner. He sits with his back to them, staring out the front window, on which surface is painted, in carmine and blue, the figure of a harem-girl dancing an improbable can-can. He is on his second bottle. His pistol on the table. Was once a Union General, one droverman claims; but another says this cannot be so.

Oh, sure it's so. That's the Blade O'Keeffe. Led the charge at White Oak. Bravest bastard in all the War. Not like one of these political Generals. He was never afraid of a scrap.

—Lost his nerve, I heard.

—You don't know beans.

—Heard tell he was frit as a runaway coon.

—Go over and tell him.

—You sayin I wouldn dare?

—Got ten says you don't.

—Twenty says I do.

—I'm a up you a fifty.

—Robbed a poorbox last night?

—Man was never a coward; play it on the level, is all. Fought his weight and come back for more.

—Not the way I had it.

—So go over and tell him.

—Wouldn waste bootleather.

—Hundred scrips says you're frit.

—*No gamblin allowed on this place,* barks the Widow, from behind the tattered curtain, behind the bowed bar. *Cut it out, you sons of bitches, or there's flies in your eyes!* She is counting the takings. A disappointment.

More drinkers drift in. A fiddler arrives: Prince Floyd Louvaine, *roulez, mes filles, C*ajun get to lovin, he the *Duc de Paris*. The girls begin working the tables. From time to time a drinker follows a girl up the crooked stairs. The fräulein goes first; that's the rule in the Widow's. The conversation continues, becomes wilder, louder, as though its subject has left, as though they are talking of a deadman. Even back in those days there were whisperings about the drinking – was his stallion shot from under him as he led the zouaves at Fredericksburg, or was its rider the worse for liquor, as some claimed? They say his temper was vicious, drunk or sober. If anything, the whiskey calmed it. But his common soldiers loved him, despite his lordly remoteness, his fightinest rages and high-tone ways. A former slave remarked, as the General rode through Tennessee: 'Yonder go a phantom. That body aint his.'

He arrived in the Territory a year ago – was it two? – carrying all its legal papers in one pocket of his frockcoat. A draggle of his veterans was his only retinue, a dozen hardscrabble Pats. 'The Apostles,' folks named them, or 'Jimmy Keeffe's Jews'. War-toughened Bowery-boys, some had Union medals for bravery; others had jailhouse tattoos. Every one of them carried a stiletto, 'an Irishman's toothpick.' They rode low in the saddle like plainsmen. You had to be Irish-born to be one of his entrusted, with kin still in the old country, traceable on both sides. It was a means of control. You transgressed at your family's peril. His supporters back in bogland would see to it.

—That's bullshit on lies. Where you heared that trash?

—Had it from a party who knows, is all.

—It dont make a bucket of spit where you had it.

—Oh, it make, chum. It make. Else you wouldn be talkin.

As he rode into St Hubert in spurs of etched silver, in Spanish kid boots and a green-ribboned black sombreiro, a trio of Cornish prospectors stared up from their panning. This jumped-up Mick was fixing to rule them. This pigmeat dressed as porco.

—Quieten your talk, fella. He mought hear you over there.

—Aint your funeral what he hears. You his Momma?

—That's a man gave his all. I'd as soon not hear him insulted.

—I wiped better than that niggerlover off my boots afore now. Better than you, too, if it come to it.

—You don't shut that reekin mouth a little closern a clam, I'll fix your flint in short time, you secession bastard.

—You boys, says the barkeep, want to tuck in your shirts. No war-talk allowed on the premises. War's over.

—Church aint out till the choir done clappin.

—All the same, Square. Not at the bar.

Drovers, saw-millers, dance-girls, the barkeep; they look at the drunkard in the corner. It is as though the air around him possesses a color. You can't approach him now. He wouldn't take it good. Miners clank in, dragging picks, sacks of tools. The dentist. The fruiterer. The photographer and his assistant. Skinny Orson Rawls, the burier of the dead, takes the measure of his neighbors as he drinks with them. And the Cajun is murdering 'La Vuelta del Marido'. The husband's return from the War.

You watch them blur behind you in the glass of the window. Darker outside. Reflections in the black. Memory stirs the pictures. Other rooms you have known. Dungeon cells. Theaters. An office in Washington. That portrait of Jefferson. That bible on its lectern. Lincoln in the crowded room.

The position of Acting Governor was put to you as an honor by the President. Of course it was a punishment; you both knew that. It had been offered to many failures, none was disappointed enough to accept it. Euphemism was in vogue. It was wartime.

Officials came and went. Markers were moved on vast maps. The President spoke solemnly of trivial things: the balladry of Moore, a book of legends he was reading, the theaters of Washington, an Irish actress he had seen. 'I have learned, my dear General, that you greatly admire the drama, as I do myself, myself and Mrs Lincoln. One hopes that our American men of letters shall one day give the world something fine in the drama.' His eyes were cow-sad, his countenance grave, and it had occurred to O'Keeffe, not for the first time, that honesty itself was a kind of act, a performance that gave a reachier punch.

Believemeifallthoseendearingyoungcharms.

Something fine in the drama. Christ.

A Hoosier fraud. So Duggan described him. The President's acid-etched face. Pockmarked, blistered, like something out of Poe; as though the digs and scratches of the engraver's burins had already gone to work on the icon. The stories of his kindness were too numerous to be collected; they obscured as much as they revealed. For he was like the whole country, so it seems to you now: kindly and rigid and self-made and dark, hard as a coffin nail, besotted with language. He valued freedom so deeply, he would repress for it if necessary; would bury half his citizens in the meadowlands they had scoped so the other half could live by the law. You think your nightmares terrible? Be grateful they're not his. What those eyes must have seen in the mirror.

'Cometh the hour, General, cometh the man.' So the President spoke, in avuncular platitudes, as though he had committed to memory some compendium of vacuity. He was dead now, the President, that complicated genius, murdered by an actor he was said to have admired, and all sorts of pieties are written about the dead and some eulogies are even true. Nobody had written what you yourself felt – that here was a revolutionary, a giant among the visionaries, who could talk to you an hour, with smoldering sincerity, without ever revealing his purpose. Perhaps that was his greatness, or part of it, at any rate. Perhaps that was what the Republic needed in those years. The subtlety you always lacked.

Larks whirled slowly in the wintry skies of Washington. You saw them through the window as you waited. And the advisors came in and went out so grave and the stenographer smiled like Lucia. She was a pretty girl, Wicklow. Greeted you in Gaelic. The bodyguards seemed edgy, aggressive. Too many in the room, steam rising from their clothes, but more kept coming, the air pungent, too hot. Reek of damp greatcoats, of rain on dirty hair. Too many to be searched. Crowding toward his desk. Messengers, detectives, usurers, spymasters. Manufacturers of weapons. Inventors. To some, you were introduced: *one of our brave Irish Generals*; to others only the President and his secretaries spoke. It was not mentioned that the General had utterly failed; that his Brigade had been decimated and then disbanded, that his tactics had been disastrous more often than not, that he had been accused of disregard for his men. Neither did the President make distasteful reference to the final controversy, the incident at Tennessee. The General had allowed himself to interpret evasion as forgiveness, though in truth it was not that, or not completely that; it was merely expediency disguised as tact – another Presidential talent.

In the era of peace, to kill Indians and renegades. To reign by the gun or its threat. *L'état, c'est moi*, said Monsieur Smith and Monsieur Wesson. *Marchons, les sans-culottes*. There will always be coercion, so Duggan once told you. It is a question of what the coercion is *for*, boy. Constitutions, amendments, fraternity, equality – all is naïvety, undergraduate sentiment; pap for Quakers and mooncalves. *People must be FORCED to be free, mon brave. In Ireland, in France, in America, every place. There is only one liberty, you Jesuit popinjay, the kind that sprouts out of a rifle. Spare me your prattle of the goodness of man while the poor are starved like mongrels*. And you tell yourself this was not what you came to America for, that you are better than Duggan, no zealot, an *idealist*, but there are hours when you lust for his certitudes. Did you cross all those waters to become killer, avenger? What have you done? What was it all *for*? Why do you persist in calling Ireland 'home' when you have not laid eyes on Wexford for half a life?

This, my home: this desolate shade. Desperadoes, secessionists, dispossessed. New Ireland, Young Ireland. Copy of the old. Mountainous, empty; fueled by drink and old hatreds, a nowhere with commandingly barren scenery of the kind to which fools attach adjectives. A place about which there will forever be arguments, whose people will always know they are living in a laboratory, their talking found exotic, collected by the fossil-men, while the rest of the world, if they notice you at all, see reflections of reflections of your clichés. Only it is larger than the old one, bitterer in winter. Apart from that difference, you are home.

Not even legally the Governor, only the acting one. 'Acting', your nickname among the clowns. You hear the word slung at you by the Cajun – ignore it. Acting O'Keeffe, the Emperor of Dogtown. *Ici vien Actin, Sainte-Vierge, boys, bow down!* You would guillotine every one of them if you thought you could get away with it. And they would do the same to you.

You do not look like a man once received by a President, who twice shook the hand of a legend. You hurried from that map-room almost drunk on your hopes, wishing only that your father could see you. Strange, fierce thought, for a married man. You walked the wet cobbles of Washington. Paperboys bawling: rumors of defeat, the Confederate armies massing to the west. You could hear the rebel cannons in the Potomac valley; see the indigo smoke of their campfires. And it occurred to you, then, that John Fintan Duggan, who saved your life, who was striped for your freedom, might be one of those choking on your name in the scorch, priming the bombs for his sons.

Then you saw her on the corner. The stenographer. Watching you. Her gaze beneath the rim of a parasol. Oh, just home, she said, to her mother's rooms. Yes, of course you could escort her. Would be an honor for me, General. And her melodious Wicklow brogue, and her humming as you walked, and her hand on your elbow as you crossed by the barricades, and the subtle way she flattered you, asked all about your War, and your plans, and your past, and Australia. How lonely you must have been, so far away in Australia. Often, as a girl, she had prayed for you. Your picture in her Euclid. Your gallows speech by heart. The other girls had teased her, saying would she not get a boy. God, the things they used to say in the convent at night. They'd have *made a Turkman blush.*

Did you see kangaroos? Were the Aboriginal squaws pretty? Was it true they walked about without a stitch on their backs? But surely not completely? Not even a shift? And how, is she allowed to ask, did you escape that isle of horrors? And is it hard for you now, being away from your wife all this time? It's raining on you, General, won't you permit me to share the parasol? In which hotel have they quartered you? Is it comfortable there? She passes it every morning, on the way to her work. Maybe some time, she says quietly, she will see inside it.

Her glove brushed your hand as you entered the park, but you just kept talking, talking about nothing, though the whomp in your stomach made it difficult to concentrate, and the closeness of her young warm body. And the girl kept talking, too, about nothing and everything. The coldness of Washington at this time of year, the troopers digging trenches over there near the bandstand. She had once been betrothed. He died at Cold Harbor. She smelt of sweet rosewater. You had never been with an Irish girl. You walked through the park toward the cannons.

And there was a moment when you paused by that nook of dreeping elms, and the drizzle was on her bonnet, and everything was suddenly silent, and you could have, but you didn't, because you gave your word – but you could have, and no one would ever have known. You walked her to the house, shook formal hands in the doorway. It was the first time you had seen a woman with a house-key.

There was lust; yes. Tempting to dress it in fineries. You had seen so many bodies broken. You wanted to touch one whole. To convince yourself, maybe, that the brokenness would one day end. Or maybe it was lust and nothing more.

'Would you come in for a minute and meet them? It would be an honor, if you had a moment. My mother is not well. I've an aunt lives with us here.'

'I had better get on to the hotel. I leave early in the morning.'

'Yes, of course; I'm after detaining you.'

'Another time perhaps.'

'I never thought I should meet you. It has been a very great privilege.'

'The privilege has been mine. Thank you for your company.'

'You are as gallant as they say. But that would never surprise me. We Wicklow girls are the fine judges of gallantry, I may tell you.'

The smoky afterglow of her smile.

Her stepping from a bed, crossing naked to a window. Her back, her behind; her hand on the glass. Her quiet, low laugh as you kiss her there again, and her fingers in the wetness of your hair.

'I had better go on inside. You'll be catching your death. Look at me, stealing your time.'

But you did not move. She met your gaze with her own. Her eyes sea-green in the dusk-light. You didn't notice it before, but her face is freckled. Her people were from Shillelagh. She says it's beautiful in summertime. You can almost smell the straw, the sun on new-mown grass. To touch her: a kind of blessing.

'So is the talk all true? About Tennessee?'

'I suppose that must depend on the teller.'

'About yourself and General Sherman. There are various versions.'

'I am afraid I have done things I greatly regret.'

'Is that one of them, so? Your regrets.'

'To strike a superior officer was ungentlemanly; stupid. To that extent, yes, I regret it. It caused hurt to my family. The talk and so on. The Shermans had been guests at our home.'

'I will always admire you. Always. My father admired you greatly. He used to wonder how you escaped from the colony. It was our story at bedtime. Your escape from the colony. He would have envied me that I had the opportunity of asking you.'

'It was a long time ago now. I'm not sure I remember. I had comrades. And money. My father sent money. These things are not heroic at all, to be honest. I was fortunate to be selected. Others had a better right.'

'They say Duggan helped you, did he?'

'Truly, I must go.'

'Go safely, then. And thank you.'

'Good-night.'

You approached and kissed her mouth, which was hot; she half-sobbed. A watchman lanterned past. She inclined her head sharply. You drew your cloak around you both. The beating of your mind. You moved deeper into the shadows of the doorway. You don't know how long you were there; bodies pushing in cold darkness, mouths conjoined and grinding . . . *Do you feel . . . the way you have me? . . . That never . . . happened me before . . . Sweet Jesus your hand.* You were shaking as she unbuttoned you. *I want you to . . . It's all right . . . It's all right* she whispered. You quaked in her arms. She held you a long time. She asked quietly if you had a handkerchief but you didn't.

And the call of an old woman from the depths of the house. Frightened. Frail. Who was there?

She stepped quickly away, locked the oaken door behind her. Shaken, you walked back to the hotel. You knew, as you arrived, as you climbed to the rooftop, where clustered guests were getting drunk and keeping fearful watch for the enemy, that the hour you had just passed would remain with you a lifetime, but you did not yet know why.

Her sentence would be seven years. The judge advised her to be thankful. Only her plea of guilty had saved her from hard labor. She was spat upon as she was led from the courtroom, she and the other Confederate spies. She would often be attacked in the prison.

It is a time of peace, of brotherly reconstruction. You sleep with a Colt repeater by your bolster. And your wife stalks the house in the cold hours of night and the businessmen fume in the fetters of darkness and somehow like an odor come your dreams of the moonboy and a lament you once heard in a filthy Irish barroom. To the air of 'The House of the Rising Sun'. A song of New Orleans bordellos.

> *Brave Lincoln, he lay dying, boys,*
> *With the bullet in his breast;*
> *'Of all the actors in this town,*
> *I loved John Wilkes Booth the best.'*

∇

CHAPTER 31

SURVEILLANCE

*A bleak progress witnessed – A fall from a ladder – & the Governor
is rescued by an unexpected friend*

APRIL 4TH, 1866. NIGHT WATCH

9.16 p.m. Subject's birthday. Subject left the salloon [*sic*] at the
Widow's Hotel and made a way by the wall to the Legislative Office.
Was visibly intoxicated & falling about. Was derided by low
persons, to some of whom he drunkenly offered violence. Was in a
pitiful, wretched condition, close to weeping like a very woman.
Was mimicked, disdainfully, in song.

Entered Legislative Office at 12 minutes of 10. Re-emerged to the street
eight minutes later with stale-ladder, bucket & rag. Appeared intent on
washing the windows but fell from fourth rung of ladder.

Lay in the shit of the street nine minutes. The boy came and assisted
him home.

∇

CHAPTER 32

YOU GONNA QUIT ME, SWEETHEART

*Elizabeth Longstreet reveals that a thing widely believed
of the child was not true*

*Peculiar child. Yes . . . You didn know what he be thinkin . . . Just scootch
around say nothin like a spent-hen i' the yard . . . Here one time I seen him
i' the black-dark of midnight chawin on a old hambone I save for the dog.
I'd fix him a supper – he didn eat none but the leftover. Didn eat enough
to make a grasshopper jump . . . It make you weep to see him. Make a
cannonstone cry . . . To think of him alone i' the world like that. Nothin
harder than a motherless child.*

*Because that was like a child never got him one ounce of love, not from
a body in the world, or never had him no mother. Nor never heard him a
kindness or a encouragement for his life . . . I ast him one time: where your
momma get to anyways? Where your people at now? Aint got you no kin?
Cause I didn know nothin of how he come up. But he wouldn talk back to
you. Wouldn talk back . . . You wasn in the room when you talkin to that
child. It like you a wisp of smoke.*

*But the curious thing: that wasn no mute . . . No no . . . Only somethin
in his mind . . . Cause he could sing just as sweet as ever you heard . . . Why
yes, sir, for certain. Like a bird come the spring. Like folks as got a stammer
sing perfect you know . . . Be singin the old gospels an storysongs you know
. . . 'Jesus Blood Never Fail Me Yet.' . . . He sing that church make the devil
shout the creed . . . Remember like I heard it this mornin.*

*Hear him round about the kitchen. In back i' the yard. Sing any old
thing. To his self now I mean . . . Rhymins. Lullaby. Cubano song. Old
nonsense . . . Them 'ballade' he get to singin, like the Quebecois got . . . Or
– whatyou call – the junkanoo like the Creole. Here one time I ast him –
cause I remember it real well – how comes it a boy like you keep all them
songs in one head? You think I dont hear you? I hear you ever day. Hear you
in the night when you singin in your sleep . . . You mustof a brain the size
of Texas in theä. Cause the way he remember all them songs . . . But never*

a word . . . But when he sing it was godly. Only child I ever heard sing a gospel and you believe it . . . Cause a child caint sing no gospel, my husband always said that . . . Cause he never lost him a fight. He too young to know the meanin . . . Sixty, seventy years since I heared that voice. But there's nights I remember it yet.

An' uh . . . sea chaunties too, he got a hundred a those . . . Was one he get to singin call 'The Wreck of the Lenoir'. Sad song too . . . Poor sailors as perish . . . Went: [subject sings, but voice very frail]

> . . . Up an he stauts, mon capitaine brave,
> An a tight little meck was he.
> O, a lover had I in the lan' of Cockaigne
> An a widow she is cette nuit, Hélas,
> Said a widow she is cette nuit . . .

'You Gonna Quit Me Sweetheart.' 'Nobody Turn Me Round.' Long as the blood run warm i' my vein I wont never forget that voice. Done cut you like a knife. Boy was born for a songster . . . Got the gift for a song. That's a grace of the Almighty . . . Lord anoint us with His blessings, we too vain and sorry to see it . . . Man dont recognize his gifts never be satisfied in the world . . . And I sure wouldof wished I could see that child again . . . Poor little feece-dog . . . Dear Lord.

∇∇∇

PART VI

THE BALLADS OF JOHNNY THUNDERS

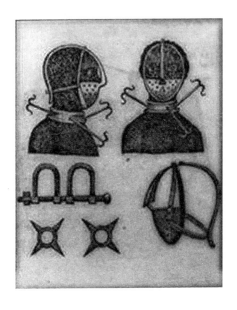

An author should consider hard before spelling a character's dialogue phonetically. It is usually a failure of the imagination. He thinks his own pronunciation the standard from which all others deviate, are primitively charming, delightfully melodious, or shamefully inferior to the norm. But this is a matter of standpoint, not style . . . He is trying, perhaps unconsciously, to tell us something significant about his creations. That they are somehow not as human as their creator. He does not grasp that his own accent could be rendered phonetically too. To others – to his characters – to most of the world – what he speaks is a bizarre Creole.

Robert Oates Ellis [Lucia-Cruz McLelland-O'Keeffe]. From her review of *Bleak House* by Charles Dickens and *Maurice Tiernay* by Samuel Lever. *The Gramercy Quarterly*, Spring 1854

Nothing reveals the dreads and desires of a nation
as does the song of her common people.

O'Keeffe. From his abandoned memoir. 1865?

CHAPTER 33

HIS FATHER'S ARRIVAL FROM IRELAND & THE BURT O' JOHNNY TUNDERS

or

DERE'S GOODNESS IN US ALL!

By *Mr. A. N. O'Nymous* †

Dear Mammy, tis Danny, I'm here in New York,
Tis a willage most big & alarmin'.
O I'm just off de boat and dey've gimme ten votes
And de ladies is poifectly charmin'.
Dere's one I eshteem, she's de right suddern queen,
An' her faytures is dark as de noight.
I don't understand 'er, but she's sweet an tender –
O Mammy, do ye tink it's all roight?

CHORUS: An it's o dear, ah musha macree!
How I loves her dushky smile.
Don't be tick, sez Pat to Mick,
Quick, waltz 'er up de aisle.
But arrah, she's from Dixie-Land
And meself's from Donegal.
Fwat harrum in dat, sez Mick to Pat,
Shure, dere's goodness in us all!

Dear Fadder O'Kelly, I'm here in Phildelly,
In nade of some holy advice;
For de love of me soul, she's de color of coal,
Ah, but Fadder, she's powerful nice.

† From *Laughter Roun' de Ole Piano: Comic Irish & Coon Songs & Hilarious Recitations for the American Family Parlor*, J. Grier Buckingham, ed., New York, 1866.

She's from Alabamee, her mammy's a sammy,
But dis is de craythur I love.
Tis it sinful mullarkey, a-coortin a dharkey?
Will dis make a differ above?

Dear Molly, me cherry, I ast ye to wait,
Till wid riches I come sailin' back.
Now I hope ye won't cry but I'm biddin' good-bye,
For de berry I druther is bl—ck (oh!)
She's me dark Rosaleen,
Sweetesht one dat I seen;
Shure it makes yeh feel feckliss an free,
When ye're kissin 'er there – arrah, don't ashk me where!
On de banks of de oul Swan-ee!

Dear Mammy, tis Danny, I'm in Alabamee,
An sendin a wee invitayshun.
Tis time you ship'd over, shure life here is clover,
In dis-here American nayshun.
We've a liddle brown Johnny, he's bright and he's bonny,
But shure, mammy machree, dat's not all:
He's de owney mul-ayto
Likes aytin potayto,
From Dixie to ould Donegal.

∇

CHAPTER 34

THE DEEDS OF AN OUTLAW

WANTED!

FOR MURDER, ARMED ROBBERY, VIOLATION OF WOMEN, & TREASON AGAINST THE FEDERAL GOVERNMENT

$10,000 REWARD

Cole John Laurence, McLawrence, or Lawrenson – alias "Johnny Thunders," "Mongrel John," "Black Johnny Conqueror," "Johnny Colonial," & cetera.

This VICIOUS BANDIT & HIS GANG are sought for numerous crimes, including armed robbery of the banks at Varina City & Westport (formerly Manchesterville), & of the Union mail stage at Blindman's Ridge, on which occasion they tortured & murdered the guards & 5 male passengers. Two women were subjected to that dishonor which is worse than death before being forced to witness unprintable horrors done the men. Southerner; sometimes described as half-breed, almost certainly is not. Possesses lethally fast draw, & his age is between 20 & 40 yrs. Has brother, Thomas Michael, his equal in depravity, and many associates of reprehensible character. McLawrenson disgraces the name of IRELAND by claiming ancestry there. Was born, so claims, in Kentucky or northern Tennessee. (Mother's name Cooney, Joyce, or Furey.) Hates the United States. Fanatic secessionist. Was once Confederate rifleman, later rode with bushwhacker mob, "The Tennessee Lincoln-Killers" in the War. Latterly rides with gang, sometimes alone. Has been seen in Kanzas, Nebraska, Indian Territory, Westn Minnesota. Stands 5 feet eight or nine inches. Long copper hair, pale complected, scrawny built, "china-blue" eyes. Is believed to know the SIOUX and BLACKFOOT tongues & to be missing portion of wedding-ring finger. On right forearm the TATTOO of a BLACK FLAG. Witnesses have spoken of his COLD & MERCILESS STARE. Is given to blasphemies of the Holy Bible. Has desecrated churches & graves. Has claimed himself to be "A Sign of God." Is armed & munitioned copiously. Should not be advanced upon except with lethal force. A LIBERAL REWARD is attainable for information that shall conduce to his apprehension DEAD or ALIVE. Apply to Acting Governor J. C. O'Keeffe, Territorial Offices, Redemption Falls, or to any one of his Marshals. All right-thinking citizens, regardless of party, are exhorted to aid public justice. Every man should consider his conscience so charged. STAND WARNED: PERSONS ABETTING THIS MISCREANT OR HIS ACCOMPLICES IN TERROR ARE EQUALLY GUILTY & SHALL BE TRIED TO THE MOST DREADFUL EXTENT OF THE LAW. FURTHER: THIS MAN IS RECKONED LUNATIC AS WELL AS BRUTALLY EVIL. ON NO ACCOUNT ADVANCE EXCEPT YOU MEAN TO SHOOT, IN WHICH CASE: SHOOT TO KILL.

Published by James C. O'Keeffe,
Territorial Governor, April 1866

∇

CHAPTER 35

THE FAUSE KNIGHT ON THE ROAD

*Eliza Mooney asks herself a question – Mormons – Her reflections on
Marriage – Three angels & a hammer – The Truest Beauty of Truro*

Three hundred miles south-east of the town of Redemption Falls, a
woman in a shabby tabard is standing on a sunken road. She has come a
vast distance, has seen many wonders. Her weight is that of a child. She
has left behind what little protection the United States might afford her,
is entering the Mountain Territory, land of renegades and runaways, but
there is nothing to inform her that this crossing has taken place, that she
is drifting over the edge of the world.

She pauses, considers the Wanted poster again. Butterpaper-yellow.
Wrinkling. It seems odd for such notices to have drawings like that: the
Face in the black bandanna. It's of limited usefulness, you can't help but
feel. Like looking at a poster of a skull.

She wonders do they use the same face on each placard they print,
and if so, who was the original model. One right savagiferous bastard,
that must have been. Probably a congressman now.

It occurs to her as she walks: perhaps it would be possible to print a
poster of her brother, nail it along the roadside as she goes. Could she
draw a sketch from the tintype? *You couldn't draw water.* Could somebody else? *Somebody else, my hole.* And where to find a printery. *And what
would they demand of you?* No doubt it would take money; a rake of
Yankee greenbacks. *And you're broke as a cockney's promise.*

And where would you advise the finder, if there was one, to find you?
And, anyways, what would you write? *Runaway brat. Eight yrs when he
kicked. Parents was Darkey and Irish. Didnt know nothin. Ornery and
stupid. Couldn find his own dick for a dollar.* My name for him when I
was *riled* was 'Little cooney bastard'. But I swear I didn't mean it. He
called me 'Crowjane Irish bitch'. There was a lithograph picture on the
wall of the cabin we lived in. The Holy Family of Bethlehem.

You can be Irish and colored together, Eliza, that don't mean shit.

Better to put black and white. But he aint a buckin *zebra*. Then 'Negro' and 'White'. But Jeddo don't look mulatto, so why mention that at all? Christ's sake, the ignorant melon-head thinks he's Mexicano. But who told him such a gum? *You did, you liar.* I never. *Yes, you did.* What height would he be now?

The shade of his eyes? Has he cropped his hair? Did he fatten in the army? *Has he started to shave?* It sprouts in her stomach like a red-veined weed – she is beginning to forget what he looks like.

The Mormons were good for alms and advice. They would talk the cock off a pirate. She became skilled at pretending to listen as they doled the soup. Well at first, she did listen; their story was wonderful. Jehovah (*or was it Jesus*) or maybe it was Yahweh. One of the Gods anyway (or *maybe it was Joseph*) one of them struck a revelation on these platters of gold and revealed them to a prophet called Smith (*or was it Wesson*) and all the true faithful had to live by those directives, else a thunderbolt up the britches was what you got comin but the Mormons didn't put it like that. And out here they had journeyed, to that flatted-out bowl of Lakeland, and built the shining city, and married many times, and Eliza had wondered if God was that much of a shake if he commended the multiplication of marriage.

For who would want to marry more than you absolutely had to? Like climbing back up on the crucifix, the nails as your footholds; the vinegar to toast your guests. To have to listen to their bellyaching, the way poor Mamo had to do, with their bleats and their aches and their get-me-this-and-that and their smiling in the lane but their fists behind the door, and the cudgels of their words, and the coshes of their silences, and your having to let them do it to you and carry their children, and fix and fetch, wash their stinking duds in ginger, and their opinions, their *estimations*, their stupidities on the world, when the most of them you couldn't trust to go out and milk a *goat* without them trying to get a suck on its titty. And never a rest. And never a kindness. And never a sympathy. And never a ribbon. I was passin a pedlarboy an I reckoned this'd be nice on you. It aint Christmas come, no, I just figured you'd like it. Go head. Try it on. Why, you're pretty as an apple. I'm glad I didn't spend it on whiskey.

Her beggings she gave for a little food at that farm – five small goose-eggs, a couple of gristly ribs – but it will have to be rationed carefully. There is no one to beg from out here any more. The land is like rubble. There are no fields, only rocks. Wild ponies come visible; hides shaggy, black-blue. Jesus and His Mother! Two buffalo!

198

Her hair is too long but she had nothing to cut it. She breaks a moldering porter bottle found in a burn-pit. Saws off handfuls she throws to the wind. The last strands she keeps, ties them into a bracelet. It is said to quell sickness of the lungs.

The mountains are terrifying, like none she has ever seen. They do not slope or slant, they are walls with no summits. They soar out of the ground: stone giants. You can walk right up to them and touch them with your hand and crane back your head to look up toward the clouds. And all you will see is a mile of black granite, a rock-protruding road into Heaven. You could walk up that road like a spider into Paradise. Where spidergod spindles the harpstrings.

The Face on the poster becomes a roadside Imp. It is nailed to every tree for thirty miles. When she blinks she sees its afterimage photographed on her retinas. She comes to know its every inkblot, every crosshatch and smudge. It is as though the masked portrayal is watching her progress. If progress is what she is making.

Lately, her aim with the catapult has been worsening, for her slinghand is developing a tremor. A palsy, perhaps; she does not know the word. Her fingers quiver like leaves. But God is good and this country is blessed. Wild grapes, blackcurrants, plums, gooseberries, buffalo berries, ground cherries – it's like walking through Eden. Trudging past a shack, she hears a song waft out, like the stench of a rancid stew.

> *O I am a gallant blah blah blah, now that's just what I blah.*
> *For the United States of Tyranny, I do not give one blah.*

They will never stop singing about their doings in the War. Like the Irish, that way. Long-memoried. Quare trickers, the Americans. You'd want to be up early to understand them. They can never let anything lie.

Colored. What does it mean? Does anyone not have a color? Somewhere are there humans with invisible skin? Jellyfish people. Like the faeries of Connemara. Their innards and bones on display. If they swallowed, you could see the food inside them. If you lay with one, you'd get magical powers. A changeling you'd be, and the world terrified to vex you. By Jesus, you'd give them reason.

Golden snow falling. A spendable mannah. She approaches the Face and is able to remove its bandanna; blackpowder dust on her palms. The mouth works, yawningly, unstiffening like a tendril, but it is unable to speak, though she pleads with it. It is wrinkled, like an old woman's, the lips are thin and pallid. She can see the doggish stubs of its bicuspids.

The artist has rendered the eyes as grubby discs of black. The cheek-bones brutally angular, the chin juts apelike, the head too cumbersome for the stalk on which it lolls. She feels, on her hand, the breath from the paper. It stinks of high summertime sewers.

—Are you alive? she asks the Face. What is your country? Ever seen you a boy come up this road like the rain?

—Cut me down, whispers a voice. I'll give you a bag of dust. I stole it owa the bank at Westport.

And the underbite is almost comically grotesque, as though attempting to gnaw the tip off the nose. She wonders if this criminal truly looks like an ape, or if the artist has tried to represent his nature, his deeds. For it's an artist's opinion that nature and deeds is the same; that's why they draw the Savior so whited and lighted, when He wasn't no whiter than a plug of tobacco, and that's why they call a bandit 'that black-hearted wretch' when his heart is pink as a pope's.

There are times when she can see them up ahead of her on the road: the trio of poster-nailers and their mule. Youngish men, gangly – they might be boys. They don't notice her, or, if they do, they don't show it. They shimmer in the heat-haze like the seraphs of Isaiah. One of them is tall; he slides his hands into his back pockets. It appears to be his function to oversee the work. Or maybe he is just lazy. It is difficult to know. His comrades appear unbothered by his scrutiny of their labor. Sometimes he hands them a water-gourd.

See me? I'm a faerywoman, you son of a bitch. I'm a no-navel, seal-buckin, tree-livin nightmare. I will magick my broomstick up your uglified ass and wave you around like Ole Glory.

Often, come sundown, they shoot at the crows, which plummet from the sky like stones. Why they'd want to shoot crows, she cannot imagine, since there is no eating in the bones of a crow. Are they showing off their marksmanship? To each other? To the birds? Who are they attempting to impress?

> *Three hundred thousand Yankee dogs is stiff in Southern dust!*
> *Three hundred thousand curs we got, afore they conquered us.*
> *They died of southern fevers, friend, of rebel steel an shot,*
> *An I wisht we'd got three million more, instead a whut we got.*

Oh shut up your hole, oh shut up your hole, oh shut up your hole again.

She seems to walk perpetually toward the trinity; their presence shortens the road. Sometimes they drop morsels of leftover bread, which she harvests and adds to her store. It is as though they are doing it deliberately. Can this be so? Can they see her in the dust, like a conscience behind them? Is it possible that they would want to assist Eliza Duane Mooney, a girl they do not even know?

And the days roll on, and the nights grow shorter, and the morsels on the road more substantial. A baconrind. An applecore. A sinewy chickenleg. The dregs of a bottle of beer.

A yawwwwwn one dawn as she clambers from the ditch. Her fingers stretching, curling, flexing, as though wishing to be plants, not fingers. Half a mile into the day she stops as though slapped. Stones on the road have been arranged to read:

HOWDY

Up ahead the angels beckon. They are chuckling, expectant. Two of them come lumbering toward her. She slinks back into a grove in a welter of fright but there is nowhere safe she can flee to. She shins up an oak. Half an hour passes. She sees them in the distance, shambling idly toward the north, slapping each other's shoulders like schoolboys on a skite, and kicking the poor burro up the backside.

She scrapes a way back down and the forest floor is leafy. A pounding in her head as she regains the road. A fold of cornbread placed carefully on a milestone. They have rearranged the pebbles, so that now they read:

SO LONG

The day has a vibration, a throb of unease. Every corner she approaches, she expects them to be in wait. Every thicket could bring a rape, each stonewall a bullet. Then a long straight lane overhung by an arcade of salleys and they materialize in the distance, maybe half a mile beyond her. One poster has been hung horizontally, another is nailed upside down. They are playing with Eliza again. She comes up to a crossroads, in the center of which, black stones have been placed to ask:

She picks up the pebbles and gathers them to her bundle. They're the luckiest she's had since Louisiana. With the first she kills a rabbit; the second fells a grebe. A third knocks a cluster of wild grapes from a tree. Balthazar's feast is hers.

As dusk comes on, she hears the percussion of their hammer. The *pok* of heavy iron striking wood. She pictures a prisoner alone in the death cell, his gallows being constructed in the yard.

Night descends. Their campfire in the distance. When the wind banks down she can make out their laughter, the scrape of out-of-tune fiddling. It's the worst sound in the world, an incapable fiddler. It would make you hate music forever.

She wonders should she approach but decides against the gamble. A woman cannot present herself to three males out here in the boonies and expect anything but a mudslide of troubles.

But that night she cannot sleep. She is edgy, confused. What are they trying to say to her? She creeps through the maze of pines toward their camp. She watches, unnoticed as they talk.

Billycans on the ground. Their fire is crackling. Playing cards and spouting nonsense about girls. Two of them have regular sweethearts, the third is only a shaver. The firelight reddening their flesh. They are out of a town called Truro, four and a half days' ride to the north; were given this work of postering by the marshal. Two bits a day and vittles – beats working, when you figure it. The money will be put toward a wedding breakfast at Moran's Hotel, for one of them is fixing to marry. The table-cloths normally provided are of red checked cotton, but for two dollars more you can hire ivory silk. The bride would prefer the latter, for ivory silk is prettier. The groom intends to surprise her.

Foxface sips coffee which he frequently spits out, like a boy who would get his ears boxed if he did this at home. Longlegs is tipsy, pluck-ing meekly on his fiddle. Cheekbones, the groom, warms his toes through holed stockings. His boots on a nearby log.

—Brother, you wanna see her in that churchdress she got. Green one with the lace. Declare she's a picture. You was cold as a wagontire, she'd come you round.

—Listen to it talkin. Big ladyin man.

—I like her sister better.

—Got a *dog* I like better.

—I could eat like all wrath.

—Wait till mornin and breakfast.

—You feel like a dance?

—Come on now, play the game.

—These cards aint too handsome.

—Quit talkin. I'm thinkin.

—Wanna shoot us some birds?

—What you reckon to her mother?

She wonders if they will mention her – they might – but they do not. What would they say if they did? She creeps back to the hollow that will be her bed. A blanket of dead, whitened leaves.

She awakens to a racket of gunfire from the direction of their bower, like the distant slamming doors of a train. It does not alarm her; in a way, it soothes her, for it is part of the music of night on the road and at least she knows where they are. Yeehawing like lusty donkeys, yodelling 'Sally Johnson' and 'The Rakes'. She pictures them dancing. Which boy plays the girl? Will Jeddo ever be married?

The dawnbirds skreeking crazily. First light coming on. She falls back into flickery sleep.

Runnels of rain on the tin roof of the cabin. Jeddo is a bat. He is roosting in the branches. *Murcielago*: the Spanish word for a bat. 'Mouse of the sky,' does it mean? Her mother is close by, but she cannot be seen. A gumbo bubbles in a cookpot. And someone lilts a lullay with a lyric she does not know, queer and dark, in a mysterious language, which Eliza is able to understand though not to speak. It is that warm kind of dream, cosy as a feather-tick, from which you do not want to awaken, though you know you must.

Christ. He is singing. She can hear it so clearly. 'Revenge for Connemara'.

She rinses her face and hands in the lake. Drinks a couple of mouthfuls, but the water tastes of chalk. The dream putters again. Sparks of the past in her mouth. You forget what the dead looked like. They go into the shadows. It's how you know someone is dead.

She looks at her mother in the mirror of the lake. Her hair like a tangled thornbush. A catfish flits through the murk of her face. She darts a hand into the ripple, actually touches his tail, but he shimmies away to the osiers.

And the road hard as hobs this early in the morning. A taste like cold ashes in your mouth. Christ, when will it soften? When does it get easier? Why do we not have wheels? In Little Rock, Arkansas, she saw a man on wheels. His uniform clean as a commodore's. He was begging passers-by with a signboard that read: A DIME FOR MY STORY OR A SONG.

Where are her angels? They must have gotten a bright start. She will gain on them later. She would miss their presence now. Cheekbones is the pretty one. Probably all the girls want him. Tawny and lean, like maybe his oulfella was a Mohawk. (*By Christ, another mane-hack, you'd be fairly one yourself.*) But his sweetheart, Tova Lunqvist, is the only girl for Cheekbones. They are fixing to marry next month. When he looks at her, he said, he feels his toes curl with happiness; and the other two laughed and derided him. He was enjoying their mockery, as a young man in love will do. They couldn't see it was making him taller.

She pictures Tova Lunqvist as goldenhaired and shapely, the truest beauty of Truro. She saunters its sidewalks like the queen of the faeries, fanning her face, letting on not to see them: her love-struck, stone-tongued, poppin-eyed apostles and their mongrel dogs on strings. This body is my temple and my chariot, she says; avaunt, you milksop grubbers. Got more chance of puttin your hand in the tabernacle of the Lord. She'd roll em down Main Street like dice. Because a boy as fine-made, he could take his pick. There's a gallantry about him, despite his hipswinging sloth. Bone-and-horn idle, but he talks real nice. She imagines him breaking a horse.

Tova Lunqvist before the window of the jeweler's in Truro. Tova Lunqvist on the road beside her. You seen my ring, girl? You seen my dress? You seen my ivory tablecloths?

Heavy, now, Christ, as though trudging through a tarpit. The suck of the road on your feet. Tova Lunqvist glides graceful in her salmonskin shoes. The decorous neckline, the kroner of gold in her earlobes; she sings in the choir on Sundays. And afterward they go picnicking out by the river and he lies in the grass picking his teeth with a twig and she rinses the plates in the waters of Zion and they dry in the sunshine of his compliments.

His cello-brown voice. His lazy, kind come-hithers. He'd give you ribbons that would reach around the world.

And they will live in a house together, Tova Lunqvist and her husband, and they will own a fine featherbed, and platters, and chickens, and their crotchety oul neighbors will visit on Christmas morning to resent what everything cost. As she bends to set out the china that formed part of her dowry, he will notice her blush – her kissable collarbone – and he will smile at her, then, and their children will be caroling, and late that night, when the old Swedes have snuffled home, to yesterday's gruel heated up by their envy, her hands grasp the slats of the bedstead he wrought, as her lovemoan fills his mouth.

For he'd roust you like a faeryman. He'd have you destroyed with the pleasure. You'd see through his skin as he nussled you. Heaven you'd see, if a Cheekbones beguiled you, and the tongue of him luscious as molasses. Cream-and-whiskey from his pores till he had you swooning astride him; swan-bosomed, love-drunk, swisser-swassering as you worked him; sucking gossam from his hair, and his pointy ears twitching, and his tail wrapping around you, winding you tighter together, and his cloven hooves clicking love-jigs. And you'd circle him, slow as sap trickling sweet from a pine, and you'd ride on his whiskers to the cold, blue moon, and you'd stallion him till the sunburst, shrieking glory-be to Jesus, *and he'd tell you he was only getting started*. Not like these miserable fuckers of the world with their sweaty-arsed songs of vengeance.

She will thrash him to forcemeat when she gets her paws on that child. Beat him red as the ace of diamonds. She will bawl like a cannon. She will roar up a tornado. She will shriek of the nights she walked the streets of Baton Rouge, begging the doorways for a clue. Rainsqualls smacking the walls of the cabin. His blanket-roll empty as a molested nest.

You found yourself watching through the flap. Rooting every hut in the lane. Peering into tents and hovels. You lay with your eye to a knot in the wall, so that even when you were asleep, you could still be watching, because probably he would return in the dark, like before; he would creep back in while you slept. You stood – don't you remember it? – at the crossroads of the shantytown and hollered his name to the winds. It was hot the month he went. You felt the sirocco on your face and the sweat in the small of your back. And you saw yourself from above, a very small animal, screeching like a Mardis Gras fishwife. *Jeremiah! I will stretch for you! W'ea you at, Jeddo Mooney? Get you here or I will redden yaw hide!* A bitch stared as you hollered. It hunkered and gawped. Pink-eyed. Its tongue like a streamer.

You searched the noisy waterfront, its cockfights and grogshops, its backyard bordellos and flophouses. The fishermen told you they had netted no boy. No dockman or stevedore had seen him. The stallwomen, the cocklers, the watchmen, the whores, the doughboys: nobody had noticed him. You implored the Yankee general who administered the town. He told you to try the waterfront, the stallwomen. *You imagine my men have the leisure to turn this cess-heap upside down? Do you know we are at war? They are targets, every one of them. Ask the rebels and traitors to assist, not me. Now get out before I have you arrested.* You hunted every passageway, every lane and mugger's alley. Then the slow-dawning dread, a kind of pregnancy in your mind. This time he will not come back.

You drove him away. The looks from the neighbors. They always feared you anyway. Wolfgirl. Changeling. Crowjane. Swampcat. Say her mother and begetter was cursed back in Ireland for they made the mother's husband a cuckold. Bastard child of an adultery can't never be blessed. Come into the world in the shackles of sin, not merely her own but the lusts of the fathers, and those of the unforgivable mothers. Women, men, they glared on your girlhood. They yanked their snotfaced children from out your path, as though you were a schooner in the pull of a reef and your sinking would drag them down. But the men came round the cabin, out back in the night, when they knew your mother was not home. Hear them scratching in the filth like gloomy hens. Thirteen you were, the first time. Didn't even know his name. *Look at me*, he told you. *That's right. Make me proud. Cause this is what you for, girl. Don't you never forget it. Only thing you'll ever be for.*

You saw him at Mass the following Sunday, kneeling before the priest to receive. His wife was beside him. She knifed you with a glower. But you understood her darkness, her hatred of the world, because she, like you, had been the prey of his body, and that would quench anyone's light. She muttered something to the priest. He shooed you disgustedly from the rail as though you were a dung-fly that might land in the chalice. You were weeping as you hobbled away, over the tombstones in the floor, past the doors of the confessionals, the ranks of tutting matrons, the tables of candles burning redly before the saints, and it seemed cruel to you, suddenly, to burn flames before the martyrs, reminding them of how they were murdered. Soon the priest would contrive a reason to visit the cabin, too. There were rumors of your sinfulness. Grave matter for a girl. You would have to confess. Did you want the fires of Hell? Forgiveness was possible but the confession must be full. Afterward you could not walk for three days.

You saw Mamo advancing the aisle, through the incense and the murmurings, like a banshee perversion of a bride. Shining like a monstrance on a tabernacle door. One hand on her hip, the other wriggling in her pocket, as though about to produce a snake as a trick. She waited for him to elevate the host, to utter the holiest of holy words, and it was then that she cursed him, and her anathema echoed around the vaults, and as the Redeemer of All Histories, who required the death of martyrs, became bodily present in that sanctified space, she raged of the body, of blood, of betrayal, and the husbands tumbled over the pews to engulf her in cloaks, and the women wept or gouged, or tried to strangle her with beads, and you watched it all happen from the back of the church, with Jeddo spitting holy water on your dress.

She stops. Turns. Sunlight dapples. Everything is about to be changed. Look at the face of Eliza Duane Mooney. The last sands of freedom are running. Why was I not there? I could have warned you, Eliza. There are false knights on every road.

The mule grazes lazily in the clearing to her left. O, the saltsmell of frying bacon. And the sweetness of last year's apples corrupting into the grass. She makes to double back. But everything is so peaceful. Birdwhillow. Foliage. A whippoorwill in the rushes. A waterfall from somewhere in the forest. Because it's louder than a river, more *constant*, somehow. Perhaps they cut a path to go see it.

Can they be so bad? Is it not worth the risk? They are little more than boys, when you think. Two of them have sweethearts. They are interested in waterfalls. She has heard them talk an hour with no woman in their company – the only test of men, their nature, their elements – and nothing they said seemed dangerous to Eliza Mooney, who knows what danger is. And you cannot fear everyone. And you cannot hate everyone. Because then, you would hate yourself.

She steps off the road. The forest is sepulchral. The syrupy blessing of sap. In the summits of the trees, the light through lace. A squirrel with an acorn in its gloves. The carpeting of pine needles drowsing, spongy. Riding-Hood wandered the glade with her basket, watched by the Arapaho, who say the oaks are the righteous Ancestors. And now, from the copse, comes the aroma of woodsmoke. She can see a tartan blanket. A water-gourd on the ground. A fiddle sitting lonesome on the altar of a rock. The hairs of its bow blowing loosely.

So quiet all around. As quiet as Heaven. The *clicket* of their kettle-lid as the water bubbles up. The soft, damp moss on her welted soles. Then the oaks start dancing a jig.

Foxface and Longlegs have been butchered in their blankets. The third, the most beautiful, betrothed of Tova Lunqvist, has been crucified upside-down on a tree. His britches knifed to flitters. He has been slashed-at, disemboweled. The gag in his mouth is bright with blood. On the campfire something leathery is griddling; a sizzle. The flames give a whipcrack spit.

This cannot. I am imagining. This could not. A vision. Now she sees – sweet Christ – that the boy is still alive, because his eyes, when you look, and she runs to him, he is blinking. And his wrecked fingers scrabbling. But what is to be done?

'Mornin,' speaks the voice from behind her in the oaks. 'Don't believe I had me the pleasure.'

The accent is Tennessee but with an insinuation of brogue. She does not turn around to meet the face.

∇

CHAPTER 36

THE AUTHENTIC WILL & TESTAMENT OF "TENNESSEE JOHNNY THUNDERS"
or
GO DOWN, YE STARS & STRIPES†

(Sung to the slow Irish air "The Rocks of Bawn")

My name is Cole McLaurenson, a desperado, me.
Rode out from farm an' kinsfolk in the spring of sixty-three.
Killed forty-seven Yankee feds an' their hangin' judge, James Blighe.
But I never once did kill no man that didn't need to die.

~

The strangers burnt my only home in the fall of sixty-one.
Come preachin' "peace an' union," down the muzzle of a gun.
Demandin' our surrenders to his vengeful northern laws,
But he riled the brave defenders of the southern rebel cause.

~

From Ireland sail'd my parents both, from famine, chains, an' death;
An' the dog who'll rule McLaurenson aint never drawn him breath.
They poisoned up my waterwell an' slaughtered half my kin;
But I'll write it out in Lincoln's blood: *The South shall rise again!*

~

They called me Johnny Thunders as I raged across the land;
A terror to all tyrants was this Irish rebel hand.
It scourged the rich an' flailed the coward: the orphan did it feed.
They seen me come, the Mudsills run, so infamous my deeds.

~

Now some do take him wife to church an' plough his rows of cane.
An' some are force to ridin' lone through whirlwind, dust and rain.

† From *A Cabinet of Cowboy Balladry & Campfire Patriotics*, ed. John Fintan
Duggan, Richmond, Virginia, 'Confederate States of America', April 1865.
Author unknown, possibly Duggan himself.

I druther been an honest man an' never force to run;
But some, they draw the punishment of livin' by the gun.

~

O mothers tell your children, not to fall so gun-beguiled;
For the outlaw is a man of grief, with neither home nor child.
The stain of Cain the murderer is branded 'cross his brow.
He wears it like a crown of thorns. A desperado, now.

~

I hated not each man I fought, if honest he fought back.
My soul is damn'd for puttin' of his wife in widow's black.
But his rulers called us "slavers all," their "free lan'" we muss join:
While, two-faced as the Pharisee, they lust for the slaver's coin.

~

I never owned no man but this! I never owned me slave!
All I had, a patch of dirt, to scrape my mother's grave.
Now the Boston dogs of privilege come sland'rin' me an' mine:
Poison up my water – while he's sippin' slave-grown wine.

~

So come all ye Harvard hypocrites, an' a warnin' take by me,
As I climb the lonesome ladder to your sacrificial tree.
When your hangman ask my dyin' prayer, I'll give the rebel's yell:
God bless the homes of Tennessee! The United States to Hell!

~

O, wrap me in the Stars and Bars; to die were finer sweet
With the banner of my felony to be my windin'-sheet.
Cut a death's-head on my tombstone, friends,
Have a Fenian keen the pipes:
This Galway air from a Tennessee boy —
GOD D°°N THE STARS AN' STRIPES!

∇

CHAPTER 37

O JESUS BREAK MY CHAIN

Metallurgical matters – Eliza Mooney's fate at the hands
of the gang – A cruel game

It is seven feet long, this zenith of the metalworker's art. It has eighty-four links, each the width of a man's thumb, individually guaranteed unbreakable. At one end is a collar-band lined with small sharp studs, at the other a hasp you can hook to the pommel of a saddle. It is designed for the restraint of a runaway slave. Its price: eighteen dollars and change.

It weighs thirty-four and a half pounds. To run while wearing it would be difficult. Soon it would be cripplingly painful. You might manage a couple of miles before finally you collapsed; a strong man, young, might make more. But in the end you would be defeated by the crush of the weight, which, although it would not kill you, was too much to carry for long. This was the genius of the chain's design: it acknowledged your mercantile value.

We do not know the name of the man who designed this apparatus, who rode home to his wife and told her he'd had a good afternoon at the drawing board, that the muses of metallurgy had smiled on his efforts that day and that all familial worries were consigned to the past just the moment he registered the patent. But we know that it was forged at Annapolis, Maryland, by the Semper Robustus Ironworks Company, for their trademark is stamped into the hasp. Fourteen thousand of these contrivances were purchased in the decade before the War. One investor in the company tended towards abolitionism, it was said; but the profit motive is semper robustus.

Chains are employed in topographical surveying, for jewelry, in prisons, on ships. On farms, in manufactories, by hauliers and armies. The Semper Robustus Company made every kind. Links of lapidarian smallness, invisible without a clockmaker's loupe. Bridge-links the size of a bull. Its principal's grandfather had forged the gargantuan chains that saved New York from the English in the revolution. Strung across the Hudson, they weighed three hundred tons. No Royalist ship ever dared test them. The name of that hero was Alastair McLelland. Grandfather of Lucia-Cruz.

How the McLaurenson gang came to possess a Semper Robustus shackle-chain, we cannot know now, and I suppose it does not matter. It seems unlikely that they would have purchased it. Perhaps they stole it. But they rode with it, always, from the days of southern slavery, when a runaway could be bootied, cashed in. And with this they chained Eliza Mooney, of Baton Rouge, Louisiana, fixing the clasp about her neck and clicking closed its deadbolts, and tethering her to the earth of her home-land at night like an animal requiring breaking. There were eleven in the gang. All gave their assent, for the shackle would have been difficult for one man to attach. Perhaps some only watched, or looked away to the horizon. But a chain always links the many.

Semper Robustus. Always Strong. In this noose of dependable iron was she starved and made to suffer, sometimes by one of them, often by more. They drew lots, her fellow citizens, to decide their turns with her. Occasionally they played poker or dice for her. At other times they wrestled as though she were a scrap of fat in an orphanage, while others took bets on which rapist would prevail. The nights of a freeborn American body in the republic of liberations.

By day, they led her with them on their peregrinations through the mountainland, that wild and unknowable realm. If she fell, she was dragged. If she fainted, they would wait. Smoking, talking, quietly curs-ing the heat, nattering like men on a dusk-reddened porch. Of their homes in the south, of their children and wives, of the girls they left behind them. All had been soldiers. Perhaps they talked of the War, though for some reason I find that unimaginable. And when she had drifted back up from the kingdom of the nightmares, they would ride on again, implacable desperadoes, hauling the booty that was Eliza Duane Mooney, who had never done a harm to any of them.

In the end came the day when one of them objected. John 'Liscannor' Murphy. Dandridge, Tennessee. A cellar-digger, before the War. Wasn't Christian, he said, to treat no woman like such. They'd had their funning. Come time to let her go. They were married men, too, their comrade reminded them, and the woman could have a disease. They did not even bury him; only left him to the wolves, a bullet through each of his hips.

In Galway, Mamo told her, they used to tether a dog in a boreen to prevent the sheep from wandering. No ewe would cross a track if a dog was there, for she'd know, somehow – it was in her nature to know – that the mountains might fall and tumble to the sea, but the nature of a dog don't change.

There are days they leave her tethered and ride away toward a town. The collar-band gnaws at her when she stirs. Her head flames with pain. Escape is impossible. She has watched them ride back and argue over the plunder. Most of them are drunk by nightfall.

She limps down to the stream. The water is cold. She kneels on the bank and rinses her shaking hands, which feel old, like dirty canvas, withered and stale; then she drinks from the water, which is sweet and woody to the taste – though, lately, the chain seems to have inculcated itself into all tastes. Everything has a tang of cold wet iron, astringent, like blackberries on the turn. A rat floats past on its back, like a human. She wonders how it would cook.

She blows the embers into a glow, fixes coffee in a can. Yesterday's grinds; their taste will be vinegary. While it boils she squats in the near-by brush. She is accustomed to it now, has been living rough all this time. She spits in their coffee and hopes it is poison. The choke-chain grinds on her scars.

She prays her incantations to the crucified God, then to Papa Bon Dieux and his acolytes. Gu, Sakpata, Damballah, Legba. John Brown the Holy Warrior; the seven sons of Mawu. Satan himself receives her benedictions. But none of the divinities is listening. He said he would wed me, so loving and bold. But my true love betrayed me, for the one who had gold.

She realizes, if they kill her, that she will be buried in the chain-and-collar, because no one will think it worth the hard effort of removal, and anyway the lock is too complicated, too efficiently made. In a hundred years' time, or a hundred thousand, a skeleton will be unearthed with a thirty-four-pound chain about its neck, and a bracelet of hair around the stem of its wrist, and the diggers of that future will wonder what offering was this. What deity was appeased by its destruction?

Their leader speaks rarely. That is part of his authority. He sleeps up a tree, like a bird or a bat, having lashed himself to the mast of a bough. He once killed a child so as to punish her father. There are no words for his fishlike stench.

And then, as the days pass, she realizes he is not leader but lieutenant. His name is not Cole, it is Thomas or Tommer. He is brother of the leader, who has departed the gang, though Eliza does not know why, or to where he has gone.

Around his neck, a gold medallion in the shape of an owl. It is heavy, jewel-encrusted, too big for a man, like something a Russian duchess would wear. He stole it from a stagecoach at Vinegar Hill. Often, he uses it to beat her.

There are times when it is difficult to damp down the pictures. A bush bursts into flames. A rock gives a scuttle. At such moments, she tries to concentrate on something graspable. A snakeskin on a rock. A buzzard in the sky. A memory of Jeddo's face one Good Friday morning when there was something to eat and drink. The terrible fervency of his hope that morning. Not long after Mamo went away.

She is shaken awake and carried to the campfire. They have been drinking again. This is dangerous.

'Beg,' commands Thomas McLaurenson. 'Say me the right word, you're free.'

Tonight's firelight game. And she does as she is ordered. He allows her supplications, while he pares his fingernails with a knife. Choral bleats, dismal mewls from the men as they watch. Blank-eyed, sucking on their jugs. *Yaw Irish. Yaw Irish. I come owda de Nought.* Her northern accent amuses them.

'You are Irish,' she continues quietly. 'I am Irish, too. My people come from Galway. Let me go and I won't tell. Your own mother come from Galway, I heared you say that before. I never even seen you, I swear it.'

'Never even seed me?'

'I swear to the Virgin.'

'You never heared lyin's a sin, girl?'

Their laughter glimmers briefly like redness in blown coals. One of them is twisting his wedding ring.

'I'll do anythin you want. Only let me go away.'

'You'll do anythin I want cause you don't got no choice, bitch.'

She will not weep before him. But it is hard not to weep. The beatings are always ferocious if she weeps.

'I am married,' she blurts. 'My husband up in Canada. Any man touches me, he's an adulterer.'

The fire spits pathetically. He looks at her a long time. She has a picture of his mind as a pool of writhing alligators, over which, on a rope, she balances.

'Think I'm stupid?'

'It's the truth.'

'What his name?'

'Patrick Mooney.'

'Oh, Mooney. That is pretty. Where Mooney at now, bitch?'

'Montréal he's at. He's workin on the docks there. He was in the rebel army. Like youse.'

Patrick Mooney, who never lived, hobbles into the camp and stands in the firelit circle. His father from Carlow. His mother from Gweedore. An aunt shot dead a landlord and was hanged. The foot he lost at Manassas, where he murdered seven Yankees and was mentioned in dispatches for his valor. Her words give him life as he limps among the shadowed host, displaying his wounds, all he suffered for the south, the medals of his lesions, the ribbons of his tears, pleading mercy for his wife, and the men seem to know him and they want to shake his hand – all except for Thomas McLaurenson.

'Mooney give you no ring, bitch?'

'Had to sell it. I was hungry.'

'Aint that the livin shame, boys. Bitch be hungry.'

'Please let me go . . . Please let me go.'

'Git you here. Where y'be goin? Don't stand. On your knees, bitch. You crawl. Cause I don't care to see you on your hinds.'

His bony scuffed knees through the holes in his pants.

'Hold me out your left hand. Where the ring use to be.'

She does as commanded. He watches her hand. And her hand is tremoring badly and he looks at it a long time, as though the hand of a woman is strange to him.

'You believe, girl?'

'Church believe?'

'Got some other kind?'

What kind of question? And what is the correct answer? But before she can think of any answer at all:

'Cause the Spirit gemme a wisdom when I come in the world. Mo ask you one time. And you listen real true. See I *know* when I'm lied to. Got the giff for a liar. So you look me *in the eye* an you speak me the truth, bein two minutes from now, you got a bullet in your throat. Hundred-twenty seconds save your eternal soul. And I want that you die just as clean as a angel. Cause you sure didnt live too clean.'

He unholsters his revolver, calmly loads it from his waistcoat pocket.

The ratchety whirr as he rotates the barrel. He rises from his squat, touches the maw to her jugular. There is a piece of leaf in his beard.

'You married, girl?'

' . . . No.'

'What you say?'

'I aint married.'

'Get up.'

She stands.

He spits in her face.

And his next act, I will not write.

Not because I am afraid to – my fear is not the reason – and not because I believe such things are better unknown; but I have already done too much to preserve in language a man that should be permitted to rot.

'Disrespect me again, you're cut up to shreds. Understand I aint lyin. Cost me more to take a breath.'

She bleeds into the earth. The fire fizzes quietly. The men quiet as statues in its light.

'Turn you in,' Thomas McLaurenson tells them.

They do not move.

'Turn you sons of bitches in. Or you're next.'

Patrick Mooney is weeping into his bloodstained hands. For shame; for having failed her; for all that was lost. His dragonfly's life has flitted to its close. He returns to the blackness he came from.

∇

CHAPTER 38

WESTERN THUNDERS BLUES[†]

What was the wildest battle
Ever shook old Tennessee?
That made the mountains rattle from Fayette to Bloody Lea?
When a bunch of greenbroke yankee dogs
Rode into Johnny T.
Said *a whoo-yip*, Johnny.
Come-ah-kie-kie; yucca yucca yay.

From the Mississippi delta
To Savannah by the sea;
From the banks of Tuscaloosa up to Californah-ee,
He rocked an rolled like thunder,
An he rode out wild and free.
Said *a whoo-yip*, Johnny.
Come-ah-kie-kie; yucca yucca yay.

His Daddy was the chaparral, his Momma was the sun.
His brother was a gallows pole, his sister was a gun.
His given name was fury. His eyes was diamond stones.
He laughed at judge an jury an he chawed on lawmen's bones.

From Suarez up to Tucson town
An back to Mexico –
The *federales* chased him
But they hadda watch him go.
His *chica* told him: *Corazón*, I think you know it well:
For a thimble of yo heartsblood sweet, they'd ride through the gates of
    Hell.

† From *Traces of the English and Scottish 'Child Ballads' in the Songs of the Western Frontier*, ed. Professor Cleve Francis Jameson, Harvard, 1921.

They shot him up in Tombstone.
Out the window he did crash;
But a bullet 'tween the shoulders
Couldn' quit my Johnny's dash.
Rode laughin' from the Forbes Hotel
Singin' "Boys, How Sweet is Life!"
On back of the marshal's big black horse
From the bed of the marshal's wife.
Said *a whoo-yip*, Johnny.
Come-ah-kie-kie; yucca yucca yay.

∇

CHAPTER 39

REVENGE, REVENGE, THE OUTLAW CRIED, WITH THE SIXGUN IN HIS HAND

———◆———

Pishkun at New Lochaber – The Indians hunting buffalo
Eliza Mooney's mark

Sometimes, late at night, she hears them talk of their departed leader. Will he ever return? Is he dead? Gone into Mexico? Why is there no word of him after all this time? He left them, she gathers, to raise recruits in the south, diehard rebels still willing to fight. Yet that was many months ago. Perhaps he is in jail. He will return, they insist. He must.

But it is late spring now. Because the flowers are in bloom. *Flores para los muertos*.

An overlook of granite. Below them a floodplain.

'Quiet,' says Thomas McLaurenson.

The sound begins. Like distant thunder. Or a muffle of drums in a dream. Now dust rises up from the treetops in the middle distance. Whoops and screams. A punctuation of gunshots. And the ground itself trembles. And the rumble is inside you. What dragon is coming from the east?

From a defile in the rocks bursts a blueblack flood. Snorting. Stampeding. Charging towards the cliff edge. The bulls blackly massive, the cows and calves ocher, the smallest being trampled by their elders. Wolf-men running after them, shooting, waving hides: harrying the stragglers toward doom.

They plummet with the strange slowness of heavy things falling: black shaggy boulders, feet working the air, or they topple, scraping hooves on the walls of the canyon, as though salvation is yet possible to the intrepid. Behind them fall more, landing hard on the fallen, and the mournful and agonized bellowings arise, and the echoing crackle of rifle fire. A calf lands backways on a jut of the ravine, which sags, and crumbles, dropping its burden to the kill-pit. Thomas McLaurenson watches from his perch, unmoving, with a watch in his hand.

With his boot-heel he has scraped a crude map in the shale. It seems to show a section of river. She hears the word 'rapids' being spoken to one of his lieutenants, a butcher called McNeill out of Nashville, Tennessee, who yawps barrelhouse rollicks when he's drunk on beer and Thomas Moore laments on whiskey. He sings out his tears, fingers clawing at the air as though meaning could be squeezed from the shadows of night, and his fellows all look like they envy his gift for the maudlin murder of a song. Eliza Mooney does not know it, but that scratching in the gravels is the preparation of fourteen deaths. A feat is planned in the Mountain Territory. A patriotic butchery.

'What you gawpin at, bitch? Fix breakfast for the boys.'

She fills the pan from the creek, sits it on the low, dull fire. Frog-eyes is leering as he whittles a bough. She turns from his scrotal face. Mutton-breath and Tierney are sawing down a shotgun. McIvor is shaving O'Leary.

Noon sees them ridden to a high, flat mesa, their bivouacs blooming in the stones. She is commanded to wash their clothing, which stinks, as do they. A pile of it is thrown on the shingles near the campfire. It is hard to wash out blood – you have to scrub with a tawstone. A cauldron is flung at her like a bell.

She fixes up a dry-line with a knotted length of lariat. She hangs their wet clothes, so heavy that they need no peg. They confer while she works. There are more maps, bits of paper. An argument begins about dates.

In the distance she sees a waggon-train progressing through a valley. She counts the yellowed canvases: there are seven: no, eight; and a cavallard of yellowbrown horses. Vessels on axles, crossing an ocean of green, and the grass growing up to the buckboards. One waggon is trailing a Stars-and-Stripes banner. The canvases pink in the sunset.

If you could only shout for help. But it's too far down the valley. And even if they heard, or saw, or suspected, what would they do for Eliza Mooney? They would not want trouble: that's the way of the world. They would say it was the shriek of a bird.

A straggler has stopped. Probably a buckled wheel. She watches as the riders emerge. Two men and a youth. They are hunkering by the wheel. And Mamo used to say the heart was a wheel: once bent, can't never be ment. The lead waggons have not seen what is happening behind; they go trundling on westward, toward the declining sun.

Suddenly she is running, dragging the chain in her wake: its thirty-four pounds feel doubled by fear and it clunks like a mallet as she bolts. There is no chance she can make the grassland, the gorge is too steep, and the links are already catching on the butts of the stones. She stumbles. Rises. Phelim Tierney grinning behind her. A whiplength of rope in his hand.

'Pullin a little hard on the bridle, an't you, filly?'

She seizes her chain and swirls it – it spins, it whoops – and smashes him across the right ear: a hammer. A strange image in her mind, of a sunflower cut down, its splash of ardent flame, its tough, thick stalk, and the slash of a machete, that bite. He falls, beam-ended, clutching his blood-spattered cheek like an actor that got slapped too suddenly. She seizes a knob of granite, beats him hard about the face, gouging at his eyes, smashing it into his teeth. Her grip on his windpipe, as though it were a serpent. Forcing the stone down his maw. She screams 'Die!'

Frog-eyes and Mutton-breath are upon her before she can kill him. Punches. Kicks. They drag her by the hair. They will murder her now but it has been worth the attempt, for whatever is to happen, whatever cruelties they can contrive, one of them will bear the wounds of Eliza Duane Mooney even to the sewer of his grave.

Remember me, Tierney, every time you see a mirror. I'll be shittin on your mother in Hell.

Her smock is reefed off. She is lashed to a tree. Tierney is reeling like a drunk in a windstorm, the slaughterman McNeill holding him up. Face-broke, lurching. Someone hands him a lasso-rope. The beating is frenzied; but she hurt him too bad for him to be able to stand up long, so that soon he hands the rope to a teenaged compatriot and crawls toward a rockpile and vomits. And the youth flails Eliza Mooney, who is the same age as his older sister, and his fellows gaily cheer their encouragement. His next act is to copy a profaning he saw visited on her before – thus, he joins the world of men. He is fifteen years old, from Lebanon, Tennessee. His home was in a country of cane breaks and cedar. Before the War he was a baker's delivery-boy.

Explosions of beer-froth salute Luke Dillon's translation, though actually they are toasting his death. Then some of his professors stop laughing and colloguing. They have noticed that the afternoon has further possibilities.

'Tommer? Got a fish. Down yonder. Take a see.'

Thomas McLaurenson and three of his riders mount up in a moment and descend on the valley already shooting. She can hear the whoo-yips of the bold rebel yell, the snorts of their horses being spurred down the rocks.

She thinks about the waggoners. She prays it will be quick for them. Let there be no woman or girl.

I will put on men's garments and away to the War. And my love who deceived me, remember no more.

V

CHAPTER 40

THE CRIOLLA'S LAMENT
FOR JOHNNY THUNDERS

Out early I rode in the groves of Dakota;
All early I rode in the dawn of the day.
When I heard a dark lady, a-tenderly weeping:
Oh whither my Johnny, so gallant and gay?

All handsome and hopeful, my Johnny so tender.
All valiant and strong as the sun in the West.
Oh false-hearted lawman that chased him to Kanzas,
Oh merciless marshal put the lead in his breast.

Come all you brave cowboys that rides on the mountain,
Come bold bandolero and motherless son.
The hope of the widow, the scourge of the landlord,
He lived by his lights and he died by the gun.

All hopeful and handsome, my Johnny so tender;
And gallant and gay as a star of the night.
He stole from the rich and he gave to the hungry,
And never a lady received any slight.

A dagger of silver he wore in his buckle.
He rode with a chain all the many miles long.
And every link held a heart that was broken
Of a girl he had spurned for the love of his own.

He said he would wed me in Galveston, Texas.
Through Galveston, Texas, now lonely I search.
He said he would buy me a bunch of green ribbands
For to tie in my tresses by Saint Mary's church.

All early I rode in the groves of Dakota;
The innocent birds whistled hymns to the day.
And I'll never forget her, that vision of sorrows,
Who wept for her outlaw; turned weeping away.

Weeping away. Weeping away.
She wept for her outlaw, turned weeping away.
Then ghostly she vanished, that ebony phantom.
As shadows of night at the dawn of the day.

∇

CHAPTER 41

JOHNNY, I HARDLY KNEW YUH

The recruiter returns – A drumhead court-martial
The knife of Lucas Tanner

One morning, after they have finished with her, they chain her to the ground and strip off their remaining clothing to swim. She lies among the rocks like something dropped from a mountainous height. The sun rises high on the Territory.

The waterfront at Baton Rouge. Praline sellers. Beggars. Fishers of men. Light glistening on the buoys in St Peter's Sound. A watermelon thrown from the roof of a gin-shop. And Mamo changed her name, will not even speak the old one. Your name is Mooney now.

The devil hunkering beside her; left hand on her forehead. He is dressed in *chaparejos* and the tattered coat of a suit, and his boots are snakeskin and heavily stitched, and there is a garnet on a pin in the stock around his neck, and his *camisa* has a pattern of parrots. His eyes china blue. His hair copper red. His wedding ring finger is missing.

'Cole. You come back,' mumbles Davey McIvor, awakening in a hammock near the junipers. He was too tired to swim. Must have fallen asleep. 'Coley, how you been?' he says.

The man does not answer. Nor does he turn. His breathing is heavy; asthmatic. A butterfly settles on the band of his sombreiro. McIvor approaches uncertainly.

'Didn't expect you fore the summer. How you been there, Cole? You get the new fellers? How many you get? Boys was just takin a swim to cool off. It real good to see you there, Cole.'

'Get her clothes before I kill you,' says the interloper, quietly, as though testing the words for their truthfulness.

McIvor hastens toward the bivouac over which her smock has been thrown. Brings the rag almost tentatively: an offering.

'Cole – me and some of the boys was just havin us a little kick. Aint no cause to go thinkin we done anythin you –'

McIvor falls dead.

Now the gangmen are straggling out of the tarn in twos and threes, in garlands of olive wet lake-moss. He sits on a rock and leans a lucifer to rasp a light. His fists a cup of smoke. Drops the match in a puddle. Fob-watch from the pocket of his black leather weskit. Holds it to his ear like a shell.

It is hard for naked men to walk over stones. They hobble like pilgrims, up the incline towards their clothes. And some of them call his name in a simulacrum of warmth, as though they have not witnessed the execution just done.

'On your knees,' he tells the air.

'Cole – '

A second gangman dies.

She watches as they kneel on the gray, mossy stones. Wet hair. Dripping beards. Wet seaweeds between their legs. He walks slowly around the circle, boots scrunching as he goes. Curlews carve a way across the sky.

'I am waitin,' he says. 'Who will speak in the defense?'

'Coley – Cole, this aint how it look.'

From his shirt-pocket he takes a copy of the Wanted poster folded, and from that he recites his aliases and versions of his surname, in the cold, tidy voice of a judge at a trial, as though announcing the names of someone else. Next he reads the charges, repeating phrases that seem to displease him, so that an onlooker might think it was the phrasings he disliked: not the fact of being accused, nor the signified crimes them-selves, but something objectionable in language. All lies, say his minions; misunderstandings; exaggerations. Yankee stop at nothing. Breed of slanderers from the womb. That murder never happened. The other was self-defense. Aint a livin one among us ever disrespect a woman. We-all know the rules, Cole. We're soldiers to a man. This girl over here – we saved her; that's fact. Got the shackle on her neck *when we found her* near Stockdale. Only naked cause she won't keep them clothes on her back. She's crazy as a whiskied Sioux.

He stops walking. Turns his gaze on Eliza Mooney.

'Show me any man touched you.'

She points first to Luke Dillon.

'Please, Coley – No – '

Luke Dillon dies.

'Who else?'

Mutton-breath dies. Truncheon dies. Frog-eyes explodes like a bursting fruit, a melon dropped off a gin-shop as a joke. Phelim Tierney's face in its bandages blooms. Three slugs are needed to finish him.

'Who else? This man here? Be real clear when you point.'

'It aint true! I never laid hand on her, I swear on my mother. Dirty little bitch be a lyin whore. Take oath on my daughter, Cole, I wouldn do such a thing. Bitch give you the pox if you did.'

'You speakin me the truth, Frank?'

'You knowed it. I am.'

'He speakin me the truth, girl?'

She shakes her head.

'You believe in the scripture, Frank? Cause you need you to pray.'

'That's a lyin filthy slut, Cole. Take her word over mine? Look at it, for Christ sake! That's a madwoman.'

McLaurenson unsheathes a knife. Tosses it toward Frank Brooks. It lands with a dull clatter on the stones.

'Mathew five,' he says placidly. 'Twenty-nine, thirty.'

' – Cole?'

'And thy right eye offend thee, pluck it out, and cast it from thee. And thy right hand offend thee, cut it off, and cast it from thee: for it is profitable for thee that one of thy members should perish, and not that thy whole body should be cast into hell.'

' . . . Cole . . . for Christ sake . . . Quit foolin . . . Will you listen? . . . '

'You all sit you straight. And open your eyes. Cause you need to witness what befall the perjurin man. Got to do what you must, Frank. Aint no other way. Or I take oath on the livin sanctification of Christ, I will cut you so it take you ten days to die.'

Frank Brooks is weeping. Looking to his fellows for help. But they are weeping too, and looking away toward the mountains. Cole McLaurenson takes a stiletto from out of his left boot and pushes it into the embers of the campfire.

'Cole . . . *I saved your hide in Decatur* . . . When the Yankees was comin . . . You was hanged that night without me, that's a fact . . . '

'You was a good soldier, Frank. Don't be cryin, it's unmanly. Sit you up straight. Aint no cause to be afeared.'

' . . . Thank you, Cole . . . Thank you . . . I knowed you'd see it proper . . . '

'You was right, Frank.'

' . . . Coley . . . ?'

Frank Brooks dies.

Eliza Mooney turns away. Clamps her hands to her ears. By the tree-line she sees a posse of maybe forty men. Some are in Confederate uniforms, tattered grays of the south. Most are wearing bandannas.

'Girl,' says Cole McLaurenson. 'We aint done.'

The stones wet and red. Only two men left. They are gibbering at the thing they have seen. McLaurenson reloads one of his repeaters to put McNeil out of agony. 'God bless you, Jim,' he says, before administering the mercy. And now there remains only one.

'Tell me not this man,' Cole McLaurenson says. Gesturing with his repeater at the last of his comrades.

She nods: yes. That man, too. Your lieutenant was worst of all. There were nights when those other men did not want to attack me. But he stirred them to do it; otherwise they were not men.

'Get up,' says Cole McLaurenson. 'You stinkin animal. Or so help me, I'll cut your throat on the floor.'

Thomas McLaurenson stands weakly, the color of ash. Damp fringe in the shells of his petrified eyes. Goosepimples flecking his chest.

'Get pants on. No boots.'

He does as commanded.

'Walk north. Get. Look back at me, you die.'

'Cole – there aint a livin town in two hundred miles.'

'I mean to count to ten, for the sake of your children. You still here I say eleven, you'll be buried alive.'

The half-naked killer sets out over the stones, but weaving uncertainly. Where to go?

'That filth is my oldermost brother,' Cole McLaurenson says. 'He's my blood. I can't murder my blood.'

'Then give me the gun,' says Eliza Duane Mooney. 'Cause he aint walkin noplace while I live to draw breath. Or shoot me right now. Cause that's all your choice. Him and me aint livin in the onesame world.'

'There will be a restitution. There will be an amends.'

'Maybe. Now give me the gun.'

McLaurenson looks at her. She is thinking of the poster. *His cold and merciless stare*. Those words do not come close to the deathliness of his expression, its lodes of cruelty seen and done, but it is not in the eyes that such terrors live, it is somehow in the bones of the face. It has all gone into him. He sweats his sins. His hand will stretch out of his coffin like a briar in a ballad of star-crossed love.

'Bless yourself,' he says.

She makes the sign of the cross.

'Own the sin. Say it now.'

'I own all of the sin.'

'On your eternal soul.'

'On my eternal soul.'

'And all of its consequence to my own account.'

'And all its consequence to my eternal account.'

He hands her a repeater. Turns his back from what is coming.

'God have mercy on your soul,' he says.

Her first shot misses his brother but it causes him to stop. The second strikes closer; it crunches off a boulder. The third clips his knee. He falls with a scream.

'Cole! . . . Coley! . . . Bitch is . . . shootin me, Cole! . . . '

McLaurenson is trudging away from her, down toward the lake, which is blue and gray and green and shadowed, and over on the far bank, a long march of pines, and waterloons are skimming and swooping. He is stripping off his leathers. He wades into the shallows. His knees. His buttocks. His waist. His shoulders.

She harvests the reddened stiletto from its cradle of cinders. Many notches are grooved in its hilt. The word TENNESSEE graven into the blade, in minuscule Gaelic calligraphy. Many years from this moment, a boy called Lucas Tanner will find it in the rocks, and his father will donate it to a museum in their town, and a senator will make a speech about what this relic truly means, what history can teach us, the importance of forgiveness, and the band will play somberly as the glass case is unveiled. But today it is only a knife.

And the blade is so hot that she can feel its heat on her face, even when she holds it at armlength. She spits on it, the metal fizzes; the air around the point seems to shimmer. And the day smells of juniper and wildweed and timothy. And he might be the father of the child growing inside her – but that will not spare him. Nothing will.

Her soles on the stones as she approaches the knee-shot man, who is crawling away pitifully as though possessing a chance, like a natterjack crushed by a cartwheel.

'Look at me, Mister.'

She shoots him through the left elbow.

'Turn round when I told you, I said.'

He rolls onto his back. Face flittered by the rocks.

'. . . I got children . . . Got a wife . . . I got money . . . Have mercy . . .'

'Beg me, bitch,' she says.

And he does as commanded, but his wounds make it difficult.

She lets fall the repeater. A gun is too good for him. The throb in her palm as it clutches harder on the hilt.

Near the islands of Lake McKinley, Cole McLaurenson hears the scream. He dives before the second one – he has heard many men die; it gives him no pleasure, never did. It is murky under the water, but there are strange ribbons of light. Your fingers in the silt feel strange, and cold. Water muffles everything except your own breathing.

He stays down as long as he can.

∇

CHAPTER 42

THE GOSPEL TRUE HISTORY OF COCHISE & JOHNNY THUNDERS†

Come cluster near, sweet nobles fair, I'll not detain ye long.
An ye love the sport of gentlefolk, attend me eloquent song.
Tis of an ancient donnybrook – 'twas fought the other week:
Where Johnny Thunders, Erin's pride, did whup the great Cochise.

Twas near the west of Africa's coast, in South Ameri-kay;
Cochise shapes up to Johnny-Jump-Up, this taunting to convey:
'Tis said you are the fightenist buck; you wears de belt, I see.
But you haven't the hogs, yeh scut of the bogs, to fishticuff with me.'

'How now,' spake Mrs Thunders' joy, the southpaw strong and true:
'Tis I'm the wildest Irish brave, which none did yet subdue.
Below the belt will punch no Celt, we'll barney till we cease.'
With that, he spat upon the gloves, and commenced to clout Cochise.

Banshee, Comanche, lout and lord: and all did cheer the show.
Pocohontas came with Cap'n Smith; Napoleon with his Jo.
Saint Patrick brought the Prince of Wales, and Lot's wife came with
    Lot.
And all did sport as peaceful friends, auld enmities forgot.

A hundred rounds, they fought their ground, and nation-pride the
    purse.
Ten days and nights, they danced the ring, still none came off the
    worse.
The sun burnt out, the moon grew a beard, the seconds cried 'hurroo.'
'By dad,' the valorous Injun goes, 'I'll puck ye black and blue.'

† From *Irish Songs & Diversions to Learn by Heart*, Minneapolis, 1878; Dublin,
1879.

'Me mother was born in the Liberties, boys. Me father come up from
   Bray.
I'm a Dubbalin lad; when I ladders you bad, tis double you'll see for a
   day.
For the Liffey is in me veins,' cries John, 'Shure there's
   Knockmeeldowns in me gloves;
And it's when I come out to America, bhoys, the ladies there I loves!'

Johnny socks! Cochise, he drops! The red-lad he's thrun down!
But bets the count, and up to mount a faresome rake of rounds.
Five hundred years they scrapped in all, and never once a foul.
Then '*Thanum an Dhul*!'† the Injun squawks, and his squaw she hurls
   the towel.

Our hero's conquered Jesse James; Geronimo he's battered.
The Sphinx of aulden Aegypt's land, the smilin' smig he's shattered.
'Auld Nick' that bakes the rakes below, flapped up the prince to fell –
But the champ's put his tail in a shamrock knot, and hammered him
   back to Hell!

Sweet muses fair, let down your hair, to noose me if I'm wrong;
If e'er a fake or falsity went uttered in me song.
So come, we'll raise the potent punch, and with it we'll imbibe:
To Fightin Johnny Thunders, friends! – the Chief of Erin's tribe!

∇∇∇

† Gaelic, exclamatory. 'In the Devil's name.'

PART VII

THE STEAMSHIP SEASON

Oh stokesman, burn them lumps a coal;
Big river roll down free;
Oh paddle spin, an bring again
My honey back to me.

Got the blackcat bone for all my joys,
Got the mojo-hand for fun.
Oh stokesman, churn your paddles hard;
Your steamboat bound ta come.

From the singing of Jeremiah Mooney,
as recollected by Elizabeth Leavensworth

CHAPTER 43

THE SAME OLE THING MADE
THE PREACHER LAY THE BIBLE DOWN

Elizabeth Longstreet remembers Lucia

There some in the world got the lightning of the angels . . . Not all of em even beautiful but it somethin in how they do. And that's what she got. And you had to look at it again. Cause you had to be sure it was real you know . . . Nothin got to do with beauty or pretty . . . It aint a thing of words . . . It's in spirit . . . But there times you get to feelin for a woman got that . . . Or a man, or a child . . . Cause it a hard thing too . . . Cause it bring a lot of people aint no good for you at all . . . Make it hard for you to know a separation . . .

Got the Spain in her blood like the Mexicana you know. Fiery lookin. Strikin. Kind a haughty like they do. Got them eyes full of light the Latina people got. An she shape just so. She got the carriage a man like . . . I would say they was handsome, yes . . . A handsome couple. Cause the General was a memorable lookin person, too . . . You seen him one time, he fix in your mind . . . Kind of brawny man. Big. Muscle-and-blood kind of man. And his wife was the beauty of the livin world. Poor Missus O'Keeffe. Been a long time since I seen her.

She was a real religious, I recollect that. 'The Light of the Cross' was her Christian name in English. Lucia-Cruz. Aint that some name? . . . Say some doctor feller back east walk in the river when she wouldn wed with him. I dunno if it so. Wouldn surprise me none.

She pray the beads and all the saints like the Catholic do. Got em a saint for ever day of the almanac. See all church got it own way of comin to the Light, like the Jew, the Baptist, the Quaker, ever one. It more churches an meetings than stars in the sky. Old Baptist get the spirit and he shout and shake. And in India the milk-cows is holy . . . See it many roads of comin to the Presence of the One. To Him be the Glory; hallelujah.

[Acetate disc is scratched here. Eleven seconds indecipherable.]

235

. . . this old cigar box and he run around collectin stones in it. Not stones exactly, but alley-taws you know, how a boy will. Like what is the word? . . . Yes, the marbles . . . He was a natural child; all he need was to be care for. Redeemer say the children to come unto me. World took His counsel be quieter.

But poor Miss O'Keeffe. She couldn fit to that boy. No, sir. Couldn fit to that boy . . . And it hard for any woman [to] mother a child aint her own. She try. But the kiddie so wild you see . . . Do any way he want to. Never listen to nobody. Run around like a dog. Climbin under the floor. Stealin papers out the desk. Run away from the schoolhouse . . . And the General reckon that was all just fine . . . But Missus O'Keeffe – she didn agree. No, sir.

∇

CHAPTER 44

SHE DON'T WANT ME NONE

*Lucia wishes to be rid of the child – Her husband wishes
to keep him – Some letters, some answers & a poem about a soldier
May to July, 1866*

To The Sanitary Commission, Washington, District of Columbia.
From The Governor's Residence, Robert Emmet Street, Redemption
Falls, the Mountain Territory, Northeast Quadrant

May 1st, 1866

Sirs:

I am the wife of General James C. O'Keeffe, Acting Governor of
this Territory. We are informed that you gentlemen at the Sanitary
Commission are engaged in the work of furnishing information to
families concerning combatants that did not return from the War.

Four months ago, an indigent boy that we think may have been
among the rebel forces was found wandering at a mine near
Redemption Falls. He is aged between ten and fourteen years and is
four feet two inches in height, with dark brown eyes, a slight frame,
and Mediterranean appearance. We believe his surname to be
MOONEY; his initial is J. He responds, we have noticed, to the
Christian name JEREMIAH. The unfortunate child would appear to be
a mute. We have the impression that he pines for his home.

Since obviously there is no place here for such a boy as this, we are
most eager that he be reunited with his family directly. Please instruct
<u>by</u> <u>return</u> as to how this may be expedited. We shall meet any costs
that might arise in the matter and offer an amount of fifty dollars to his
parents.

Sincerely,
Lucia-Cruz O'Keeffe

▽

May 27th, 1866

Dear Correspondent:

The Sanitary Commission possesses no records of rebel combatants.
We are, therefore, unable to assist.
 Faithfully,
 R.F. Madigan

∇

To the Law Offices of Kiernan, McBride, and Love.
52 Mulberry Street, 14th Ward, New York City

May 11th, 1866,

My dear McBride:

Hope you are keeping well and crime continues to pay. All here in the
Territory is good, or at any rate not bad. We shall have to entice you
and Her Ladyship for a royal visit some time. Lucia would be delighted
to see you both again. We shall bring up the trumpets and drums.
 Condifentially [sic] Old Stick; I am in want of a little lawyerly advice
from a man I trust, and since such a one is unavailable, I thought that I
had better turn to yourself. To be serious: Lucia and I wish to adopt a
child in whom we have taken an interest. Be good enough to let me
know a little as to the proceedure [sic] and what must be done, will
you? I mean is his birth certificate necessary, & cetera, & cet. I suppose
there is a balls-aching amount of penpushery involved, but let me
know. We mean to act on it quickly.
 Forgive brevity, old friend, and remember me to La Reine.

 In haste but as ever,
 O'Keeffe

∇

'SUBSCRIBER-ADVERTISEMENT'
PLACED IN SOUTHERN NEWSPAPERS
BETWEEN June 3rd and 7th, 1866

FOUND!

One boy, J. MOONEY at Redemption Falls, the
Mntn. Territory. Approx 11 yrs. A mute. Possb.
Irish. Apply to: Mrs J.C. O'Keeffe, (Private,
Confidential). Redemption Falls. N.E. Quadrant.

∇

To the White House, Washington, the District of Columbia

IN REGARD TO PREVIOUS CORRESPONDENCE

June 8th, 1866

Mr. President, sir:

I trust that you will excuse a brief interruption. A month ago I wrote
the Secretary of War about the case of a vagrant boy. To date
(irritatingly), I have received no response. You might be good enough
to have someone attend to the matter immediately. The boy must be
repatriated to his family.

My father, Peter McLelland, a supporter of your Presidency, would
be grateful for your personal intervention in this case; as of course
would

His daughter,
Lucia-Cruz McLelland-O'Keeffe

∇

REFERENCE: 'REPATRIATION' OF INDIGENT BOY

June 29th, 1866

Madam:

I am instructed by the President's aide-de-camp to reply to your
communication of June 15th ult (and three previous). You will appreciate

that the President, who is helming the national reconstruction, has not the leisure to involve himself in such matters as the one you raise.

The President adds his hope that your husband's continuing employment as Acting Governor of the Mountain Territory is adequately expressive of his gratitude for your family's endorsement. If that is not so, I may say, Mrs O'Keeffe, that his resignation will be accepted without objection.

You might consider writing some person at the Sanitary Commission, or subscribing an advertisement in one of the southern newspapers. But the question is your own to manage as you will. This correspondence is now concluded.

Faithfully,

[*unsigned*],
Undersecretary

Post script: Your use of the term 'repatriation' is quite inappropriate, if I may say so, and has given offense in certain quarters that were better unoffended. You will have noticed that a war has of late been fought among our people to decide the problematical question of whether or not the United States is one country. It is.

∇

FROM A LETTER TO AN IRISH PRISONER
IN MANCHESTER JAIL, ENGLAND

. . . He is a quiet little pup, rather inhibited and sad; but I must say I have taken a fondness to him. L, for her part, reckons him a wonderful apparition and has quite fallen in love with him, I believe. Never thought I should be interested in children at all, and am not, in a sense – beastly little ****ing *******s† – but there is an expression he has at certain moments that rather disarms the heart. No, that is not correct. I don't know how to characterize it. But I do not need to describe it; as a father, you will know it. One feels – how to say it – protective and so on. He is satisfied with little and brings much.

Since we have no children of our own, we should very much like to

† The letter was censored by the prison authorities.

help him; and we hope he will remain with us happily. He has one or two little ways that want a certain degree of regulation – how could he not, given the life he must have led? – but L is really a most adaptable creature (in that way quite unlike her lord and master!). She will make him an ideal mother, I know. One has always felt that motherhood would be her gift, her ideality. And it shall settle something in her to have a function at last. You know how very ************* they can grow without one. My plan is that all treats shall be administered by yours truly, and L can mete out the correction . . .

∇

To Mrs. John Fintan Duggan, Rose Cottages, Merchant Street, Richmond, Virginia

June 30th, 1866

Dearest Martha:

I should have written very much sooner to say that we were absolutely sorry, Con and I, to learn the heartbreaking news of the deaths of the boys. We remember them day and night in our every prayer, and we condole with you, even so belatedly, for your dreadful loss.

James we shall always remember as so handsome and strong, Con as the gentler, with your own tender spirit, and also your loyalty and exceptional goodness. This terrible and wasteful war will take us all a long time to recover from, dearest Martha; but perhaps we women can somehow cut a path.

Martha, I had hoped to have your counsel on a delicate question. We have found a boy here in the Territory – a southerner, we feel certain – and wish very much to return him to his family. He was caught up in the war and may have followed a southern Army. I wonder if John would have any suggestion as to where we might turn. I am quite at a loss, and obviously the child can not remain here. Might you ask John to advise me, if he would?

Fondly,
Lucia (L.C.O'K.)

∇

July 11th, 1866

Rose Cottages, Merchant Street, Richmond, Virginia

Mrs O'Keeffe:

If ever you presume to write me again, which I wish you would not, take note that my name is Mrs Lieutenant John Fintan Duggan. Only friends are permitted to address me by Christian name; and I no longer regard you, or anyone belonging to you, as any friend of my family.

Talk of loyalty and goodness comes strangely from you, Mrs O'Keeffe. Do you think we hear nothing in the backwoods of Virginia, or that the south has no eyes in the streets of New York City? The world knows of your touching wifeliness in recent years. I will take no homilies from a woman of scandal.

For your further information, Mrs O'Keeffe, my sons did not die in any 'wasteful war'. Their cause was correct, their courage manly; and the crocodile tears of a secretly gloating enemy are nothing but a debasement of their memory. I can only hope and pray, as they breathed their last, that the horrible thought did not occur to them, that their godfather, your husband, was among the legalized murderers who came to spill their blood.

Recently my attention was brought to a so-called poem, which appeared below your initials in an abolitionist northern ragsheet. Had ever I thought, when foolishly I regarded you as a friend, that you would pen such an affront, I should have shunned you sooner. My husband, in prison, said this contemptible dirt could not have been produced by you; but I have long suspected you capable of despicable acts. You are the sort of woman no man can ever truly see through, for the turn of your ankle or the flash of your eyes creates a most useful diversion; but I, Mrs O'Keeffe, see you clearly enough. The beauty given you by God you have turned to a mask, like your husband's oratorical patriotism. Samson, it would seem, was not the last fool brought low by a painted appearance. You will recall from your Milton how a once great man ended: 'Eyeless in *Gaza* at the mill with slaves, Himself in bonds under *Philistian* yoke.'

Are all soldiers, in any war, to be measured the same? Is the invader, with his battalions and armaments and bombs, with a treasure-house of filthy dollars to support his crime, the double of the one who picks up a stone to defend his aggressed homeland from the trespasser? I thank God that my sons regarded the world rightly and knew the distinction between evil and goodness, black and white. Were I a more charitable person than the Almighty has seen fit to make me, I should pray that you, too, discover it one day. Such a knowledge might improve your morals, as well as your poetry.

I am,

Mrs. Lieutenant John Fintan Duggan

▽

WREATH FOR AN ENEMY SOLDIER
by 'L.C.O'K.'†

Who will say *traitor* on this lilied corse,
Which lies neath weeping salley bough?
Shall we disdain this fallen force?

See, the mercies yet allow
The zephyrs kiss his bloodied brow.
Who will say *rebel* on this lilied corse?

Lost, the gallant boonfriends now
Whose boyhood valor did endow.
Shall we deride this fallen force?
He had his cause. He chose his course,
As all we must, who know not how.

Who will say *liar* on this lilied corse,
So stillèd side the watercourse,
Hush'd lips yet framing loyal vow?
Shall we defame this fallen force,
To count it cruel and count it coarse?
Then come, his betters – mock him now.

Who will say *traitor* on this dead child's face,
And laugh upon its sacrifice?

▽

† This was the only one of Lucia's poems to be published 'below [her] initials', so presumably is the one to which Martha Duggan alludes. The 'abolitionist northern ragsheet' in which it appeared (on October 7th, 1865) was the *New York Times*. James Duggan, 19, was killed at the Battle of Shiloh/Pittsburg Landing, his brother, Con, 16, at the Wilderness.

CHAPTER 45

THE CHILD WITHOUT A FATHER

Treating of events in Redemption Falls between May and August, 1866.
A selection from the Archive of J. Daniel McLelland, Professor (Emeritus)
Department of American Literature and Folklore, Columbia University.
Comprising transcripts of field-recordings from surviving Redemptionites,
letters to Professor McLelland, and other documents.
Recordings made in the field in the summer of 1927 unless
otherwise indicated. Letters individually dated.

ELIZABETH LEAVENSWORTH, née LONGSTREET,
DOMESTIC SERVANT
Recorded 1928, Monrovia, Liberia

Steamboat season come in round the end of the spring rise . . . Dependin on
the year but that's May, early June. When the melt-snow put water enough
for sailin in the river. And late May's about as early as that ever happen – it
change from year to year but generally May. And that's how I remember what
happen with the child. Cause come time the season over – so August, like I
said – that house was about fixin to boil.

PENLEY O'GRADY, CATTLEMAN

Yeah, you'd see em in the town. O'Keeffe and the shaver . . . Remember it
like it was yesterday . . . Two of em goin along with the dog . . . Wolf-hound
dog O'K had him that time . . . Kind of funnylookin curiosity, O'K and the
kid, cause O'K was this mountainy sort of a sight – big nurly Fin Macool in
his general's duds – where the kiddie was about so high, no more . . . Piece
of work he was too . . . What I recall about him now, he's curious as
all-get-out. Stare you right in the face. Or at what you was doin. Hadn the
manners of a Irish hog . . . But O'Keeffe didnt seem to care.

FRANK DUNNEGAN, FORMER BARKEEP,
THE COSSA-ON-SHOOGAWN SALOON
Recorded June 1931, St Peter's Hospital, San Francisco

. . . I mean there's people can do remarkable things. Forgivers and peace-
makers. Bring folk all together. You moughta got one in your family, in your
place of work. Me, I got a theory there got to be one of em in a marriage,
else you aint gonna stay married too long, Jack. But you know the type I
mean. Compromise people. Point bein, O'Keeffe wasn't one of em.

Not by a jugful. Tough son-of-a-bitch. Glare you like a sidewinder if
you crossed him. And brother, I mean glared: the thousand yard stare. Your
balls'd wither up in their holsters [when] you got that one. Remind you of
one of them old pagan druids. Not a character for funnin around.

Man told me, in the War he saw him shoot a prisoner one time. You know
forwhy? For singin a rebel song. I dunno if it's true – I suspect may be not.
But Old Hard-Stuff was capable of cruelty, you know. That's what they
called him in the War. Kill a man and no compunction: least none you'd get
to hear of. So he didn't have too many exactly loved him.

No, I don't say him and the small-fry was friends exactly. Folk tell you
they was like father and son – that's bunkum. I seen em together plenty and
that aint the way it was. It was more – how'd you say it? – they could be in
one another's company at all. Have to tell you, it was a remarkable thing.

ORSON RAWLS II, UNDERTAKER AND AUCTIONEER

My father was undertaker in Redemption Falls at the time. Come up from
East Texas in the spring of sixty-five. Couldn fit to the negro walkin around
bird-free. Come up to the north cause it cold up here in winter an he
figured the negro wouldn never follow the cold . . . He was prejudice when
he was a youngfeller. He changed some later. Come time he died, he hated
ever one about the same. I guess you'd call it progress.

And I recollect seein the kid in the town right around then. Went to
school with him a while. Right there in Redemption. Well, it's a ghost town
now. Sad, sorry place. Schoolhouse was there on the corner of Fitzgerald,
just down a little ways from the logjail. John Connolly's Dublin Quartzmill
was up there afterward, right where the main street was at when I was
a chicker – but that's all fell down too. No, I dont care to go up there,
now the folks all gone. Nothin but rats and ruins up there. My grandson

goes sometimes. He'll dig around with his cousin. No, me, I dont go no more . . .

Melancholiest face you ever did see. Always lookin sad. Never spoke him a word. Stone-dumb he was. Cause he was born without a tongue. Say his mother was a certain type down Atlanta Georgia, took the snakeroot or somethin for syphilis. So he was born deformed. He once showed me inside of his mouth. Well, not actually me, but my cousin Jimmy Cultrane. And Jimmy swore me blind he was tongueless as a fish. Which was about the most disgusting thing I ever heardof up to then. I dont rightly know why. But it was.

Matter fact my Pa got this scheme cooked up in his mind about the scudgie. He seen in some old book where the folks over in England hire these kiddies for to walk at a funeral. 'Mutes,' they was called. Cause they go along silent. Cause those miners, you know, some of those boys liked a fancy funeral. Your Irish fellas especially, and your cockneys. Mean they'd fool away a fortune, send a buck on back to Momma . . . But come time to go above, they'd pretty much want the whole pony . . . Wreaths and a catafalque and ever damn thing . . . An a stone you wouldn cut for a sultan . . . Well I believe he ast O'Keeffe if he could hire the whipper for that: set him walkin behind the hearse in a little black suit and topper. But O'Keeffe wouldn suffer it: dont rightly know why. Heck the youngun might have enjoyed it a piece you know. Might have give him an interest. Took him out of hisself. Believe it was a book of Charles Dickens he seen that in. But now dont you go quote me, could as well of been Twain . . . My Daddy was always readin the hell out of some book or another. You got time on your hands when you're undertakin you know. Folk dont die just to order I guess. You tend to be waitin around some.

OWEN McDONAGH, TAILOR AND GENTLEMEN'S OUTFITTER

My store fronted onto the main street. Tone Street, they called it then. Wolfe Tone was some big britches over in Ireland I guess. He fought the Limeys, yes sir. Give em fifty kind of trouble.

So my wife and me would see em of a mornin and I openin the store. Lord now, I dont know, sir; good question; I dont know. Just . . . mullockin along. Doin a business in the stores there. Or seein him to schoolhouse for I know he went up there. Kit Doherty run the schoolhouse. Kit's alive yet in

Grantsville. And Kit was about the prettiest girl in the mountains that time. Sweet as a pudding. Just a really nice girl.

O'Keeffe was a heavyset fella – you probably seen him in pictures – so the boardwalk out front of the store would sag when he walked on it. Sag just like that. Cause it wasn ever made true. See the wood was all bowed and bent dont you know. Queer the things you remember when you come to an age. Cause I always figured he'd break it.

But they was kind of a nice sight, I always thought so, yes. Like a father and son. Closer in some ways. Give you a Christian feelin to see it, just the two of them mousin along. And he seemed a mannerable little fella – to me anyways. So he didn't say much. What matter?

I knew O'Keeffe, of course. No I wouldn't say friends. My Grandaddy come out of Wexford where he come from himself; but I dont know why, I dont remember ever talkin to him about that. But yes, sir, I cut him a uniform or two in my time. He'd go for your fancier uniform: lots of braid and so on. 'Chickengut' we called it, the yellow braid a general got. Man had enough chickengut on his arm for a coop. My wife use to call him General Chickens.

He come in latish enough one evenin for to get the child fixed: I mean woolens, good boots, a trapper's fur kepi. These shirts we used to carry that the miners wanted. Strong canvas you know. Oh, those was shirts. We'd get those in from St Louis; they was tough as a tent . . . And my wife cut him a little tucker jerkin of a wolfskin, I recollect that. Because we never did make one so small before. And we measured him a rain coat, I suppose a slicker you'd call it now. And as well a Sunday best for the chapel and so on – and that was a story, because we hadn no frieze for to make it. But O'Keeffe would have a suit for him and that was all about it. Then Julia says what about that suit we cut before that time, you know the one I mean, for Tommy Brogan, Lord rest him. Westkit, britches, coat and bockers. And I wrought that suit for a poor child as died out by Morton's mine. Tommy Brogan was his name. But the poor cavvy drowned. And here it fit this little feller like a godmade skin. So O'Keeffe said he'd take it and not to let on. And I dont know but it made me feel good to see this newboy goin around in them clothes. Maybe it shouldnt have. But it did. It just caught me . . . Cause you take a consolation from a sight like that. You dont know why exactly; but you do.

SEAMAS 'JIMMY' FOLEY, COPPERMINE OWNER

The ladies liked O'Keeffe. Oh, they liked him fine. He cakewalk down Tone Street and the flutter of lashes was like a damn flockin of butterflies. Fine clothes on his back. He be baited for widow. Catnip, he was. Nearabout knelt and adored him . . . And he had an eye on him too but I dont think he ever strayed . . . Say he took the starch out of a duchess or two before he was married . . . More luck if he did . . . Who wouldn't? . . . But you know how it go when a man showin kindness to a child. Dont matter if the fella's ugly . . . Probably helps a piece if he is . . . I mean, there's somethin in the ladies, they see that goin on, it's Daddy won't you carry me home . . . It's nature, is all . . . It's the way of the world . . . Mean, there's times you'd see him with the child, I'd of about jumped him m'self and I aint so inclined, not at all . . . You take Ingrid Schmidt. Ever hear tell of Ingrid? Well, Ingrid run a hotel if you know what I mean . . . Exactly . . . That type of hotel . . . Do the can-can in there and it come to the chorus, they bend over and show a little understandin . . . And I mean Ingrid – Lord forgive me – it aint Christian to say it – but this was one scarifyin, evil-lookin old pullet of a woman. She's haggard, pale – bowlegged, limp. Bout as ugly as a sore on a hog. Brothers Grimm woman, if you know what I mean. And also not a particularly nice person . . . Give that strapper an orphan, she'd about eat him on rye. But she'd see O'Keeffe and the little squirt just scootchin along Tone Street and I dunno but she'd come close to a smile. Well, close to a smile as Ingrid ever did get. Which weren't all that close. But still.

ANNE-KATHLEEN O'LEE,
née DOHERTY, SCHOOLTEACHER
Letter, 1887

The boy did not speak; this was the difficulty. At least, this was the obstacle around which other impediments cohered. I was aged only nineteen and found the situation troubling and difficult. I am certain that I did not manage it very well.

It became evident to me, quickly enough, that he knew how to read. Moreover, I would say that his reading was already quite advanced for his age; yet because he did not read aloud, it was impossible to know for certain. He was happiest – if he was ever happy – sitting alone at my table, scrutinizing, always silently, whatever primer I could find for him. His fingertip would trace a progress through the lines of the page. Sometimes his lips would move.

He took no part whatever in games and suchlike. He appeared not to notice the other children. Often, they would rag him and call him hurtful names. (I am afraid Redemption's children were not unusual in that regard.) He only stared at them as though they were somehow not real . . .

Miss Longstreet, then in service at the Governor's House, used come to me in the evenings for reading lessons. She told me several times that she had overheard him singing. I cannot say that I myself ever heard this singing, and I asked him very often if he wished to sing. But there was a sort of concentration in his gaze when one of the other children sang. He did not look directly at the singer, or, if he did, I do not remember. But he seemed present in a way that was not always the case. His eyes would lose fleetingly their dreamy expression. And then, when the song ended, it would return. The same effect was observable if a poem or rhyme were chanted aloud, in the singsong way that children have. Something in the rhythm seemed to arrest his attention. It was not that it gave him pleasure. More, simply, that he had noticed it.

PETER MICHAEL TIERNEY, MINER †

See, you get a child the likes of that one, he make folk feel nervous. They get to reckonin he's watchin em – takin in what they doin. Ain nobody care for that much, not your Westerner inyhow. We'll thank you for a little shake-room if you know what I mean. Mostly a pile of sugar gets in your stories of the West. Most all-fired courteous people you ever will meet. Help you out with your ploughin, takin in a crop. Dont care where you come from: any place you ever heardof. Cut off his own head before he ask your religion, or whoever you vote for, or things of that nature. Dont care if'n you're black-man or white or blue – that's my experience of it any ways. Tell a frontiers-man 'I'm sweenied' you get every neighbor in the county ready to make a

† From an interview recorded in Pitman shorthand in 1924, when the subject was aged 81. Tierney, born to penniless Tipperary parents on a ship in New York harbor, became a gold billionaire in the Klondike. He had prospected near Redemption Falls from 1865 to 1867, where he lived in a bivouac and often begged, on one occasion having his life saved by Blackfoot Indians when he was lost in a blizzard on Great Smokecloud Mountain. The interview was conducted at Cashel House, his mansion in Edwardstown, which was said to be the largest private residence in the United States.

fist of helpin you get fixed. Biggest toad in the puddle [or] no seat in your pants. Your westerner's neighborly as all get out. But he dont want you right up in his bidness neither. He'll thank you for keepin a distance.

Oh sure, I remember his appearance real well. Handsome little scallawag. Knee-high to a bee. Feller here told me he was a semaphore-boy in the Lincoln War. Lot of curiosities went on. That War was a thing. See these younguns got no idea of the history now. And bully for them. Whyn hell should they care? I was young now myself, I could care less for all that gum. Be out there chasin tail and makin a spectacle. But it dont mean it didn happen, that's what my wife always says. Aint nothin ever come out of nothin.

The things people done. Things as had to be done. Cause I could give a damn less what it tell in the books, but this is your land of the immigrant, brother, and your immigrant tough, and your immigrant hard as jackoak, cause he had to be, see, to get where he's at. Had to leave someone behind. Loved ones. Kin. Crawl over the poorman to get where he's at. Like my father-in-law was a Noggie,† best man you ever met: told me one time he left his likely girl behind in Tromso, every soul of his kin, so-long and much obliged. Not a once had a regret in all his born days. Claimed not to, iny-ways. Got to do what he must. Westerner get hungry, he gonna pull foot real fast. Find him some little seven-by-nine of a town, he callin it home the day after he ride in. Oh, he singin about the old country but that's all it is. Wallerin in the beer. Done it plenty myself. But that's all it is, the barstool blues. Cause he hightailed it out like a weasel up a rope. Stand outta my road and bury me decent. And that's why this country wont never turn Red. Cause we come a long way to get what we got. It's me and it's mine and brother dont you figure on takin it, nor ask me to share it with some hoeboy I dont know. Some vaquero layin in bed and scratchin his whatever while I'm workin my plot for his keepin and beer? Thank you, Mam, no. Shut the latch on your way. Bible tell you the meek shall inherit the earth. In Paradise maybe. Not in the West. Cause I'll draw you a line call the hundredth parallel, and left of that, brother, the meek inherit shit.

Russia they do it different. Good luck to em I guess. But this-here aint no Russia. Aint even the States. We're out here singin solo, that's the way we tend to figure it. Dont want no politician. We rustle us own grub. Washington never done for the man of the West. I'd've care as much for China if you want the Christ's truth. So I dont say the kiddie was good nor wicked. He was like ever one else. He did what he must.

† A Norwegian.

'LITTLE' JOHN RAWLINS, BARBER

Short back. Short sides. Soldierly I guess.

Funny thing, but it made him look younger. Yeah. Like time was going backways. [Laughs] Hated gettin it cut but a boy that age will. Mean I'm two-fifty now but I was two-thirty already then. Magraw the size of Rawlins comin at your head with them shears, you aint gonna be feelin too tranquil. O'Keeffe and Calhoun had to hold him down in the chair. Oh, he'd squirm, sure enough. But a little bub will. We had us some rassles, me and that boy. He'd about kick the belly off you. Bite you. Any damn thing. Let fly with a kick like nothin to nobody. But likeable with it. Spirited.

Nice little face. You could see more of his face. Neat little ears, kind of a long broad forehead. And these very strikin eyes, kind of maroon yellow I guess. Believe he had Mexican in him. Was his mother one maybe? I believe he was born in El Paso.

FLOYD LOUVAINE,
MUSICIAN & GENTLEMAN OF LEISURE

They was like as two peascods.

BILLY CORISH, DRY-GOODS STOREKEEPER

They looked nothing like each other.

DANIEL HANAHOE, BLACKSMITH

. . . And I dont know if that kiddie is alive or dead today. But I do know – and you can believe this or not – entirely up to you – that my brother told me he seen that child's ghost in the street there last winter. All these years later. Still the size he was then. Right there on the prairie by where the Governor's House used to be. With a saw in his hand. And he aint the only one ever claim to see it neither. Always a saw. Make of it what you want. I'm only sayin what I was told by my brother.

SISTER MARIE-PAUL LEFEVRE,
MISSIONARY, SISTERS OF CHARITY
Letter, 1894
(Translated from the French)

They made a comical pair, O'Keeffe and his foundling. They were like nothing so much as a couple of improvisatori [clowns]. The townspeople often mocked as they witnessed. Boy would walk behind man, at a distance of some paces, in the lolloping gait of a graceless child; his long arms swinging, gaze on the ground, pausing only to hitch up his britches. He seemed to find the wearing of clothes difficult; it was though he would prefer nakedness. His protector, meanwhile, would rarely acknowledge his presence, only scarcely conceding a glance at the pursuing boy. Yet curiously, there was a sort of counterpoint to their movement. One stopped when did the other. They walked in harmony. And soon – this was noted by many who saw it – the bearing of the boy became a pitiable facsimile of the General's, even acquiring the elder's slight limp.

It became the boy's practice to accompany his foster, as the General would ride out to the outlying farms or to the mining camps that then surrounded the settlement. A pony was procured for him – a surefooted little beast – 'an ambler', they used to call such a pony at the time – and many a curious miner looked up from his digging at Irish Quixote and his beardless Panza. The boy was not a good rider, and was thrown many times. He was once chased up a tree by the pony.

They came to the Station one day when I happened to be there. The Governor's horse was lame. There was of course no man among us but Sister Michael shod the bay quite as capably as any blacksmith in the Territory. We shared with them whatever refreshments we had. The little [fellow] went into a corner to play about with a kitten.

They remained with us two days and we were happy to have them as our guests. We took them to see a titanic cascade one of the sisters had happened upon, very deep in the fir forest near Loomington Mountain. Its fall was quite nineteen hundred feet. The boy was so excited – it was marvelous to see. I remember the General saying to him, in a somber and soldierly way: 'Jeremiah, you may be the first boy in the world who ever feasted his eyes on this wonder. Look at that glory. You shall tell your grandchildren of this moment.' And his large, manly hand on the little [child's] shoulder. And the little boy wide-eyed with awe. And then the General carried him pick-back home to the Station with the little fellow waving a cutlass of switch.

He was so proud of the boy, I found it rather touching; but he would accept no compliment for his care of him . . . The General spoke to me in excellent finely-accented French, inquired as to our situation out here. He helped us buy mules and a sawmill for our work and to manage all the documentation to bring the machinery up from Wilmington. I must say that I found him, always, a courteous and sensitive man. Others would differ; but he was kindly to us without fail. I feel he should be remembered in the round, as it were. Some accounts of him do not give a full picture.

MYLES AND PETER CASHIN, SAWMILLERS

[MC] *Oh sure, sure, he'd take the kid in a saloon.* [PC] *Nobody said no mind to it, neither.* [MC] *Nobody said no mind to it, neither.* [PC] *Get a bullet if you do.* [MC] *A bullet. That's right.* [PC] *I recall this one time, I was in the Shoe-Gone with some Kanzans.* [MC] *That's the name of a saloon, the Shoe-Gone saloon.* [PC] *That's the name of a saloon.* [MC] *The Shoe-Gone or the Ropes.* [PC] *When in come Old Hard-Stuff and the doagie behind him.* [MC] *In come the two of them. This is one good story.* [PC] *And here's this magician feller on the stage doin a bullet-catchin trick.* [MC] *Where his gal shoot a gun and he catch the bullet in his teeth.* [PC] *It's a old bunko finagle, he got the bullet in his beak already.* [MC] *Hid under his tongue.* [PC] *That's it.* [MC] *So the girly shoot the pistol and bang, there's the trick.* [PC] *Magician sput the bullet right out from between his tusks.* [MC] *And O'Keeffe draws his pistol and shoot that magician right in the ass.* [PC] *And you know whut he say?* [MC] *'Catch that.'*

BARTHOLOMEW BONAR, CABINET-MAKER

They tell you that yarn? The 'catch that' story? . . . Yeah, they spin ever one that gum as comes along. Why, them two old blowhards is so brimful of bull it's a wonder they aint drowned in it yet. They didn't even move *here till seventy-two! Never seen that child in their life, sir . . . I could tell you things about them two buccaneros curl the hair on your head. I reckon they aint even brothers, is the truth of it.*

JOHN F. CALHOUN, STATE GOVERNOR
(formerly DEPUTY MARSHAL)

There was a funny thing one time when the kid tried to ride that damn wolfhound. Up on his back just as brave as you want. That aint a smart move with your Irish wolfhound . . . Kiddie done him some runnin that day . . . [Laughs] So I asked around, see if we couldn find the boy a horse would ride for him. But he was so small you know. So we got him a pony . . . Little pinto, that's right. Nice-gifted fella, too. Cause the Spokane would breed those. And he would ride it, sure. Try to any ways. [Laughs] No, he weren't no rider. I could not say that. Saddle would turn or I don't know what exactly. Well he wouldn ever listen when he was bein taught to saddle up. Wasn't inclined to listen, prettymuch period.

Your aunt was tolerant, or she tried to be, I guess. See, me, I don't care for Lucia bein talked down. People got to have a villain. Saying this and saying that. Never stop a living second [to think] if they'd do it any different if those was the choices they was looking at. There's people should be ashamed, and they know who they are, for things they said about Lucia O'Keeffe in this country. But sure: it was real clear she had a dislike for the boy. Maybe that puts it too strong; I wouldn't want to be unfair to her. Mean, he can't have been easy to like, that boy. But Con would have him, and that was all to it. And you didn't argue the call with Con O'Keeffe; not if you didn't want trouble. Stubborn son of a so-an-so. Used to call him 'Old Hard-Stuff' in the War. Get the fire in his eyes when he was riled.

Because I always say it about Con: you got to understand the War. I don't like to get boresome but it wants to be said. The whole story about the boy and him and Lucia – you got to remember the War. Cause it changed folk forever. Every last thing they thought. All of your givens was changed.

I mean me, I was with the unit went into Andersonville at the close. You see men like living skeletons. And other Americans in charge . . . Thirteen thousand soldiers they got buried down there in Georgia. Near enough a thousand not even a name on their graves. I don't know . . . It's above my bend . . . That's your brother human being . . . If there's honey in the marrow – I dont know – that sucks it out.

I was one of them put to guarding Wirz on the train to prison – that's the man was in command – they hanged him in Washington. And I ast him one time how it all come to that. Because I truly couldn't see how it would. And you know what he says to me? 'I was followin orders.' I mean, what can you make of that?

And that was the cruelty, do you know, of the times. For sure there was valor. For sure there was courage. But there's cruelty in war and you always got to mind to that. And a man like Con – I don't know what to tell you . . . I think it shook him right down to the soul, to be straight. To me, he was never the same again. And it come to an insistence. Fixations I guess. The trees, not the wood. Small things seemin bigger. A man that's been in combat, you will see that in him, often. Get a little out of kilter on you. His proportions come to change. You have asked that man to do some pretty grave things. Country? Yes. Cause? Okay. But that isn't where your mind's at when you're doing those things. Because brother, you're dead if it is. And the boy just went into that whole picture someway. And Lucia, I don't know if she could see what was happening. He got fixed on the child like a last chance at the world. And I truly believe she didn't see that comin down the pike. Least not till it was all too late.

Way I saw it myself, the more she give him the sharp side of her tongue, more hellbent he come to keep him. And then it's a stand-off and the both of you biting the bullets. And talking about where you are comes to seeming a weakness. And that's not a great aspect for anyone in the picture, child nor Con nor Lucia. And a child in the middle and ever thing running to that. And I asked him one time: 'Con, you fixing to be a father to that boy?'Cause a father int somethin to take up and put down. Well, he pretty much told me he reckoned that out already. He was determined. You'd have to give him that much.

How the kiddie felt about it? I don't honestly know. He took off a few times but then afterwhile he always come back. I guess, he didn't like it, he'd have took off for keeps. Mean he wasn't in prison or nothin like that . . . He was one lonely little feller. You'd never forget him if you saw him . . . I guess he didn't have too many choices.

LAWRENCE NEWCOMBE, PHYSICIAN, SALT LAKE CITY
Letter, 1892

I think I saw him four times while visiting the town, on the first occasion for a stomach flux, the second for bedfouling. From memory, I also pulled a couple of his teeth. But there is nothing about that in my notes, so perhaps it is wishful thinking.

I did not care for him at all. He was rather a loathsome child, entirely lacking in finesse. He looked like one of those boys that eats clay and nettles, the sort that will do anything for a dare. He was slovenly, unappreciative, and nauseating in his habits, to an even greater degree than is the case with most boys of that age. His breath reeked of pigsties. His teeth were crusted green. If you will pardon it, the feeblest essentials of bodily cleanliness were as mysteries to him. His garments, his bedding, his every accouterment was ruined by filth. He ate at his fingernails and picked at his ears. Redemption was at times quite a memorable parfumerie; every frontier town was, at that distant era. But that boy had an atmosphere, a pungency all his own. His stench seemed to orbit him like a moon.

The Governor entertained notions which I found rather naïve; that the ungrateful little cur would be finally revealed a saint, as kindliness worked its magic toward the end of Act Three. But that is not what happened. It never does, in my experience. The boy expectorated on floors, urinated where he pleased, thieved from his protectors, broke or dirtied everything he touched. He would enter the Governor's study at any hour of the night and disorder or steal his papers. The servant, so she told me, found him early one morning, doing in the cookhouse what a dog does outside. There is only one course with a boy as lost to human society: very frequent caning and a diet of milky foods; but the Governor would not have the former and the latter proved fruitless. Were I in his position – it is not Christian of me to say it – but I would have put the child from my house and on the road for his pains. Which, I think, Mrs O'Keeffe wished sorely to do. But a husband wore the britches in those days.

Most disturbing of all – Mrs O'Keeffe found it horrifying – were the reports of cruelty in the town. The boy had been witnessed, so one settler insisted, stoning a lame calf until its hide was all cut to pieces. A dog had been captured, a blind old bitch, and subjected to appalling tortures on a fire. A mule was killed and mutilated – nobody could say by whom – its very innards bedecked about a tree like streamers. On the evening of the day when I had heard this last tale of horrors, I happened to be departing Redemption Falls on the six o'clock stage, when, at dusk near Sullivan's Creek, I myself saw the boy, cleaning off a knife on his boot-soles. He glanced up as we passed, and I shall never forget that expression. One felt that one was looking at pure, hard evil. My dreams, for several nights, were uneasy in the extreme. He was grinning quite gleamingly as we passed.

HONOR MORAN, FORMER DOLLAR-A-DANCE-GIRL, THE ODALISQUE HOTEL

Twas never proven it was the child done all them things. He got the blame for every wrong was ever done in that bugtusslin dump. Nothin would ever do them bar pointin a finger. That's my brave America.

Behind the door at home they're up to anything you want. Then covered in holiness beyond it.

CON LAWLESS, PROSPECTOR, VARINA CITY

I'll air up to you, Mister, I did not like that child. I'll tell you right now, that child had evil in him.

It was the way he had of looking at you. Not a screed of human shame. Like here this one time I seen him and I on my way to my Jimmy Cashin's and he sat by the springbranch, drawing with a stick in the dirt. Well, when I seen him I had some feeling for him and over I go. 'What you got, sunbeam?' says I, and he covering it with his hands.

You know what it was? Upside-down crucifix.

Look disbelieving as you want, but that's the God's truth for you now. And I never did care to see him again after that day. Get the shudders to think of it yet. Devil's own child. That's what they use to call him. And that aint a name to put on any child in the world. That's a mother's own son, and I raised my children that way. Didn't walk in the shoes, you be wise not to judge . . . And no one's ever needed the forgiveness of a merciful God more than the man's sat talking to you now . . . But when I heard what happened afterwards . . . I can't tell you it surprised me. It was never coming any other way.

GOVERNOR CALHOUN

I'm not saying they never had a quarrel. Not by a ways. Know marrieds can say that much, they're either liars or saints. But sometimes your little ruckus int the worst thing in a house. Clears up the air a mite, you know? I see my secretary laughing over yonder. What you laughing at, sweetheart? . . . She thinks I'm full of it I know . . . She aint married yet, that's for why . . . Oh marrieds is rarely closer than when they're having a quarrel. It's like jumping into bed together, only without the fun.

DOCUMENT WRITTEN IN O'KEEFFE'S HAND & NAILED ON THE WALL OF THE COOKHOUSE†

I: *Thou Shalt Not Suck of Thy Hands, nor Shalt Thou Chew of Thy Fingernails.*
II: *Thou Shalt Not Consume the Detritus of Thy Nostril. It is unclean.*
III: *Thou Shalt Go About Thee QUIETLY, in especial at night-time.*
IV: *Thou Shalt Bathe Once the Fortnight, with Soap, which shall be provided Thee.*
V: *Thou Shalt Not Eat With the Blade of Thy Knife at the Table. Neither shalt thou slurp, nor gnash, nor gulp, nor issue forth sounds from thy fundament. It is abominable.*
VI: *Thou Shalt Sit Thee Up STRAIGHT with thy mouth SHUT FAST.*
VII: *Thou Shalt Put on thee Laundered Garments each Sabbath Day morn.*
VIII: *Thou Shalt Not Pick the Crust of Sleep from Thine Eyes, then to eat of it in thy mouth: it is injurious to the Lord.*
IX: *Thou Shalt Do as Thou Art Commanded, obeying all orders, at all times, with a good heart, & learn the habits of a clean & obedient boy, & pray for those that protect thee.*
X: *In especial: THOU SHALT DESIST FROM PURLOINING THE GOVERNOR'S DOCUMENTS. THERE IS AN ABUNDANCE OF CLEAN PAPER IF IT IS REQUIRED.*

ANNE-KATHLEEN O'LEE, SCHOOLTEACHER

There was a story at the time – the old people would tell it – that the coyotes contain the souls of the dead. Perhaps it was a piece of Indian lore. Anyway, westerners always loved ghost stories. Well, I remember the day I was telling the children about it in the schoolhouse. I happened to glance in his direction. His face was pure white. He seemed terrified by what I was saying. It is something that I have never forgotten.

† Original on display at the County Museum. (Replicas are sold to tourists as souvenirs.)

JUERGEN SCHULMEISTRAT,
TYPE-SETTER, FORMER MINER
Recorded Seattle, Washington, 1929

With my cousin. Yeah. His name was Heinrich Mantel. He died maybe ten years ago in Frisco . . . Oh, the two of us saw them in the street, I would say every day. We thought he was father of the boy, or an uncle or something like this . . . He was an alright boy. I never saw nothing amiss with that boy . . . We got a bunk down in Limerick Lane. They called it Kleinedeutschland back then. And we lived there six months, Little Henry and me. But then Henry took up with a girl and took off to La-Source-Des-Femmes, that's up there a ways past St Joseph . . . Sure, sure. Saw the child most every day. We give him a quarter to fetch a newspaper, something like this. Or a beer or a porter from the Shoogawn or the Bone. Because that's hot work, mining; you sure enough get a thirst. Some days you carry yourself home in a bottle. We come home all cover in dust and dirt and whatever and here come-up the boy with ice and drinks for a sale. [Laughs] Now that's a millionaire! . . . He was an Irish kid, yeah, or his father was Irish, maybe. But the Mickeys in the town, they didnt seem to care for him, or some. He was a most beautiful singer, this I remember. Someone told me he went to prison after, for a murder was it? But I left the town by then and never went back. No, I never heard nothing about him again. I believe he was hanged in Dakota; is that right?

ELIZABETH LONGSTREET, DOMESTIC

Yes, I knowed what they got to sayin about that child afterward . . . that he come up a murderer an a devil an all such. Heard ever thing they said. I dunno how it come that way. All I can say for my own self: I never once saw him do no cruel thing. Just a boy never got him no chance is all . . . I aint got no more . . . No, I'm feelin weary now. I got [unintelligible] to do later . . . See this man here he callin me . . .

INTERVIEWER: *Well, then. We surely do thank you, Aunt Bessie . . . If I may call you . . . Yes [interviewer laughs] . . . Aunt Elizabeth . . . Do you have may be . . . well I guess a word . . . for the young folks that's comin on now? . . . Or a witness or a word for the youngsters and their families? Because some of us get to feelin . . . I don't know if may be you feel this yourself . . . that bein young right about now is a hard thing to get straight.*

SUBJECT: *Read you the scripture.*

INTERVIEWER: *Read you the scripture.*

SUBJECT: *Morning and evening new mercies I see.*

INTERVIEWER: *Well amen, amen. I don't know would you maybe . . .*

SUBJECT [interrupting]: *And they are many more wonders which Jesus did: the which, if they should be written ever one, I suppose that even the whole of the world could not contain the books that should be written.*

That's the last verse of John. That's all I got to say. Glory Alleluia. That my word.

∇

CHAPTER 46

SHE IS FAR FROM THE LAND WHERE HER YOUNG HERO SLEEPS†

A letter from Lucia to her sister Estafanía – The sadness
upon the end of a marriage

The Governor's Residence
Robert Emmet Street
Redemption Falls,
The Mountain Territory

August 19th, 1866
Sunday midnight

Cherished Heart, my own Malinche,

Your MS. came as a mercy and an answer to prayer. A blessing to know
that things are better for you now – at least a little – though your words
made me yearn all the more to be home in Manhattan again. How I
wish I could see my own Steffa even for an instant, to be lost among
the lights and reflections of the city. I should like to walk with you on
the Avenue, or to the Battery at twilight, with my arm in yours, the two
of us speaking together of small things. How I long to see the harbor at
that chiaroscuro hour, the lanterns being lighted on the ships; the
shadows on the water. All other cares should be as nothing, then. It is

† Letter bequeathed to the editor, Prof. J.D. McL., by his aunt, Mother
Anuncion of the Carmelite Order (Estafanía Maria McLelland) on her death in
1894. Written in Spanish (on official gubernatorial notepaper) in a cryptogram
code devised by the sisters and two of their Toledan cousins in childhood. Lucia
was able to write remarkably fluently in this cipher, even drafting some of her
poems in it, as surviving MSS at the New York Public Library demonstrate.
'*Malinche*', a family nickname for my aunt Estafanía, is a crimson-petalled
Nicaraguan flower, the jacaranda.

so quiet here tonight. One can almost hear the pulse of the silence. It is like the beating of an insect's heart. How I hate this place and almost everything in it. I die here [*Muero aquí*].

It was a relief to learn that David is recuperating. I burn a candle for him every dawn before the icon of the Virgin, the little malachite one Mama brought from Chinandega. When he learns to manage with the walking-cane, his spirits must improve, and the unhappiness you see in him will surely be lightened. Poor, good-hearted David, and poor Malinche. When one thinks of how he loved beauty, the gaiety of the world, and the rose of the world that is you. Never to see again must be the worst of all crosses. How he bears it with any grace is a miracle. But do not be afraid of his sadness, my heart. Let time do its healing and all shall be well. David shall make you in every way the loving husband you deserve. I only wish my own choices had been as wise as yours. But there it is. I must to bed.†

Dear Bloodflower – Oh my Host – that you were here is my wish. Soon it shall be dawn. I hear the miners on the road.

Five hours of the watch have passed since I commenced this letter. I have put it away, and taken it up, and put it away, all the night. Several times I have thought to tear it, and yet I cannot seem to. I have tried to sleep but can find no rest.

Steffa – I am in trouble. I need you to pray for me now. There is a very painful matter, which I must disclose to you honestly. I have anguished too long about whether or not to tell you; it is not an easy thing to say and will cause hurt to several people; but after long unhappiness, which has defeated all resolutions, I have come to the decision to break from Con.

What a small, terrible sentence. I have dreaded its writing, for it makes everything real, where before it was a shocking dream. It is a horrible thing to own – to be owned by – a secret, and to walk about with it corroding your spirit as you go. One puts on a masque of

† David Daniel Kobor (1841–1868), Lieutenant, 88th Pennsylvania. Twice decorated for bravery, he died in New York three years after the War, having never recovered from the effects of prolonged starvation at Andersonville Prison Camp. The Kobor Foundation for Immigrant Children, of which Lucia was lifelong patron, was named in his honor. Estafanía entered the Carmelite Order four years after his death, working the remainder of her life among the poor of New York and, later, Central America. She died and is buried at Mexico City.

blandness and calm, but behind it one is rotting like some forgotten thing in aspic, still holding its shape as it putrefies.

Heart: You are the only one in the world to whom I can entrust this – the only living soul on this earth. Dear Christ, how I wish I could fly the thousand miles to your side. I would be there tomorrow if I could.

Our parting has been inevitable for longer than I can concede to myself. The truth is that we have known difficulties since soon after we married: very troubling difficulties, of an insoluble kind. Some of these were my fault; some poor Con's. And some, I suppose, were nobody's fault, only that flaws in each of our natures have conspired to make them worse. I was not so foolish as to think any marriage can remain free of small, intermittent trials. One sees, in the married people one knows, that a couple, I mean spouses, are like the hands of a clock: sometimes together, many times apart – sometimes even as opposed as the poles – but the fulcrum of loyalty holds them both in the same circuit so that they must again meet when a little time has passed. But there is no meeting now between Con and I. If ever there was a lynchpin, it has broken.

The matters between us have grown larger and ever more complicated, until they have become insurmountable – I do not exaggerate. Since coming out here to be with him I have learned, to my loss, that a severance is the only course that can let both of us remain sane; and this lesson, sorely learned, must be acted upon bravely before further hurts are done, which might never be healed.

The last steamship of the season departed yesterday forenoon, and the route by the stagecoach is closed for the present time, for the outlaws are menacing the roads. I will remove to an hotel in Edwardstown in the coming days, and shall return to New York as soon as I can discover a means.

Now you know, Little Red [*Rojita*]. I have failed in all I wanted. I feel anger and guilt and shame. I try to be brave, but there are moments when I am very afraid of the years to come. I pray to Mama, then. I know she will help me.

I think you have suspected – I know you have, wise Steffa – that all has not been as it should between C and I. You hinted as much when you saw me good-bye at the station, or I thought you did, and how I longed to tell you everything. Instead, I spoke sharply and spoiled our farewell. Forgive me, dearest Steffa. You deserve a much better sister.

What I am about to confide must always remain between us; but I know I do not have to ask it, for you would anyway assume it. You are so very good; so slow to pass judgment. I wish I had even a shadow of your merciful kindness. In any case, I do not wish to condemn Con. He is the man he is, a good one in his heart; but I knew, when we married, that being his wife could never be easy. Heaven knows I had been warned of it, not least by C himself, but by others, also – and anyway I knew it. The world thinks him self-possessed, I dare say even arrogant; but nobody can carry the wounds of such a life and be complete. I wish I could write you that I do not love him any more. How much easier that would be, were it true.

For as long as I can remember, and especially since Mama's passing, I have longed for the day when God would permit me to be a mother. Con's avowal, during our courtship, was that he would like us to have an army of children. But very soon after our marriage, he changed. He grew sullener of spirit, more silent and secretive. At length he confessed to me the reason for his darkness. During his time at Tasmania he had married a native woman who bore him a daughter, but the infant had died at eight weeks. The woman, he told me, took her own life some time subsequently, not long after he escaped the colony. He had thought himself recovered from the grief of the loss but could now see that he was not; since marrying again it had returned. Steffa, I was shattered he had never told me of child or mother – and I saw that I had married a man who was in thrall to his secrets, who would always keep them, no matter the hurt to others – yet what choice had I now but a blind hope in providence? But my prayers were not answered. He grew more distant all the time. Men would call to the house for him at any hour of the night. He would not say who they were, nor reveal their purpose, nor open a letter in my presence – and there were many from Australia. We had not been married a season when he told me he could never again be a father, was too broken in spirit, too afraid. It was beyond my understanding, this terrible refusal. I begged him not to sentence me thus.

Our quarrels grew dreadful. Yet they did not kill my hope. God help me, Steffa, I have been so stupid and self-regarding. I could not take him at his word, preferring a vain trust. Time would assuage the hurts he carried – of this I attempted to persuade myself. Yet all the while he became more ardent, he would not be a father, ceased approaching me as a spouse at certain weeks of the month, denied that this was the case. I wished to 'trick' him, he said, to disrespect his wishes, or to cancel 'by wiles' what he called 'our agreement'. Those years, which should have been happy, passed in enmity and vicious words. Worst were his silences: unbearable repudiations.

There are privacies in any marriage, which God forgive me if I disrespect. But I cannot go on dissembling; it will send me mad. The truth is that Con and I have not lived as husband and wife for nine years, since even before the War, since he started traveling away from me. Our marriage is a shell, a husk of itself. We are a nothing in a crevice. I think we always were. I have come to doubt his reasons for wanting to marry me – even, on occasions, to think Papa correct. 'Fortune-hunter' is an ugly, a despicable name, and in saner moments I cannot make Con fit a pattern so unmanly. But always comes the doubt: I must have had something he wanted. If only I knew what it was.

Some time ago, Steffa, I made a mistake. You will think very low of me. But I must tell the truth to someone. I allowed myself to form a friendship with a person in New York: worse, a patient at the hospital. He was – is – a good and kindly man, an officer in the Corps of Cartography. He endured Hell in the War: unimaginable suffering. His face was so disfigured when he came to the ward that he could not bear to look on his reflection.

We would go walking together. We spoke of poetry, of beautiful things. He paid me compliments. My vanity permitted them. I think loneliness was part of it but that is no excuse. Before long – I do not know how it happened – our feelings ran deeper than friendship. I should have broken the attachment but to my disrepute I did not. I found, in fact, that I was unable to. I longed for our meetings as blessèd hours, telling myself they were innocent, yet knowing, were they guiltless, there was no need for them to be always kept secret. He began speaking to me as a suitor addresses a girl he loves [*una novia*]†, made declarations I should never in honor have permitted. But I did permit them. And soon, I returned them. But you yet do not know the worst of what I am.

One night, it was last spring, he asked me to transgress further: to meet with him privately at a dishonorable place. I knew what he wanted. I knew it very well. I am not so pure as everyone imagines me. He implored me to go to him. I said I could never. He told me he

† Novia: a betrothed woman, a sweetheart. It can also mean a bride.

would be there, would wait for me there. The morning came; then that afternoon. I prayed and walked. I went to make confession. The priest, a very old monk, was so kind that I wept. A mistake had been made. Loneliness was not sinful. But the error must not be compounded; the friendship must end. I went directly from the chapel to the place of which the man had spoken, the incense still scenting my clothes.

In that room we spoke. At first there was nothing more than speaking. I told him that we must part, could go no further with this wrong. But even as I uttered these unfelt negations, I longed for him as a lover, more than ever before. The room seemed a world possessed of its own laws. I wished I were someone else, or that this man was someone else. Or that he was a girl, and I a man, with a man's capacity for self-forgiveness. We shook hands, in farewell, or so I thought, but soon kissed, and our caresses became forbidden intimacies. Steffa, I felt no shame – and no shame for feeling no shame – but the joy of being desired by another. It was all I could do to arrest the misdeed. I must beg the man to cease. It was only the thought of betraying Con that prevented me from acting on my wishes. The man spoke of love, the forgiving morality of love, was gentle and tender as he asked and asked. Had he asked but once more, I know what would have happened. My sin would have been greater, would have been the ultimate of a spouse. But I know, I became an adulteress that night. My presence placed that unforgivable stain to my account. No – it had long been there.

In the coming days he wrote to me. I returned his fiery letters. He wrote again. I beseeched him to desist. I told him that I was coming here to be with Con, to whom, for better or worse, I had vowed my loyalty. I had made a mistake, had compromised my word. But the error must be put in the past.

I had hoped, when I came out, that we might start anew. But the hope was in vain. All our way is eroded. Our quarters here are separate. He has insisted it should be so. We eat, we live – we go about alone, like a broken old bachelor and his spinster sister who roast on the flames of one another's disappointments. Our days are become reflections of our friendless nights. We hardly speak a syllable to one another any more, nor even sit quietly in a room with the other. I come in; he departs. I go out; he enters. What might have been hoped the intimate friendship of a married couple has been supplanted by cold loneliness in every way.

I try to content myself with my writing, with walking in the hills. I visit the poor sections, arrant hypocrite that I am, and play in the role of the Governor's wife; but life here has been dismal with no hope of reprieve. I cannot write anything but dressmaker's trash, derivative nothings only fit for the kindling. I have tried to speak candidly with Con many times, to ask how I disappoint him and how I can improve. At these moments his rages become absolutely terrifying. No prayer I can contrive reveals any course.

In the silence of the night the worst possibilities have loomed around my bed. There is one that came constantly; I know I do not have to name it. So accustomed I grew to wrestling with this terrible thought that, now I have overcome it, I almost want for its companionship, for it would be a relatively simple thing if only it were true; at least it would be understandable. Of course one hears rumors in a place as small as this – there are looks of almost violent sympathy from some of the ghastly women, and snickering comments from the brutish men – but I know Con's nature is loyal, unlike my own, and faithlessness of that kind he could never countenance. In any case, I believe – forgive me if I speak plainly – that no mistress would abide his mercurial demeanor. Such a woman always wants the best of the man she has taken, not his weaknesses or disenchantments, whatever disappointments he carries. Some event, some doubt, has invaded him like an illness. He is not the man I married. I do not know what he is.

He wanders the periphery at night like a ghost of the battlements, convincing himself that Indian attacks impend, or that outlaws gather in the darkness. Even the beggars laugh at him, the basest drunkards. They call him vile names and have worse ones for me. He does not seem to notice, only continues drifting the outskirts, gazing on the sierras even as the nightfall obscures them, as though the rocks might come to life with the departure of the sun. Last month he ordered a watchman of the town to be imprisoned, a boy of only nineteen with a mother to support, who left his post a moment to pass some innocent nonsense with a girl. His men whisper that he has a scheme to encircle all the settlement with a moat-and-breastworks, and to construct an iron caging around this whole house. Twice he has mustered the Guard to ride out to the mountains in the dead of midnight, only to return, weeks later, exhausted and sun-sick, with no prisoners taken and no weapons found, and his men ridden halfway to the grave. He walks all night and sleeps half the day, and often it is the dark of evening before he rises. I pass his door at noon to fearful cries from within. His drinking has become – no, has long been – excessive. I have even come to fear that his mind may be imperiled. Steffa, he had the servant remove every pier glass from the house. He told her, so she confided to me, that he could see 'specters' in their glasses. She will not be alone with him here any more and prefers to stay at a cabin in the town.

For a time I thought the cause must be something that happened in the War. I know he saw obscene sights, was responsible for some of them. You and I can imagine, from those dreadful nights at the hospital, what horrors he must have witnessed. He is tortured, I know, for so many of his men having died, and wracked by thoughts of their widows and children. He feels that he abandoned them, betrayed them in some way; was the very worst General in all the War. Every penny of his remuneration goes directly to a fund for them, and much of my allowance for these last several years, and almost all of the capital I have thus far received. (I beseech you not to speak of this to Papa or Attorney Graham. They would crucify me had they any inkling as to the truth of what has happened.)

His reluctance to discuss with me anything of the campaigns served only to fuel my impression that some unspeakable thing occurred, about which I did not know, and from which he wished to protect me. But when I ask him, tranquilly, as coolly as I can, he roars that my imagination will always be my curse and he had rather fight ten more wars, and lose another brigade, than to go on having to be 'its victim'. And there is a freezing, steely logic in his outbursts at such times, a pitiless hatred I cannot recognize. He will go again to Panama and this time not return; will go again into Nicaragua or Cuba or Mexico, where he claims to have associates but he will not tell me who they are, nor how they live, nor anything they do. And these threats I dread, for when he went away before, I had not the slightest idea as to when he would come back, if at all.

Then I must discover more of what happened at Tasmania, that accursed country whose very name I loathe. Some time ago, when I was on my passage out here from the States, I found a way of opening a box of his like a pitiful little sneak. I do not know what I sought: a reassurance, perhaps. What I found was a journal containing certain recollections of Con's. Passionate, adoring, full of longingly devoted sentiments. I should never have read them. I curse myself for having done so. But I think that he loved his first wife far more deeply than he had told me and perhaps has not mourned for her, and even still longs for her. Steffa, on my life, if a haunting is possible, that poor unhappy woman has crossed the oceans to this house.

I have heard him call her name from his room in the night, and the name of their poor dead child. It is a chilling sound. I hurry on by. I do not like what it makes me feel. I know that he keeps their anniversaries, even after all these years, and puts on black, and goes to the chapel, telling me he commemorates some relative in Ireland, or a comrade killed in the War. But it is those two sorrowing souls for whom he mourns; and I think he always shall.

Some time ago a boy was brought here to the house: a war-waif found by C and his deputies at a derelict mine last Christmas. Nothing is known of his parents, not even if they are living, nor where is his country, nor what can be his history. The child is a mute and we think a southerner. It is thought that he was a camp-follower with the rebels.

'What of that?' you will ask. Must we not remember charity? Oh Steffa, I can see your mild and beautiful eyes and feel your kind reproach. It has scalded me to the soul that the same man who has forbidden me a child could be fatherly to a boy that came out of the night like the rain – an associate of those who would have murdered him if they could – an urchin whose name he does not even know. Too well I am aware that I should be kinder, more forbearing – believe me, I loathe myself for my wretched selfishness – but *I cannot bear it more*, no matter how I have tried to. I have come to detest the very sight of the poor weird child, who comes and goes, and goes and comes like a spider. The sight of him is a reminder of all that has been prohibited. He appears in my dreams. He is everywhere I turn. As I eat, as I bathe, he comes out of the floor. Every knot in the walls, his eye is behind it.

Last night we quarrelled violently, C and I. Terrible things were said. I told him that the child must leave without further delay. He retaliated that it was impossible, ridiculed my wish, excoriated me for having expressed it. I contended that Con must find him a place at one of the mines, or with some merchant of the town who might want for an apprentice. These proposals were hurled back at me with screams of hatred. He would rather *I myself* forsook the house. Why could I not go? Did I not know he detested me? The sound of my voice. My snobbery and conceit. That he would visit – Steffa, he said this – with a woman of the town, before ever again he would come to me as a husband. These, and other cutting terrors he roared, until he drove me by his curses from the room. It is too heavy to bear. I will not bear it more. This is not why I am alive in the world.

I cannot ask you to lie, but if you could not tell Papa – at least not for the time being – I should be more than grateful; until I discover what to do and how I am to return to New York. I shall write him in a fortnight or so, when I know better what to say. Dear Steffa, pray for your girl. Life is thin.

The sun is risen. Pray for me, Malinche. And pray harder for Con, I beg you.

Your loving and sorry sister,

L

∇

CHAPTER 47

SURVEILLANCE

A stranger in town – A fire burns long in Redemption

THURSDAY, AUGUST 23RD, 1866. SECOND WATCH.

10.14 a.m. O'Keeffe left the residence and proceeded towards the Legislative Office, accompannied [*sic*] by the boy. There conducted meeting with man identified as Captain James Fitzgibbon, United States Navy, though the latter in civilian clothing. Boy witnessed repeatedly in window of office.

11.35 a.m. Departed the office and went into John Grady's Alehouse, taking the boy and the dog in their company. Purpose of Fitzgibbon unclear. Has been in the town approximately one week. Rumors of secret shipment? They were encountered by Patrick Vinson and other disreputables in the Alehouse. Vinson started a quarrel about his pay.

Observer II notes: at five minutes of noon, three carts drew up before the residence, each driven by a masked man. One took up a sentry position at the southern end of the lane with a pistol forbidding access. His fellows entered the house and quickly set to emptying it of many furnishings, books, a camera & tripod, etc, loading same into carts, directed by LCO'K. Presently Marshal J. Calhoun arrived and challenged man acting as sentry. Tore off his bandanna. The man was a Chinee. Said he had been hired by the Governor's wife.

Calhoun entered the house. Left four minutes later and ran toward Legislative Office. At twenty-one minutes after noon LCO'K emerged from the house, tearful. Was pursued by the Negress who was pleading with her not to go. LCO'K entered the second of the carts. All three drove away quickly toward the south.

Subject did not return from the Legislative Office until ten after four. Visibly inebriated. Extraordinary scene ensued. Over two hours and a half, assisted by the boy, he removed a very large quantity of domestic and other items from the property – books, furnishings, lady's clothing, hatboxes – made a pile of them to the rear of the house and set it alight, dousing the whole with a flagon of lamp oil. A large painting of a savage, brought by LCO'K, he smashed to pieces with a wood-ax and threw same onto the flames with the rest. Calhoun came and tried to stop him. But he would not be stopped. The fire yet burning as I write.

∇

CHAPTER 48

AND HERE IS A RING, A RING OF GOLD, SET WI' THE PRECIOUS STONE. HE PRAYS YOU COME TO SILVERTON WOOD AND ASK THE LEAVE OF NONE

A Goodly Priest – An assignation with outlaws
The traitor Patrick Vinson – A plan to go into Canada

On the night of August 26th, 1866, Father Jeremiah O'Reilly is awoken by three callers to his cabin. He is hand-bound and hooded and taken away by the men. They ride for perhaps two hours.

He is unhooded in a clearing. The surrounding pines are thick. By the moonlight he sees an assembly of heavily armed guerrillas. A Confederate banner has been slung between two junipers. Someone is strumming a guitar.

No harm is plotted against him, one of the masked men assures. He is needed for a work of God. An apology is offered with food and drink – a little wine only, for the sake of the stomach. He may walk about the camp but not stray too far. He is asked, if he will, to be patient.

He walks about the camp, speaking to any man who greets him. Some of them request to pray. He speaks quietly, gently, and he finds that his apprehensions are diminished by the starlit prayerfulness. He does not ask questions. It is obvious who the men are. For a son of the gospel, no person is untouchable. Every sinner is some mother's child.

From the tent comes their leader, who is aged about thirty. His eyes are a striking china-blue. A Catholic, he wishes to make confession. He kneels on the forest floor and asks forgiveness of God, for his sins have been many and brutal. In a time of war, hard things are done, and he

273

did not always pause to examine his conscience before doing them. He considered himself a soldier, though they have called him a murderer. If a murderer is what he is, he is sorry.

Next from the tent comes a ghostly girl, clothed in the apparel of a man. She is pallid and looks ill. She is with child, she tells the priest. He gives a general absolution, for she cannot now remember all her sins. Among them was the fact that she had prayed to voudoun Gods. She has lived a fallen life.

The ways of the Lord are mysterious, reflects the priest. Unwise, the man who questions them. Happy night when two souls are returned to the claim of the Prince who bled between thieves.

There is one further service he is required to perform. He balks. It is impossible, he says. Such a thing cannot be done without adequate preparation. There are rules, procedures: it is a matter of canon law. It is explained to Father O'Reilly that the requirements of the Pontificate will have to be set aside in this case.

They are married, Eliza Mooney and Cole John McLaurenson, by a priest with a gun to his temple. No McLaurenson child will enter the world a bastard. God, it is hoped, will understand. The bride has seen the cruelties of the world to the fatherless. Her child will have the protection of a surname.

It is hard to speak the rite in such circumstances as these but it is made clear to him, repeatedly, in unadorned words, that the sun will come up on a matrimony. When he inquires of the bride if she will take this man, she answers, with calm firmness, that she will. Quite sure, she says. She has not been compelled. As a matter of fact, she was instigator. She is owed amends for a deeply grave wrong. This marriage is what she has demanded. The father of her child may have been kin to the groom. He is now deceased, it is sworn. The ring is a quarter with its center shot out. She greases it onto her finger.

The priest is taken back to his cabin near New Lochaber, given seven hundred Yankee dollars for his work among the Cœur d'Alènes, and warned that if ever he breathes a word to deny this marriage, his head will not be found for burial. He must write in his holy book that the ceremony was performed, the date, the names, the names of the witnesses, and register that paper with whoever needs to see it, and never in his life refute it. It is not the last shotgun wedding at which he will ever officiate, but it will probably be the only one, so he often reflects, where the weaponry was wielded by the groom.

The Register of Marriages records the bare facts. *Eliza Mooney, spinster; Baton Rouge, Louisiana. C.J. McLaurenson, smallfarmer; Tennessee.* There is an addition to the document, a poignant detail: 'Only daughter of Mary Mooney, of Connemara, Ireland; missing, presumed deceased, in Louisiana.'

Eliza McLaurenson and her outlaw husband retire to their separate tentquarters. They are kin now, they have agreed, but since there is no natural fondness, she will not be forced to conjugal servitude. It is better, for that promise, that they take their rest alone. Man awakens beside a woman, so her husband avers, nature and his loneliness can conspire in the darkness. It has been six long years since he lay by a girl. He might not be capable of battle.

'I got lusts,' he says. 'The devil ever which where. I told you the thoughts blow through my head ever day, you'd think I was evil itself.'

'I seen evil,' she says. 'Seem the whole world got evil.'

'Seem to me I got more of it than most.'

She has no interest in hearing his truer confessions; but he seems purposed to tell her, so she listens. There will always be men who assume you wish to attend to their guilt, especially when they have paid for your time. They think you will be relieved only to have to listen, but sometimes it is less taxing to lay down for them.

'I's married one time . . . She's Irish as me . . . People was Donegal County. Not a drop of Yankee in her. Good; pure. But come to where I was false to my wife. Had a fancygal I go to trickin with in Clarksville; in a "house". I's sixteen an a half. Figured pretty was the thing. But pretty aint the thing. Who you fix to is the thing. And my wife got took away I believe for a chastisement. Weren't wedded two year, she got a snakebite and die. Cottonmouth in a river, where they don't never bite. Washin her hair. Then she dead in the water. And our child in her belly, so the doctor said me later. And that what come out when a man break his vow. Mountain of judgment on his head.'

'Why you tellin me anyways? I dont care to know it.'

'Moughten care to know it but it wiser you do. No one ever gonna harm you – ary that child in you neither. And I give you my oath-of-blood. You remember it, girl. Whatever way you want it, that's how it gonna come.'

'I told you before. Only one last thing I want.'

'Be warmer in Mexico.'

'We aint goin to no Mexico.'

'This brother of yourn . . . You know where he at?'

'If I'd knowed I'd of told you. Canada's all I know. I dont hardly know that much. I'm guessin.'

'Canada bout the size of the moon, is all.'

'He's my blood,' she says. 'Aint no one belong to me left.'

'He want that you find him?'

'Kinda question is that?'

'Then, that's what you want – that what's gonna happen in a while. Got a fish to catch me first, couple things want done. Then Canada sound fine for a season or two. Party up Quebec owe me money.'

She lies on her palliasse looking up at the stars through a rent in the canvas roof. Strange wedding night for Eliza. She is thinking of her mother. Miss Havisham in the burning gown.

It is three hours before dawn when the camp is awoken. They ride out in a hurry, some of them hardly even dressed. It is clear to the forest-bride that most of them don't know what is happening. She herself does not know. But she follows.

There is a new man in the company. Another Irishman she thinks. They call him Patrick Vinson. He looks edgy and cold. Sudden noises make him uneasy. And some of the other men do not seem to like Patrick Vinson. There are murmurings behind his back.

You cannot trust a turncoat. *He's right enough, hold your pike.* Man betrays his friends, he'll turn us in, too. *Cole knows what he's at.* Sure as Hell hope so. *Trust a traitor bout as far as I could spit me a rat. For that's all he is. A vermin.*

They stop at Poulanassy Cross to give the horses a breath and for some of the men to use the bushes. Dawn on Gallows Mountain. A broken fingernail of moon. She sees Vinson remove an object from the pocket of his longcoat and toss it among the rocks by the roadside. Curious, she dismounts and picks it from the stones. It is a tin-colored star, heavily scratched and bent-out. The badge of a deputy sheriff.

Onward they ride, toward the string of the Missouri, now visible in the scree valley below. And off it, a narrow tributary wends toward those rapids. You can see the whitening frothcloud even from here. Where are they going? What violence is coming?. The snorts of the wearying horses.

She is asked to fix breakfast of a brace of shot rabbits for her husband and the traitor Patrick Vinson. She watches while the other men hack down the oaks on the bank, toppling them into the river. They work

276

quickly, efficiently, in tight, small teams: two men sawing, a third with a sledgehammer, a fourth with a tackle-and-chain. They go to singing as they sweat but are ordered not to sing. By eight of the morning, the river is barricaded. Not even a canoe could pass.

The crakes whistling fiercely. A wolf ranging the cliff top. The toil-stained, silent men.

'You boys done a job,' her husband says. 'Aint a slackerman the whole crew round. Today we give the Yankee a sore, hard lesson. Sore, hard lesson he won't never forget. I expect ever man here to conduct himself with honor. Valor aint enough. So's you know where I stand. Ninety-nine and a half won't do. We are soldiers of the Confederate States of America. Blood of the patriots is not to be dishonored. Remember it today and be true to the cause. Would you gentlemen do me the honor of kneeling with me a moment? And I wish we would all raise a hand.

'Lord of Battles, God, by whose alone power and conversation we all live, and move, and have our being, we are gathered in the glory of Thy creation. We are come of many corners of this darkened Republic, justified to the work of the righteous man. We pray mercy on the enemy who this day shall see Thee; Thy courage to ourselves, Thy praise be ever on our lips. May not a one of us stray in the errors of rapine, or bring shame on the name of his parents or place. Did we stumble, give us heart. Did we fall, raise us high. Let Thy vengeance be mighty but swift. Gentlemen – patriots – free men of the south: here beginneth the end of that horrid abomination – that vile Satanic scheme named the United States. Shall we gather at the river?'

Mumbles of assent.

'*Shall we gather at the river?*'

'Woorah! . . . Yeah, sir! . . . Fontenoy! . . . Faugh-a-balla!'

'Let me hear an Amen, boys.'

'Amen. Amen!'

'Did I hear a Gloryglory?'

'Glory-oh. Glory-high!'

'*An't* there witness here among us know how to *shout* a littlebit?'

The rebel yell rises as they stand to their feet. That high, cold sound like a Connemara keening. The leader punches the air as they whoo and yip around him.

'Come time to hunt buffalo,' he tells them.

Vinson crosses himself beside him, looking gray, enfeebled. In his bearing, the loneliness of the defector. Sometimes he glances at her, as though he knows her from someplace. She finds herself looking away.

You cannot stare directly into a Judas's eyes. Mamo used to call it bad voodoo.

∇

CHAPTER 49

THE WRECKING BY THE CONFEDERATE BANDIT COLE JOHN MCLAURENSON OF THE SECRET FEDERAL STEAMSHIP WILLIAM H. HARRISON NEAR FORT CODY, THE MOUNTAIN TERRITORY, IN 1866

or

THE LAY OF THE LONESOME OAKS

'Grampus?' the innocent ast one night, 'on the road next t'Whippoorwill
    Creek,
There's a spot, Momma hold, where we mus' hurry by, and nevermore
    tarry to speak.'
Wull, the old-timer smiled at the curious child but his eyes was grum
    as the dawn.
It happen back sixty-six, he said: the summer your Momma was born.

Wull, a bunch of us buckies was whompin it up at the Broken Bone
    Saloon,
When in through the shove, with a pistol in glove, hurries Marshal
    John Calhoun.
'Honest men! Laivee ho! up to Liberty Falls, for to see what them
    renegade done!
For they've wrecked-up the Federal steamship, boys, and away to the
    mountains run.'

Out rapid we rode, long the Sullivan Road, and we went a precarious
    speed;
For McLaurenson's men muss be ridin' again, to have wrought this
    nefarious deed.
Sixty oaks did they fell on Ole Muddy's high swell, for to barricade up
    the wide course,
And the Federal goldship *Harrison*, boys, they've wrecked without speck
    of remorse.

Her pilot, Tom Hanley, they've shot from the banks, her paddle-wheel
    riddled with lead,
So the ship did careen in the current so mean as she spun to her
    treacherous bed.
She was broke on the rapids at Donegal Gulch; o'er the rocks to her
    doom did she thunder:
Over Liberty Falls into Whippoorwill Creek, where the outlaws was
    waitin to plunder.

All survivors was murdered with nary a prayer by McLaurenson's
    pitiless pack;
And her load it was stole from her smashed-open hold, as she sunk in
    the torrent so black.
As he rode from that water, that whirlpool of slaughter, he's cussed
    them in cruel farewell:
'God drown all Yankee vessels, you dogs – and wreck them down to Hell!'

Ingelmann, Connolly, Livingston, Cox: pray pity upon their wives.
Phelan, O'Donnell, McTaggart, McNeill, and Colclough lost their lives.
The brothers Dinneen, John Hall, freed slave, brave Captain James
    Fitzgibbon.
In the year of eighteen sixty-six, on August twenty-seven.

Fourteen friends met their end that dawn, in Missouri's crimsoned
    foam;
And fourteen mothers did weep for sons that would nevermore sail
    home.
Sorry luck to that hand an' his stone-heart band to commit such a
    cowardly wrong;
For they've wrecked-up the Federal goldship, boys; and away to the
    mountains run.

Now there's some as believe, on a wintry eve, as you ride over
    Whippoorwill Creek,
When the swell runs high, and the wind blows mean, you can hear an
    eerie shriek.
Not a seed ever growed by that cursèd road near the murdered
    Harrison's rest –
But fourteen lonesome, withered oaks, where fourteen vultures nest.

∇∇∇

PART VIII

THE MAPMAKER

Erin go Bray: An Irish Field Officer on his Charger
Print displayed on the office wall of John Knox Trevanion,
newspaper editor, Redemption Falls

This disgusting Celtic viper . . . and his troop of yammering troglodytes have made the town a capital of drunkenness, corruption and filth. He has no allegiance to anything save his own depraved ambition. His flag is a greenback, his emblem a whiskey bottle. No robbery, great or small, is perpetrated in this Territory without tribute being paid to this loathsome despot. He flaunts love for the Union, now 'respect' for the South, 'forgiveness' for her admirers when we are not ashamed but PROUD. He would line the banks of the Missouri from here to St Louis with crucified Negroes if he thought it would preserve his power. We have lately finished a war. Do you wish to start another? . . . Take a heed now, Sir, for we shall not warn you again. It is time that his subtraction from this Territory were effected, else the consequences were a matter for your conscience, not ours. An Irish jig is a memorable thing to watch. Particularly when its performer is suspended from a tree.

Sir, we are

Certain Vigilant Citizens.

Letter about O'Keeffe,
sent anonymously to President Johnson, September 1866

CHAPTER 50

SURVIVING PAGES FROM A JOURNAL

'BY CAPTAIN A.M.W.'†

Room IX, Hotel Freundschaft, Redemption Falls.
October 31st: All Hallows' Eve, 1866.
Fourteen minutes of midnight.
Night III

I have just now returned from my first visit to the Governor – an Irishman by birth as well as in certain regrettable habits. The night is extremely cold – minus 14 degrees, a significant diminution from the seasonal average, but the wind they call 'the snow eater' is coming from the west so that the morning may commence a thaw. A tornado is said to be drifting southerly from Alberta. The natives blather of ancestors.

The proprietress, a widow, a raw-faced Valkyrie, is hurrying about the premises, nailing closed the casement shutters. Below me, in the saloon, one of the miners is singing queer ballads: serenades to Lady Bottle and the outlaw Johnny Thunders. An out-of-tune banjo spangles like an abscess. I would strangle my mother to stop it.

I fear I am unwell. The shingles are clattering. Some creature lollops nightly in the crawlspace of the attic above me; I hear the scutter of its claws on the boards. All about me, this very edifice gives out windblown creaks and groans, wheezing in the blow, whimpering, juddering, as a vessel snowed under by tumultuous seas. My lantern flame twists with every slam of a lattice, with each remote blow of the widow's hammer.

† Written on a noteblock of graph paper of the stamp used by the US Corps of Cartographers, these are the only pages remaining of what was perhaps a much lengthier document. It would be stolen from Winterton's room at the Freundschaft Hotel on Christmas Morning, 1866 (possibly by Frieda Perlmann, a prostitute with whom he had passed much of the night), and later found in a midden-heap in the town.

Weird, black-dark, these songs of the miners. The seams in which man roots for his distractions.

> *The child did say, What shall be my name?*
> *Good steward, tell to me;*
> *Thy name shall be 'Poor Disawear',*
> *Thy fate shall crueller be.*

My dreams, since I am fevered, are grown macabre as a hermit's. Yester-evening I had a nightmare in which this room was plunged into churning water, so that I and my bunk were lofted upwards at the rafters. Aghast, I screamed out; yet my voice was not my own, but the death-wail of a Confederate trooper I saw disemboweled at Chickamauga. Next, I was astride a roofbeam of the drowned garret, being tumbled down the Niagara that the street outside had become. Onward we plunged, here capsized, now upright, spinning in the spume like a dismasted boat. The mountains encircling us at every turn seemed to liquefy as I watched them to gargantuan waves, to breakers the size of alps. To the north, I saw the pitiless eye of the sun. A voice was beseeching: *Murder me, brother!*

> *Oh father dear, I long to hear*
> *You speak of Erin's isle.*

There are trees a thousand years old in this Territory. When Chaucer was in swaddles, they were groaning. The wind screams down over dog-towns and wheel-ruts, over tepees and cabins, through mineshafts and deserted forts, from Lewis and Clarke's Pass to the shores of Devil's Lake, obscuring man's efforts in dust and snow.

The acid-yellow stink in the streets revolts. The Gods of sewerage go unobserved here.

In all the immense continent of North America, I do not believe that there can exist a wilderness more woebegone and storm-swept. Death Valley would seem a Parisian garden beside it, the wastes of Alaska a pleasure dome. There is but one gazetteer, and this unfinished; it was commenced by a Piedmontese Jesuit – this we are told – who ventured into the badlands to convert the indigenes. A fur-trapper happened on his skeleton six months afterwards, lashed to a tree, manuscript wedged betwixt its ribs. The epistle was published within the month (of course), dismayingly unproofed, & in many pirated editions. It is frightful, blowy stuff, an ecstasy of adjectival slobbering. Perhaps the killers were literary critics.

Awesome this MASEJTY, these catedrals of rock,
the falls of her cataracts, diamond-rainbow'd,
thunderous, cascading as though from the
cerulean haevens. Witness, Traveller!, and know
thou art DUST. Astonishing landscape!
Psalmody of mother nature! Hosanna the
TERRIBLE GRACE of thy Creator!

Poor reverend Punchinello, if ever he existed. As to which, I may say, I have the misgivings of doubting Thomas. Show me the wounds, friend, show me the wounds, else re-scabbard your exclamation points. Yet maybe he did. Unfortunate Loyolan. If his saint gazes down from some zone of the hereafter, may piety console for the want of his royalties *in secula seculorem, Amen.*

The veracity of his words I am forced to concede – of some of them, at any rate – precision, Quasimodo! – but I cannot find it in my constitution to care for such a very wilderness. Its beauty is exhausting; its scale too epic, its shapes too uneven for the admirer of our gridded-out American cities, where even the baffled immigrant, still finding his land-legs, may discover an immediate way. In any case, the word 'landscape' should be reserved, exclusively, for paintings. It is decidedly not a cartographical term.

I am told that, in the summer, the sun pummels this country like a steam-hammer, that beasts drop dead of thirst, and men see visions that madden them; but with a mean temperature of 86 degrees and a half – the data are patchy, nonetheless one can estimate – one cannot help but wonder can it be truly that severe. Tonight, with the crusting of glaze-ice on the mere, and the plangent mewling of the chinook in the sequoias, such tales, at least to me, seem scarcely possible to credit. I imagine they are told in order to perturb the interloper, for the Redemptionites, like all colonists, love to do that. It appears to give them pleasure to disconcert the outsider. Or perhaps it binds them tighter, for they themselves are outsiders, and always will be strangers, did they live here a hundred years and stamp Pappy's cognomen onto every last pebble. They like to watch us dance within their circle of horrors. Well, that is all right: Quasimodo can dance a little.

And many of these fictions boast a recurring protagonist. The Governor 'drinks blood.' He 'lay with a savage-woman' at Tasmania. An 'Houngan', a druid of the vudoo cult, schooled him in Louisiana to call the dead from their graves. He is an eater of hashiesh. His presence sickens livestock. He is 'Grand Cyclops' of a sect of behooded apostles, which congregates on Gallows Mountain to chant 'the black Mass.' A cyclopaedia of spookery the Governor has inspired: County Wexford's most infamous warlock!

Damn this racked body, how I wish I could escape it. The bowel spasms which I suffered at San Francisco are come at me again, now I am into this Republic of stones. My temples smolder. My *fingernails* throb. (Can that be possible, or do I hallucinate more?) It seems to me, now, that my very eyeballs sweat. I am almost disinclined to display myself in the street downstairs, so perpetual the extruding of my fluids. The widow advises that I must take *ein Schluck Wasser*, but yet, when I do, it tastes fetid completely, of liquefied gun-smoke or wrung-out rags. This pain behind the sinuses, it scours and scalds; this thirst will not be slaked. Drank one of the barbiturics I had of the wheelwright. Little effect. Think I was swindled. Doubtless, some witch of the locale could concoct me a medicament. *Die Witwe* speaks often of puissant herbs, would herself have been formerly candidate for the kindling. She has taken rather a fancy to my person, I believe, & often smiles (I think it is a smile) benevolently (I think it is benevolence) as I shuffle her ominous corridors. Remarkable, I have found: how some women admire a hideous looking man. Dear Christ, for the reassuring tedium of the east, where trails are straight and widows wartless.

Here we shiver tonight, in this crater of blasted gulches, encircled by fastnesses and reeks so colossal that their pinnacles disappear into veneers of stratocumulus. Some of the higher peaks have never been scaled. Most of even the lower have no track the fleetest mule could go. How ever they are to be triangulated, measured accurately, eludes me. But a solution must be contrived, and it will be.

> *If, as in epochs long immemorial, before ever Christian illumined the Paganlands with the LAMP OF GOSPIL TRUTH, those crags were to groan and quake them but an inch, all trace of mortal intercourse with this unfathomed dominion should be obliterated, fossilized in ghostly remembrance.*

Ghostly, indeed. As though ghosts remember anything. Suffering such bilge, such agitated strainings, one would imagine the Enlightenment had never occurred. Oh, scrupulous Mercator, you would loathe it out here; you would hate what it *does* to those who describe it. And yet, when one walks a league unaccompanied in this country, one approaches a comprehension of why description crumbles to cliché. Land is like music, for it resembles nothing but itself. We can only speak about it in translation: for this reason we have poets – also, as it may be, maps. This mountainplace is a fugue of despair and fracturedness. But I shall make of it Bach . . .†

. . . Today, in the austere foothills that outcrop west of Arroyo de Maria, I stopped to replenish my gourd and correct some calculations in my notebook, when I observed, in the creek, gliding out of the osiers, a strangely shaped fish with silver-scarlet scales, which belonged to no genus my amateur biology could name. Its little graceful ballet of the shallows quite enchanted, and I sate me on a boulder to attempt to sketch it. So still was the scene, so silent the surrounds, that one fancied one could hear even the minuscule bubbles as they lipped and broke asunder in the brook.

Foolish, foolish. Allowed my thoughts to wander toward her. Our time at New York. Certain hours we trudged together. Like a schoolboy and his first sweetheart on some glum little tryst and no money to go in someplace out of the rain. Funny little habit, that she would never say my name aloud. Often wondered why not. But she never would tell. An intimacy too far, perhaps.

Since my descent among the Redeemed on Monday afternoon, not a trace of my prey in the town. No one mentions her, ever. She is like a bad smell. No one answers any question, whether subtle or blunt. She does not leave the house or appear in its windows. Not even to the chapel goeth my saint.

Had hoped not to alarm her; to communicate that I was come – perhaps – sweetest thought – even to meet away from scrutiny; to beg one last time would she hear Quasimodo's case. I could wait no longer. I must go to the residence tonight. The bubbling of the stream was not softer than her laugh. The thought of her lips was as a drug-dream.

Suddenly there was a plunging of water – no, a fantastic explosion! A big male eagle, as beefy as a chimp, had swooped, and seized my piscine model in one of his talons, and already wheeled away, even as I sputtered and spat. Drenched, I watched the lordly animal ascend towards a

† There follows a great deal more of this sort of material, in essence pointing out that the Mountain Territory is mountainous.

distant summit, now beating with steady might, now borne sidewise on the windstream, until it and its quarry were infinitesimal specks, and the glare of the sunlight on the snow-silvered fleetings meant I could watch no more. What a death!, I thought, if death must come. But then I saw something just every degree as startling.

High on a granite precipice, half a mile into the skies, a thread of purple smoke was rising in the air from some eyrie. A tiny man was up there: a human ant. I saw the glint of his scope as he studied me.

What hideaways must abound in those clefts and giddying canyons. Imagine what the eagle's cold eye reflects! Desperadoes and their hoards. Deserters from the war. Mountain-men whose collation of favorite choice is the liver of a strangled Blackfoot.

> *I'll be the man to lead the van,*
> *Beneath the flag of green.*
> *Then loud and high, we'll raise the cry:*
> *Revenge for Skibbereen.*

Down here in the colony, the settlers look like the savages: craggy, resentful, whipped. Not every one is bad; indeed, most appear industrious – but few enough inhabitants of such a dolorous outpost are not on the lam from something troublesome. In this I do not condemn them. Nor do I differ from them. It is an American entitlement, to go where one will. To resume one's story over if the plot does not thicken to one's taste. This should be the motto of our reconstructing Republic: The maps are not agreed. The atlas is unfinished. It contains so many extents that are consolingly blank. Come hither, pretty pilgrim: fill me.†

Prussian, Irishman, Frenchman, Hollander: all Europe is here, in bedraggled embodiments, with Confederate sniper, Union dragoon, disgraced overseer and manumitted slave. Hucksstresses, mountebanks, carpenters, card-sharps; Chinamen, gold-diggers, dealers in insurances. None is what he appears. All wear a mask. The slave-catcher now the gunsmith, the defaulter the churchwarden, the wife-poisoner sells millinery, the bigamist now a bachelor. The butcher, who avows himself long a friend of the Union, danced a jig at the news of Lincoln's

---

† Winterton's empathy with the desire of certain of his fellow citizens to 'go where one will' may have been deepened by the fact that he had left gambling debts of almost twenty thousand dollars in New York at the time he wrote the journal.

slaughter. The meats in his window are every day arranged in such a manner as to form the bloodied characters 'S. S. T' – many who pass can decipher their covert meaning.† Aye, all possess knowledge of some secretive variety. They nod at one another like disciples of a craft. Even their children seem withered by knowledge. They glower up as one rides past, ironed out of innocence, somehow. And the Governor lords it over this rubble-strewn Lilliput, 'high on ze goose', as the widow's parlance has it, despised by nigh on everyone he subjects. In this, at least, he fulfills a useful function. They prattle of him like Hottentots in the shadow of Baal, as tribesmen presided over by Nobodaddy. Truly he brings unity to this cavalcade of the murmurous. Having now made his acquaintance, I understand some of the stories.

His residence is set apart, at the northern periphery of the settlement, a two-story log-house with cut-stone chimneybreast, in a section whose shabby groggeries and suicide saloons are rumored nearly all to be brothels. Erected by navvies on a government contract, it was burned, & then bombed, before the builder was murdered by secessionists. Over its lintel is nailed the bleached skull of some long-extinct thing. A bannerless flagstaff stands sentry in the yard. All hail, thou lonesome totem.

A *mulatresse*, I presume a cook (she had bile on her apron), hauled open the front door, which is cast of studded iron, and at first seemed disinclined to concede me admission, even when I presented my carte-de-visite and rain-spattered papers of credential. She and Modo traded incomprehensibilities for a considerable time. Indeed, she appeared not to understand the English language, or, at least, my eastern manner of speaking it. Presently I became aware that Nubia and I were chaperoned. Out of the dimness behind her, I could detect the unmistakable rhythm of breathing. Some weighty presence was holding its counsel in the black, one sensed, and would not be the first to speak.

'Governor?' I ventured. 'Is that you, sir, within?'

No salutation came back from that lightless recess.

'My name is Winterton,' I said. 'I am on Federal Government business. I am come to see the Acting Governor. Is he in the house at present?'

---

† A curious sentence. The initials noticed by Winterton (and by others in the town) may have alluded to the words *Sic Semper Tyrannis* (Thus always to Tyrants), said by some witnesses to have been uttered by the assassin John Wilkes Booth from the stage of Ford's Theatre moments after shooting President Lincoln. The phrase is the motto of the state of Virginia.

The world exploded white! Terror squirted through my spine. The creature I had reckoned a man lunged forward from the gloom and sank its fangs into my glove, uttering a chain of petrifying snarls. I tore back from it, cursing, almost pissing with shock. Thank God, it had a shackle affixed to a clasp about its neck; but the ghoul tested the fetter severely as it strained toward my torso, maw dripping beads, 'til it was choking. Here was an extraordinarily massive and grubby dog – an Irish wolfhound, I think its breed is called. It had the dimensions of a small pony, of the kind used down pit-mines in England, and its eyes were the jasmine of butter gone rancid. Worse, the thing had a tumor on the side of its cheek, a furuncle or pustule of livid ruddiness, the size of a possum's head. No carnival of capering, God-abandoned freaks ever boasted such a dollar-maker.

'*Duggan*,' spoke a male's voice from the darkness behind the brute. Instantly it slunk down into a supine attitude, though it sustained an inhospitable scrutiny.

'I am not wounded,' I managed to call out. 'It is nothing. A graze only.'

From the passageway loomed the silhouette of a thickset man, his left hand clenching a twist of the fiend's chain in preparation – whether for restraint or release was not quite clear – the other clutching a stump of guttering tallowflame, the light of which refracted itself over his visible flesh.

'General O'Keeffe, sir?' I asked.

He gave me a meaning look.

'Who wants to know it?' came the sullen rejoinder.

Here loomed before me 'O'Keeffe of the Blade'. Old England's sworn foe; Young Ireland's banished hero. How many bitter nights had I prayed for his snuffing, that one, only one, of the millions of bullets that flew in the War would free her.

His face is dark, almost Romany-dark, with black eyes quite sunken, although with a penetrative, distrustful glimmer, and a flaccid gray mustache that makes him look somehow defeated. The hair is a web of chaotic dirty curls, thinned severely at the temples, Apache-braided at the rear. There is something of Davis, the crushed rebel president: the deeply graven frown-lines, the air of lugubrious dignity. He holds himself stiffly, a degree too erect, as a boxer attempting recuperation from a painful beating & not wanting to show himself whipped. The line of the nose is strong, vaguely Roman (lends hauteur), but the jowls quite slack like those of a bloodhound. He is not corpulent, exactly, as has been reported in the dossier, but perhaps five sizes stockier than in the wartime daguerreotypes, and wearier of countenance, and a little oily looking. The handsomeness is still evident (the ghost of it, at any rate); but the Governor has aged markedly since coming into the Territory. Did I not know he was forty-three, I might have added a decade to his span. His shirt was disarrayed; he wore no coat or stock. The leggings were of buckskin and were remarkably unclean. He had on him a firearm in an underarm holster: a Remington 1859, I am certain, from the shape and length of its butt.

'Captain Allen Winterton, sir, of the Corps of Cartography. I wrote you to say I was coming from Washington.'

He regarded me intensely, as though I had uttered some affront to him. Cerberus clanked over and commenced investigating my snow-flecked boots, now my cuffs, now my private person. A stomach-churning odor arose from its pelt, of ash and grease and dampened filth.

'I wrote you several times, General, but received no reply. Perhaps my dispatches failed to reach you. I am informed that there have been difficulties in that regard.'

'In which regard?' Now he watched me assessingly.

'With the mail. I mean with mail robberies. With the savages and so on.'

For what seemed endless moments he remained soundless as a Hindoo fakir. And an eerie sensation stole over me, soon, for which I can record no rational support, of impending violence of some fiercer kind than before. Putting plainly, I felt certain he had in mind to murder me then and there; and I realized I was thinking of ways to escape him. As though choked in the grip of a medium's presentiment, or magicked into a scene from some syphilitic's screechmare, it seemed that I saw myself fleeing through snow-blown ravines, with the Governor and his familiar in ravening pursuit. I can only put it down as some fleeting delusion my lately suspected fever had enkindled. It is odd (as we know) what the mind can do. Illness, I find, can sophisticate a thing.

'Are you armed?' he asked morosely, and I came back to myself. Now I could detect the curdled reek of whiskey on his breath.

I said that I bore a small pistol and unfastened my greatcoat to reveal it. His eyes did not stray southerly to take in my gun, but remained glued (their jellies rheumy) on my own.

He uttered a phrase in some weird language to the observing lacquey, whose only acknowledgment was an unfathomable nod; then turned about and hobbled back toward the interior quarters, trailed by the low-tailed, dismal hound, which paused now and anon to lick at the naked floorboards or push its dripping snout into crannies in the walls. I was not certain whether or not I was intended to go after, but since the cook did not shut the door against me, I mustered courage and entered.

I had not taken two paces over the door-stones when she commenced gesturing at my belt, in a manner of greatest insistence. I understood her to mean that I was to surrender her my weapon. This I did soon, for she was most persevering. I held it in her direction but she did not at first accept it. Suddenly, I apprehended that the woman was having some difficulty in seeing, and I was sorry for having erewhile thought badly of her.

Venturing down the corridor in the Governor's wake, I approached and entered after him into the house's core: a spacious if ascetic room, lit but dimly by candles and by the sputtering flames of a log-filled fire. Fuliginous and rank, the air all about us, and tainted very heavily with a choking redolence of scorched dust. Over the inglenook hung a work in oils, depicting a naval scene from the Revolutionary War; but zagged across the canvas was a faint smudge of dribbled magenta, as though a measure of hock, or a spurt of gore, had bedashed those cangled frigates. A Cheyenne head-dress did its wan best to decorate a pilaster, its feathers withered down to blanched-out stalks. There was a hideous example of the taxidermist's crime: a jackrabbit-head with the antlers of a young stag fixed on. Around this nightmare's neck depended a string of wolf's teeth. How vicious we are to the animals.

At the core of the *studio* squatted an unvarnished oaken table, substantial in appearance, though its plank-boards deeply excoriated, and defaced extensively by the spherical taints observable on the surfaces of bars in low saloons. As well, I noted an assortment of jagged abrasions in the tabletop, as though it had at one time been employed for butchery. Around it perched a half-dozen finely made chairs, which looked to this untutored eye to be Louis-Quatorze and brittle. An uneasy polygamy, these courtly Mademoiselles, with the uncouth old frontiersman they surrounded.

The remainder of the apartment was Dominican in its want of appurtenance, so that the effect of French frippery was to accentuate the severity. Puddle-stains were visible here and about on the floorboards; the worst had had sawdust haphazardly flung over them. Wind gusted coughingly through numerous apertures, some of which had been occluded with bungs of rag and other matter; but the drafts wavered the

294

candle flames which tussled weakly with the shadows, and the room seemed to wheeze like a moribund. This was far from the Fifth Avenue, from the mansions of Manhattan; one might have wandered into the shack of some boot-chewing prospector. There was no rug or dresser, neither chest, clock or bookshelf (which deficiency surprised me, given the Governor's literary bent, his celebrity as an *homme du monde*): nothing intended to supply more than frugal endurance. I formed the immediate intuition that here was a sanctum unsanctified by the recurrent presence in it of a lady. *Ubi est*, I wondered? Where was the beast's belle? A sickening idea licked me – that she had died.

The Governor was seated in presiding place at the board, his frockcoat draped untidily on the upright of his chair, at his hand a stone decanter and the remains of a repast. (The vittles had been toyed with, rather than consumed.) He had a wallet of papers opened before him on a little lectern, like a priest's. These he appeared to be studying with engrossed attention. A heap, promiscuously assembled, was amassing itself by his plate, for when he had finished reading some, he would toss them there.

For almost six minutes he perused, and some documents signed, and others impressed with wax and seal, bethumbing this, inscribing tinily on that, without condescending to glance at me even momentarily or otherwise concede my attendance. The man whose papers are of unavoidable importance – this was the attempted rôle. The performance did not surprise, far less offend me, self-abnegation being seldom encountered in persons of the political class. I have seen such overtures played out before, especially between men of relative power who do not know, as yet, which of them has the upper hand. One rather respected his efforts.

'Whiskey or mezcal,' he muttered bleakly, after a time. 'We can't get claret, which I'm sure you'd prefer.'

'Thank you, I am content with a cup of watered beer.'

'Be content with what you are offered. We have whiskey or mezcal.'

'Nothing, then, thank you, sir. I do not use the spirituous liquors.'

Now the eyes burned me again, baleful, inescapable. Here was the stare from which duelists had fled. One felt as a camphorized butterfly being skivered to a parchment. One could comprehend how men had marched into blizzards of cannonade at his directive; how striplings had bared breast to the foeman's bayonet rather than rake their commander's wrath. As well I could credit, which previously I could never, how the halls of our Republic had thrilled at his oratory in former times, how soberest burghers, neither sentimental nor susceptible, had stood up in parterres from Louisianne to the Pacific, the better to ovate his verbal firestorms. In short, he seemed possessed of lionly allure. It came clear to me why ladies had thronged at stage doors, there to plead a lock of his mane or a button of his weskit. And yet the metaphor is not quite an apposite figure, for cats slink subtly and thrive by outmaneuvering, whereas this Celt, if clever, has little craft. What he has is brute force, this grog-wrecked Vesuvius. Were the Governor a schoolmaster, he would not actually whip you; but the undeclared threat that he might change his mind would be violence enough to advance scholarship.

'You are from?'

'Boston, Governor.'

'I said where are you from?'

The fire was smoldering low in its grate. 'I was born at Deptford near London,' I allowed. 'My father, a tailor, came over in '49.'

'And how does England and England's queen?'

'I am American,' I said. 'My country is Massachusetts.'

'Empress of Ireland and India,' he scorned. 'I wonder the hag does not garb herself in a sari and Arans.'

'Trust me, General, I am no admirer of monarchies.'

His gaze was chilly as a beadle's before a beggar. 'Snow shall fall in the mountains of Hell before ever I trust an Englishman,' he said.

He went to slivering at a hank of elk with what appeared to be a hunting or fisherman's knife – it was at any rate a knife not invented for table-work – and tossing gristly scrags of it to the gulping dog, which had lain at his feet with its beard on the floor. At least, I assumed the hound the sole beneficiary of gubernatorial benevolence, but, as my eyes accustomed increasingly to the murk of the apartment, I was startled to perceive, in the shifting shadows of a corner, *the figure of a hunkering child*. Whether male or female I could not quite discern, for there was a strange girlishness about the features, so it seemed in the firelight. But the clothing was that of a boy.

The child regarded me sleepily, blinking like a calf. The face was so emaciated, so pitiful of expression, that it might have been fathered by the pen of Maestro E.† But alas, since the War, we know only too well,

---

† Possibly George Eliot, pseudonym of Mary Ann or Marian Evans (1819–80). Her novel *Silas Marner*, published 1861, featured a waiflike foundling boy. A copy was given by Lucia to Winterton as a gift during his recuperation at St Mary's Hospital, New York.

such urchins may be noticed in every county and quarter. But now – *mirabile dictu* – this seemed no kind of orphan, but a miniature fac-simile of my laconic host. The same dark complectedness, lack-luster demeanor, and worms of lank dirty hair. It occurred to me that the Governor had once sired a child, product (I refuse the usual word, for it is not the infant's fault) of the Australian, the Aboriginal attachment. It could surely not be possible? But no. It could not. My watcher had that peculiar solemnity, that gravity of outward show, which one observes in the physiognomy of the criminal orders, also in certain varieties of mendicant, and in southern Italians, also cockneys. Grimy nightgown and cap. A bone in the hands. The feet were unshod, the wrists twig-thin. All about, on the floor, was a rough circle of papers, some of which were scribbled upon with a charcoal. Mute as a stockfish the child looked at my face, but not as the world habitually gapes on my repulsiveness. I conjectured that this might be an invalid, or perhaps an unfortunate idiot of the kitchens, for my gaze was given back with the disturbing innocence of such persons. It was entirely, in short, as though I were not there; or as though I were innocuous weather.

All the while I regarded the apparition, and it regarded me, the Governor kept at his reading. I found myself wondering what foolscaps they were that so commanded his attention, but I feared that, did I inquire, he might fling them across the table in my face. The mastiff gave a start and growled resentfully at the hearth-light, as though some genie of the sparks had offended it. It padded into a corner, sniffing, slavering, and appeared to attempt copulation with a pillar. And soon it was performing an act upon a part of itself, which, if a man could do, he would do so often, that he would rarely egress from his rooms.

'I hope I do not interrupt at an inopportune moment,' I said at the last. 'I took the liberty of calling several times in recent days; but you were always away. There was in any event no answer.' And I added, I hope tactfully, though my eardrums were thumping: 'Mrs O'Keeffe, I assume, was also away.'

'The door is forbidden to be opened when I am not in the house. I have many enemies here. It is not like Washington.'

'Oh, a man can make enemies in Washington, too, sir,' I ventured, thinking a little levity might allay the somewhat Transylvanian ambience. He regarded me mirthlessly. 'So I see,' he said.

'General,' I recommenced, and I made to move toward him. 'Where you are!' he snapped drunkenly. 'Do not presume to approach my person without a bidding, else by Christ, sir, I'll school you in cleaner manners.'

One found oneself adopting an attitude of erect concentration, as an unkempt private recruit before his bawling better.

'Fasten the buttons of your coat, you insolent sloven. *Is this how you present to a General?*'

I did as he commanded, while he continued to regard me as something found under a rock.

'Your purpose, Mister. And fast.'

'I am come to make a reconnaissance for the mapping, General,' I told him. 'My information was that you had been informed. Forgive me if there has been a misunderstanding. The endeavor is to commence in the springtime, when the Missouri is navigable again. I am to survey this whole Territory from Fort Galloway to the *portage* at Inundation Pass.'

'Are you indeed?'

'I and my men.'

'What men are those? *Stand straight when you address me!*'

'They will come in the spring. My letters explained it. Men – an entire brigade – and cartographical equipment. A battalion of sappers. It will be a very great undertaking.'

'How valuable to learn, as Governor of this Territory, that our lords back in the States reckon us worthy of their admeasurement.'

Evidently, our encounter was going to continue difficult. Soon I wished that I had contrived our introduction to take place during daylight, for it was plain that any discussion under the present head would eventuate in discord, and I was very tired, and sick. But once into a scrape, we must press to the close. I could not depart the house without at least some news of her. Yet how to ask it without seeming to. My trade.

'There is the question of the outlaw depredators,' I took up. 'It was thought, by the Government, that you might require assistance in the matter. With the savages, also. The Government wishes you to enjoy its help.'

'Does it indeed? A Damascan conversion.'

'There is concern. That is, a feeling.' I stopped and began again. 'This character McLaurenson – this "Thunders" by soubriquet – is causing disquiet in high places since the piracy of the *Harrison*. His maraudings must be punished. The plunder must be recovered. It was thought that the existence of a comprehensive map must make the writ of the law run cleaner.'

'I have hunted that robbing rat whithersoever he rides in this Territory.

Run him down into Kanzas and over to Nebraska. Perhaps the Government would care to come here and see for itself that our criminals seem averse to present themselves for the gallows. Neither do they present for election.'

'I will emphasize your efforts in my report, sir, I assure you.'

'What report?'

'Why, nothing, sir. Nothing. My report to the Government.'

'Is it maps you scribble, Captain, or reports to the Government?'

'General, I – '

'Speak it out, Mister. Spare me evasions. You are come here to find my enemies a hemp for their noose.'

'I am not, sir,' I insisted peacefully. 'I know nothing of such matters. My interest is only in the lie of the land.'

'How many men have you killed?'

'None, sir,' I told him.

'I suppose you served in the War? In which campaigns?'

'I had not that honor, General. The injuries you see unfitted me. A substitute went in my stead.'

He gave a disdainful scoff and stabbed at the roast meat before him. And I thought I heard him imprecate, but could not discern his words.

'The man was well paid,' I insisted on saying. 'He was a poor man, an immigrant. He needed the wherewithal.'

'More than he needed his life, do you reckon?'

'I am not in a position to say what became of the man. Whether or not he fell, I mean.'

'Men do not *fall* in a war, sir. They die! Do you mind me? *War is not a map. It is real.*'

The volume, but more the wolfishness of the snarl quite shocked me. A string of saliva moistened his goatee and he wristed it away desultorily.†

For a moment I was beaten as to know how best to respond. As though detecting my indecision, he spoke again, loathsomely, talking himself the while into a profundity of anger, which seemed, as often happens, to

---

† By far the strangest passage in Winterton's journal. I have never been able to explain why Winterton represented himself to O'Keeffe as a non-combatant in the War. In fact, as a professional soldier from 1858, he had seen a great deal more combat than had O'Keeffe himself. There must have been a reason for such a calculated falsehood, but it is beyond me to know what it is.

generate no relief in the speaker but merely to stoke itself harder. To reproduce the obscene soliloquy would require several paragraphs, but I do not intend here to record the locutions, a good number of which did not comport with the decorum of his office, and in truth I should like to forget them. It is not a fair thing to put down the spewings of a man when he is under the influence of a regrettable indulgence. It will suffice to note that their conclusion was the following couplet, which was delivered as though to some long-detested foe; not to a fellow servant of the United States government whose wisdom, after all, had placed both of us in that room.

'A cancer, you and your ilk of Catholic-hating cowards. To think I sent boys to the shambles in the name of such trash.'

It was then that I saw into the depth of his unhappiness. And I resolved to grope beyond the venomous fruit of his slight, to whatever execrable root bore it. My dossier has made it clear that he was raised under the dominion of popery, as are by far the greater number of his unfortunate countrymen. And yet, as we know, they love this Republic fiercely, and are not unintelligent, be they quick to emotional eruptions. Any fair-minded man can conceive how bitter their fate has been: to have had to flee their birth-land, from starvation and despotism, from that same hideous tyranny of hereditary princelings which once held our own fathers in bondage.

Unhappy Ireland. Her unhappy sons. Where ever should we be without them? Moreover, one can but imagine the pain of such a man as the Governor, the thoughts which must have tortured what was then a taut mind as in chains he watched the mountains of her receding coast. It was in this spirit that next I spoke, as placably and comradely as I could in the circumstance, for sometimes it is necessary to bite on an insult, the better to eat the bread of fellowship again.

'Forgive me, General, if I someway offended you. Your service during the War was exemplary, and that of your countrymen. All of us who love liberty owe you a debt. If I may say so, it is an honor to be able to thank you in person. You and of course Mrs O'Keeffe.'

Nothing to my maggot. The shark did not nibble. I heard a party of roisterers pass by in the lane. They were singing a mocking song.

'As to creed,' I continued (hoping to overlie the scornful serenade), 'my father was a Methodist; my mother's people were Northumbrian Quakers. They tried to assist Ireland in her years of hunger. I know that many of your motherland's patriots were of the reformed tradition, as are many of your friends, who write and speak of you admiringly. They speak of a man without a grain of bigotry. They speak, if one may say so, of a hero.'

He answered me not. Perhaps he knew – I think he did – that some of what I had said was more obsequious than accurate. Indeed, had his command not been terminated under difficult circumstances, probably he would not be sitting in this forlorn Territory tonight. None of this I mentioned to him, naturally enough. I did not wish to wrench the poultice from the wound of his ambitions. Few of us, truly, would survive that experience. I, for one, would be destroyed by it.

'Permit an apology, Captain,' he said, never uplifting his countenance. 'I should not have spoken as I did. I disgust myself, always.'

'Sir, I beg you, please do not speak of – '

'I am loathsome. I ought to know it. In the War, I was nothing. I let thousands who trusted me die. I should have told them to go home. You will have heard the talk at Washington. The talk of my failure and removal.'

His words were louchely slurred, and I felt sorry for him, I own it. It is wrenching to see a large-bodied man in distress, as awful as to see a frightened child. My conscience was ashamed for the wrongs I had done him – nigglingly ashamed – a glow-worm's light – and for the graver robbery yet to be committed. I could see, when she came away with me, that it would murder what was left of him; and I wished some other denouement were possible.

'My prayer, sir, like yours – my sincerest hope – is that children such as our companion, that little one by the hearth, will be spared the terrible experience, for all their lives, of war between American brothers.'

No reply he offered. No clue as to the fire-elf's identity. And I played a rather reckless hand.

'Your child is a credit, if I may say so, sir,' I said. 'Possessed of the father's bearing.'

He gazed up at me as though I had spat upon him, his features distended by pain. And I was harrowed to see those insensate eyes, whose pitiless stare had so recently disconcerted me, now dampened by an excess of feeling. 'Brute,' he spoke bleakly. 'How is my child here?'

'Why, there, sir – ,' I began, but now the Governor lurched from his seat. A moment passed. I felt rather afraid. The flagon of liquor he dashed from the board, his whole body shaking with the mute vehemence of despair.

'My child is not here, sir. No child of mine is here! I shall never behold that innocent face. Never! Never! Never!'

And now – I cannot explain it – but a perplexing thing happened. For I turned about, and nobody was there.

The fire burned low, the wind bellowed in the eavesdrops [*sic*]; but in the place where I had seen our cohort but a moment erewhile was only a swirl of turbid shadows. One felt as a miser who seeks his burgled gold, rubbing his eyelids, knowing the trove must be there, but anyway not seeing it, so staring the harder. The child must have stolen away from us while I engaged with the Governor; and yet, I heard no door unlatch, nor even the faintest of footfalls. Were one tended at all toward weakness of mind, one might have fallen foul of girlish suspicions that the tattlers of the town had wisdom in their gibberish; that forces praeternatural (malicious, et cetera) were ruling that reportedly Faustian roost.

'I implore your pardon, sir, truly,' I said. 'I am not well, I think. My wits are upset.'

He had crossed to the hearth and had sunk onto a bench before it, quivering with anguish, burying his face in his hands. A log fell in two with a fizzle of scarlet sparks. 'Get out,' the Governor said.

I vacated the house directly, thinking I had best. He can be contended with by-and-by, perhaps better in the light of day.

On my trudge back here, the tempest began to blow up harder, so that presently I was forcing through flurries of smarting hail. The road was a very soup of adhesive filth and ordure. Miners with storm-lanterns were dragging a terrified horse from a ditch; but the effort proved no good, and they must end its agonies with a pistol shot. This execution I watched. It was sad; very sad. There was a quite tremendous quantity of blood.

Watching, I bethought myself of a line I had happened upon in some poem, wherein love is likened to the star of the north. 'Constant as a star is my darling dark.' But the stars are not constant. They flare out and burn up; and the entire of the momentary nothing they sparkle, live always encircled by out-and-out darkness, which encroaches, as it must, until all light fades. A star is merely an explosion seen from a great distance, and, like all distant violence, may be attributed significance. But that is all it is: a cruel event. And we poor fools pen poems about it.

I can write no more this night. I tremble and blaze. The perspiration from my brow drips onto the parchment – blurring.

∇

CHAPTER 51

THE STORM
or
LINES AFTER QUARRELING NEAR THE SECOND AVENUE

To a dear friend who must be nameless and who asked
a greater intimacy than a kiss

A constant star, my lonely dark.
Lightning racks the night.
Lost, we roam'd the cloistered streets,
Escaping worldly slight.

No haven, this forbidden bond
With all its wildest hopes.
'I wish,' he whispered. 'Say my name.'
'No words,' the other spoke.

Tender, rousing hands and eyes
Evade the heartless light.
Raveling illicit hopes,
The sheets of rain tonight.

O friend unnamed, I spoke not true;
Now – alone – I storm for you.

Charles Gimenez Carroll [Lucia-Cruz McLelland-O'Keeffe]†

∇

† This sonnet appeared in the January 1864 number of *The American Gentleman's Monthly* under Lucia's *nom de plume*. It aroused controversy among certain subscribers, not for its technical immaturity, but because some read the piece as being addressed by one man to another. As to the identity of the 'friend

CHAPTER 52

BEWARE, YE RARE AND LISSOME GIRLS, THE COAXING WORDS OF A SOLDIER

*The outlaws' hideout – A strange language – Patrick Vinson
makes a mistake that will cost him dearly*

A beam of cave-light, dust-filled, opaque, comes coursing through an aperture in the roof far above her and shines like a visualization of the power of God in a prayerbook intended for children. The dripping and gurgling of underground water. A field of eroded stalagmites like unhatched eggs. Lichens on the walls, and the chiselings of a people long moved away or died.

And the bandits, like the undergrounders, have departed, too, in the weeks and months following the robbery. Ridden away for their homes, in twos and fours: her husband's accomplices in piracy. Back to their families, or to gangs they call brothers – to mountains, villages, campfires, burnt schoolrooms. Yes, one of them is a schoolteacher – or he was, before the War. Come up from Virginia, she thinks.

Each guerrilla took his share, having sworn an oath-of-blood to use it solely for the Confederate cause. Some will purchase arms. There was talk of explosives: a plan to bomb the White House, to assassinate the entire Government. She suspects it was bluster. They are only desperadoes. Some of them will never go home.

She bathes in the rockpool. Weightless; waterborne. The scald of the ice-cold water. The fruit of her womb is ripening in its husk. She feels it rolling inside her. There are two simpleminds to protect her – John Fox

---

unnamed', I had been returning to the poem for many years before a wiser reader noticed the secret in its structure. To my wife, Ruth Ginsberg-McLelland, I am indebted for pointing out the fact that a downward reading of the first letter of each line is revealing. It would appear that the dear friend is not unnamed, after all.

Galligan and a Tennessee farmboy called 'Bubba' or 'Dunne' – and the traitor, Patrick Vinson, who has no place on earth he can think of to go any more. Every time she looks up, he is watching her from the shadows. His peasant's ruddy face.

'How you feelin, Eliza?'

'Whut you care.'

'Got somethin agin talkin?'

'Let me alone, Mister. I'm readin a book.'

She has seen him light a flambeau and make into the depths, his light growing smaller as he goes. He feels there must be gold, that the realm is a treasure-house, if only one knew where to seek. He returns, hours later, with not a grain of gold but with tales that freeze the sportings of the fools. A cavern at least a mile away with a dragon-shaped rock. A vault that looks *worked*, for its floor is smooth as glass. A toadstool he saw, the size of a stagecoach. A ledge to which he climbed with strange runes on its slabs. He copied them onto his shirt-collar with a nub of charred wood. He has forgotten that the natives do not write.

Y ‡ î Ω ‡

'. . . Eliza? . . . Eliza? . . . You seen what I found?'

'Got a bale on you, don't you? You turn deaf as well as dense?'

'You don't want to see it? . . . That's a Indian language . . . Give a ransom to know what it mean.'

'Mean go and suck your momma's, cause you aint suckin mine. And get out of my light. I'm readin.'

'I don't mean to vex . . . Real sorry if I did . . . '

'Quit lookin at me that way, Mister, or I'm tellin Cole.'

'Cole aint here, girl . . . Cole aint never here.'

'He'll be back soon enough.'

'You reckon?'

'I know.'

His eyes always watching. Taking everything in. That day she slipped on the rock, had to bandage up her knee. Him pretending not to look as she undresses.

'You was mine, I tell you the one-thing: I wouldn't never quit you. Be here to take a care of you. Do anythin you want.'

'You got nothin I want you to do, nor say. Cept get out of my road. I'm readin.'

He does not move away. He does not move at all. He stands by that pillar of flaking, wet limestone, watching Eliza Duane Mooney read. The Governor told him one time – they were arguing violently –: 'You're not unintelligent. But you're *stupid*, Vinson. You will always be stupid. That isn't the same thing. And you're never going to change, because a fool never changes once he reaches the age of reason.' He is wondering whether or not to speak the words in his mind. The sentence with which he could overcome her.

He has carried it a while, a key to a pleasure dome. Anticipating the pleasure of its use. He has thought about the words, the right moment to speak them. Her gratitude, her malleability upon hearing them.

Her dress is dark green. Her feet are naked. There is a tenderness in how she turns pages. She licks the middle fingertip of her smooth right hand, for the flimsies have a way of sticking together in the damp; and the grace, the womanly tact, with which she gently separates them, and her lips moving silently as she reads. The beautiful ribbons in the spine of the Bible. Cave-light on the side of her face.

'Only I seen that boy,' Patrick Vinson says quietly, as though somehow uncertain if it is true. And the words float out of the cave of his mind and into the must of the cavern. They can never be unspoken. They are part of the world, like the odor of the lichens, and the plinking of water, and the whiteness of her toes on rock. And the tiny, jagged swellings on the wet gray granite, and the plasterish taste of the air.

'You got a tintype over there. I heard tell it's your brother. I seen that boy. I know where he's at. Aint three days' ride from there to this. I know that boy. I'm sure on it.'

Eliza looks up at him. The man who played his card. He appears fearful, as though about to be wagered a stake he doesn't possess. Something is making him tremble.

'You seen my brother?'

The traitor nods wild-eyed.

'Name Jeddo. So high. Be sure of it, Mister.'

'Certain sure, I swear it. Even talked to him a few times. Twas myself found him in April and he making into Canada.'

'Where?'

'Canada.'

'No, where he at now?'

'Well, see – that's the matter – Oul memory aint so good this weather . . . Figured . . . mebbe you'd help me remember.'

Patrick Owen Vinson, County Louth and Red Hook, Brooklyn. As he dies, he will remember this moment. The instant he collaborated with the power of coercion and thereby wrote his sentence.

'That the way it is, Mister? I don't lay for you, you don't tell me?'

' . . . Eliza . . . There's no call . . . It dont have to be like this . . . I care for you, Eliza . . . Let me talk to you, Eliza . . . '

'What you want of me, Mister? In the dirt on my knees? Stick it up me like a sow? That what you want?'

'Eliza . . . '

'What piece of me you want, Worm? Say it. I want to hear it. My hand? My mouth? Where my child gonna come outof? My breast that gonna suckle? Cause I want that you speak it. You so ugly and low you can't get no woman to touch you but rentin one hates the livin sight of ever thing about you?'

'It aint rent. That aint right. I never said aught about money.'

Echo of 'money'. Vowel-howl.

His mouth on her own; his grip on her waist. She snaps away from Patrick Vinson, as from the gush of a fireball. Her back to a wall of spore-puffing moss that sags as she connects with its jellyness. The ball of her wrist wiping his taste from her lips. And sudden as a sting, he sees the family resemblance. It isn't in the eyes but the curl of the mouth. It's the way she grits her teeth.

'You dead, Mister. You know that? One word from me, you gone.'

'That happen,' says Patrick Vinson, 'you never see your brother again.'

'Cole gonna beat it out of your filthy skull. Then I tie up your noose myself.'

'That aint gonna happen,' Patrick Vinson replies, unholstering his Colt repeater.

So heavy, the repeater. Like an anchor in your hand. The effort you put into buying it. The drinks undrunk, the girls uncourted, the nights you stayed home counting pennies in a cigar box, yesterday's suppers, the worn-down boots, and all of it brought you to this moment in history that will never appear in any record. You would not have thought it possible in your youth, Patrick Vinson, that you would come to be the subterranean man.

Water dribbles down the clefts in the parapets of rock. The mushrooms glistening: russet. The plash of something echoed from those transepts of granite and the chuckles of the simpleminds dicing someplace you can't see. It is not too late to turn away from this cross-roads you have cut, but it is harder with a gun in your hand.

'Rape now,' she says. 'You some playboy, aint you, Mister. You hard with a gun in your hand?'

'Aint rape! Don't be stupid. You don't think so good, do you? You pretty but you don't think so good.'

'What I think is, I'm gonna enjoy crushing your eyeballs for grapes. Like grapes, you whore's leavings. I'm gonna drink their juice.'

'*You don't understand,*' Patrick Vinson interrupts. 'This gun int for you. *It for me.*'

'Ee-aw-ee-,' shrieks the cavern behind him. The clatter of a stone onto stone.

His hand with the repeater is shaking very badly, as though he wishes someone would take it away from him. Sweat slickens his cheekbones. He licks his thin mustache. He looks like a prisoner in front of a firing squad, groping for the last precious memory.

'You don't come round to my way, then so help me Jesus Christ, I ride out of this hole in short order and straight into Canada. McLaurenson catch me up, I put a bullet through my head. And you'll never know your whole life what I knowed about that boy. And you're young. Life gonna be long.'

The fool John Galligan has appeared on the outcrop below, dancing by himself in longjohns. His friend Dunne, or Bubba – who knows his story? – is sawing on an invisible violin. The light-beam alters subtly, as though the unseen sun has been obscured by the hand of God. She hears Vinson's breathing; strained, uneven. He is sweating like a fungus in heat.

'I give you choices,' he says. 'A yes. That's all. And I take you to your brother. Your blood.'

Behind him the invisible damned, all the men who ever used her, by force, by currency, by the currency of force, a number so great that she has long stopped counting; behind *them*, all the users of her mothers. They live in the blackness. You can hear them in the night. They gabble their strange languages, one to the other, but everything they say comes out the same in the end: *Would one more make any true difference?* Because this is what you're for, girl. All you'll ever be for. No point in saying anything but yes.

'I won't,' she says. 'Not for any child on earth. Not for no one's ever lived, or ever's gonna live again. Not the child in me now. Not my brother. Not no one. Not Christ and His mother. Not the world. You can make me, I guess. You can try to, I guess. You look like you're strong. I'll hurt you ever way I can. And you better be ready to murder me dead. Cause if I live, I *will* kill you. Some day I will kill you, though you live to a hundred and figured you was safe. One night you'll open a door. Turn around in your bed. I'll come out of your fuckin mattress. You trust on it, Mister. Cause I won't say yes, not if you put a bullet through me now. Tell me, or don't tell me. I say no.'

Stalagmite Vinson. He wishes he could weep. The oak for his coffin is felled already. He hears it fall in his mind.

'If livin ever meant you was more than a dog – think hard before you put your hand on me, Vinson.'

∇

CHAPTER 53

I'LL NEVER WISH TO TARRY MORE, FOR LOVE HAS FLOWN AWAY

An angry letter from Lucia to her husband

Con: Since you very well know my whereabouts I will not trouble to write them down. Your spies will be able to inform you of my movements. You would be judicious to tell them, should any man impede me, I will shoot him in the head without compunction.

Every day I go to the stage office and ask for a ticket to Salt Lake City. Every day I am refused by the Manager. This morning I was informed that you have issued 'an official order' continuing the suspension of all stage routes for a further two weeks. Apparently you are prepared to bankrupt and cripple this Territory if that is necessary to frustrate my wishes.

I give you notice, if no other means of leaving become available by the close of a fortnight, I will make a way out of this Territory on horseback, or on foot, if I must, and I will go through the Indian Territory, or any I choose. The consequences, if any, were a matter for your conscience. You know me better than to believe I would not dare it.

Furthermore, I will tell every person who asks me along the way that I am the wife of James O'Keeffe, who reduced me to these straits for his pride. When I reach New York – if I reach New York – I will write of your treatment in every publication that will accept me. Every newspaper in Ireland will receive a copy of my chronicle, as shall every last one of your friends. Already I have written to my father and his attorney, instructing them to withhold any further payment of my capital. Keep me like an animal in your private Australia and I can assure you, you will pay the cost.

It is nothing less than pitiful that you would stoop to punish me in this stupid and childish manner. You will not succeed in your endeavor; be certain of it, sir. If you wish to fight a war, I will give you one.

Lucia.

∇

CHAPTER 54

OH WHITHER MY LONG-LOST GIRL?

---

*More from Winterton's journal – He searches the town for
his departed love – & sees a stranger who resembles a former comrade
of the Governor – Reflections on aspects of one of Redemption's
principal languages – & a new friend is made among the citizenry*

5. XI. 66. Redem. F.

Frequent and violent alterations in wind speed and direction.

Find, since the War, that memory is shot. Simplest things flit away. Details in especial. This morning happened to think upon my coming into the Territory and could scarcely recollect route without writing it down. Rather concerning; even upsetting. Dearly hope it passes. Wonder if a doctor could do anything.

Four days and nights abed – pulsingly vivid dreams of her – but the fever has broken now. Queerly sensate after one has been sick of a fever. Purged of many vile elements, or layer of epidermis stripped away. Smells, tastes, even touches electric. One wonders if this is how an infant feels on arrival into the world. Or dying man about to leave it.

Little rickety in the forenoon, still sweating like a hog, with stools not firm, and tongue slick and ashen; but by twelve of the clock was able to face into a walk, and by one to take a glass of pale beer. Found it vivifying, although it tasted disturbingly earthy or nutty. Christ knows what they put in it. Best not to.

Sallied out to Perryville Cross. Made sketch of the ruins. Thermometer has malfunctioned so that I can enter no accurate record. But air very cold & sharp & enlivening. Keener appentency ensued: merely to breathe was a relief. But I could not keep much down.

Town crowded during the morning with Koötenais traders who remained beyond the midday curfew. (Apparently he turns a blind eye to their presence.) Elk-furs, bearskins, some nicely enough got up, trinkets, little fixings wrought by their women. Shabby pinto ponies no one would want to buy. Purchased a coon-hat with ear-muffs from one super-annuated rascal, he was almost quite naked, the cold notwith-standing. Asked me by gestures (at my pistol) could he have bullets rather than coin. Demurred & he looked most chapfallen. Not a tusk had my mercantile in his painted noggin. One wondered how he chewed his meats at supper. His 'pard' showed a mawful of blackened broken stubs. Like looking at a thunderstruck graveyard.

Lost a little at Spanish monte in saloon called 'The Shoogawn'. Considered a hand of poker but resisted in the close. Cheat among the pack, I could see what he was doing. Clever. Would be hard to best him.

Noted a number of striking expressions employed by the whites. 'Knight of the ribbons': a stagecoach driver. 'Blackleg': a gambler. 'Bugscuffle': an insignificant town. 'Raw-mashe:' nonsense or (perceived) cant in speech. 'Gutty': a street-boy. 'Jonah': bad luck. 'Here's your mule' is a sentence they utter very frequently: a phrase, so far as I under-stand it, possessing no meaning *per se* but employed as a sort of amiable punctuation. They have many others of these, indeed a remarkable number; the Hibernians have a veritable Websters of them: 'Who'd be a soldier?' 'There it is for you now.' 'Shure, what can you do?' 'Go on to God.' 'Go up the yard.' 'Is it yourself I am seeing?' 'Mary and Bridget, when you think of it.' One hears conversations, some lasting a very considerable time, where absolutely nothing substantive is said. One suspects that it is a matter of where the emphasis is placed. Like the cantor in a synagogue, perhaps.

The snow proved brief, which brevity was auspicious, for the town could not withstand another proper battering of the concentration it is reported to have suffered at Christmastide. Already there are too many empty dwellings – tumbledown and melancholy; little better than hurley-houses; the population is diminishing by the week.

Today, as I limped the streets (*church bell is clanging, I think it must be midnight*), I noted an extraordinary sight: family of immigrants walking the road. Father grunting in the thill-shafts of a dilapidated donkey-cart, their meager hillock of possessions roped on like a pedlar's junkshop; poor Bridget and a dirty Negro boy drudging along behind, laden like miserable pack-mules. Most striking was the face of the Moses hauling between the shafts. Were he not a prisoner in Virginia, could swear it was none other than *John Fintan Duggan*, the rebel lieutenant, onetime friend of O'K. Most astounding similarity I ever saw. Truly every man has a double.

Since reports of very large gold seam discovered near Jacobite Mountain, the diggers have been fleeing like bats from dawn. One must wonder, indeed, as to what can be the future of despondent Redemption, and of many other tin-towns in this Territory. Perhaps something of it could be rescued, were it demolished and built again suitably, employing the grid from the outset, and passable surveying, with sewers, macadam roads, a marketplace, measured lots, and all befitting a civilized settlement. This piecemeal method will not do long; for a town, like a human, must grow from germ to a design, or the defects inhering in the seed destroy it. (House divided, & cetera, & cetera.) But none of these obdurate blockheads would listen to such a reasonable proposition. O what matter, I suppose. Let it fall into ashes. Everything will, at the close.

Hobbled about a while. Intermittent shivers. Ague in the gut went and came. Violent crisis had me discovering an alley but felt better for having uncargoed. At one moment – Christ – thought I saw her in 'Tone Street', buying bundles of kindling of a Chinee. Followed like a fool. Almost called out her name. But she turned, and it was not my angel. Considered collaring one of the Negro mudlarks and saying I had a letter for the G's W; could he enlighten as to where she might be found? But it seemed a little perilous, since I had no such letter, and anyway he would merely direct me to the house. Loitered over an hour but did not see her anywhere. Felt downhearted mood. Very low, and it grew worse. The clear, unruffled composure of despair. Always wrong in poems.

Thoughts flying like a bird: landing here, flitting there. Could settle in only one tree. Forced myself to take a wash at a cowpokes' bathhouse, perfect symphony of filth. Grimy tub of hammered tin. Towel threadbare and stinking. Poor homunculus, I think Russian, employed to fetch the water, which was tepid & the color of urine, literally, owing to gold-ore in the mountain (he maintained). Offered to scourge me with tree-branch. Claimed it capital for the blood. Told him *nyet*. He looked disappointed.

Met one Calhoun, acting marshal. Would give me the clew to nothing. (Born 'Colquhoun' in Ireland. 'Too hard for Yanks to say.') Decent, dignified sort, unruffled luster about him; an astuteness that has not panicked. Does many unobtrusive charities, so the townspeople attest. Even the Confederates respect him. One meets his likes in every hamlet of America. When they are men, they humble, make one wish to do better. When they are women, as often, perhaps even usually, one feels life might even have a purpose. How such people came through the War, I think I shall never know. Fortunate: the children of these.

Returned to hotel at quarter of two. Widow presiding at altar of the desk. Invited me to take a brandy with her in the *Büro* to assist my recuperation. Said I did not use brandy. Offered me 'English tea'.

Talked of the War. Nothing notable. (Claims to have supported Union, though others say she went with the wind.) Knew nothing of the piracy but what had been written in the paper. Had lost no sleep for it. Did not intend to do so. Had not the smallest interest in political questions, she said. (Drowning sailors – a political question?) Continuously apologizing for her English, which in fact was serviceable enough, but it seemed to please her to apologize and receive the usual reassurances, so we played the tennis of bogus courtesies a while, and the tea, although sour, was not vile. Told her one had a smatter of her mother tongue, in fact. Out of practice, of course, but one had had, in that impressionable twilight, *ein Kindermädchen*, a nanny, of Bohemia. She blazed with delight to hear it. One sensed doors open, as it were. Was sorry for not mentioning Beate previously.

Stood up on a bench and procured from a sandy shelf a volume of old *Volkslieder* or Germanic folk songs, entitled *Des Knaben Wunderhorn*, or the Youth's Magic Horn, macabrely illustrated with the customary wood-cuts of agricultural-looking persons and other lechers. This tome she had fetched with her from Hamburg in '53, she confided mournfully. Vati, a compositor, had made up the type. Handsomest man in Westphalia, she alleged. But every woman thinks Papa a *Meisterwerk*.

Did one's best to emit the required grunts of endorsement as one perused her progenitor's *magnum opus*. (Crow-black inks, cornucopia margins: the whole, one must own, rigorous and beautiful, but one must be in the whole of one's humor for such starkness.) Consider, *bitte*, plate seventy-two. This said with some force and I obeyed. Repugnant troll, thigh-deep in a bog, crossed eyes, hooked beak, gruesome protuberance about his hosiery. Did it remind one of anyone, she asked with possibly a grin. Impertinent slut, one thought. But no, it was not Modo reflected in the parchments. A certain Irishman of some influence in the town? Cruel, but one could indeed recognize the burgermeister to whom she alluded. In the midget's gnarled paw was a sword.

Commenced speaking to me of *der irische General* in a somewhat sly and sidelong key, a favorite register of his constituents. He was a para-doxical conundrum: she did not concur with his every policy, but had nonetheless to admire his *Festigkeit*. Did I know that word? *Aber Ja*, I said: 'firmness'. Beate had illustrated it in a most memorable fashion as we blackberried on my seventeenth birthday.

Had heard, so she said, that I was a former comrade of *der General* in the War. Corrected her on this misapprehension. She seemed pleased.

Was a cold-hearted *Teufel*, quite ferocious of temper. Had often been overheard scolding his wife. Had driven her away from him, thus ran the rumor. *Aber Ja*; she had been here. Did not know where she had gone. Some said to Fort Braintree, others to Freshet Falls or Cleburne; others, back to hellfire where she belonged. Had not been liked in the town. Many airs & graces. Flaunted like a duchess among raggers.

Der Irishcher had told his marshals to put it about the settlement that she had gone to avail herself of the healing waters, would return in a little time – but two months had elapsed since a reportedly hurried departure. Please God, (archly), she must be healed by now, of whatever unfortunate ailment had sickened her. Their marriage was a pretense: this was the whisper of the town's idle tongues. He had wed her for the *Geld*; she had been magnetized by his fame. The Governor had fathered bastards in every state of the Union. His wife, God be good to her, was no better.

Ja his wife was 'a haff-breed', everyone knew it. Product of a slave-woman and an overseer. Had been taken, out of charity, into the house of her so-called family, who had passed her off as their own. It was why she and O'Keeffe had never reproduced. Any issue they would parent might be more Ethiop-toned than she – science had proven reliably that such throwbacks happened, often – and her secret would become legible to the world.

'Gracious,' I said, with what I hope was an unforced smile. 'Madam's biology is commensurate with her beauty.'

I had heard (she said thinly) the speculations, of course. Replied that one knew nothing whatever of them. That was better, she opined. They would affect my opinion of the Governor. *Gott behüte* that she should stoop to the dissemination of hearsay. All the gold in Yankeedom could not persuade her into gossip. If his wife had set the Governor in the cuckold's cap, that was nobody's business to discuss. Oh, I was not aware of these matters? Well, enough, enough. The woman would face her Maker in the end of all. Those who play the courtesan when their husbands are away at war perforce must give answer in the hereafter.

Ja sicher, ja sicher; it was known throughout the Territory. Her behavior, her morals, had been *skandalös*. My confidante, the widow, had had it from a reliable authority. There were things about the Governor's wife too appalling to be spoken; the vilest whore on earth did not deserve such calumnies. When no other accomplice was available to satiate her lusts, she would go about the waterfronts of Manhattan habited in a common woman's clothing, importuning young soldiers by offering herself cheaply, or gratis, in cases of distress. She was also, misfortunate lady, a slave to the opiates. Alas, it was the gospel truth.

'Surely not,' I contended, adding, not untruthfully, that one had heard many tributes to the lady in question, indeed paeans to her honor and goodness. Had she not nursed in the War, performed uncountable acts of altruism? (Affordable prostitution not among them.) Did not hundreds of men owe their very lives to her ministry? Was not tittle-tattle unchristian; the disparagement of the envious? We were all presumed innocent until convicted.

The widow uttered a hoot at one's touching naïvety and supplied herself another tincture of brandy. There was a reason why that contaminatrix had volunteered at the hospital. I could imagine what it was. She need not spell it plainly. To make herself appear a saint of high-toned morality rather than the coin-bosomed trollop she was. But an idol of gold could be filled with filthiest poison. (The leopard, its spots, &cetera.) Medicals, a Negro orderly: she had not been selective. Not even the ways of Nature had this vixen respected. She had pursued and steadily seduced an eminent surgeon's wife: a staunch Christian woman, the most beautiful and devout in New York. Her good husband, on returning home early from his work, had been so shocked by the culmination unfolding in his lady's private library, the corruptress in recline, skirts unconventionally arranged, being administered the gift of tongues by her genuflected if corsetless convert, that his beard had turned quite gray by morning. The adulteress had plumbed so low – surely I had heard this? – as to deprave one of the wretched patients in her charge.

One paused in mid-sip. It seemed remarkably unlikely, I ventured.

On the contrary, it was common knowledge. But let no more be said. The thing was too improper to be discussed beneath a decent roof. A milky young trooper, *in Gottes Namen*, but a few pained breaths from his grave-cloths. Had truly I never heard what the dogs of the street were barking? Why, if not, it were better; she would not enlighten me further, for to sully a neighbor's reputation was *verboten* by the Commandments. But it was a mercy, she said, that that monstress had quit the town, for there had even been whisperings here. A farmboy at Lake Allen. The gunsmith's idiot son. Why, the very brat at the Governor's house would be next of her victims, just the moment he commenced shaving his cheek. The woman was eaten rotten by her jungle appetites. Had it a pulse and wore britches, she must ruin it. But yet, we must always be charitable; must we not? Let the one without sin cast the *Stein*.

Did not know very much about the child at the house. A boy, she confirmed, and a bad one. Could not remember when he arrived – maybe last Christmas. *Ja sicher*, last Christmas: out of the storm like a spook. Had heard he was once *mit der Armee des Südens*. Did not know if it was true. Did not much care. As to why the General had sheltered him – it was a mystery all insoluble. Who could explain the doings of such a mercurial man? Truth to tell, he was half the time *stockbetrunken*.

'. . . ?' I asked.

'*Mit wizky. Ze hootch. Die Branntwein.*'

Ah.

Beate's tutelage had extended very comprehensively, I smiled; but Germanic terms of inebriation had not been part of it.

Obviously, she said, she did not object to a man drinking, not even occasionally to excess. But overindulgence, she insisted, should always be in moderation, otherwise it could go too far. (I think that I know what she meant. Anyway, I nodded ardently.) The Governor would get utterly *sternhagelvoll*, sometimes even *sturzbetrunken*. At such times, the foul-mouthed *Säufer* could not be approached without trouble. Some took a charitable view, saying: '*Worte eines Betrunkenen sind die Gedanken des Nüchternen.*' But mein hostess did not think this any adequate excuse for offensive behavior. Did I?

'Indeed not, Ma'am,' I replied gravely, though somewhat in the dark. But she seemed gratified to be recipient of my solidarity.†

Inquired of my work. Went over the ground in brief. Seemed touchingly interested, & not at all slow in apprehension. (*Kartenzeichner*: a cartographer. *Eine topographische Übersicht*: a survey.) Wished to know in some detail how a map was made, the denotations of the symbols & lines & cet. The chains employed for surveying would be fifteen miles long, each link the size of a hogshead (I said). Then showed her my sextant and she operated it briefly, uttering bleats of quite childlike awe. Turn the lever and you shall lengthen the barrel, I told her. She turned it. It extended. She cooed.

Ugly wrigglings of ideas bestirred in one's swamp. Stirred soberly at the coagulation of one's tea.

---

† The adage with which Winterton is agreeing is: 'A drunk man's words are a sober man's thoughts.'

There was a matter, she said – she supposed it a confidential matter – but a matter which she felt our friendship might permit to be aired. It touched upon my project, but was of interest to her, also, as a personage of enterprise in Redemption Falls. A great number of soldiers would be coming into the Territory, she had heard. There would also, she supposed, be officers. They would all of them require accommodation, feeding & watering, and so on. The quarters required by the Officer Corps must be first-rate in every way.

Natürlich, I agreed. If possible.

I would be well placed, she supposed, to offer recommendations to the Federal Government as to where such excellent lodgings might be found. What one would doubtless have in mind was a superior establishment, not one of the flophouses or groggeries or glorified slums of which the County could afford a plethora. Naturally I would be compiling a list of possibilities, several of which might fit. She had heard it said in the town (she could not remember by whom) that her own was placed neck and neck with another establishment in my present estimation. She was hoping that it would become firm favorite.

Ah, I said.

Aber ja. Aber ja.

I believe, I said tactfully, that we understand one another.

The fact that I was assembling no such register I thought were best unmentioned.

She smiled, rather violently, and looked at me a while. I must own, in a certain light, she is not entirely repugnant to me. A gossip, yes, but who has not gossiped? Malice is but a forgivable pastime of the provincial mind, as superiority is for the cosmopolitan. The north face, to put it politically, will never be her fortune, but the southern latitudes display a not unpleasing range of elevations. Rather suckable Vest Wirginia. Her Appalachian amplitude. Not unpleasant – to have her measure.

There is something of a bulbous bird, very probably flightless, almost (or quite) extinct – but with the curved nose, heavy eyelids, and prominently molded chin of those whose moral energies are incurably European. A doleful, a melancholy mien this lends, a slack-jawed despondent sagginess. But she is also, importantly, a person of wide experience, possessed of an understanding of the world. They whisper that her widowhood was accomplished with the aid of the Vigilantes; but one has little doubt that the infidel deserved it. He was discovered, so it is attested, drowned in a barrel; gagged by an intimate garment of a pubescent seductee. Hell hath no fury like a hoodwinked frau. They say that she herself nailed the lid.

She asked if one was lonely, so far away from home. One confirmed that this could occur on occasion. Warbled at me a while about the burthens of duty. Serving the American citizenry, whilst the greatest honor to which one could aspire, was not entirely without its stresses (she had frequently supposed); its frustrations must be many and aggravating.

Indeed so, one agreed. I had her every sympathy. Some of the gentlemen at her establishment were pleased to have a friend at trying hours. A burden shared was a burden halved. Would be no difficulty to arrange it. On the *haus*, of course.

Said one wished to be frank: there was the question of one's appearance. Most ladies would find one a chillying prospect. One was a man of the world, and so on and so forth, had served in the army, & cetera, & cetera, but since sustaining one's injuries, one had visited no gentlemanly establishment, for feelings of shame and so on. No difficulty arose on that front, she discreetly insisted. Her ladies were selected for their kindliness as much as their pulchritude. A *Mann* was still a *Mann*. He would always be a *Mann*. 'If you prick us,' said the widow, 'do we bleed?'

Gave me an album of daguerreotypes, the perusal of which she recommended in my quarters. It offered an artistic depiction of every beauty in her charge, she enlightened. Would call on me presently to see if anything bestirred my interest. Most arresting volume. (Rather more than the Youth's Magic Horn.) Photography, one feels, is an exceeding promising discipline – particularly when practiced by an aesthetician.

What harm? one felt. Not as if anyone would ever know. Gift horse, & cetera, & cetera.

Selected a plump pretty *Fräulein* (I suppose for reminiscence). Affable and competent, Wisconsin farmgirl, but the usual gloom after she departed. Cannot have been pleasant for her. Looked at my face in the window. Never pleasant for the girl, but they are ordered to feign. Unmanly really, when one thinks on it any length. Leaves one with less than one had.

And what becomes of them afterwards, when they are old and tired? And if one met her in the street, with her children and a husband, what would one say, after all? Pretend, I suppose. All sham and pretense. And the greatest of these is marriage.

Witwe asked me, at supper, if all had been satisfactory.

Lied that it had, *danke schön*.

An honor, she smiled, doing business with the government.

Und so, at last, to bed.

∇

Sweet Christ – A terrible dream, the worst ever I had – It seemed that I crawled some constituency of the damned – through a sludge of gristle and putrefying flesh – with the Governor on my back, riding me like a jockey – his teeth chewing lewdly through the carapace of my cranium while he spewed the cry: 'Death to the traitor!'

Hard by were ranked the legions & battalions of the war-fallen: whole armies in Union blue and in butternut gray – weeping, howling, worm-gnawed number extending in ranks to the vanishing point. – Scourged me to a high crest overlooking a river – on which sailed a barque of clowns and child-ghouls – Here a medal was nailed to my breast by a boy in fiery rags; the word graven into it was 'Coward' – It scalded my flesh but I could not pluck it off – He was the urchin I had seen at the Governor's.

Awoke a moment ago – flailing at the coverlets; the counterpane and bolster saturated with perspiration – For a moment, truly, did not know where I was – Jesus – What terror – Pulse in my throat beating fit to burst my jugular.

Someone walking on the landing. A man I think. The night is tomb-quiet. Snowing.

Twigs at the window. Down in the street. Looking up at me, the boy. Appeared laughing.

Someone has been into the room while I was asleep: the candles quenched and a washing-jug brought in. Creature in the loft is shifting, scraping. Shall not sleep again this night.

Wish to Christ redeemer I had something to read.

But have just now remembered: I do.

∇

CHAPTER 55

O I AM A VALIANT FELON, BOYS MY COUNTRY DID I LOVE

Winterton's reading material – A biography of sorts

INTELLIGENCE STATEMENT
SECRET & CONFIDENTIAL
DO NOT READ OR POSSESS THIS DOCUMENT
UNLESS AUTHORIZED TO DO SO†

Caveat Lector. Certificate is unverified & may contain errors of fact.

GIVEN NAMES OF SUSPECT: Giacomo (a.k.a. James) Cornelius O'Keeffe.

ALIASES: None. (Certain familiars address him as 'Con'.)

BIRTHPLACE & DATE: Wexford County, Ireland, Unit. Kdom. April 4th or 5th, 1823.

WARRANTS & BOUNTIES: Warrants outstanding for his arrest in any territory or possession of Great B, by any agent of her govt.

APPLICABLE PUNISHMENT OF WARRANT(S): Death by hanging, drawing, quartering. No right of appeal.

FATHER (if known): John Downing O'Keeffe. Grain merchant; Lord-Mayor of Wexford 1827–1829, briefly Member of (Great B) Parliament. Well-connected.

MOTHER (if known): Annalena Margarita Rugierro (b. Pordenone, nr Venice). Descd, Dublin, consumption, when subj aged five months.

SUBJECT'S SCHOOLING (if any): Rowanwood Coll., Kildare County, Ireland; Stonesglade Coll., Shropshire, England. Frequently disciplined. Boothman Medal for Shakespearean Recitation. Expelled (allegedly possessed opium: denied).

---

† Document found in a search of Winterton's clothing after the massacre at Fort Stornaway, January 1867. It had been sewn inside the brim of a hat.

PERSUASION: R. Cath., not practicing. Some anticlericalism in speeches, writings.

MARITAL: Current legal marriage. Previous irregular situation. See below.

DESCRIPTION: Five feet 10 inches. Eyes dark brown. (Iris of right slightly darker than left.) Swarthy. Graying hair. Prominent jaw. Beetle-browed. Mediterranean type. Bloated & gouty. Faded tattoo-mark on left breast shows flaming sword with entwined scroll reading 'Erin go Bragh.' ('Ireland for Ever,' in the Erse or Celtic language.) Slight limp due to fracture; fall from horse at Fredericksburg.

INFORMATIONS: On expulsion from Stonesglade Coll., traveled in Europe (knows Italian, some French); returned Dublin, became militant, 45–48, of fanatical sect purposed to destroy crown rule (operating under guise of Literary Club). Attributed Irish famines to English misrule. Extolled French revolutionaries, summer 48. Devised 'Irish tricolor' banner. Praised 'Chartist' agitators & has spoken from platforms with them (Manchester, England). Writings, orations advocated armed revolution, for which he gained soubriquet 'O'Keeffe of the Blade'. (Attribd to English belletrist W.M. Thackeray.) Plotted insurrection summer 48. Betrayed by informant. Charges: treason & 'countenancing the death of the monarch'. Death sentence, Clonmel Assizes, Tipperary County Nov 48. Commuted on petition (by his father), life-transportation HM Penal Colony, Van Diemen's Land, Australia.

There enjoyed privileges. Owned livestock, sailboat, farmstead at Lake Comfrey. Permitted gentleman's apparel, excused punitive labor. Established household with Catharine (or Kathryn) Foley, half-breed Negro, one daughter, confirmed deceased two months. Subject absconded March 52. 'Wife' died by own hand, Hobart Asylum, Tasmania Oct 55. Subject md Lucia-Cruz Rodríguez Y Ortega McLelland, 1 the Fifth Avenue, NY, of the respected steel family, Jan 1856. No issue. Marriage unstable. (Subj drinks. Women also? Investigate informants, brothels, & cet.) Has visited Central Amer isthmus on long sojourns of uncertain purpose. (Canal rights, gold-fields, mineral exploration?) Intensely disliked by father-in-law, who regards subj as fortune-hunter. Known to be kept by wife. Investigate further. On four occasions in the late 50s he inquired of subversives in New York if a passage back to Australia could be clandestinely arranged. Informants were not told why. Revolutionism?

WAR SERVICE: Southern sympathies, secessionist associates (cf: John

Fintan Duggan, Richmond, Va.), & has refused to 'stigmatize' slavery; but sided with north. Raised company of 'Irish Zouaves' for Union 61. Brig. General, Irish Brigade, 127th New York ('The Con O'Keeffes'). Charged with drinking while in command at First Bull Run. Exonerated by inquiry. Fair Oaks, the Seven Days, Gaines's Mill, Savage's Station, Malvern Hill (his men in brutal hand-to-hand battle fought with bayonets), Antietam (Bloody Lane), Fredericksburg, other engagements. Brigade destroyed at Chancellorsville: only 31 survivors. Brief service Eastern Tennessee Command. Stripped of rank for striking superior officer (General Sherman), conduct unbecoming, & reckless disregard. Request for brevet Generalcy refused. Is not entitled to be styled 'General'. Is not entitled to wear uniform of US General, preside at inspections, receive salutes, award decorations. Is to be styled as civilian: 'Mister O'Keeffe or James O'Keeffe., esquire.' ON NO ACCOUNT is permitted to raise troops without WRITTEN orders from Washington. Any attempt so to do is to be prevented by the immediate detention of subject or BY ANY MEANS NECESSARY.

WHEREABOUTS (if known): Redemption Falls (formerly Joliet Gulch), Mountain Terr, Nthn Sector. Appointed Territorial Secretary Feb 65 (unbeknownst to subj, wife petitioned incessantly for him to receive governmental position.) Is Acting Gov. To be DISMISSED as soon as practicable. Informants ****** & ***** report subj widely resented. Govship has seen lawlessness, summary executions by 'Vigilante' band; worsening outlaw & Indian depredations. Legislative matters unattended to. Waggon trains undefended. Bitter Party feuding. Railroad not progressed. Interests of capital unrespected.

SUSPICION: Subject suspected of criminal conspiracy in grand larceny: viz, piracy of secret Federal shipment of gold bullion and sapphires, Fort Galloway, August 27th, 66. Strong intelligence indicates subj is clandestine ally of perpetrator, Cole John McLaurenson, alias 'Johnny Thunders.' (Confederate blackflagger.) Subj will attempt to use share of plunder to purchase weapons for long ambitioned invasion of British Canada or Ireland.

RECOMMENDATION: Send Field Intelligence Agent directly. 'Cartography Division.' He is both to prepare an expedition & learn what may be learnt. Preferably unmarried & a volunteer.

V

CHAPTER 56

A-ROVING SHALL I GO

Winterton's Fieldwork – A meeting with Natives
A visit to Fort Braintree – An assignation in a cowshed

Nov. IX. 66. Temperance Hotel, Kinsella's Crossing

Two days' hellish ride north-east, badly saddle-galled & exhausted, but no knowledge of her whereabouts in the town or at any settlement along the way. Asked at every crossroads, saying I had news of a onetime friend, a Colonel whom she had nursed in the War. Wife (Mrs Blackmore) had borne the Colonel a daughter; had called her Lucia as an honor. Perilous strategy to speak so openly of her name; but disquiet becomes a spur.

Every stage office closed and many locked up. Notice on a door at Levintown:

ALL ROUTES SUSPENDED INDEFINITELY BY EMERGENCY ORDER OF GENERAL O'KEEFFE, OWING TO FREQUENCY OF HIGHWAY ROBBERY & MURDER. PERSONS LEAVING THIS TERRITORY ON HORSEBACK, OR BY OTHER MEANS, STAND WARNED. YOUR PROTECTION IS NOT GUARANTEED.

Strange, my compass has joined the thermometer in failing to function. Must be sitting atop a lode of magnetic matter. Broke a trirrup† coming down, godblasted nuisance. Saddler in the town perhaps.

THOUGHT: World where carnal and social intercourse were reversed. Sweethearts met furtively for conversation, literary criticism, & cetera. Conversely, at supper-party, would be acceptable – indeed considered bad form *not* – to sexually gratify one's hosts, or whichever guests happened to be placed either side of one. Débutante balls would be organized on the principle of pleasure (as opposed to being business

† Presumably a stirrup.

occasions with an orchestra). 'Miss Amelia, you look quite radiant since your return from Venice. Might you permit me the singular honor of the Last Rogering of the evening? If your card is not already completed, of course.' Would be less of that dishonest poetry where swains warble on about fen and field and daffodil and lake, when what they would secretly like to immortalize is the bush, rock, mesa, Alp, & cetera, near where Daisy, or Dorothy, or Micky Muck, or Matteo was desired to, or almost, or actually did, suck on country pleasures. Unlikely to come about very soon, I suppose. Pity. Better for us all. Only that whoremongery should soon become quite as dull as most conversations now are. And then we should be longing to talk to one another.

Spent the early morning *solus*, taking readings near Lake Inishfree. Saw Koötenais watching my labors from Devil's Backbone. One of them ventured down a little, in my direction, as I supposed; but when I raised my staff in greeting he ran away very quickly. Almost goatish in their fleetfootedness. Saw them again before long. Five males, approx 25 – also a boy. More perhaps hidden, I suppose. Felt not exactly fear, but sudden weight of being alone. Could not have outrun them had they struck.

About 11 of the forenoon was attempting some fieldwork, as much to quell anxieties as for any other purpose. It is becoming too apparent that we have greatly underestimated the number of surveyors required, for vast tracts are heavy going, swampish or steep, and many of the forests almost literally impenetrable, so that to map them might mean their destruction. Was sketching a shallow fish-shaped gorge, about half a mile long, to the N.N.E of Mc Dermott's Farm, when was approached by two besoiled old coots. Monitored me for a time, like schoolboys observing the distress of a scorched centipede through a lens. One attempted to disregard them, as one ignores the first shudderings of an illness. But this quadruped of filth would not be ignored.

Was I this-hea government feller? Was I writin up this-hea map book? Did I know that this-hea gorge was known as Ducksfoot Canyon? Told me ludicrous lies about how it received its name. (Had once been a lake. Flock of Canada ducks landed thereupon. Feet froze to surface. Could not escape. Flew away in a body, taking the water with them. As though they done planned it out.)

I fear such men. Not alone for their lies, but for the fact that they appear to believe them. 'Dang me if nature aint cruel,' Coot II blurted, as though the first earthly sage to have had revealed to him this nodule of trite undergraduate snots; while the other, my Virgil through the underworld of banalities, continued his peroration.

'Remarkable,' I said.

'Aint it now.'

Spat frequently, copiously, loathsomely, the goat.

Had many other facts that would interest me, he missupposed. A floodin (I assume he meant a flood) of such biblical forcefulness that a surtn house in these-hea parts wuz carry there fowteen (I assume he meant 'fourteen') mile by the deluge, and the owner and his bub *still inside eatin hominy.*

Indeed, I said. I had heard that fact already.

I had?

Yes. The owner purchased the land beneath the spot where the house came to rest and he resideth there happily now. Extraordinary. I also had the story of the orphan raised by wolves, the floating stones, the three-breasted squaw, the squaw with an organ of generation in her abdomen, the talking apes of Idaho, the water-dragon of Liverpool Lake, and the grass that causes famishment to any who walk on it ('till they'd ate their own childer to be full').

The mammalia looked at one another. Then the two of them looked at me. 'Captain Ghoul at service,' I did not actually say, but things may be said by a stance. I had taken off my hood, the better to permit them appreciate my full beauty. They appeared almost femininely wonderstruck.

And away toward some adjacent latrine they staggered, thumping one another on the back like music-hall idiots, pitching and yucking with repugnant hilarity. There are moments when I am greatly troubled for the future of this Republic. Not that those two diseased old imbeciles will be part of it very long.

Completed my calculations and sat by the river a while. Saw specks of gold in the water. Was weary, so that I nodded off into shallow of sleep. Uneasy nights of late. This not remembering very troubling. Or holes in the recollection as in a cake of Prussian cheese. Jolted back to the world by whinny of a horse.

At least a score of Blackfoot observing me from a line of oaks. Heavily armed from what I could see (with rifles and bows). Made immediately to walk toward them, hand outstretched. Arrow whipped into the scree before me – not half a yard from my left boot. Backed slowly away with gloves raised high. But others were approaching from behind. Tallest, a leader, emerged from the body. Walked up to me without uttering a word. Eyes lined with cobalt paint, like a buccaneer's mask. Crow feathers in his hair. Necklaces and an amulet. Fully a minute he scrutinized my person, gesturing that I was to turn about before him. Had me empty out my pockets but did not thieve anything. Squinted very disgustedly as he looked at my face. Rather shaken by the encounter . . .†

. . . Later, was walking in the principal street (dirty soldiers drinking; skinny old horses) when I lit upon a nymph of the pave. Irish. About 25. Five feet four approx. Wantonest smile I ever saw. Followed her to barns down an alley behind the livery stable. Murphy Bros. Bounden slave.

Cows enstalled, staring like a row of nuns. She pretended innocence. Drove me demented by her coyness. What was Mister's profession? was he a professor or a minister, for that was what he looked in them fancy black duds. Was a lawyer, I said. (I do not know why.) She said three. I agreed. What did I want of her? That would not be possible. Was there anything else that might suffice? Loosening a corona of russet hair. The very naughty Mister I was, to be sure, to go askin a nice girleen such a badness. And myself brought up in the church and all, unstaying the lacings of her chemise.

Redeeming Christ. There now, Allanah. We shall have a little fun, rest you easy. Permitted no kiss of her cranberry *bouche*, but to touch her face and hair. Was gibbering like a Bedlamite as she unfastened me. Lay in her palm like a slug on a Giotto. Anxious, I suppose. But she did not ridicule. Soon had me tiptoeing on the spot. (Christ Above; what must they think of us?) Asked me to quiet down, I suppose for fear of arousing the curiosity of some slack-jawed Pat of the pitchfork and the torch-bearing bibulous bros. Cupid's couch was in a closet of damp, old hay; she forbade not the anointing of Venus. Beelzebub & Moloch, prepare thee my skewer, I shall roast on it happily till kingdom come – or unhappily, despairingly, whichever is required. Only baste me in the juices of a redhead's sins, and season me with the salt of a bishop's.

Seconds of bliss & one's joys ranneth over. Washed at a trough, serenaded by the horseflies and the intermittent philosophical low. Had a child at home, she told me, husband died at Mechanicsville; had to take to this profession for there was none other she could do. Hoped to marry again come Martinmastide; go into California with her new beau. She requested, and I did not forbid, a smoke of my meerschaum. Poor

† There follow two and a half pages of trigonometric calculation.

lamb was soon coughing like a broken-down train, & needed to have her back rubbed, which was delicious to do. Most exquisitely made shoulders I ever touched in my life. A sacrilege even to look on them. Before long one felt the want of a return to the fray. Maneuver I wished would cost another three, she insisted, for it was an intimacy only permitted her beau. Smoldering stars – exceptionally generous. One was practically speaking in Gaelic.

As she fastened herself afterwards, asked me what part of England I was from. Told her I was not of that country, but from Boston in the states. There was a whole rake of Pats beyond in that place, she said. Confirmed that this was indeed the case. Did I know the bossdog of this Territory was a Pat itself? I said that I heard of the fact, but knew little of the gentleman. He was 'a man and a half' – this she told me proudly. Done a powerful lot for Ireland. Done a lot for the poor. It was awful sad when you thought about the talk of his late private troubles, for his wife was a fine person, too.

'Your neighbor,' I ventured.

'How, Mister? My neighbor?'

'Oh nothing, dear girl. May I assist you with your lacings? It was only that I had had it, I cannot recollect from whom, that the lady you mention is in residence at Fort Braintree.'

'Not at all, she stays at Edwardstown. At the Plains Hotel. They say she will go back to New York when the spring rise come. For that is where her people are living.'

I was kneeling in the straw with one of her shoes in my hand. I looked up at my backyard mavourneen.

Told me the Governor lived separately from his wife ('a rare beauty'), who had journeyed from the east in the summer to be with him. But the intimate atmosphere between them had not been a happy one, it was whispered. The Governor had a mouth on him. He could be violent by times. He would not raise a hand but his words could be cruel.

'Oh, dear.'

'So they say. I never met him.'

The lady had removed to the aforementioned coppertown, a pleasanter settlement than Redemption Falls, since the former was constructed on a peaceful tributary of the Missouri, while the latter, a hellroaring mining camp, had scarcely a Christian in residence, and was infested by doxies, slingers, galoots, and indigenes of the County Limerick. It was currently the Territory's capital but would surely not remain so for long.

'Poxbottle' would be the better name for such a conurbation. Little wonder Mrs O'Keeffe could not stick it.

At Edwardstown she wrote poetry, sometimes painted, and photographed. She was said to be an artistic lady. Moreover, a small controversy was said to have fleetingly energized the town when she had invited a grist-miller of Bremen to model for one of her Grecian studies; and not, as it were, in his Lederhosen. She was not, one might say, a person of narrow convention. Always wanting to kick at the traces. And devil the harm in that, when you thought. The poor woman had suffered so greatly.

'You seem well informed,' I smiled. 'Are you a spy, perhaps?'

'Sure it's known the world over. My beau saw her once. 'Tis said she's the handsomest creature in all the creation; but lately awful sad, so that she do hardly go out. Don't hardly ate a biscuit, but above in the rooms. They calls her the Ghost of the Plains, so my man told me that time. For that's where she stay, the Plains Hotel. 'Tis said it's the finest in Edwardstown.'

'This Edwardstown you mentioned? I do not know it.'

''Tis a fair piece from here. A week's ride by any road.'

'Through Redemption Falls, did you say? I am unfamiliar with your country.'

'Aye, Redemption, and south on the Carlow road. They do say it's a town of wonders. But I never seen it myself. But my man was there once. He said it was strikin. Why, have you business down that run of the country, Mister?'

'No, no, my dear. No business at all. I was speaking out of curiosity merely.'

'Do you mind and I ask you, Mister, what happened your poor face? Was it something in the War itself?'

I looked at her a while. But something confused me, I think. Presently I became distressed so that she must ask me what was wrong. In truth, I was not weeping for any pain of my injuries. It was that I could not remember, no matter how I searched, how or where I had come by them.

'Gettysburg,' I said in the close; and she sympathized.

Found it a very frightening experience.

V

CHAPTER 57

THROUGH ALL THE GROVES OF JEOPARDY THE LITTLE PRINCE DID WALK

A sighting from Donnelly's Cliff – A disagreement among newlyweds

'Wounds of Christ,' says Eliza.

'Told you I seen him,' says Vinson.

'That's him.'

'I knowed it.'

'That's him, Cole.'

'You sure?'

A boy in velvet britches is trudging toward the schoolhouse with a gunnysack of books on his back. He retrieved them from the study of the man who protects him. They are heavy and thick. Their authors were paid by the word. He is unaware that he is being watched from that copse on Donnelly's Cliff. He staggers under the weight of his booty.

'What can we do, Cole?'

'Take him, I guess.'

She hands her husband the telescope. He peers through it a time. ('Sure don't look like no kin of yourn to me.') Vinson, meanwhile, regards her with bleak anticipation, but whatever he might expect is unclear.

'Take him and what?'

'Can ride with us, caint he? Take him down to Arkansas when we go.'

'Arkansas?'

'Yeah. We're goin into Arkansas.'

'But . . . what about Canada?'

'I dunno. What about it?'

'It's a home the child needs. Not a gun and the prairie. Or sleepin in a saddle and runnin from lawmen.'

'Aint gonna be like that. Not for long any ways.'

'*How* long?'

'Girl – Christ Almighty, if you don't ask a question. I'ma go down Arkansas, do a thing I gotta do. Some boys I know – why? Is it any your concern? Since when I gotta ask *you* before suckin a breath?'

'That aint what you promised – how much more money you need?'

'*More.* That's how. You don't like it, take off!'

'And maybe I will! Direct to the marshal. What y'think about that, you piece of grovellin shit?'

'Keep workin that maw, girl, you gonna know plenty what I think.'

'Aint afeared of you, McLaurenson, nor any of your ilk. Lift your robbin hand to *me*, I'll shove it wet down your gullet.'

His glove to her throat. Slamming her backways against a boulder. Her feet lifted clear of the stones.

'You mouthy little nothin. Talk to *me* like some houseboy? Give you a cut of my beltbuckle if you want it! You hear?'

'Cole,' Vinson says. 'She don't mean no harm by it.'

'Mind your business! You're warned. Stand away or get dealt.'

'Christsake, McLaurenson, there's a child in the woman.'

'*You told me you want the boy. You want him, I'ma git him. Fix up your mind, girl. Cause I'm tirin of your mouth! I'ma go-down to Arkansas, rob me a train. And that the way it is.*'

∇

CHAPTER 58

THE DAWNING OF THE DAY

———▶———

The Governor dreams of a lady – A backstage priest
The Thunder-makers – Ophelia in Shropshire

He awakens in half-light to see a woman in his casement. Her back to his gaze. Has she returned?

Lucia? Catharine? His thirst is broiling. She revolves in the volutes, as though having heard his thoughts. A curtain-veil of lace obscures her.

Sleeplessness and bourbon and an afterimage from a dream. A meadowlark gliding over furze. If a dream can have a shape, this one seemed to him a conch shell. And he is inside it, somehow. Drifting spirals of coral. The whiteness of its recessed polyphonies.

His mother, he sees now; but she is clad all in rags, like a wretch in an etching of the Famine in Ireland. Her hands tensely cupped, as though holding a butterfly. When she opens them, a minuscule light like a star, and it smolders with blistering clarity as it rises above her palms and moves slowly around the edges of the room. He does not know which to watch, his mother or the light – he feels one of them can tell him something important. There are sounds in the walls: the scrabblings of mice. He finds himself unable to stir.

Unmoving in his chair. Booted feet on the floorboards. The crusting of sleep in his eyes. There is madness in his family. He has always feared it. Dread of the chains and the jacket, and then? A peasant-fear, Duggan said.

'*Nel mezzo del cammin di nostra vita,*' she whispers. '*Lasciate ogne speranza . . .*'

Once, as a schoolboy, with the Jesuits in England, he auditioned for the part of Othello. He was not given the role – his accent was too Irish – and was told, instead, to present himself behind the flies. He had wanted to weep for humiliation and anger. The gaiety of his classmates at his retreat.

A Father, a Belgian, onyx-headed and tall, welcomed him to the wings with kindly words. As though here, and not the stage, was the realm of truer miracles; as though to be out of the action was the highest vocation.

Strange and dark, this blue-place of drapes. Musk of the mothballs, old priest and blackface.

He showed the boy a skull. Canvas breastplates, a jester's bells: these were displayed to him with druidical somberness, as though components of a long forgotten sacrament. The more flippant their purpose, so it seemed to the boy, the greater the priest's solemnity as he explained them. Daggers that retracted into their hilts. A trunk of opulent costumes. Trapdoors.

The mysteries of illusion. Bloodlike dyes. Helmets and monstrous masks. Here was a drum filled with tiny stone marbles. If you rattled it, the gush of a rainstorm. A tincture of this compound touched with a heated nail and a fog would result, which could make a scene more enigmatic. People like not being able to understand things straight away. What was life itself, but an appearance not comprehended? And look – a pane of metal, which when shaken with vigor gave out the rumble of thunder. The squawking and parping of an adolescent orchestra, and the scrape of his house-fellows' boots.

Father Liebhart made the rainstorm and the boy made the thunder; and collegially they watched, through gaps in the curtains, as the capering deluded who thought they were significant revealed themselves as painted puppets. 'Some only act,' Father Liebhart murmured. 'But others make the thunder. You will always be one of those, James.' He learned an important lesson, that year he turned fifteen. We see what we wish to see, unless we are backstage; in which case, there is nothing invisible.

For no reason it comes back to him, as he eyes the woman in his room. In the shadows of his dressing-screen by the corner nearest the door. She has acquired a garland of lilies from the air and she blows on the embers of their withers. Ophelia of the west. Boy who played her at Stonesglade? But Ophelia is not in Othello. To speak and purpose not. And if all of this is lunacy – as it seems to him it could be – might not madness be a kind of relief?

He swallows. She is gone. He elbows up in his chair. The bed not slept in. The bottle half-drunk. His dog on the floor, asleep.

The skreeking of a chalk-nub on a square of slate. The boy must be awake – on the landing. He howls for him to be silent. The scraping stops. Tumble of stocking-feet down the staircase.

He will describe the troubling dream to Desdemona. And then he remembers. And awakens.

∇

CHAPTER 59

THE MEETING OF THE WATERS

A schoolteacher's account – Tidings of the boy are requested

It was a Sunday afternoon, I remember, for I had been to chapel that morning and it was the day the banns were read for my younger sister's marriage. In any case, I am certain it must have been in November. I have reason to recollect the date.

I was walking not far from the town in a place called Farrington's Meadow, with my fiancé John O'Lee; later my husband. We had had a little quarrel of the kind young sweethearts will have and had gone out walking together to make it up.

We were sitting, John and I, by the meeting of the two streams, when we saw that a young woman was approaching along the track. John happened to notice her and he wondered aloud to me who she was; for between our families we would have known fairly everyone in the County but neither of us knew this girl.

I would say that she was nineteen or twenty, very pale and poorly. She was a pretty girl, you could see that; but she was not in a good way. Her dress was worn to rags and she was expecting a child. It was terrible to see her so poor in that condition. I would have thought she was six months gone.

Well; she came up close to where we were seated on a blanket in the grass, and we saluted her and she bid us a good day. Her accent was strange to me; I could not name it, but there was the states in it anyhow, and something eastern. There were a few pleasantries about the winter sunshine, nothing of consequence. She did not seem to want to continue her walk. I saw her looking at whatever little bits of a picnic we had, and I felt sorry for her, then, and troubled. My sister-in-law was expecting to have a baby that Christmas, and all I could think was how frightening it would be to know want at such a time that should be happy for any young woman. I asked if she would break bread with us, for we had plenty enough to spare and it would bless us to share it, if she wished. She said in her way that she would not care to interpose, but I pressed the invitation and she sat by us.

I could see that John was a little vexed with me for having invited her, but when she sat and took a morsel to eat, after a while I could see that he was glad. If you had seen her, it would have broken your heart. It was as though she had never been given anything in her life. And to be honest, I found it difficult to keep a conversation, it was so sad to see her hunger like that. But John was very kind and could see the way it was with me, and he went to talking away with her, drawing no attention to anything, like any gentle friend. It is a strange thing to say, but actually, at that moment, I could see why I wished to be his wife. There was a German boy in the town who had been paying me attentions; very hand-some and amusing and all the girls loved him; but I could see that he would never be John.

Well, the poor mite ate a little and she drank a cup of water. She said her name was Mary Jane and she was going into California. And this did not surprise either John or myself, for we had a great number of migrant people, many of them poor, journeying through the Territory after the War. One took care, I suppose, not to ask them many questions, for often they were leaving a past of which they did not wish to speak. My mother always told us that it was holier not to inquire of them, for to tempt a Christian to lie was the same sin as lying, and in some ways would go worse for the tempter.

She inquired if I was Miss Doherty, the schoolteacher at Redemption Falls, and I said, I suppose surprised, that I was. A shopwoman in the town had mentioned me in passing, she said. She could not recall her name.

She asked me pleasantly about school-teaching, was it difficult and so on. I think I said that it could be trying, but was also pleasing in its way, but that I did not know if I should care to do it after I was married for I should likely have my own family, then. And John made some joke or another about that.

Then she went to asking me about the children and what they were like. She had seen this one and that one as she went about the town. We had a little Chinese girl about whom she inquired. And we had identical twins there, Karl-Heinz and Edmund Schiller. And how would a body know them apart, and so forth. And there was a boy who stayed at the Governor's and who sometimes attended at the school. Was he a good boy at his lessons? How often did he come? I laughed, for this famous boy was forever being asked about, and I said he was as good as ever he might be. Why did she wish to know it? Oh, it was only that she had seen him hither and yon, she told me, on his way to the schoolhouse, and had wondered what he was like and if he was happy in himself. Did they feed him at the Governor's and take good care of him there? Did he have nice clothes? Did he sleep in a bed? Was it true he had a horse? Had he doctoring if he was ill? She appeared to know something of General O'Keeffe, and to respect him considerably, which John and I did, too, very much. I said, which was all truth, to the best of my knowledge, that the Governor had come to regard the boy very naturally, almost as a father his son. So his situation was happy, then? I said yes, I thought it was. There was a look I shall never forget in her eyes.

Had he a mother? she asked me, then. I said that he had: a very kindly lady of a well-to-do family. For there were rumors in the town of difficulties in the marriage of the Governor and Mrs O'Keeffe but I did not think it proper to share them.

It seems strange, all this time later, to write it down, but it did not seem so at the time, that she would be curious about this child. The whole of the County was inquisitive about our foundling personality. She was far from the first to have asked of him.

After a while of I suppose half an hour, she stood up and bid us good-bye, for she had an appointment, so she said, at some distance. We wished her safe travel and she thanked us for the food and went off in the direction of the town. I felt that she was distressed for she had departed with an uneasing suddenness. Of course, I did not know why.

A man was waiting for her at the verge of Tiernan's Woods. I saw him very clearly, although he was so far from me that I could not make out any feature. He was clad all in black, like a priest as it might be. John never saw him but I know that I did.

I said: 'John, that girl did not tell us something. I wish you would go after her and see to her safety.' But he said that he did not want to do that; I was taking a notion, and besides he was tired, for he had been building a corral the day before with his uncle, and wished to rest and talk.

To be honest (he told me), it was better that she had gone. He had seen that kind of girl during the War. It would not do in the town if we had been observed to address her. I remember asking him, for I was green as an unsunned pumpkin, despite thinking I knew nearabout everything in the world, how could he tell she was that kind. He told me that he did not want to discuss it but felt sorry for her, as any Christian should, for the life of such a girl was entirely without hope. The crime was the man's, and not the girl's, he believed. He had seen things in the War that were terrible. It was the first time that John and I had spoken of the War, for I knew that he had come home hurt by it, not in body, but in heart. And I do not believe we ever spoke of it again after that day. He never attended commemorations, or marches, and so on. He used to tell our children that he could not remember any of it. He had a medal, but it lived in a drawer.

And that is all I can tell you. For I never saw her again. John and I remained at the Meadow until dusk was coming on, and then we walked back to the town. We were married not long afterward, rather more expeditiously than pleased our mothers, and our daughter was born nine months subsequent to that day by the river. We were married fifty-two years. He was my treasure in life. Every minute of every day, I miss him.

∇

CHAPTER 60

SOME KILLERS WIELD A SWORD OF STEEL, BUT OTHERS PLY THE PEN

The mapmaker returns to Redemption Falls
An encounter with a hangman – Cartography rebuffed
A commercial proposition – A warning

XII. 11. 66

Arrived back here 11 last night, too fatigued to continue southerly. Widow answered my pounding: same quarters, lower charge. Fell asleep with my clothes on, even my boots. Did not awaken for nine hours.

Scorching head-ache when I arose, as though I had been hard at the barkjuice, or smoking French cheroots – which surprised me for I had indulged neither vice the night preceding. But body is as body does. Drowned my head in cold water. Did not do.

Saw the Gov and the boy passing below my window. Holding the lad by the hand. Heading southerly, slowly. To the schoolhouse I suppose, for the boy was carrying a string of books. O'K paused to buy him a pear from a stand outside the grocer's. (Corish his name. Unusual.) As he looked up, the Gov saw me – I have very little doubt of it – but feigned, for some reason, not to have done so. A number of passers-by appeared to laugh at the duo as they went. The G is so large, his ward so small, that their juxtaposition is indeed rather taking, in its way. Poor old broke-down waggon.

Wrote my notes and a letter and accounted my money and considered what is to be done. Not easy; but several reasons for optimism, after all. One must steady one's eyes on the prize.

Tried to say a prayer but it was difficult, difficult. Was thinking on poor Papa. His anniversary today. Such a good good man, by any and every measure. Worked tirelessly hard for us, never a thought for himself. And when Mama was ill. All those nights at her bedside. Wish we had been in the way of better friends. But one never thinks of such matters when young and selfish. Always seems there will be time to atone.

Descended to the purgatorio of spitballs that is entitled the Dining Room. Had it entirely to myself but for the flies and other crawlers. (Menu being happily eaten by a biscuit-beetle.) A slattern came in and regarded me morosely. She looked like a person, if such a one exists, professionally employed to frighten children. I requested of it sustenance. It shambled away rattling its chains (not really). I must not exaggerate; it is foolish.

Strange giddiness; but it is the enemy. Difficulty in killing it. Thought of seeing her again, I suppose. Still, one must be prudent of demeanor and go about quietly; for recklessness, truly, could undo.

Before leaving, a few days ago, I had pinned on the staging-post outside the hotel a notice soliciting a number of helpmen. No answer had come in regard to my plea. This most inconvenient; indeed downright irritating. Too frequently, alas, it seems that our American citizens, rightly the envy of the world in multifarious ways, yet have much to learn when it comes to recognizing what is in their – our – better interest.

They – we – are like infants sometimes.

They – we – need a boot up the britches.

At my breakfast, which was ghastly, a congealment of *frijole* beans and eggs (this concoction has been my daily visitation since coming into the Territory), I asked the Widow to make certain there had been no applications. She returned moments later, having inquired of unspecified lesser daemons, with no information that might sweeten the bitchdrool served me as coffee, but wielding a placard which she intended to display in the saloon window of her premises. On this specimen of intrepidity she sought my opinion. Here is how it read, verbatim:

Drunk for a dollar. Dead drunk for three. Clean straw to lie on.

Told her I esteemed it a piece of real poetry. That did not seem to much gratify her, but she put it up anyway.

Breakfast digested, or at least not yet regurgitated, I betook myself to see the editor, a Mr John Knox Trevanion, at the offices of the *Redemption and Edwardstown Epitaph*, and discussed with that gentleman, who is Scottish by birth, the numerous requirements of my coming endeavor and how he might assist me to fit them. Specifically, I asked if

339

he would consider a proposal: viz, to print for me on his presses a number of poster-bills, which might be pasted about the town and environs.

Mr Trevanion is leader of the O+O men in the County, a fact one is not supposed to know, though everyone seems to.† It was odd, indeed, to be conversing with an executioner. They say his particular skill is with knots. His fingers were plump and often moved about on his inkblot, in a manner that called to mind a spider or crab. Scuttling tarantulas and a tartan cravat. A blackwatch beetle; balding.

He was at first a little obstinate, which surprised me greatly, and indisposed to converse candidly on the reason for his position. But presently, he became a shade less obtuse. I had been observed, so he told me, entering the Acting Governor's house.

'What of that?' I asked mildly. 'One wished to see him, after all.'

The Governor was not much admired in these parts (Mr Trevanion said), which was every degree as enlightening as if he had confided that King Henry the Eighth, decsd., London, was not much admired in the Vatican. The reason why he had been sent here was not at all apparent; he had never administered anything efficiently, including himself. It was his, Trevanion's, view, and that of his paper, that any friend of James O'Keeffe was an enemy of Redemptionites.

'You misunderstand,' I replied. 'One could hardly name oneself his friend. One is in the employ of the Federal Government, as he is; that is all.'

'Is it, sir?' asked the Scot, in the blunt fashion of his country. When a Caledonian of Mr Trevanion's sort addresses you as 'sir', unless he is a waiter or a ghillie (and commonly even then) he is making it plain that he despises you.

'I have met the gentleman only once and the meeting was brief.'

'Pontius Pilate met the Savior of the Universe only once,' retorted Mr Trevanion. 'A great deal of treachery can be accomplished in one brief meeting.'

† 'O+O Men': a flag of convenience for Vigilantes of the locale. The origin and meaning of the term is unclear. A memoir published by Trevanion himself in 1895, while fervently denying that its author had been a Vigilante, is striking for its insider's knowledge. He elucidated the name 'O+O' as standing for the Spanish *ojos y oídos* – the eyes and ears. Others have maintained that the name contained a typographical warning, that the figures 'O+O' resemble a pair of watching eyes and a funereal cross. Whatever the characters meant, they were not something you wanted to see painted on your door.

I looked at Mr Trevanion. Mr Trevanion looked at me. I was thinking of the numerous great men of his homeland: the surgeons and scientists and colossi of the intellect, the thinkers and philosophers and jurors and poets. And then I was thinking of Mr Trevanion.

The townspeople were not happy with my presence among them in the Territory, said the Missing Link. It was rumored that my mission could cause them certain difficulties. It would meet staunch resistance; I may as well know it. It would kick at a nest of hornets.

'Why, sir, maps do not instigate difficulties,' was my amused rejoinder. 'If well-made, they solve them, or at least make solutions the clearer.'

'No map is wanted here, sir,' Mr Trevanion said coolly. 'We live tolerably well without one.'

At this assertion, I own I was astonished, completely. How could knowledge of our Republic, the measurement of her form, ever be regarded suspiciously, rather than welcomed with gleeful gratitude? This is proof, were it required, that our people need urgently to shake themselves out of certain regrettable peculiarities. I said that the Ordnance Survey of Great Britain was our motherland's greatest glory ('motherland' was a mistake, I could see that immediately) and that no less a titan of letters than deathless Wordsworth had floated its praises in the comet-streams of Pegasus.

'Of?'

'Pegasus,' I clarified. 'The wingèd horse. The figure, the emblem of poesy.'

Mr Trevanion said the matter was not so simple as all that. Out here in the west, I would find that the horses were wingless. (Prim, tight smile. Christ, poor Morag at the hoosie. Imagine its dawn-lit pawings.) The only Wordsworth with whom he was acquainted had been a sharp-shooter in the War, whose boast was of dispatching more Yankees than had Jesse and Frank James. Mr Trevanion was in regular contact with this poet of the Winchester, he added cryptically. If ever I wished to see a display of marksmanship at close hand.

Here in this Territory, what a man owned was his. Often, he had crossed the world for it; commonly had fought for it; and his property, or any claim he might have to same, was not properly the business of any other person or agency. Such had been the situation obtaining for a number of years; it would be a most foolish government that would license its representatives to set foot over the fence-lines of a freeborn citizen, still less to record anything which might be found there. It would be, as it were, to put a hand in the fire, a head in the crocodile's jaws. Cartography was a euphemism for conquest and thievery; how the burglar inventoried his pickings. There was also, to state it frankly, the question of taxation. The citizens of the Territory were not idiots.

'How do you mean, sir?' I asked Mr Trevanion colorlessly.

'If we are measured, we shall be taxed,' the Pict replied. 'Only a child does not know that this is what maps are truly for: to give assistance to governments in strapping their people. Governments and the sneaks who work for them.'

'Sir – '

'Sir, nothing, sir. Nothing! They spout fineries in Washington, while out here we fight to endure. There is hardly a man in Washington could point to this Territory on your precious map, yet he wishes to dictate us how to live in it. He crushed down the south, then burned her to ash; when her people were defeated, he ground his heel in their faces. Is this what shall calculate us, sir? This parcel of Judases? Tell your paymasters, sir, to think again.'

Judas. The Savior. The tax collector. Pontius Pilate. It was becoming quite the biblical day. One anticipated unfavorable comparison to the Whore of Babylon, but that title, one realized, probably was owned by another in the Territory. I had a passable idea of who that might be.

One was aware (one said) that life could be difficult in the Territory. The desperadoes, for example. The piracy of the *Harrison*. When one thought on how those unfortunate sailors had been murdered so callously. Truly, it was a monstrous affair.

Patently I was fascinated by that matter (he countered deviously), for it had come to his attention, and the notice of certain others, that I had been asking many questions about it, in all the town.

Had I?

Aye, I had.

I had not been aware of it.

It was almost as though I were a marshal, or an agency detective, or an insurance man in the employ of the steamship company. Alas, none of these exhilarating avocations was my own (I chuckled); one had merely been arrested by the event on reading of it back home in the States. Like any honest citizen, one hoped the miscreant would shortly be fetched to justice, of course; but apart from that hope, one's interest was uninvolved.

He would never be captured, Mr Trevanion replied. Not while James O'Keeffe held power.

The certitude I found striking. Why did he feel that?

'Because my enemy's enemy is my friend,' he said gnomically. 'But I will say no more of that man. So do not ask me.'

He would not be persuaded on the matter of the poster-bills, no matter what argument I advanced to him. A consideration of a hundred dollars, then a hundred and fifty I mentioned. These he refused as though having been offered a brimming spittoon. There was no price on this earth that would persuade him to prostitute his principles (he enjoyed the alliteration, as his type of Scotsman always will). If there was nothing further for the present, he would bid me a good day, for he was preoccupied by the necessity, the regrettable obligation, of having to labor for his bread. Irony, I believe, was being deployed by the Laird Trevanion, of that particularly thin-lipped, self-preening, supercilious, Edinburgh debating-society kind.

One was tempted to inquire if his unprrrostitutable prrinciples extended to a prractice called frreedom o' exprression. Instead, I asked him placidly if he did not think that his readership might be entrusted with the ventilation of two sides of a case. His nation, I made myself say, esteemed civilized disputation (when not gutting one another with claymores, I did not say). Why not place my suggested text in the columns of his organ, and counter it, if he wished, in an editorial or introductory? That would satisfy me quite adequately, I said. Unless of course, he were afraid of the joust.

No flight to the bull ever shafted so sweetly. An outraged squirrel. A chipmunk libeled. The cheek-pouches bulging with winded affrontedness. Celticism wounded is always memorable. He would have me *know*, sir; would yield before no calumny; ancient name of Trevanion, doomed charge at Culloden, & cetera. Cornish, Welsh, Manx, Caledonian, Bretons, Hibernians (the worst, the very worst) – the whole predictable box. Moping, self-piteous, skirt-wearing ninnies. Only know where to tickle and they gasp for you.

Immediately he consented to place the advertisement in his pages: *soliciting the application of fifty strong men, miners preferably, or possessing a sound knowledge of the local topography;* these to be drilled by myself in the rudiments of surveying, and some, if sufficiently sharp-witted, in trigonometry. Mr Trevanion appeared surprised by the latter proposition, but my own policy on such matters is clear. Our sad war is over; we must henceforth aspire to newer (to better) manifestations of equality. Cannot a miner be taught to figure his numbers as well as the Harvardian? If not, then all the wars in the world were fought for nothing – so it seems, at least, to me.

I said that I would also have employment for a number of guides and pathfinders, probably Indians, but at this proposition Mr Trevanion determinedly drew the line. 'Savages, sir, do not read the *Epitaph*,' he averred. I did not supply the obvious rejoinder.

His talon, which felt limp, accepted the offer of my hand. And I had a strange desire, the like of which I never experienced previously with a man, to take him tenderly by the sideburns and kiss him passionately on the mouth; not out of desire for congress of that (or any) sort with him, but simply so as to see what he might do. But I did not prosecute this fancy. Perhaps it is just as well. One has rather grown accustomed to respiration.

He would find me at the Widow's, he offered in farewell, the wee, sleekit, tim'rous beastie. In a few days, one said. One was going to Edwardstown. With a mickle & a muckle, one made to depart.

Only this: that as I opened the door, he said something very queer. It was calculated, I feel certain, to disturb.

'You are a gaming man, I believe, sir.'

'I would not put it that way.'

'Six hundred dollars, is it now? Your debt at cards in this Territory?'

I made no reply, for that was none of his concern.

'The outlaw McLaurenson. You inquired of him to me.'

'Did I?'

'That man walked the streets of the town this day. I saw him from that window. Himself and a girl. And then I saw *you*, sir. You have been ten paces away from him. Have a care how you play, sir. You are watched in this County.'

'Always,' I said. For I would give him no satisfaction.

There were men in the street outside.

∇

CHAPTER 61

ON LOOKING AT A PHOTOGRAPH
BY MR O'SULLIVAN[†]

~~The Finishing~~
November snow benedictions the boy.
In the chill gray smoke, the lost stallion ~~seems~~ ghostlike,
Or vision of horse. Some ridden-down symbol
Of bit-grinning fears that gallop through nightmares.
It nudges its bridle toward where he lies
Among the reeds. But the boy is still.

Perhaps a girl expects him, still.
Watches the road for her homecoming boy,
Who joked of love but told no lies,
And laughed on Hallowe'en, so ghostlike.
Riding now, among the nightmares.
Not representing. No loaded symbol.

No banner; no cross. No adult symbol
Translates the shattered frame, so still.
Only the crows, black-winged as nightmares,
Enshroud the broken, beaten boy;
The pallid prey entirely ghostlike.
Harvest of hatreds. Watered by lies.

Come, captains, make oration on the bower where he lies;
Erect him a stone. Interpret him a symbol.

† Signed 'C.G. Carroll' (Lucia's then pseudonym). Unpublished. Written in pencil on sheet of cream pasteboard torn from pad manufactured for sketching. The title refers to a photograph of a dead Confederate at Antietam, made by Timothy O'Sullivan, son of New York Irish immigrants, a pioneer of American war photography. (He photographed O'Keeffe in April 1861.) The Chief Archivist of University College Dublin is gratefully acknowledged for permission to reproduce the manuscript.

He cannot hear. It is we who are ghostlike,
Who rage in the chains, while he remains still.
He had little to remember, this barebacked boy,
But the gifts of the grown in the wrappings of nightmares.

How do you sleep through the necessary nightmares?
How do you speak the courageous lies?
You have no son, perhaps? Have you loved no boy?
Of what is your own flesh the sentimental symbol?
Send his mother a medal. Can you know so little, still?
Look at his face – not living; ghostlike.

The horse and the soldier. The monochrome ghostlike.
Metaphors an easier language than nightmares.
All ordered in columns; in their lines stone-still.
Words follow orders and hear no lies.
A bullet smashed him; no high-flown symbol
Of freedom. No simile. Another boy.

Look on him, General. See where he lies.
Unchained, at last, of battle's hot nightmares.
The son you had not. Your body. A boy.

~~The son you refused me. My body. A boy.~~

November, 66. Edwardstown.

∇

CHAPTER 62

THE SLAVES

*At the Plains Hotel, Edwardstown – A memory of statues
The visions of Judith Purefoy – An unexpected visitor*

The proprietress's macaw croaks *comment allez vous* as it hops disconsolately in its cage.

And at night there is music from the dancehall across the street. Waltzes, hornpipes; Epsom Reels. It is dismally played – banjos, a fiddle, an out-of-tune piano, a thudding bass drum – but she finds it a sort of consolation.

Sometimes she sits in the window and watches the men approach. Drifters, plainsmen, bankers in their suits. There is a Judas-hole in the oaken, studded door. A coin to the heavy and he admits you. She has never been inside a dancehall, tried to enter the other night. But the doorkeep would not permit it.

'I wish only to see.'

'No ladies allowed.'

'Do the gentlemen waltz with each other in this establishment, then?'

'No ladies, Ma'am. Rules of the house.'

The bedroom can become hot, is often airless at night. A reek of food lingers – stale meat, stewed collards. She does not dine downstairs, prefers to eat alone, for in the dining room someone always wants to join you. That salesman out of Poe, with his unctuous eyes and the pearl-handled revolver in his armpit. Frequenter of the dancehall – she has seen him trudge across. An hour or two passes; the men come and go. The laughter of women, but you never see them go in. A separate entrance in the alley, she assumes. Then his doleful return to the hotel around midnight, the click of his boot-heels down the corridor. Watcher of the street. Connoisseur of schoolgirls. She has hung a pillowcase over her keyhole.

On the wall is a watercolor print of *The Broad-tailed Hummingbird*, with the rose-magenta throat patch of the male. Every room at the Plains has an identical picture, thus Monsieur Gauthier informed her proudly.

He bought thirty of them from an Irish pedlar, a quarter the piece, is proud of his bargain but prouder of his taste. He would like every room to be identically furnished. The pedlar, he smiles, knew nothing.

The poem about the photograph has taken her two days. The form is difficult. Even now, she is not certain the piece is finished. Strange, the word 'finished', for it means completed but also dead; or doomed to die, or sentenced. Or the climax of sexual pleasure. It means so many things. Should the poem be entitled 'The Finishing'? It is not completely bad – one or two of its images want to live – but there is something she does not care for in its tone. A want of absolute clarity. A vagueness that sinks it. A poem should be like a snow-grain, clear and cold; unique, worth looking at again. Or a root-strand of the poet's hair in a phial. It has business to exist if those standards are met. But her efforts are only rearrangements of things already said. Mirrors held up to mirrors.

Once, in Florence, at the Giardino de Boboli with Mamma, she saw the statuary Michelangelo intended for the mausoleum of Pope Julius. Night-time, stormy, near the end of the season; the gardens had only been opened because Papa knew someone, or paid someone. Lightning over Fiesole. The sputtering of rain on umbrellas. Slabs of butternut stone, austerities of mass. She had tried to make sketches but her hands were shaking as she drew. It was difficult to make the shapes, she was so moved.

The pieces were said to be unfinished; Buonarotti had abandoned them. Or perhaps he had died before being able to complete them – she could not remember now what the *Professore* had said. In the pearl-like rain, four studies of slaves. The sound of the rain smacking marble. Ghosts seemed to press at the surfaces of the stones as though frantic to escape their interiors. Those fingertips and lips. The suggestion of a limb. That shape in the seam? Was it a crown? The first *The Young*, as though writhing in his torments, was awkwardly stooped, uncontoured, too smooth – 'which may explain why he is considered "the young"', the *Professore* said, with a smile at Lucia, who was sixteen. And then *The Awakening*, as a petrified explosion, caught in its struggle to wrench out of its own limits. *The Bearded* was scrupulously worked, Michelangelesque about the torso, other extents left blank except for a quarryman's rough chisel-hack. Then the slave known as *Atlas* – the one that had moved her to tears. Only the slightest indications of eyes and nose, but the stance indicating he was steadying himself under some terrible weight. And since there was no world visible above his faceless head, no planet of stone, no gravities of nations, it had seemed to Lucia that it was his head itself (something held in his head, some colossus crushing mind) that was the burden he must bear forever. 'Atlas,' said the *Professore*, 'perhaps more than the other prisoners, seems to express the energy pent up in marble. Sad, my friends, that these wonders were never completed.' But it had occurred to Lucia that the *Professore* was wrong. They were not uncompleted. They said everything required. Their maker had found the only language in which to speak of such a subject. Completion would have rendered them useless.

The waste-basket by her desk contains many abandoned drafts. There is perhaps only one reason why this one will be preserved. That reason is approaching on the road from the north, will be here before nightfall, though she does not know it is coming. The man who went to India with his bride to make maps. The scholar of triangulations clops closer.

The couple upstairs are honeymooners from Rhode Island, awaiting the stage into California. She sees them walking the town, always beautifully dressed, the slim-waisted girl in her trousseau of bustles, and her groom, a minister of religion, in frockcoat. At night, you can hear the percussion of their bed. And once, as she lay in a weltering sleep, a whimper of powerless pleasure from the cathedral of their room. Raw western dawn; the silence of the Plains. She was weeping as the small death came. Everything living wants to escape the body. It is why there are poems, and stories, and songs, and drink and churches and oratorios and children. Why marriages last. Why marriages happen. Why people go on being married after love has burned away. Because we cannot be alone in the stone.

She leaves the Plains Hotel, walks the riverbank a while. Out, out, past the extent of the town, and slowly through the rushes towards the forest to the north where solitude is a sharp, cold pleasure. The boots are too big for her – she had to borrow them from Monsieur Gauthier, for the store in the town has no ladies' boots in stock. The weather does not change; the dawns are still late. The snows are not melted; the Missouri is low. She can hear it in the night from her bed at the Plains. No steam-ships are returning from the east.

Forest-peace is calming. She moves through the pines, where the hummingbirds, in the summer, pitch their homes and harvest grubs. She would like to see an American hummingbird but that will never happen. By the summer, when they come, she will be gone.

On a stump-top, the graven shape of a diamond. Garlands and religious pictures have been placed in the mulch, and rosary beads weighted with pebbles. A thirteen-year-old girl, daughter of the blacksmith, saw the Virgin appear on that tree-stub. The girl, Judith Purefoy, is whispered to have Cree blood. Stockmen bring her to sick cows; she is said to be able to heal them. Humans, too. Tooth-ache and colic. Weakness of the nerves. Fragility of the lungs. Menstrual aching. Barrenness.

She is thinking about her husband, that shipwreck of a house. Is the boy still with him, she wonders. Do they eat together in the evenings? Has the child learned to talk? What do they talk about? Has the roof been finished? If only he had come to her; asked her to return. She would not have accepted, it was too late for that. But his asking would have meant that some screed could be rescued, a memento of all they had hoped for.

She walks back to the town by a different route, circling by Tiernan's Paddock. The struts of a new chapel are rising from a cornfield. St-Mary-the-Virgin-in-the-West.

To the Stage Office again. The manager is sympathetic – a dapper little Glaswegian who whistles as he saunters the town – but the position remains as he previously described it. The passenger route is suspended. Murders on the highway. There is no way to leave the Territory, at least for the moment, and anyway, there are no drivers now. Since Harran was lynched at Redemption last Christmas, few men will face the risk of the job. The manager sees no future in the stagecoach business. He is thinking of opening a saloon.

The clank of a bent cowbell. She makes a way toward its call: along the new-built street, over the stile in the stone wall, through the feathery grasses of Loman's Meadow, the hems of her skirts knocking mushroom spores into the air. In the distance Three Giants Mountain with its trinity of peaks. The mauve of snow on the slopes.

By the time she arrives, the barn is almost full. Old Loman is on his feet, with the slateboard behind him. His students are mostly men, but today there are three women, and a cluster of children in rags. He is talking to them of the alphabet, how it is the key to all knowledge. There are twenty-seven people in the barn today. Only two of them have never been property.

She helps him to distribute the battered, spineless primers, with their drawings of apes and bees and cows – all through the bestiary to zebras. The children look up at her. A girl touches her dress. They chant a way through; it sounds like a prayer. Old Loman practically sings it, in a faltering tenor, clicking time on the slateboard with his walking stick. A boy calls her 'Mistress', which subservience makes her uncomfortable, but Loman has advised her not to make an issue of such nothings. *What they call us does not matter. She must try to understand this. Our pride must be left at the door.*

> *Lucia: I do not care what you do, nor where you go, nor whom you go with, nor what should befall you. You may walk into a lake for all I would care. Your disloyalty is no surprise, since I have long been accustomed to it, but your arrogance and presumption are beyond belief. It is a very great respite to be delivered of your pathetic mewling. Go to Hell and take your threat-letters with you.*

She paces the aisles of box-crates which do duty as desks. Fly-zizz. Sun-glint through the roofbeams. What, in truth, would she like the boy to call her? Lucia? Mrs O'Keeffe? Mrs General? Changeling? Are all those women the same?

In the corner is her camera, cloth thrown over itself; like something hiding, ashamed. It had been her intention to make photographs of the school and its students. The thought seems intrusive now.

An old man rises from the mound of sacks where he sat. He is the age of her father, she realizes. His clothes hang limply. He leans over a cane. As a boy, he was beaten so ferociously by his owner in Tennessee that he lost the hearing of one ear and went lame. She has seen him in the town shining boots for the bossmen, on the corner of Second and Foley. He progresses as far as 'o, p, q' – 'stout man, Jonathan,' Loman encourages – but suddenly becomes confused and gapes up at the roof as though consonants might be roosting in the rafters. A few of the younger men, and two of the children, raise their hands to offer the solution; but Loman commands them to remember patience, and the old man mumbles: 'ess?' The teacher corrects him and assists him to the zee. He sits back down on the cairn of sacks. There is a murmur of approbation.

The boy in the photograph, did he know what he was fighting for? Had anyone ever told him? Were there moments when he realized? It occurs to her now that perhaps he himself could not read. Can his parents read his tombstone, if he has one?

At the close of the lesson, a spiritual is sung. Loman, a Quaker, is not supposed to like hymns, but she finds it affecting to see him lilting quietly along with those who believe in the power of the alphabet to free. And like any other God, you would have to doubt it sometimes. But today, in the barn, it is believed.

> No more auction block for me,
> No more, no more.
> No more auction block for me,
> Many thousand gone.
>
> No more peck of corn for me,
> Now my Jesus set me free.
> No more auction block for me,
> Many thousand gone.

At the hotel, she reads over the poem again. It seems drained of any life it ever had. My poem about a corpse is a corpse, she feels. As she goes to tear the page, she happens to look out of her window. And down in Laforge Street, the impossible.

A dust-covered man on a dust-covered bay.

He is wearing a hood, like a Venetian during carnival. His movements are familiar as he heels his mount's flank and pats her on the veiny neck, cajoling. The horse appears exhausted, is slickened with runnels of sweat.

But it cannot. It is not possible.

She rises from the bureau.

She is aware of the pumping of her blood. As though swimming in cold water.

The first impulse is to vomit. The second is to run. But where would she run to? The forest? The barn? She watches as he dismounts, ties the reins at a hitching post. He bends towards a trough, dips his gloved hand in the water. He raises its sopping wetness toward the face she has kissed. As he does, he pulls off the hood, as if this were a moment in a cheap play. In a way, she realizes, it is.

She is dreaming. Yes. She has dreamed of him before. Writhing like the wraiths in those altar-blocks of stone; his hands, and his unmarked child. A mosquito *zits*. You can dream a mosquito. But no; there is no fragrance when you dream. Those wildflowers wilting in the jug on the bookshelf. The sickly redolence of their petals.

Could she reach the lobby before he enters? What would she say to the clerk? I am not here today. Tell that man I have departed. Tell him I was *never* here. You have never heard my name. You will know him by his face; he was burned, is disfigured; I am not here, do you understand? I will give you twenty dollars.

She rushes to the bureau, pulls open its drawers. It is ridiculous. She is searching for currency. Poems. Notes. A cup of blackened coins. A twist of withered orange-peel. Abandoned letters to her husband. She must get away immediately. She will go to the Lomans. Let me hide in your roof until he goes someplace else? I want no man, at all.

She returns to the window. He is talking to Sheriff Arkins, who is pointing out the hotel on the corner. She flinches from the light as the two men look up. It is as though they have heard her pulse.

The saddlebags over his shoulder.

The *ting* of the desk-bell.

The Irish maid's footsteps on the staircase.

She looks in the mirror, awaiting the knock. She thinks of a prisoner in the death cell.

∇

CHAPTER 63

SURVEILLANCE

An incident in the tea-room is witnessed by a spy

By the time I could get there, they were at a table near the window. I sat as close as I could without alerting suspicion. (Believe she may already suspect as has been asking at the desk what sort of salesman I am, where from, et cetera. May be necessary to replace before long.) Could not always hear their words. Noted what I could on back of menu. Wrote them up immediately afterwards, as follows: (X is him, O her. **** is where I could not hear them.)

X: Who are all these biddies?

O: Why are you come here?

X: Lucia: do not affect. We are grown-up people.

O: You wrote me you were to marry. To go to Indiana (?) in the spring.

X: Our engagement must be ended. It was not fair to the girl. It would have been wrong to continue a deception born of hurt.

O: You ******** to your fiancée?

X: Do not lecture me on broken promises.

O: ******* ********** ********* *************

X: We had not the intimate feelings that spouses ought to have for one another. Such marriages do not last. One would have thought you of all people **** **** *****.

Here they talked heatedly approx one minute. Could hear nothing owing to boys in street. Then:

O: For pity's sake, there was never any fiancée. Do you think me a damned fool? Your intention was to stir me to jealousy.

X: You are suddenly expert on my intentions? Then know, Lucia, that my intention is that you leave this Territory with me.

O: Will you ****** ***** your mouth? There are people in the room.

X: Then let us go to another where we can be alone.

O: Are you quite insane?

X: I meant only to talk.

O: Can you not see that there would be gossip? This is a respectable place. ********* your voice for pity's sake.

X: Respectability, now. From the free-thinker herself. I can think of several occasions when your respectability *** ***** ****.

O: Stop it. I warn you.

X: Feelings you confessed to me. Do you wish them repeated? Because I remember the words, I could never forget them. You were not playing the Carmelite, then. *** ****** *****.

O: I do not wish to be alone with you. I do not know why you have come here. I understand that you have feelings, but the time for that has –

X [*mighty sore*]: How dare you? How dare you? You will never know what I have lost for you. You can never know my feelings. By what right do you dismiss me? The nights I have wept and thought to end my life –

O: Let go of my hand. You are hurting my hand.

X [*with paper from coat*]: Read that, Lucia. You wrote those words freely. You wanted to write them. You wanted me to read them. You know it is true, it is a matter of gravity. If it is a sin to ***** *** **** then the sin was ours the both. You may attempt to deceive yourself but it cannot be changed.

O: If once I was mistaken. I do not want you now.

X: That is a falsehood of the kind I had never suspected to see in you.

O: It is the literal truth. I am sorry, you must go.

X: Then you will change your mind. I have upset your equilibrium. I have come to you too suddenly. You will change your mind in time. *******

O: Never. You are deluded. I do not know **** **** *****. You must leave this place immediately and never return. If ever you cared for me, I tell you, do as I ask.

Here the proprietress approached their table, perhaps alerted by looks from other patrons.

P: Is everything quite well, Mrs General?

O: Quite well, thank you, Madame Gauthier . . . Captain Winter (?), a family friend . . . He was just leaving, as it happens . . . You might show him to the door.

The man appeared riled as he stood from the table.

X: I will never leave this Territory without you, Mrs General. I make
   you that promise. No matter what else. I have come too far. And so
   have you. The time for deceptions is over.

He looked at me as he left. But briefly, I think. I was reading a newspaper.
He went away.

∇

CHAPTER 64

I SHALL SEE MY DEAR MOTHER AGAIN

*From Winterton's journal – The fate of an immigrant family – The fear
of a pursuer – The resurrection of a ghost near Redemption Falls*

[*Several pages have been torn out and the manuscript resumes as indicated*]

. . . told me that he had once ridden into the Yellowstone Valley, and
of some of that region's astonishing sights. The bones of enormous
creatures, and their many-toothed skulls. A cataract so immense that its
plunge was surely fifteen hundred feet. And he had happened upon a
trail-waggon, entirely ruined, the skeletons of its poor passengers still
sitting in the buckboard in gnawed tatters of clothes, the reins of the
stolen horses yet held in their fingers. The telling seemed to affect him
for there were tears in his eyes as he spoke. It was evident, he said, as he
had examined their meager belongings, that these wretcheds had been
immigrants from his homeland.

Later in the day, I walked three leagues out of town, bringing only my
theodolite and a couple of books. I intended to scout out a number of
elevated vantages, which might serve as expedient points from where to
commence a triangulation.

I was looking through my scope, and by that means I noticed, about
a quarter of a mile away from me, I think north by northnorthwest,
three men riding the crest of Aerly's Hill. They looked like Five-Points
hooligans; all were clad in black. Each was copiously armed, more than
any miner needs to be, with bandoleers, machetes, short-handled
shotguns and sawn-downs. More remarkable (so I now saw), one of the
trio was a woman. Or, rather, a girl of about twenty.

They paused as I watched them. Both men dismounted; one of them
urinated on the trail. The girl then dismounted. She had on canvas
chaparejos and a rough-cut cloak. In her hand was a long-blade knife.

She hunkered and picked up a glove-ful of earth. There was conversation between her and one of the men, the other remaining silent I think.

357

She stood up again abruptly. There appeared to be a quarrel. The girl and her adversary exchanged vigorous shouts but I could not make out their words. The other man was making placatory gestures.

They mounted up and rode away toward the north in a body.

I mounted quick as I could and commenced to follow. They were headed in the direction of Redemption.

∇

Vinson reins his mare. Twists his head like an owl. Staring over his shoulder at the track they have just ridden. It is arched by a tunnel of low-grown cottonwoods. He looks panicked. His horse gives a whinny.

'What matter?' asks McLaurenson.

'We're dogged,' Vinson says.

'Wean't dogged. Who's to dog us out here?'

'I'm tellin you, we're tailed. Look at the birds over yon.'

A rising of crows in a cloud from the woods. Raucous. They whirl like ashes.

'Cougar,' says McLaurenson. 'Coyote may be.'

'This far over? And no water in thirty mile?'

'Whut are you – '

'Listen! . . . '

The crows croaking dully as they circle above the forest. Eliza says nothing, only heels at her horse. They have a ways to ride this evening and cannot afford delays. But she has a sense – inexplicable – that Vinson is correct.

She looks back down the trail. The birdcalls have ceased. A disc of dusty daylight at the end of the tunnel.

'Ride on,' says McLaurenson. 'Aint a body back there.'

Vinson is staring at her as they go.

∇

At a quarter after four, the boy is witnessed in Tone Street, leading James O'Keeffe's horse, which is lame. He goes into the cobbleyard of Johnny Boylan the blacksmith, who will testify that the boy seemed 'his usual self. Quietlike. But he didn't look troubled.' Boylan and the child come out to the street, where the horse is quickly examined before being brought into the yard. The boy crosses to Corish's, where he buys two apples. Corish will say 'he looked fine'.

He walks back to the house and unties his pony from the hitching-post.

By now it is twenty minutes after four. He is asked by Elizabeth Longstreet to do an errand at the grocer's but he gestures that he has just now returned from the town, is unwilling to go back there again. The errand is not urgent, so that she does not scold the child. He heads away from the house by the north-eastern lane, not riding the pony, but leading it.

Two former slaves see him as he passes the field where many of their fellows have their shelters. The wind blows his hat off. He chases it; picks it up. He is feeding an apple to the pony.

'Jeddo,' says the voice. ''Tis me. Your oul pard.'

The boy stops and looks at him. The Yankee sheriff. But different now. Thinner. More frightened. Like a scarecrow of himself, to be burned on a bonfire. A traitor about whom there will be songs.

'Were they askin where I go to? In the town? I suppose they were. See, I went to see a pard of mine. Would you like to come and meet him? His house is up yonder. He got a visitor you'll want to see.'

Always watch the eyeballs, Mamo used to say. You can tell they're lying by their eyes.

'It's a someone you'll want to visit with. Up above in the hills there. It's your skin-and-blister, Jeddo. It's Eliza.'

The pony is wandering away, trailing his lariat in the grass. Wind moves the rushes in the streamlet. The Great Smokecloud Mountains look true to their name, for their slopes are gray and vaporous.

'Don't you care to see your sister? She's after coming a fierce way. Will you go by and take supper with me, there's a good boy?'

The child does not move. Because Eliza is not here. She is in Baton Rouge, Louisiana, on the other side of the moon. But this lawman knows her name. Can he read your secret thoughts? Like a faery ill-met on the road.

'Lookat here . . . I got someone else. Someone you int seen in a long time. Wants to see you again, son. She's over there in yon trees. Shure, she's heartbroke to see you. So I told her I'd ask you . . . It's Mamo, son . . . She's after coming back . . . She wants you.'

In the meadow by the cow-byre a farmer is girdling elms. Come the spring he will burn them. The grass is flat and yellowed.

As though drawn on a rod-line, the child walks towards the forest. Vinson puts an arm around him. No tears.

∇

CHAPTER 65

I SHALL HAVE THE PLANTATION OF THOSE GODLY FIELDS

Found painted on the schoolhouse door at Redemption Falls
on the morning after the boy's disappearance

HYPOCRITS I AM HERE
I SEE EUERY THING YOU DO

RAISE A HAND TO TAKE THE BOY FROM ME
AND I WILL SLAUGHTER EUERY MALECHILD IN
REDEMPTION & TO THIS I TAKE OATH THAT I WILL
MURDER EUERY LAST OF YOUR SONS & THEIR
BLOOD SHALL BE ON YOUR HANDS

TAKE NOTE THAT ALL WHICH ASSIST
IS GUILTY & PUNISHED

I SEE EUERY THING YOU DO

YOU ARE HYPOCRITS

- MK1025 -

∇

CHAPTER 66

LES ADIEUX

The lonely death of Patrick Vinson – His funeral – Lucia's return

They found Patrick Owen Vinson at Willowcreek woods. He had received a single gunshot to the head. At first the searchers reckoned that he had taken his own life, but his onetime friend, Marshal John Calhoun, pointed out that no man ever shot himself in back of the head. He had been victim of an execution.

He was buried in the churchyard at Redemption Falls, his casket afforded military honors. O'Keeffe himself gave the oration at the chapel, though he had not slept in days, was exhausted from searching for the stolen child. Patrick Vinson had been his comrade in the War, he said. A good and brave man, he had fought the lion's fight. The Governor had seen Patrick Vinson run into a burning hospital-barn in Virginia and save sixteen soldiers from death. Some were Confederate prisoners. Some were Union loyalists. Two were former slaves. Four were children. He had carried two infants across a river in Tennessee because he could not bear to leave them parentless.

He was born in County Louth, in the Cooley Mountains. His parents had died in the Famine. Aged six, alone, he had stowed away on a packet to Liverpool. He had spent many years in English prisons. In the winter of '58 he made a way to New York. He had worked as a waiter at Brooklyn. He had scrimped to bring an aged uncle and aunt from Ireland where they were living in desperate straits in the Cavan poorhouse. He had been the first Irish-born immigrant to enlist for the Union, rising quickly to the rank of Corporal.

He and O'Keeffe had later had differences – it could not be denied. But the rumors about Patrick Vinson were wrong and cruel. Traitorship was unimaginable in the heart of such a fighter. If Vinson was a traitor, so was every man.

The congregation of nine attended in silence to the Governor. When it came time to take the coffin from the chapel to the hearse, nobody

361

volunteered to do this honor. O'Keeffe and Orson Rawls and the priest and an altar-boy carried the remains to the empty street. Out of loyalty to O'Keeffe, John Calhoun then joined the funeral procession. Those five were the only mourners at Patrick Vinson's graveside. The Stars-and-Stripes from his casket was never claimed. Nobody knows what became of it. In the coming years his tombstone would often be defaced. Memories proved long in the Territory.

∇

Late the following night, from the south-eastern trail, a woman rode into Redemption Falls. She looked weary and pale, for she had been traveling since dawn and was unaccustomed to the roughness of the Territory's roads: its want of bridges, its unmarked fords, its tracks through burnt-down forests.

He was alone at the table, back to the door, as she entered with the slow-moving cook.

'General,' said Elizabeth. '*Stróinséir a ta ann.*' His Gaelic for a visitor. A stranger.

For some time he did not move. Then he montioned for Elizabeth to leave. He reached out a hand to the bottle on the table and unsteadily filled a glass.

'Have you come here to gloat?'

'Con – please . . . '

'You are happy now, I suppose. Your wish has been granted . . . You must tell me the saint to whom you prayed for deliverance.'

'I am sorry,' she said. 'Nobody would have wished harm to the child.'

He stood, went to the fire, tossed a log in the flames. She was surprised by the cleanliness of his clothes. She had been expecting to see him broken, but he was clear-eyed, neat. He had shaved off his beard. He refused even to look at her. He sat at the table; began writing.

'Is there news, Con?'

'Of what?'

'Of the boy, of course.'

He continued at his paperwork. Unfolded a parchment bearing a diagram. She watched him crosschecking figures in its margins. Other documents were sifted while she stood in the firelight. He pressed his seal into an envelope.

'Might I have something to eat?'

'Are you addressing me? Or a servant?'

'I am hungry, Con. I only wanted – '

'Elizabeth will give you something. If we have it. In the kitchen.'

'The kitchen?'

'That is correct. I am working here at the table. My work is important. It cannot be interrupted by inconsequential disturbances. Was there some other matter before you let me alone?'

'Might I stay here the night, Con? I have been riding since early.'

'Wherever the Hell you want. I could care less what you do.'

Elizabeth was not there, but had left mutton broth on the stove. Lucia ate alone at the servant's table. The soup was sour; there was no bread. She climbed to her old room, found a nightgown in a drawer. Bare soles on the rough-planed floorboards. She heard him some time later, entering the cave of his room. The quoits of her bed as she turned in it.

She slept for a while, but shallowly, uneasy. There were many boxes in the room; piles of books, old cartons. She supposed he was using it to store unwanted things. They seemed to draw the goodness from the air.

'Lucia,' he called. 'Would you come here a moment?'

There were clothes on his floor. Spider webs in the windowframes. A gun-belt hanging on a peg.

'I apologize,' he said, without meeting her face. 'Thank you. For coming back. It cannot have been easy. I am grateful to have you here tonight.'

'It is not a matter of gratitude.'

'Yes, it is. To me, it is. I hope you have been well. I am very sorry for what has happened between us. I was lonely without your company. I should have said that when you came. Forgive my stubbornness if you will. I have not been very well. It was bloody of me.'

'I was lonely without yours. Your company, I mean.'

Perhaps suspecting merely courtesy, he made no reply for a moment. Wind racketed a door downstairs.

'Would you stay a while in the room? I have not been sleeping very well. If the idea would not disgust you. I expect it would.'

'Of course it would not. How can you say such things?'

'Would you come closer to me, Lucia?' he asked.

Unfamiliar nakedness. The loneliness of being in a body. The picture we refuse of our parents, our ancestors, of people who lived long ago, who were not like us, who did not have our feelings, whose desire is so frightening because it is that from which we came. And there will one day be an anonymous poem where this moment is approached: its disquiets, its misgivings, a woman's breasts being kissed, his fingers in the lacings of a nightgown full of metaphors, for the body is a fund of metaphors in the hands of a versifier, who knows how afraid it makes us. Broken in war. Touched in love or want. Longed for in the night. Imagined in the street. *This living hand*, wrote her most beloved poet. *I hold it out to you.*

There is gracelessness, for they are unaccustomed to reading one another any more. No rhyme, no meter; nothing scans. A candle overturns and extinguishes on the dresser as they clunk like the couplets of a youthful sonnet. His hands are ungainly, as though bandaged in apprehensions. The dresser scrapes the floorboards as he kisses her abdomen, but he has forgotten how to pleasure her, and she has forgotten how to feel, or to trust, or even to know what pleasure is. The thing he is doing is too intimate now, and the mirror against her arching back feels cold and strange, so that the feeling is an incursion, unreal as shaking hands with a spouse, and with her hands she asks him to stop. He rises to her mouth but he seems reluctant to be kissed himself. Somehow he has opened his clothes. So strange to touch his neck, the cleft of his collarbone. To be intimately touched herself, to be touched by him in any way at all. He turns down the wick of the lamp.

In the dark they kiss untidily, and his sex tastes of ashes, and he maneuvers her wordlessly into a way that does not especially please her, but she remembers how fiercely it arouses him and she permits it. And there is a tentativeness, if that is possible, as well as a desolation, in the silence and then in his sounds. And it surprises her, before long, how he remembers the way that was always best for her, and asks shakily if she would like that now. But her pleasure, as it begins to rise, seems too much for him to be part of; he is too quick, and it hurts, and she is dazed with dissatisfaction as he finishes. He himself does not seem very satisfied either. The rhythm of his breathing; he is feigning sleep. It has been almost nine years since she last shared a bed with him, the only adult on the earth with whom she has ever shared a bed. What stirs in the cauldron of his head as he breathes? How unknown, that body now.

Sea-flower. Anemone. Coral. Australia. A shark's fin cutting water. An enemy. In drifts of a dream, she sees him alone on the island and some-how she is there with him, they are sleeping on the stones.

'. . . Con? . . .'

His breathing.

'. . . Would you like . . . Are you tired?'

That hour you watched him swimming. A night you did not sleep at all. Was that love? Does the body remember? The words cried out, or

364

whispered, or withheld. Intimacies of lovers. Unwritten verbs and nouns. A night you awoke to his touch and he wanted you both to be silent; and all night long you were silent together, except for those seconds when it was impossible to be silent. Those days when you were new married, before everything changed. Those hours you walked together in Washington Square Park scarcely able to wait for the nightfall.

Looking down on the dot of the bed from a stupefying height; then dropping toward it suddenly through interstellar space. Around her, as she plummets, hurtle ribbons of light, which are palpitant, somehow, with the earth-aromas of their bodies. Elizabeth and Winterton coupling in a stagecoach. A hospital ward in the War.

She awakens with a judder to find that he has lit a candle on the dresser. She looks at the clock. She has been asleep three hours. His white, flaccid shoulders; his untied hair. The body of a man past the mid-point of a life. As though everything he feels – has ever felt, perhaps – has enwrapped him like a caul of unwanted flesh. Faded scars of Tasmania across his back.

'Do you think the boy is dead, Lucia?'

'– Con . . . You must sleep.'

He nods without turning.

'Yes.'

'You did your best for him, Con. You must never think – '

'I cannot . . . seem to speak of it. I am sorry.'

'Are you sick? You look pale. Won't you come away from the window?'

'Not sick. I am very thirsty.'

'Can I fetch you some water?'

'You're not tired.'

'It would only take a moment.'

'Thank you.'

She rises, puts on her nightgown. He does not look at her as she does. The house through the darkness, the ghosts of the kitchen. The guillotine of an ancient mangle. Something scuttles by the door. From the press she takes a jug of water left to cool by Elizabeth, who is sleeping in her chair by the embers.

The palliasse in the corner. Its blanket triangled, as though the kitchen were to be inspected by a sergeant. The boy's trousers and a shirt folded neatly by the pillow. A book he was reading; face down.

'Lucia?'

'Yes?'

'Do you think we should not have married? I should value your complete honesty. Has it been a very great mistake?'

'I suppose . . . I have sometimes been confused. You are not an easy person to be married to . . . And I am not an easy person to be married to, either.'

'We did not know each other very well. When we married, I mean. Perhaps we should have waited longer, as your father would have wished.'

'Perhaps . . . That would have been wiser . . . I suppose all married people must have such thoughts from time to time.'

'Do you think so, truly?'

'I don't know . . . Is that strange?'

'You were very young when we married. I used to think about it in the War . . . Sometimes, do you know, one of the fellows would get married . . . They seemed so young; like children, often. And sometimes I would think: that is the age Lucia was.'

'I was old enough to decide. Or I thought I was.'

'Once you told me I was a soul mate. It did not prove true. Did it?'

'Con . . . '

'There is nothing to be afraid of. I promise. Speak honestly.'

'I suppose . . . if it did not prove true, it was not true for either of us. It seems a very long time ago now.'

'Yes. A long time ago. It has all gone so quickly.'

'And you had already met your soul mate long before you met me. In Tasmania. It must have been terrible to leave her.'

He hesitates. Touches the window, as though he finds the cold glass strange. 'I do not believe in the idea of a soul mate any more. I don't know that I ever did, not truly. When I was in prison I used to hope that I would live to be extremely old . . . To have all that time given back, do you know . . . But I don't hope that now. Damnedest thing. Not that one should want actually to die, of course. More that one would not be afraid.'

'Don't say such things, Con. They are tempting of fate.'

'Fate . . . Yes . . . We must not tempt that.'

He takes a drink of water. They are silent for a time.

'I know you wish to go home – it is not very safe – but since you do want to go, I can arrange a posse of bodyguards. They will be men I trust. I shall ask John Calhoun to lead them. He is a good man, intelligent. They will see you to Salt Lake City. Perhaps, soon afterward, the stage route will reopen. They say that the weather will break.'

'I can stay until there is news of the boy. You should not be alone.'

'It's generous of you. But no, you had better go soonest. It will only be more difficult to delay.'

'All right. If you think it best . . . I will go in the morning.'

'Yes, best to be cleaner. It will only be more difficult to delay. These things can be done in a civilized manner. You would like to be home for Christmas, I am sure. Estefanía and your father should be glad to see you again. You will need them now. You must let them help you a little. You are sometimes too independent, if you will permit me to say so. You must try to accept their support.'

'You do not wish? – I mean Christmas is . . . If you wanted me to wait?'

'Better to be brave. We will be thankful for it in the close. I will write – if you wish it – to your father in a while. There will be the matter of your settlement to be returned and so on. And the legal aspects. I shall write to the lawyer. We have land, still, in Ireland. There is the house at Dublin. I can arrange for the trustees to see to everything.'

'We should rest a little while, then . . . I should go to my room.'

'There was something I wanted to say to you.'

'It is very late, Con. We can talk tomorrow, before I go.'

'One night in the War, I was in Washington alone. A girl looked at me admiringly. I was lonely and afraid. It was the night before they thought that the rebels would come. And all would be lost. Do you understand?'

'Con – '

Tears are streaming in the grooves of his face. A sight she has never seen. His anger, his laughter, his want, his fearfulness. Lust. Pride. Other feelings called sins. The tears he wipes away with the back of his hand.

'There is nothing I need be told, Lucia. Nothing at all. There is nothing you could say, and nothing you could do that could prevent me from loving you the rest of my life and after my death, if that is possible. You are the very finest person I have ever known. It has blessed my life to know you – even the little I have. And I am sorry that I was not the husband you deserved. It was my fault – not yours. It has all been my fault.'

' . . . Con . . . '

'I should like to sleep beside you a last time . . . May we do that, at least?'

He crosses to his wife. His head is in her hands. Cold wind from the north in the cottonwood outside. The creak of withstanding too long. Some matches are made in Heaven, so poets believe. This one was made on earth.

▽

CHAPTER 67

APOLOGIA

I have wronged you, yes; I do not apologize.
You did not deserve betrayal. I do not apologize.
I am sorry, yes; I do not apologize.
I will never wrong you more. I do not apologize.
What is done is done. I do not apologize.
I ask your forgiveness. I do not apologize.

Apology is an asking for the speaking of lies –
To be told it does not matter.

I do not apologize . . .

Fragment in Lucia's notebook
Redemption Falls
November, 1866

∇

CHAPTER 68

O GOD PROTECT MY CHILD

A plea

REWARD
$5,000 (IN GOLD)

A BOY was abducted from the northeastern outskirt of Redemption Falls on Monday, November 21st, at about quarter of five of the evening, while he was walking a pony at Joseph's Field. He has not since been seen, despite searches of the surrounding counties.

The perpetrator of this EVIL, whose name is known to all, has added to his crimes, which already were INNUMERABLE, the taking of a troubled & friendless child from the only mother and father he had.

Every man in this Territory, no matter his party, will REVILE THIS DESPICABLE ACT. Every woman will repudiate it. Every American will disown it. Every neighbor is implored by Governor & Mrs O'Keeffe: think on your own children, their happiness & safety. Is there anything you know, or suspect, of this wrong? Be it ever so small, will you impart it to the authorities, or to some trusted person, for example, of religion?

This man himself we here entreat: whatsoever you have done in a time of War, fall not to that INFAMY where the child-hurter must dwell, despised by the world forever. Think of your mother & father, who gave you life. Think of the name of Ireland.

The Governor offers to treat with you, AT ANY PLACE in this Territory; at any time, & in any circumstance. He is ready to surrender his person into your custody, in place of the boy, if required.

We implore that any tiding of the boy be communicated without delay to Governor O'Keeffe or his marshals. A CONSIDERABLE REWARD is offered WITHOUT CONDITION. This is an innocent child that has done no wrong.

In conclusion: it has been evident that a number of the citizens have of late formed the view that a change of governorship is wanted. For the common good of the Territory, the Acting Governor now proposes to step aside, and has tendered his resignation to Washington. THE HOUR THAT THE BOY IS RETURNED TO REDEMPTION FALLS, THE GOVERNOR & MRS O'KEEFFE VOW TO TAKE HIM & REMOVE FROM THE TERRITORY. They undertake, further, never to return, & to accede to any other stipulation.

V

JOHN F. CALHOUN

Distraught would not cover it. Man was out of his mind. Don't believe he slept more than a couple hours all that week. Seen him up in the roof any hour of the night. Prowl the outskirts with a rifle. Walking arpents of prairie. Waiting for sun-up, so's he could start searching again. That was one week I don't care to remember.

And we turned that Territory downside up. As best we could, with only the number of men we had. Farmsteads. Houses. Under bridges. Barns. The islands on Lake Liverpool. The reservations. Ever place. Got a tracker – a Blackfoot. Couldn't pick up no trail. Got dogs. Same story. Nothing.

And I guess for a week or ten days, I thought it might work out all right. But then it come to a fortnight and still no word. And I pretty much was coming to one conclusion. I just didn't want to be the one had to tell him.

Then your aunt come down to the jail that Sunday morning and ast me come up to the house. I could see she'd been crying and you don't like to see that. She told me the news. She was cut-up.

I quit whatever I was at and went along with her to the house. Because I always had a liking for Lucia as a person. And I didn't care for the talk about whatever went on. You ever heard of a marriage where the parties was always saints, that's a marriage to put in a storybook.

Weren't too pretty at the house. I don't care to talk about it much. He was sittin in the dark with the shutters all closed. You can imagine it I guess . . . No, I won't go into the details if it's all the same. Let's just leave it at saying it did not look good.

I got coffee in the man, but it didn't do. I said something like: 'Con, this gonna have to stop, or that bottle be your end' and other things of that nature I guess . . . Cause I lost my own marriage through the bottle, so I knew. But there wasn't no talking to him that day.

Well, the house-gal, Elizabeth, come in after while and says there's a stranger out front to see the Boss. And that was a surprise, cause it was a Sunday morning like I said, and most people would be home with their kin. And I probably told her to scoot more sharp than I shouldof, but anyway here she come back in, and said this bub at the door, he wouldn't take no for an answer.

It was Johnny Creed come in. I knew him, sure. Well, I knowed who he was; I'd see him in town, but we wasn't what you might call too good friends. Been a sharpshooter with the rebs out of Biloxi, Mississippi. I guess he'd be what, twentyfive, twentysix at the time. Big feller. Scotch-Irish. Worked a claim up by Eliot's. Kind of kept to himself, or mostly.

Said some of the boys and him got to talking things over. Yeah, yeah, other Confederates. We had plenty in the town. Johnny didn't reckon it was right, what happened with the kid being took. He was married himself. Very pretty wife. Cajun girl she was; she'd had their second daughter that year. And his wife, she encouraged him to come on up. Cause she didn't think it was right.

Said if there was anything he could do, why, he wanted to do it. Had one or two other rebel men felt about the same way. And this wasn't no choirboy, I can tell you for sure. Killed a whole lot of Yankees, Johnny Creed in the War. Was in it at Fredericksburg, Marye's Heights you know. Could shoot the damn date off the nickel in your pocket. Plenty of Con's boys he put in the grave at Fredericksburg. Irish as he was himself . . . And some of those boys, those was boys and no more . . . Sixteen, seventeen . . . Children.

No, I don't remember them shaking hands. I suppose maybe they did. Con told him he appreciated that he come on up. And Johnny said sure and went home.

I don't suppose I should say it. But sure. Con cried. And I was crying myself . . . Powerful thing . . . [*Subject becomes distressed. Brief silence before continuing.*] . . . Even talking about it now . . . As you see, upsets me yet . . . Me and him sat in the dark . . . And we cried, all right . . .

Because Johnny didn't know it . . . But the news come the night before. The kiddie'd been found hanged in Canada.

∇

CHAPTER 69

JESUS, JESUS, DON'T LET ME DIE ALONE

Obituary for a soldier of the rebels

IN MEMORIAM
A BOY

After midnight on Saturday last, a certain man of the North called at the home of Mr J.K. Trevanion, editor of this publication. The testimony he gave would appear to corroborate certain rumors, which had gone about the Territory in recent days. The little guest who came among us we shall never see more in this world. This man, who is known of old to Mr Trevanion, had himself seen the child's remains.

Mr Trevanion went at once to the Gubernatorial House and had the hard duty of conveying what he had been told to the Acting Governor and Mrs O'Keeffe. They bore it with bravery and asked privacy for their grief. This notice is published, with the Acting Governor's assent, to put a cease to all further speculation.

We have lived through War. We have lived through sorrow. Little thought we then, that we should live us to know the most monstrous wickedness ever done in this Territory. All of us, without exception, are diminished by this barbarity. Some, who did not welcome, have most on our conscience.

This paper has not seen eye-to-eye with the Acting Governor and his associates. We have opposed him zealously at every turn. We retract not one word: that is the way of a Free Press. We do not affect regret that he shall soon quit this country. But this morning, as human brothers, we offer him our prayers, as must every Christian person in this Territory.

The prayers of a friend are easily tendered. The prayers of a foe may matter more. Let us pause, this day, to remember in mourning:

Jeremiah Mooney
boy soldier, Louisiana.
Aged 12 or 13.
R.I.P
✝

CHAPTER 70

AND MY TRUE LOVE EVER QUIT ME, I SHOULD SURELY FIND ANOTHER

The last surviving pages of the cartographer's journal
A change of heart – Future prospects considered
A restless horse – A challenge

Violently windy day. Riders wearing kerchiefs and bandannas. Grit and broken twigs like confetti.

Saw party of his men searching a house near New Blackheath. Heavy-handed. Rifle-shots in the air. Threatened family with eviction and burning if they did not tell. Pulled out the little sticks of furniture + smashed them in the yard. Had been rumored to have hidden the boy.

Saw notice they were posting re reward & c. Took a few for my satchel. I don't know. Feel sorry for the poor bastard. Every rumor has the child hanged. Devil's own work. To do such to a child.

Beggar on the road told me he saw them in Edwardstown two days ago. On their way to church. He looked broken; she brave. Will return to New York, thence to Paris it is said. The French admire him, apparently.

Have not the stomach to go on with it, now. Whole scheme seems the devil's work. Seeing her again, I don't know, rather unsettled one. More prim than I had remembered. Tighter. Tougher. And one never thought she loved him, but for some reason she appears to. Madwoman + Madman = Madness squared.

Suppose shall return to the town, preparation of survey, investigation of piracy, & cetera. Who knows where might lead. Proprietor of profitable hotel and saloon. Fluent German not beyond one. Quiet little life. And many attendant benefits.

Guten Morgen, my dear. You would care to be employed here? Won't you join me in the parlor? Frau Winterton is occupied just at present. Come, come, sit by Uncle. That's right. A little closer. Now Liebchen: let us talk about *you*.

Blessing, in one degree, that it all came to nothing. For had rarely truly liked her, if honest. Fond of her in a way, + understood her, I think, but thought of marrying her sans benefits rather chilling. Felt Pappy would pony up tin enough to guarantee a fat life – money buyeth not happiness, this, alas, we know, but it does buy a better quality of misery. But he might not have, after all. Said to be a hard one. Even if he did: life sentence.

Stunning to look upon, must be gasp-inducing undraped. Once would have been pleasant, certainly. But rather too indomitable and insolent for my liking; overly-determined, also a portion on the thin side. Prefer a bit of meat. Skinny females untrustworthy. Goodly; knowledgeable; but too well-read for a woman. Gives them uppity ideas and never stop talking. Give a man the blue mopes, a tongue as incessant. Would never have known peace. And then what?

Bastard? Yes. Then, God, stand up for bastards.

Fellow passed me on a horse. Grunted a salutation, as did I. And I noticed something strange as he did. Raised his hand briefly to tip at his hat.

His wedding-ring finger was missing.

I wheeled about. He appeared to hear me turn, & took off at a gallop toward the north. I followed him hard but my own Bobby was very weary and I could not keep the other in my sight. Several shots, I think four, rang toward me in a volley as I made a turn in the road. Could not see the position of the gunman, at first thought he must be in some trees, but then, ahead of me on a bridge, he loomed into view. Small. Twisting as he fired at me, still riding hard away. Kept after him as best I could.

Evaded me but I followed his dust round a bend in the track and down into a field of broken mine-works. Nobody in the field. At least none I could see. Crept about for a while. Many broken equipments. Very thick grass. But I . . . [*Page of manuscript rotted away.*]

. . . the mouth of an abandoned tunnel, perhaps the shaft of a mine. Could hear the echo of water, see the mangled steel of rails. Queer fungi growing all about the mouth.

Considered entry. Did not seem wise. Had a strange realization, of piercing intensity: nobody on the earth was aware of where I was. Could be killed in two minutes. No one would ever know. Was not her I was thinking about, then.

Retreated to coppice and tied up Old Bobby. But he was restless, stampy, would not be soothed. Considered shooting him but difficulty that they might have heard the shot. Also, to be without him could present extreme peril, since no mode of escape if attack came on; but his fretfulness was compromising my position extremely and nothing I did would calm him. In the end took the decision to unloose and scare him. He bolted toward the lakeshore to the north-east. Felt exceptionally vulnerable without my good old fellow. Yet hoped he would not drift back.

Lay covered some hours with eyes trained on the field. Darkness approached. Must have fallen asleep.

Moonlight. A girl came out, largely pregnant, *accompanied by the boy*. Definitely him. Recognized his clothing. Appeared weak enough health. Coughing badly.

Too young to be his mother. But resemblance. Cousin? She led him to a ditch that I had not previously noticed.

The night very silent. Two simpleminded men. Idiots. Innocent. Leader must be still underground.

Was thinking of how they trained us to lie still ten hours, a thing I had found almost impossible. Story about Irishman a fellow once told me. Hid him in a bog-hole fourteen days and nights while the redcoats were burning his townland. Would sink him into the slime if he heard them approach. Breathe through a length of straw.

—*Who is there?* she called out without warning.

Did not move. They exchanged some words. She produced and shot a pistol.

—*Who is there? I know you are there. Stand up or you are dead.*

One of the idiots went away and came back with three storm-lanterns. Features very monstrous in its glow. Gave a light to the girl, who raised it on a pole. Eardrums by now drumming hard. I saw John Cole McLaurenson come from the cave. Positive identification. No question whatever. He was bearing a sawn-down which he loaded.

—*Counting me to ten. Get to eleven, you're a deadman.*

Rope was produced by one of the imbeciles. The girl slung it over a bough. She started to count. Very clear, cold voice. Accent of Brooklyn. Unholstered my pistol.

McL heard my Bobby. He ran toward him firing.

The girl and the idiots followed.

All the while, the boy was lying very ill on the ground. I could hear his frightened tears.

∇

CHAPTER 71

TO BAIT A HOOK YOU NEED A WORM, TO LURE A MAN, A PROMISE

Message delivered late at night to the Governor's house – scribbled on a shred of the reward notice

Eight minutes past Midnight – *Christmas Eve*

General O'Keeffe, sir,

I call'd to your house this instant, but you were not at home, and the servant did not know your whereabouts. I thought it improper to ask for Mrs O'Keeffe, who had retired – but perhaps, given the circumstances, I should have press'd the matter. If I have not heard from you in a couple of hours, I shall take a liberty & return – We must confer before dawn at the latest.

Forgive – sir – my unruly hand – I have ridden six days & nights from the north with only the briefest respite. I should see you most urgently on a subject of profoundest importance.

Am at the Widow's Hotel – Send a man the very moment you receive this – and I will come to you immediately – Or come here yourself <u>no matter the hour</u> – Insist with the widow, sir, that I be awaken'd the instant you arrive. She will attempt to protect me but for God's sake brook no opposition.

Your marshals & militia need to be muster'd without the least delay & every last man you trust in this Territory. I believe, firmly, that we have not a single minute to squander.

Thankful, sir, to have an opportunity to prove myself

Your friend –

A. W., Capt.

▽▽▽

PART IX

THE FINISHING

. . . It being almost midnight, and dispatches yet to be written, he excused himself and retired to confer with his Captains. As he took his leave courteously, I put to him a parting query, emboldened, no doubt, by the lateness of the hour. He pondered a while, as though my question had surprised him, and his thinking eventuated in the following response: 'My ambition?' he said, 'is to know a contented family life. To be a kindly father and husband; to deserve the blessings I have been given. I was at one time a revolutionist. I am now a soldier for the constitutional. But I would be, as soon as possible, a quiet and private citizen.' He added, after a moment of further contemplation: 'And for my people to be free. To know they are as good as any other. I cannot see my brother live and die a slave. If I do, I will have wasted everything.'

From 'A Sketch of the Handsome Irish General on the Eve of Battle'.
New York Times, August 29th, 1862.

CHAPTER 72

AN EXTRACT FROM
'CONCLUSIONS of the COMMISSION OF INVESTIGATION into CERTAIN EVENTS, WHICH OCCURRED LAST YEAR at FORT STORNAWAY, THE MOUNTAIN TERRITORY, & at sundry other PLACES'

Two hours before dawn on Wednesday, December 26th, 1866, a posse set out from Redemption Falls, the Mountain Territory, for Fort Stornaway on the Missouri River ($47°49'10''$ N; $110°40'11''$ W). The collaborators stole in silence, their lanterns unlit, the hooves of their mounts muffled with wraps of wet sacking, down the passageway behind the quietest of their settlement's four streets, and westward, through the quarter-light, to the County's remotest outskirt. There a trio of associates, who had been waiting in a certain house, slipped out and added their number to the assembly. The hour was now approximately a half-after-five. The order was confirmed: ride north.

Black hoods were worn by some, bandanna-masks by others. Others, again, had obscured their features with dirt. Most were bearing carbines, rifle-muskets or revolvers; behind them, hauled on a gun-carriage, was a 12-pounder field howitzer, and, mounted on a trail-wagon, an empty cage. A miner on the road, returning from the sickbed of his brother, happened upon the queer company and took them for vigilantes. He was advised to walk on and banish the encounter from memory if he wished to live long enough to see the sunrise.

Presently they came to the ridge near Brogan's Prospect. There they took an old mule-trail that winds northward for twelve and a half miles, through overgrown terrain, along a precipitous undercliff, to a long derelict burial ground of the Pend d'Oreilles Indians, making campfire adjacently around half-after-ten. The horses were watered. A plan was argued out. The howitzer was test-fired. Around noon, they rode on.

The mission was anticipated to require seven days and nights. At its head rode former General James Con O'Keeffe, Territorial Secretary and Acting Governor, who had commanded the 'Irish Brigade' of the Army of the Potomac, and later served briefly, we might add controversially, at a desk in the headquarters of the Eastern Tennessee Command. The Mountain Territory extends to a dauntingly vast area, much of it unmapped, most of it inhospitable, but the Governor, no stranger to reckless judgment, refused wiser counsel and pressed his scheme.

Certain parties came and went in the course of those days; but the core of the posse was as follows: Acting Governor O'Keeffe; nine men of his purpose; a tracker by the name of Eye-John Thorn Berry; the Governor's wife; a federal cartographer; and a maidservant, one Elizabeth (freed Negro). It is deplorable that the participation of women in such an operation was ever countenanced, over precarious country, in a treacherous midwinter. The solitary mitigation is a meager one indeed: that the circumstances and objective of the mission being unique, Mrs Lucia O'Keeffe had been adamant that her duty was to accompany her husband to its end. Loyalty is a commendable, a wifely quality. It is second, however, to obedience.

Information had been garnered by Acting Governor O'Keeffe that an infamous brotherhood of outlaws captained by one Cole John McLaurenson – styled 'Irish Johnny Thunders', a Confederate renegade – was hiding in a cave system accessible by abandoned mineshafts lying northwestward of the town of Fort Stornaway. (*Map coordinates: 30/ix/f*). The gang's crimes in the Territory had been numerous and brutal, the most monstrous being the murder, on the 27th day of August, 1866, of the entire crew and command of the Federal steamship *William H. Harrison*, when that vessel was wrecked with callousness and cowardice and pirated of four hundred thousand dollars' worth of gold and uncut sapphires.

But the truer instigation of the Governor's mission was his own: that a friendless orphan, one Jeremiah Mooney, in whose improvement a benevolent interest had been taken by Governor and Mrs O'Keeffe, was abducted near Edwardstown in late November, 1866, reportedly by the gang's principal, McLaurenson. The child had been widely reported dead but the Acting Governor held to hopes that in actuality he was alive. The intent of this expedition was to liberate the boy Mooney, to fetch his captors to justice, or to kill them. It is the conviction of this Commission, having weighed the available testimony, that the latter was the option favored strongly by the Acting Governor. This was, in all but name, a mission of execution, and was understood so to be by at least several of its participants, who regarded themselves as a fellowship above the reach of that law which some of them were employed to defend. That men who had sworn an oath to the United States Constitution suffered themselves to be members of 'O'Keeffe's Apostles' – that they addressed their leader by the title of 'General' – conducted themselves, in fact, as a quasi-military body – these are grave matters indeed. There is but one legal army in this Republic; its Commander-in-Chief is the President.

The mission was insufficiently informed and was to prove ill fated. The catastrophic consequences are known and need not be repeated here. It must only be noted that Acting Governor O'Keeffe, some creditable service in the War against the rebellion notwithstanding, acted in a manner that warrants, and here receives, the severest possible rebuke of this Tribunal. Furthermore [*the remainder of this paragraph has been heavily scored out, and the subsequent nine pages are missing from the file. The document resumes as follows:*].

. . . to anyone who wanted to know of it. The personal reputation of Mrs O'Keeffe *** ******** ******* ** *********** ** ********. We are satisfied, entirely, that this allegation is unfounded and deplore that it sullied these proceedings.

Many questions linger unmet at the conclusion of our deliberations. The Commissioners have noted the vague recollection of certain witnesses, the dubiety of the evidence offered even by some under oath. For a lawman to depose with less than complete forthrightness brings dishonor on the badge he wears. Our investigations have been further impeded by the refusal of certain parties to testify, the absconding of one witness (reportedly into Canada), and the failure of Acting Governor O'Keeffe, in breach of the law, 'to make and keep and maintain for the people a record *in writing* of his works'. It is difficult to avoid the deduction that particular persons, of whom a great deal better might have been expected, have attempted to dam, or at least to divert, the flow of revelatory truth. These charges we place sternly before the magistracy of private conscience, since we have not the legal authority of dismissal.

The facts uncontested, inasmuch as we have been capable of

ascertaining them, are above set out in brief. Four conclusions, merely, shall be placed on the record:

I) Acting Governor O'Keeffe's mission was NOT authorized by the United States Government.

II) The United States Government denies EMPHATICALLY that it had hand, act, or part in the events at Fort Stornaway.

III) The coming into the Territory of one John Fintan Duggan had little, if anything, to do with these events. This Duggan, nevertheless, is to depart the Territory immediately, his holdings to be confiscated (without compensation of any kind) and appended to the Koötenais reservations.

IV) The proceedings of this Commission, and all papers which it considered, and all evidence gathered by dint of its powers, are to remain CLASSIFIED and UNPUBLISHED for a period of no less than seventy years.

The names of these Commissioners are never to be revealed; and the matter, now deemed concluded, is never to be revisited.

Signed: **** ***** (Brig. Gen., Presiding);
***** **** **** (Maj. Gen.)
and ***** ********* (Major)

Given this day, XII January, 1868,
At the city of Washington,
The District of Columbia,
The United States of America.

∇

CHAPTER 73

THE LAST RIDE OF THE APOSTLES

FIRST DAY OF SEVEN
Wednesday, December 26th

Her husband stumbles out of the coppice with a Colt repeater in his hand, having convinced himself, wrongly, that he heard a rattlesnake in the bracken. His face is leathery. He looks traumatized and tired. The vein in his forehead is rope-like.

The Indian tracker is angry with the Irishmen, one of whom is translating his signs. He is a mute, the Indian, or so he claims, though Lucia is not certain this is the truth. It is a desecration to discharge a weapon in this locale, he insists. The burial ground remains holy even though it has not been used in twenty years; to disrespect it is to spit in the faces of the dead. The Irishmen pretend to listen even as they are priming the fuses. He warns them they will be sorry, will bring down a curse. They laugh; push him away. They say his smell is the curse.

They do not understand that cannon, she knows. Her husband is trying to explain its workings, but she is not sure he understands it either. He cannot leave anything mechanical unexplained. It has always been one of his shortcomings. The squabble grows louder. Some of them are shouting in Gaelic. Elizabeth looks up at them from the river.

He saw them used often during the War, he insists, for breaking up bunkers, for digging out diehards. When they get to Fort Stornaway this machine will prove its worth. There is a rat at Fort Stornaway will need digging out.

Creed, the former rebel, looks hard at her husband. He does not like the equation of 'diehard' with 'rat'. She can see that her husband regrets his choice of words. Creed lets it pass. Stands away.

The explosion rocks the ground. The whiz of the mortar. It sails into the forest, over the crests of the sequoias, and a wrenching splintering bursts from the woods as it lands in some place unseen. Birds soar out of the burning pine-tops. Some beast utters a shriek of abjection.

'Guess she's workin,' Hannigan says, slapping the barrel of the cannon as a farmer the haunches of a milkcow.

Hannigan is the one who most enjoys machinery. Face blackened with smoke and cinders. They say he murdered rebel prisoners: she can imagine this happening. They say he has a wife someplace. She feels pity for his wife. The thought of him naked is terrifying. Only a few hours since they rode out of Redemption and already she is feeble with the cold. It blasts you in this Territory, needles a way into your pores. It is like a torturer finding out the secrets of your body. The thought that this stupidity will last seven days – incomprehensible now. How did she agree to it?

Winterton sits on a rock near the streamlet. He appears to be sketching the Indian.

∇

EXHIBIT 21A:
ANONYMOUS LETTER TO JOHN FINTAN DUGGAN
WRITTEN BY IRISH CONFEDERATE SYMPATHIZERS IN
THE TERRITORY
INTERCEPTED & COPIED BY THE FEDERAL AUTHORITIES

Prisoner 435v
Richmond Prison,
Virginia.
May VII, 1866

Honored Lieutenant, Sir:

We are a committee of private citizens of the Mountain Territory, sons of Old Ireland all. Providence has favored our endeavors since we came into this country, thus we dare, who deeply admire your patriotism, to frame this impertinent interruption.

You cannot know our delight to have learned that your release impends, for which to God we offer thanks, and to you, sincerest congratulation. Our joy for you and Mrs Duggan has been tempered, nonetheless, by a matter that has troubled our consciences.

Dear Friend – if we may presume to address you thus: we hope that a desire to assist does not prevail over tact, the courtesy due to any so far above us as you stand; but we have read that you experience a certain difficulty at present, an impediment that has been known by many great men, and by lesser such as ourselves, in former times, when family and love of country were the only wealth we knew. Treasure it was, in those leaner days, to have the example of John Duggan to shine before our children. We wish, if you will permit us – we dare to ask that you do – to assist a staunch friend of Ireland.

Some of us own a plot of land in a north-western Territory, which we wish you would accept as your own. Furthermore, the deed is already completed; you will find it in this packet, and shall see, when you study it, that title rests entirely with you and your heirs; the conveyance merely awaits your signature before an attorney. The property was purchased, we vouchsafe, with honest money, some years ago when land in the Territory was inexpensively had. The plain truth is that one of us had hoped to mine the plot for silver, but it proved entirely worthless for that purpose.

No mortgage or lien outstands on the property. It comprises a couple of acres, with outbuildings and a log-house, which latter, though in poor repair, could be built up again. It might do very neatly, but, even if it proved wanting, you would have sufficient of land on which to build a better; and of assisting hands a plenitude. It is not, Respected Sir, anything approaching what you deserve; but you would be among friends who love you.

A tributary of the Missouri waters the acreage. There is adequate fishing and hunting, so that a man and his wife may eat. Lest it be thought that the burdens of farming might be too much to take up, at these, with profound respectfulness, the years of most maturity, we should say that the hiring of a boy or two would lighten the load, with perhaps an overseer to boss them. We have among our settlers many Irish of every county, often knowledgeable on culturing and animal husbandry. We are adequately stocked with Negroes, most are biddable and clean, for the disruptive meet rapid correction. We have Swedes, Danes, and Germans, and the men make good hands. Our Norwaymen, also, are large-framed and strong and will work an honest day for a dollar and a grubstake. We might add, for it will concern a man of your piety, that Christians of the white race predominate here. Indeed, some of us have determined to have us a little south in the north-west, with her courtesies, traditions, and time-proven ways.

Your vista would be a wild one of mountain and lake, agreeable to any Hibernian who ever reminisces of his motherland. Our savages are quelled; submission has been schooled into them. Our country is large.

Here a man has room to go about. He may choose his own society and live by his own lights. Down-easting Yankee doctrines on the intermingling of the races, fashionable among the guilt-ridden hypocrites of New England, are regarded out here as dangerous sheckoonery. There is never any need, for the man of the West, to meet one he wishes to avoid.

Honored Sir, lest there be any question of disinclination to accept a charitable hand, which reluctance we know would be the prime impulse of any manly Irish heart, permit us to state, on our solemn honor as your countrymen, that no condition appends to our proposition. Nor even do we wish to be identified to you at the present, for we feel certain, forgive our discourtesy, which is not intended, that you would attempt, out of pride, to reverse or cancel our deed, whereas we, stubborn men, have determined to press it. We shall welcome you delightedly when you are come to be our neighbor. Our wives shall greet Mrs Duggan, in excellence their model, as a respected, a beloved sister.

We beg you, Honored Sir: think not our proposal any benevolence, but an expression of our profoundest gratitude, a private act of friends. We can think of One greater than any of us here, trodden by invaders, punished by Imperials, who spurned not the shoulder of the Samaritan when it came, feeble and unneeded though it were. No man is an island, entire of himself. You have had to be, we own, when the turncoats deserted you; when the onetime friend, the posing patriot, chose for gold not glory. But know that you are at the center of a vast archipelago, which will one day be united again.

Honored Sir, there is a book more we would wish to write, but we have presumed enough by now on a great man's patience. Only know, Esteemed Friend, as you reflect on our proposal, that there are thousands of us out here who never prostituted our birthright, who never bowed a traitor's knee to Jonathan Yankee or Britannia. Our touchstone in those times was John Fintan Duggan. It would be the deepest honor of our lives to have assisted him.

God keep you in the coming days. We shall never forget your sacrifice. God bless Ireland and the Confederate States of America, which, both, shall rise again.

Sir, we are – we have the privilege ever to remain,

Your countrymen and admirers in the West.

P.S. We are many days' rough ride from Redemption Falls. No troublemaker out of that miscegenated Sodom ever darkens our country. Did he dare to, he would not return home.

∇

SECOND DAY OF SEVEN
Thursday, December 27th

A fierily cold dawn. Ice on the fleetings. He is stiff from the night in the tent.

A hundred yards ahead of him rides Winterton alone. He has stopped and is standing up hard in his stirrups, as though something unexpected has captured his attention. His horse wheels messily. Winterton doubles around his neck. He is pointing, shouting. Hannigan and English ride up to him hurriedly, pistols drawn and aimed at the horizon. It is only a rare bird he has sighted.

On through the foothills. The temperature falls. Ice-beads form on the riders' bandannas, and the snorts of the horses come harder. To the north, a mile-long snow cloud. The Indian advises great caution. They take refuge in a grotto and wait for the storm but it does not come and the men are irritable. Time has been lost. It will be dark in four hours. They ford the Missouri at Crow Creek.

Through an ice-glazed forest where once, many years ago, the Koötenais fought with the Blackfeet. Spear-ends and arrowshafts still stuck in the trees. The clavicles of a long-rotted tepee.

If Calhoun were among them, the Governor would feel a little easier. But someone must remain to keep order. A good man, Calhoun. He had wanted to come. There is talk in the town about John Calhoun and Lucia. The Governor knows it is empty.

They enter a cavernous valley with gray limestone walls. The cold diminishes slightly, for the wind is shielded out, and its gusts far above them sound organlike and strange, a basso continuo, he thinks. There is a faint eucalyptus smell and something else – smoke? A long-dead tributary has scored out a track. Above them a loon utters an echoing squawk. The wheels of the gun-carriage canting and slipping on the stones. Scarves of snow on the cage's bars.

There is unease between the riders. He can see it in their bodies. The rebels keep to themselves when the camp is made, rarely speaking to the

389

Yankees or the Indian. Winterton moves subtly from group to group. Ingratiator. Always seeking information. And Elizabeth and Lucia form a group of their own, although they, like the rebels, rarely converse with anyone else. They talk to one another quietly, in Spanish, about food. Lucia has proved a passable teacher.

Grief bubbles up in him. He is thinking about Demonsland. Why would he think of it today?

∇

FROM LUCIA'S JOURNAL

Thursday Dec. 27. 66. Elizabeth unwell. Severe pain of the head. Hope the reason is not as I believe.

Men dislike having us here. Sly glowers. Collegial grumbling. C not helpful. Hate the way he joins in their remarks. So desperately wants to be one of the filthy mob when he will always be one of the elite.

I can ride as well as any + better than most. I do not know why they look at me.

∇

FROM THE EVIDENCE OF EYE-JOHN THORN BERRY, TRACKER, A BLACKFOOT

*The witness, a mute, gave his testimony in sign language. It was interpreted for the commissioners by Corporal J**** O' B****, who is himself of Indian blood.*

EXAMINER: Do you know the English language?
WITNESS: Some words. Not many.
E: I would like you to take an oath. Here is the Holy Bible.
W: The truth should be spoken at all times: not sometimes. No oaths are wanted between men of honor.
E: That is all very fine, but –
W: You have no powers to compel me to take an oath. This is written in your own law.
E: Very well, then. You were employed by the Acting Governor to assist in this mission, were you not?

W: My people do not call him 'Governor'. We call him 'Irish General'. That is what everyone in the Territory calls him.

E: In any case, will you tell us why he asked you to accompany him on this ride?

W: His man Calhoun came to me, I cannot remember when. He said they needed a tracker.

E: You were on friendly terms with O'Keeffe?

W: He was willing to pay.

E: And the General told you he wanted to find this boy . . .

W: I think you mean the Acting Governor. You are not employing the correct term.

[*Laughter from some of the Commissioners but not from the witness*]

E: Clearly you know the English language better than you led us to believe.

W: You are wrong. I know only what you told me.

E: What were you told had befallen the boy?

W: That the night-man had stolen him.

E: You mean the outlaw Cole McLaurenson?

W: I mean as I said: the night-man.

E: And on the second day of the mission, just before dusk, you detected a track, did you not?

W: Three sets of horse-prints. They were headed north-east.

E: You are skilled at tracking?

W: My father was skilled. I can track a little.

E: How do you do that?

W: By looking.

E: In which sense?

W: By looking at the earth. And opening your eyes. How else would you recommend? By looking at the sky?

E: You do not care for being questioned . . .

W: I was ordered to come here. I have come.

E: Don't you want to assist these gentlemen?

W: I do not know who they are. They have not spoken a word to me. They only sit and appear stern while you ask your questions. [*Witness here used a phrase that the translator said he did not know.*]

E: They are very important men who have journeyed all the way here from Washington. That is in the east. A mighty and powerful city. You will have heard, perhaps, of the great white palace, where the chief of the white man –

W: I know what Washington is.

E: The gentleman in the middle is General ——. To his right is Brigadier General ——. And on the left, sipping the glass of water, is Major —— ——.

W: Are those medals they wear for bravery?

E: They are brave men indeed.

W: They murdered many south-men? In the War between your peoples?

E: Each of them has done many heroic things. The word 'murder' is not –

W [*interrupting*]**:** When some go to war, they are called beasts and savages. When others go to war, they pin women's ribbons on one another.

E: Do not be impertinent. Will you assist the gentlemen?

W: Do they need a tracker?

E: In a manner of speaking. They are attempting to track the truth.

W: Then look at the earth. And let them open their eyes. The truth leaves a mark if you know where to look for it.

[*At this point, the Presiding Judge interjected. It was felt that the witness had little beneficial to bring to the proceedings. He was told to stand down and excused from further attendance. He and his brothers left the room.*]

$$\nabla$$

THIRD DAY OF SEVEN

Friday, December 28th

'*Buenos días*,' says Elizabeth Longstreet, glancing up from the fire. Her face is grimy, her hair tied in braids. It occurs to Lucia that she has never asked Elizabeth her age. She might be thirty. It is hard to tell.

'*Buenos días, Elisabetta. Deben comer.* You ought to eat.'

'*No tengo hambre, señora.¿Quieres desayunar?*'

She ladles out a mess of frijoles and offers it to her mistress. The mush tastes acrid, as though cooked in rancid water. She eats it down anyway. It is all there is.

The Indian walks slowly around the circumference of the camp. Sometimes he looks at the stones.

O'Keeffe is conferring with Hannigan and English. Shortly afterward, each of them saddles, then rides out alone, English to the east, Hannigan west – Lucia does not know where they are going, or why.

She fights a feeling that none of them will ever return from this journey. The plan is too vague, too dependent on luck. She does not want to see anyone innocent die. She does not want to see death, at all.

That private – from Wicklow – who had crawled into a corner and turned his back to the ward so that nobody could see him. She had gone to him, knelt behind him, in case he wanted a companion; but he had never turned around. He had died alone.

It was the day that the news had come from Appomattox. The War was over; Lee had surrendered. In his submission there had been defiance, or what southerners called gallantry. His beautiful uniform, pressed as for a ball; his gloriously accoutered stallion. The conquering troops had watched as he stepped down to their level. His buttons were so polished that they glittered in the sun. Grant, the victor, had on the attire of a private. It was the beaten man who looked like the champion.

When the surrender was signed – it had not taken very long – the rebels had stacked their arms in a pile on the road and crossed to where their vanquishers were standing. The northerners offered handshakes, parcels of food; bandages. Then the rebels had gone home to their families. Those who owned horses were permitted to keep them, so that their farms could be worked again. Six hundred thousand dead. The south in ash. All it took to end the killing was the crossing of a road.

Winterton approaches from the tent near the elders. How can he be so clean in this filthy cold? Does he wash his clothes at night? Where does he do that? The ghost of how he looked before his injuries wrecked him. His eyes marble-green, his hands young and strong. She has an intimation of how Winterton's child would look: like its father, but without the wounds.

'I thought I might take a walk,' he says.

'Where shall you go?'

'Into the forest over there. I should like to make some measurements. I shouldn't think it will require longer than an hour or so.'

'Shall you take one of the men? It might be safer if you did.'

He lets his disappointment at her rebuff become visible in his expression. That is one of his skills: communicating plenitudes in silence. In that way like her husband; and in other ways, perhaps. But what did he expect? A walking companion? He sets off with Flor Savage in the direction of the woods. She looks at their footprints in the snow.

And she wonders was he telling the truth that night at the house. Had he truly seen the child? Is some game being played?

They are talking about the cannon again. She wishes they would stop. The Indian is troubled; she can see it in the way he walks.

As though the weight of the firmament is pressing down on his head. He toes the ice-glazed stones.

∇

THE TESTIMONY OF JOHN TREVANION,
NEWSPAPER EDITOR

[The witness agreed without objection to take the oath. This done, the examination commenced.]

E: Is your name John Trevanion?

W: John Knox Trevanion.

E: Where were you born, sir?

W: In Dumfriesshire, Scotland. I have resided eighteen years in this country.

E: And you are editor of the *Redemption and Edwardstown Epitaph*, I think.

W: That is correct.

E: Could you speak up a little?

W: Yes, I edit that paper.

E: Would you tell us what happened on Friday, 28th day of December last? That was the third day of the Governor's expedition.

W: I had ridden up to the Chelsea River with some associates of mine . . .

E: Associates?

W: Yes.

E: And?

W: I had ridden up to the Chelsea River with some associates of mine. We wished to survey a parcel of land in which one of us had an interest. It was a gentlemanly excursion. Nothing much more. We had gone into the forest near Clonmel Cross because we had seen a she-bear, a grizzly. We thought we should have a little sport.

E: You are quite the huntsman, I believe.

W: I do not understand your tone.

E: The pursuit of a quarry rather excites you, does it not?

W: Hunting is a gentlemanly pastime. I would not see much else in it if I were you.

E: Please proceed.

W: I saw O'Keeffe and a party of others riding past the clearing. Or perhaps he saw me first. I cannot recall. In any event, he rode over and asked what I was doing in these remote parts. I said I was doing nothing that was his concern, only hunting a bear. He became offensive in his language, which I did not appreciate.

E: When you say 'he became offensive' – what did he actually say?

W: I should prefer not to repeat the words. They were odious.

E: Did he say: 'You crawling whore's vermin. You worthless shit-ass coward'?

W: It was something like that.

E: 'You are a traitor to this country and everything decent in it and I shall see you stretched from your own filthy noose'?

W: I believe so.

E: Why did he say that?

W: You would have to ask him.

E: To be sure, you have an opinion. A man of your intelligence.

W: My intelligence, if I have any, is insufficient in this case.

E: Did you threaten that you would murder the Acting Governor?

W: That would be a remarkably foolish thing to say.

E: Did you threaten that you would murder the Acting Governor?

W: I suppose one might have said it in the heat of the instant. One was taken aback by the ferocity of his insults. A Celt can say injudicious things when his blood is up.

E: An exculpation that does not extend to the Governor, presumably.

W: Your point is noted, Lieutenant. I am not especially proud of what I said.

E: To revise a moment: I wish to be certain. You saw the Governor and a party of other men riding past the clearing?

W: Correct.

E: How did you recognize him?

W: I knew him all to pieces.

E: The Governor and his party had on bandannas for the cold. So how, I wonder, were you able to identify him?

PRESIDING JUDGE: Please answer the Examiner. Take a moment to recollect if needs be.

W: As I said, perhaps he saw me first. I do not know. I cannot recall.

E: I suggest that you and your party of gentlemanly associates had been tracking the Governor all the way from Redemption Falls.

W: No.

E: That you knew of his expedition and intended to warn his enemies of it.

W: No.

E: That you wished to make clear to the Governor and his men that you and any supporter of the defeated Confederacy would hold sway in the Mountain Territory.

W: That is a ludicrous fabrication from prolog to fin.

E: Did you ever, in your newspaper, write or publish one line repudiating the depredations of Confederate outlaws?

W: I have not committed to memory every sentence I have written.

E: Did you say on various occasions to people in Redemption: [*Examiner reading aloud from a confidential document*] 'Any wind that shakes the tree of Yankeedom is good for our cause'? Or: 'John Cole McLaurenson is a hero of the white race'? Or: 'One man's outlaw is another's soldier for liberty'?

W: You seem to have a catalog of my reputed sayings. I do not remember ever having said any of them.

E: 'McLaurenson is the finest man ever to set foot into this Territory. You would not think he had any Irish in him at all'?

W: That does not sound like a sentiment to which a wise man would give public voice.

E: Are you now, or have you ever been, a Vigilante?

W: I decline to answer.

E: Forgive me; I did not hear you?

W: Amendment Five to the Constitution conveys the right to decline.

E: This is not a criminal trial, sir.

W: I decline to answer.

E: You are leader of the so-called Committee of Vigilant Citizens, or the 'O-and-O Men', as this fine body is sometimes termed. You have been responsible, in this Territory, for the 'lynching' of numerous persons. Flynn. John Harran. James Dunne. The list is legion. Your quarrels with the Acting Governor on this matter are widely known. You have written vilely about him in your newspaper and slandered him about the Territory. He had the audacity to oppose you. He must be punished.

W: I hope I do not write vilely. But I am entitled to free speech.

E: You are quite the constitutional authority.

W: No, sir; I am not.

E: On the Fifth Amendment only.

W: I am no kind of authority.

E: Do you champion the O-and-O Men?

W: I defend my neighbors.

E: Do you defend their contempt for the Government's laws?

W: The Government is in Washington, not here in the Territory. Were we ordered by the Government when to sow and to reap, we should soon starve to death in our fields.

E: A most touching parable. Which Vigilante said that?

W: Thomas Jefferson said that, sir. I will forward you the reference.

E: You bracket the likes of these hangmen with the father of this Republic?

W: The bracketing was yours, not mine.

E: You will know that the Constitution bestows the right of due process.

W: I am not here to –

E [*interrupting*]: To seize a citizen with no trial but a drumhead pretense. To carry him into the night, with neither friend nor advocate, and to torture that person and put him to a beast's death. Is that properly constitutional, to your manner of thinking?

W: I have not been to Law School. You tell me.

E: You think this a matter for levity?

W: I decline to answer.

E: Were you party to a conspiracy to burn the gubernatorial residence at Redemption Falls?

W: No.

E: You have heard the Governor say that you were.

W: A lie.

E: Did you ever sketch a plan of that house for a man?

W: No.

E: Did you cause a man or men to engage in surveillance of that house? And of Mrs Lucia O'Keeffe at the Plains Hotel, Edwardstown?

W: I decline to answer.

E: Did you conspire with others to bomb that house?

W: A lie.

397

E: Did you murder one Devlin who was employed to build that house?
W: No.
E: Did your party disrespect, and then cause to be destroyed, the flag of the United States at that house? Did you on many occasions despoil a lesser house, the home of a person formerly a slave, with secessionist and other slogans touching her race?
W: I decline to answer.
E: Do you love these United States, sir?
W: I hope I am a good patriot.
E: That is not what I asked you.
W: That is my answer.

[*The time being five minutes after four o'clock, the proceedings were adjourned.*]†

∇

FOURTH DAY OF SEVEN
Saturday, December 29

Lucia's journal

Elizabeth told me the reason for her illness. It is as I had suspected, alas. Started some months ago, in left eye, she says. Bad aches, sometimes dizziness. Vision comes and goes. Told me there are moments when she can barely discern her hand before her face. I asked: 'Can you see me now, Elizabeth?' She answered: 'Your shape only.' I moved closer to her and asked again. She said nothing.

Told her we would fetch a doctor. It would not achieve, she felt. Asked me not to speak of it to C, but I felt I had no choice but to do so.

He came in and spoke to her decently. Said she would be kept on. No question whatever of dismissal. She said she could be of no use. He insisted. I saw a kindliness I used to see in former times. A gift, to be able to talk to people. Wish I had it.

† John Trevanion failed to present for questioning the following Monday morning. A marshal went to his home but nobody was there. A 'suicide note' was found at his place of work. Its author was seen in Montréal fourteen months later. He lived to ninety-three and died in his bed, having made a fortune from his memoir *Strong-Handed Justice in a Wild Frontier* (reputedly Queen Victoria's favorite book).

Later, told him my news. That perhaps he and I are to be parents. He wept. Said he was happy for it. Pleaded with me immediately to return to Redemption. Told him I would not, for the moment.

Two more men joined us tonight. We are now fourteen.

∇

A REGISTER OF THE RIDERS & THEIR FIREPOWER
COMPILED FOR THE TRIBUNAL-OF-INQUIRY BY US ARMORY DEPT.

Jas. C. O'Keeffe: 43 yrs. Austrian Lorenz Model 1854 rifle-musket, .54 caliber, re-bored to .58. Two Colt repeaters. Regimental saber of Queen's Own Hussars, with 'Genl. J.F.O'K' etched into blade (gems missing from hilt).

Patk. Edwd. Hannigan: 37 yrs. Acting Sheriff, Varina County. Veteran 127th New York, 'The Irish Brigade'. Colt Army Model sidearm 1861, .44 caliber. Surgeon's scalpel (x one) by Weis of Bond St, London. Modified to be scabbarded down a boot. Also garrotting chain.

Daniel Neyland Moody: 24 yrs. Acting Sheriff, Truro County. Veteran 127th NY (decorated sharpshooter). Long-range bench-rest rifle. Lethal to 1,800 yards. Machete knife (one) with serrated blade.

Owen (known as John) Creed: 31 yrs. Confederate veteran. (1st Mississippi). Spencer rifle, metallic cartridge, primer builded in. 12 rounds per minute. Bowie knife.

Denis Arkins: (Veteran 2nd Mass, 12th Corps, 1st Division.) Acting Deputy Marshal, Edwardstown & Thomond Counties. Sharps 1859 Carbine (short barrel, breech loading). Belt of Chinese throwing knives, star-shaped.

Michael Francis English: 32 yrs. Veteran 127th New York. Acting Sheriff, Canada Borderlands. Two x Starr revolvers, .44 caliber, six-shot, double-action weapon. Also sawn-down shotgun. 'Erin Forever' carved into stock.

Joseph John Mounrance: 26 yrs. Veteran 127th New York. Acting Sheriff, Skibbereen County. Bespoke 'figure 8' revolver, claimed to have smithed it himself (while prisoner at Pentonville Gaol, London, England), .36 caliber. Not thumb-cocked. Dependable.

John 'Flor' Savage: 46yrs. Veteran 29th Indiana. Acting Marshal, Sequoia County. Le Mat Revolver, 'cap and ball', two barrels.

Francis William Dwyer: 34 yrs. Veteran 32nd South Carolina. Model 1861 Springfield Musket. $15 to $20. Springfield Armory, Mass.

Allen Winterton: 34 yrs. Captain, US Corps of Cartographers. Enfield rifled musket, manuf. England. Bore diameter .577 inches, 9 lb. 3 oz. with bayonet. Fires similar to minnie ball. True to 800 yards. Small pistol: unknown make; now lost.

Michael Martin Joyce: 52 yrs. Veteran 21st Georgia. Whitworth rifle, British manufacture (retrieved from fellow Confederate rifleman at Spotsylvania). Fires hexagonal 'bolt'. Delivers terrible wound.

'Eye-John' or 'I-John' Thorn-berry: Age unknown. Blackfoot Indian. Colt-Root Model 1855 percussion repeating rifle .64 caliber. (US Army issue, stolen.) NOTE: DEFECTIVE WEAPON: HAS BEEN DESTROYED. (Prone to fire all cylinders at once: severed finger from rifleman's forward hand when test-fired.)

Lucia-Cruz McLelland-O'Keeffe: Starr carbine rifle with 21 inch .54 caliber barrel. Zero misfire rate, unfailingly true. Small jewel-handled dagger, Spanish design. (Twenty diamonds in hilt, antique, used as an aide-mémoire for prayer, each diamond representing a mystery of the Rosary.)

Beth: Freed Negro. About 30 yrs. Unarmed.

OTHER ORDNANCE & WEAPONRY & cetera

Bear-trap cage, cast-iron, with chained gate & deadlocks. Williams breech-loading rapid-fire 'Mechanical-gun' built for Confederate War Dept, used at Seven Pines. Prone to overheat & jams its breech. Has been destroyed.

One very savage hunting hound: property of the Governor. Has been destroyed.

∇

FIFTH DAY OF SEVEN
Sunday, December 30th

They left camp shortly after dawn and rode most of the morning, resting only measured minutes at a time. At a farmstead near the Cricklewood River, English was waiting with fresh horses, but fodder was scarce by now.

The farmer and his wife, Thomas and Kate Prunty, were Fenian sympathizers born in Liverpool. They regarded O'Keeffe as a hero, his presence as an honor. For this reason they had invited a number of Irish neighbors to their home, despite having been asked to keep his visit completely secret. He refused to meet any of them, indeed flew into a rage with his hosts and betook himself to the barn with his men. Lucia appealed to him to greet his admirers, asserting – perhaps questionably – that they were more likely to be discreet if the request came from O'Keeffe himself. At any event, he remained in the barn all day. There was a heavy fall of snow in the afternoon.

Food, drink and blankets were brought to the barn, with coats and a few pipes of tobacco. Still he refused to see his hosts. It grew dark by four o'clock. O'Keeffe slept a while in a blanket-roll. The men played dice or poker quietly; others rested in the stalls, or cleaned their guns. They had been ordered not to drink, but some did, surreptitiously, for the oncoming night was bitterly cold and no fire could be permitted in a barn. At midnight, O'Keeffe conferred with Savage and told him of an alteration of route. The plan had been compromised. He was convinced they were spied-on. They would not be proceeding directly to Stornaway.

Winterton was behaving oddly. He seemed highly-strung, visibly nervous. Flor Savage of County Cork, who was emerging as O'Keeffe's right-hand man, would testify at the Tribunal that the mapmaker had not slept all that night, had sat awake in the barn, repeatedly searching his clothing and haversack. At dawn he told John Creed that he had mislaid an important journal. Creed helped him to search for it. It was not found.

About an hour after sunrise, as they made to set out, Elizabeth Longstreet became too ill to continue. Lucia insisted she remain at the farmhouse with the Prunty family, whose son agreed to see her safely back to Redemption Falls as soon as the weather permitted. He would ride the thirty miles for the doctor in the meantime. It was snow-blindness, said the farmer. Distressing but not serious. They would take good care of her, he promised.

O'Keeffe bade her good-bye at about a quarter-past eight. It was New Year's Eve, 1866. She would never see any of the riders again.

∇

SIXTH DAY OF SEVEN
Monday, December 31st

It was a dim, bitter day as O'Keeffe led the posse through Gunmetal Gorge, down Two Mile Hill, then over the flats of the snow-covered prairie by the north-east trail toward Canada. They must have ridden past Lake Union, which was surely frozen solid, and its sprinkling of tiny and overgrown islands. They would have had to negotiate O'Malley's Gulch, no easy thing in fair weather on the strongest mule. In midwinter, on horseback, with the stones rolling like cannonballs, it must have been a frightening traverse.

The temperature that day was seven degrees below freezing. They passed the ghost town of Silverlode Spring. The river was forded at a place called Simoon, which Thorn Berry had been told of, but had never previously seen. By now, some of the men had an idea of where they were headed. Three, perhaps four, were unhappy.

They stopped to rest the horses at Milestone Landing, a pass connecting a tributary of the Parfleche River with a branch of the Redwolf to the west. O'Keeffe was approached by a deputation. If their assumption was correct on where they were headed, about half of the men would not accompany him further. He did not give them an argument but agreed they should wait for him here. He would return, he said, in two hours.

O'Keeffe, Lucia, Winterton, Savage and the former Confederates continued. The Pend d'Oreilles track they took is no longer in existence; at the time it was narrow, little more than a footpath, so that they rode single-file with O'Keeffe to the front and Savage, gun drawn, to the rear.

Five drumlins of stones. A fallow black meadow. At first they were uncertain this could be the place. TRESPASSERS WILL BE SHOT announced a placard on the gate. And then, through gusts of swirling smoke, a tattered Confederate flag.

Chickens grubbing at a midden-heap, tugging worms from its depths. A rooster prancing slowly near the kennels. A jennet tethered to a stake, which it was circling in a grim plod. Many sacks of unsown seed.

As they rode toward the cabin of whip-sawed white fir, they saw a man in a nearby field, digging with his back to them. He might be forty or sixty: it was difficult to tell. Near him, a black child was sitting in a barrow.

O'Keeffe dismounted first. The steader did not look, though he must have heard the crunch of their hooves on his stones.

The smoke was from a bonfire of brushwood and pines that was crackling in a hollow near the creek. The fire shot sparks. There was an odor of boiling pine-sap.

'John,' said O'Keeffe, to the shoulders of the man. 'An old rebel is come to see you.'

Still he did not turn. He only dug the harder, grunting as he cut, his neck reddening lividly with every thrust, then whitening again as he straightened. The child looked up at O'Keeffe and Lucia, as though waiting for them to tell him something important.

'I hope Martha keeps well. Is she here with you or still at Richmond?'

The man made no answer but footed the spade. Its rasp sounded harsh in the schist. They could hear his breathing, so uneasy it sounded painful. He had always suffered badly with his lungs.

'I meant to come before. To wish you fortune in the Territory. What with one thing and another I rather – '

'I know why you're come.'

'Then you have heard of what has happened. The outlaw and the boy.'

'I know why you're come,' he repeated.

'This man who has wronged me. He was once a Confederate soldier. I thought, if I may speak frankly, with your standing in the south – of all you gave in the War and so on . . .'

'To liken my sons with a gunslinger. Is that what you thought?'

Now he turned to face O'Keeffe.

He was a short man, stocky, with a graying tattoo on his right forearm. A man that had once been handsome. You could tell from his accent that he had lived in different lands but that Ireland, Ulster, the city of Derry, had probably once been his home. He stood with a slight stoop, had done so for many years – result of the floggings he had received in Tasmania. The worst one he had gotten, two hundred lashes, for assisting the escape of the figure now before him.

'I'd as lief you'd explain,' said John Fintan Duggan. 'Do you liken my sons to that killer?'

'Of course I do not. I meant only to say that any southerner would surely listen to one of your standing in his country. If you were prepared to intercede. There can be a peaceful outcome. The boy is only a child. If any harm came to him . . . '

'You dare talk to me of harm? After what I have endured?'

'The day has never passed that I did not pray for the boys. Your sacrifice – and Martha's – it was too much. It was cruel.'

'Do not speak of my sons, sir. You are not worthy to speak of them. The prayers of your kind are not wanted here.'

'They were fine boys, John. A credit to you and Martha. I know they will have fought with courage, always.'

'And their godfather in the vanguard of the assassins that savaged them. How much "courage" did it take you to turn on your friends?'

'John – if I have wronged you – I ask your forgiveness.'

'It's yourself you've wronged, sir. It's yourself'll pay.'

The threat seemed to bounce on the stones between them. Wild geese clattered from a cottonwood.

'Tell me, General O'Keeffe, or whatever you call yourself now. Do they know your little secret? Should I tell them? You hypocrite. You posing, posturing fraud.'

'John – '

'Then I see you have kept it quiet. That is what I had heard. Was that difficult, sir? For all of these years? Even a liar as filthied as yourself must surely have his moments in the night.'

'Con,' said Lucia, 'what is he talking about?'

'Aye,' said Duggan. 'What am I talking about? Tell her, why don't you. Or should I?'

Each man faced the friend of his youth. One night in a cell they had cut open their thumbs and mingled their blood in an oath. The older looked at the younger with the impassivity of a magistrate whose conscience is untroubled by passing sentence.

'Do you feel that fear, sir? That is your judgment. I would walk into Hell for the remainder of eternity before I would spend a single night in your mind.'

Duggan motioned to the child, who slid out of the barrow and approached him with a gourd and a bundle of rag. He poured water from the flask into Duggan's cupped hands. Duggan plashed his face, dried his hands with the rag; took a couple of careful quaffs from the gourd. He had the neatness of a man to whom water is scarce, the neatness of a man who has been in many prisons; who might one day be prisoner again. The boy shambled back to the wheelbarrow and sat in it, crossed-legged, like Buddha observing the nothing.

'Was there some other import?' Duggan asked the ashes around him, which rose and fell and fell and rose and adhered to his flesh and his spade. 'I've a claim needs working. Some in this country must work. We receive no Judas dollar of the Government.'

'I come as an old friend who is fallen in trouble. I will beg for your help if that would persuade you. I am in very great danger. Some I love are in danger. The days to come, they might well be my last.'

'Then, winter where you summered,' John Duggan said, and turned back to slicing his dirt.

An eagle scudded slowly down a turret of wind in the northernmost quadrant of sky.

'Con, come,' said Lucia, taking his arm. But he seemed reluctant to go. She beckoned to the men.

John Flor Savage brought O'Keeffe's horse up by its rein. It was restless, twitching its ears at the cinders. The riders were silent at the repudiation they had witnessed. It was a hard thing to have had to see.

'Can you shake my hand at least, John? For the sake of better days?'

Duggan refused to turn. But he rose from his work. He seemed to be looking at the eagle as it banked; he had always loved birds, found them beautiful and strange. O'Keeffe stepped toward his back tentatively, right hand proffered.

'James and Con, they would surely have wanted – '

The next thing would be remembered for many a year by every one who saw it happen. Lucia gasping. Savage's pistol being drawn. O'Keeffe's hand restraining him. A horse rearing up. A screamed obscenity. A black child doing nothing.

O'Keeffe wiping the spittle from his face.

The woman had come up so silently that nobody had noticed her approach. She was small and thin and pale. She was habited all in black but her clothing was old, so that its black was bleaching to gray.

'Black day they didn't cut you to pieces,' Martha Duggan wept, her shoulders tremoring violently. 'An I'd known what'd come of you, I'd've whetted their knife. You are filth. Do you mind me? The lowest of the low. When I think of the men you deceived into following you. Now hie your vermin out of this land – *or be buried in it.*'

It was Winterton who came to lead the Governor away. The black child watched them ride out.

W: Couple hours after the Duggan place, we come to Bunclody Ford.
Boss was in a blue; even for him. We pitched camp up above but he
took off a while by himself. I suppose a couple hours. He went into
the forest. He looked poorly when he come back down.

E: Poorly?

W: Here [*indicating face*]. I don't know. Feverish I guess. I don't mean
he looked moonsad or nothing like that. But body-peaked, you know
. . . His eyes was fierce rheumy . . . I heard one of the boys – I think
English – asking him if he was sound. He said he was sound enough,
just he tucken a bad chill. Then English asked him if he was sure we
was going on with the plan.

E: What did he reply?

W: He said: 'Clapper's in the bell, Mick. Let it ring.'

E: In what spirit was that said?

W: I guess trying to be chirk.

E: Chirk.

W: Cheerful. Trying to buck up the boys, I would say. Or his self.

E: Some time subsequently, you overheard a quarrel between the
Acting Governor and his wife.

W: I guess.

E: About?

W: I don't remember.

E: You remember very well. What was the matter between them?

W: I didn't hear all of it. It was something about Australia.

E: It was a violent quarrel about the secret to which John Duggan had
made reference. Do not prevaricate, man. You heard every word.

W: No, Sir.

E: Mrs O'Keeffe raised her voice, was extremely distressed and
weeping bitterly. She employed abusive language towards the Acting
Governor, did she not?

W: I don't recollect one way or the other.

E: Mrs O'Keeffe struck the Acting Governor in the face, is that not so?

W: She might have. I couldn't say. Then she went into the tent.

E: I think you remember a great deal more of this incident than you
are telling.

W: No.

E: After she went into the tent: what happened?

W: The Boss ast me if there was a Post Office where we was headed.

E: At Stornaway?

W: Sir.

E: He did not know?

W: Well: there was some question if it was stationed or not at the time. I said I was pretty sure it was. Cause I know Iggy Gilchrist – that's the marshal of Stornaway – and he was after mentioning to me about a man I knew in the War was working there. So the Boss told me get him some paper and a pen. And see he wasn't disturbed. And a drink.

E: A drink?

W: Believe it was a bottle of whiskey he wanted, yes. But we didn't have no whiskey left.

∇

FROM LUCIA'S JOURNAL

Should have suspected before.

    Should always have seen it.

    He asked my forgiveness. Was too shocked to speak.

∇

CHAPTER 74

SURVIVING LETTER FROM THE GOVERNOR TO A BOY IN TASMANIA†

To Master Robert Emmet Boland,
in the care of Mr. and Mrs. John P. Boland,
Blackwatertown Farm, Nr. Hobart, Australia.

December 31st, 1866

My dear son, Robert:

I send you a New Year greeting and my hope that all [*missing word*] along well with you there. Please forgive my so dilatory [*missing word*] to your last, which took fully ten months to come from your hand to mine. The mail is often extremely tardy arriving here in the Mountain Territory. The frequent severities of weather and our geographical remoteness see to that. Also this year we have had difficulties aplenty with Indians attacking the steamships.

If I am not as attentive to our correspondence as I ought to be, Robert, I ask your forgiveness, and promise to better the attempt in the future. I should say, especially since the War of the Rebellion has concluded, with the victory of the United States and her valiant northern armies, that your father is become a tremendously important bore here in America, with many onerous duties, and many eminent drones always desirous of his ear. But such is the yoke of the victorious General. Success, like failure, brings its trials.

I trust that you are being a good scout for your guardians and attending to your lessons and not being otherwise an out-and-outer.

---

† From the private archive of Professor J. D. McL. Five sheets of official gubernatorial notepape, written on both sides, in O'Keeffe's handwriting, with the address of the residence scored out on each page except the first. Small burn hole in first page, possibly caused by cinder. Final 'page' is a shred torn from a flour-bag.

Allow me to applaud the notable improvement in your cursive. Looking at it I cannot credit that you are aged only fourteen: I should have proclaimed it the script of some scholarly graybeard. Possessing the ability of writing neatly is sometimes described as being the accomplishment of a fool, but be assured by your father that only a shite-hawk possessed of no accomplishments whatever would say such a witless and jealous thing.

Proceeding to some of the weightier subjects your mention letters [*sic*]: I have considered your sentiments carefully, and I think that I know what you mean. I am sorry that you have been upset by the silly boy you mention. Try not to notice him, for to pay such nuisances any credence serves only to encourage their ignorance.

You must not think it unmanly to have written to me of your feelings; on the contrary, your frankness does you credit and only confirms, which I already knew, that you are the sort of boy who will grow to a manly and admired adult. A boy's father is the best friend he shall ever have, even in the strange circumstances in which you and I have found ourselves placed; and, in any case, proper manliness is not stoniness.

Every mortal man who was ever worthy of his sex, from Cuchullain to Wolfe Tone, to Bonaparte, to Abraham Lincoln, to the very great patriot who bore your own name, knew the limitless universe of human emotions, sorrow and heart's pain among them. Alexander the Great who conqured [*sic*] his whole world is accounted as having once wept. Did not the bravest hero that ever stood on the earth weep in the loneliness of His passion? No, it is not girlish to weep at times. I myself, when I think of how you and I are parted at present and have been for so long – yes, I have wept.

My own mother, like yours, was taken from me early – I can remember feelings of lonesomeness when I was the age you are now – so that you and I can be brothers in that hard experience, as well as being father and son. It is hard for a boy whose mother has gone to Paradise. We should be happy for her because she is receiving a beautiful reward in a place where no more hurt can ever be done her, where the color of our heart, not our flesh, is the measure; but we think of the loss of that kindest friend, and are lonely sometimes and afraid. You are a good natural boy and a feeling one. Never be ashamed of what is in your soul, for what is found there will always light you a way. Cup your hands around that flame and ever protect it, Robert; for when it extinguishes, a man is lost.

Proceeding to the question which, understandably, has troubled you the most: the filthy words employed by that boy for your late mother, and for those of her skin color, including yourself. Any person that uses the term 'half-breed' about his fellow human being requires our prayers and our pity, for he is a failure. Such words reveal the aching emptiness of those who speak them. How dismal, the mind of such a boy.

At the outset, let me say this, Robert, and know it is the truth. Your mother was a person of peerless character, beautiful and gracious-hearted for all the fact that she was born of lowly degree. I made her acquaintance in no 'pub' or 'den', as that boy imputed, but through a doctor friend to whose children she attended as nursemaid. Her father was not 'a criminal' but a goodly settler born in England. Her mother, an Aboriginal woman, was a lady of extraordinary kindness, one of the finest I have had the honor to know. As for what Father Moran told you about fighting or 'coming the rough', you must reach your own verdict, but I can tell you that I do not myself concur with him. No boy should permit a slur to any lady to stand unchallenged, still less to the one whose very being protected him as he formed within her body, and gave him the gift of life. It is not pleasant to fight; but sometimes we must, else the bully thrives, and his brother, the braggart, and good people suffer the trampling of their hopes. And when that violence is done, good people turn wicked, and the hatreds of our inheritance are amplified.

But since you are troubled, let me reassure you in a clear and clean way. Your mother did not 'trick with men' to employ this crude boy's parlance. And if it is a crime to have had forebears who were not of the same race, then your father, Robert, can stand with you in the dock. The fact is that I myself have Caribbean blood, from an ancestor who was once established at Jamaica. So you see, dearest Robert, I am myself of 'the Negro race', whatever those words might signify. And I am the same man, now, that commenced this letter, shall still be the same when I end it.†

Your sadness has brought to my mind a dear person whom I wish you had known. She was a lady called Beatrice Collins, who was our nursemaid in Wexford. A Negress, she had once been a slave in England. She came to us after my mother's passing. 'Aunt Beatrice'

† This claim, often made privately by O'Keeffe to friends, has proven impossible to verify.

we called that beautiful friend. She is in Paradise today with Our Lady.

She was kindly, devoted, gentle Aunt Beatrice, the rock in the tempest of our frightened lives. She was – I do not exaggerate – as a mother to me. My little childish troubles, without exception, were hers. If I cried in the night, she soothed me. I was sent away to school, first to Kildare, then to Shropshire, but whenever I returned, I could see that she was happy to be near me. We got on tightly together. I liked her very much. She was one of those quietly reliable people who gladden us merely to know them. Even my father, who could often be severe with us, mellowed a little in her company. Indeed, as the seasons passed, Father and Aunt formed a friendship. They would sit together in the evenings. They would read to one another. Sometimes they would walk an hour on the quayside. They would have liked, I learned later, to marry. But the shameful prejudices of the world prevented this. Their friendship, if not ended, must be conducted in secrecy – so a priest of the town insisted. Thus the sanctified slum of the pious mind held sway. How woeful, these prisons of bigotry, Robert. The friends unmade, the lives impoverished – the deathly and terrible wastefulness.

I am sorry that you have heard, and will hear again, the terms with which people of color are insulted. It seems to me, Robert, that there is absolutely nothing I can do for this. You yourself must decide your response. But it is also important to say to you something. The color of your body is beautiful, Robert; it was drawn by the Heavenly Artist to be loved. That same Supreme Intelligence, which designed all creation, decreed its crowning masterpiece to be various of aspect – but ignorant man, that has made so little of what he was given, presumes to question His wisdom. Every giraffe looks the same, every worm and every zebra. Only Man has the variety of godhead. Humanity is of the palette of the Beautiful Mathematician, who, when He came to the earth in corporeal form could have chosen to do so in any. A lion of Judah; an angel; an eagle: or in some dazzlingly lovely shape never seen in this world. He did not choose thus, nor to be any of a white man. He walked the dust of Palestine, an African-Hebrew. As immortal Milton tells us, *He took a darksom house*. The Holy Bible itself, as you will see when you study it, is principally a book about African people.

The bravest heroes in this country are of African ancestry, indeed are, in my estimation, the future of this Republic. Often during the War I had the honor to witness their valor: bold, impressive, comradely,

disciplined, lion-hearted, indefatigable men. Through the cruelest
torments, they had not surrendered dignity, through the vilest
oppressions, they had held. It had been attempted to cut the heart of
them. They had gainsaid the knife. So hold your head high. Be proud of
your patrimony. Tell any pitiable bigot who crosses your path that a
black man will be elected President of these United States one day, and
when that day dawns, that beautiful day, this Nation will be released
into the greatness of its promise and will shine as the lighthouse of civilization.

All the time I was in captivity, your mother was loyal. We lived in the
little shieling I built by my own hands at Lake Comfrey – it might yet
be standing. Ask Uncle Boland to take you there. I thought we should
have a happy life by its waters. Whole days would pass in almost
complete tranquility in that oasis. I learned to fish and to hunt, the
names of the creatures. There was sadness, yes: our little daughter did
not live, but was taken home to Heaven only weeks after her birth; but
your mother was brave – much braver than was I – and in time even
that pain was accepted.

I have been fortunate, Robert. Always fortunate. I know what it is to
be loved. All my life – I do not know why – I have had friends who
were loyal and good, who protected my confidences, perhaps too long.
But there is no soul on this earth, there never was and never shall be,
that I loved as I loved your mother. She was my east and my west. My
hopes for us were endless. There were numerous occasions when I
thanked whatever is in Heaven for my exile, for without it, I could
never have known my soul mate.

It will seem inexplicable to you, I know, that I departed from your
mother. It was a terrible, a terrible decision. Love of country, which is
second only to the love felt by some for the Maker, calls us, sometimes,
to the sacrifice. There is an impulse, a profound one, not to tell you of
this, and which hates the very notion that such words could ever be
written. I have seen where they lead – these easily repeated words – to
the graves of the young and the poor. For like all kinds of love, love of
country has its seasons. It burns hottest when we are young; we can be
infatuated by it. There is blood in our eyes for desire at such moments,
and we cannot see the ghosts by the road. I do not know that I would
do it now – but I did do it then; and must always live with my choice.

Robert, it is not difficult to manipulate words, to bend them to their
opposite meanings. I could write you that I had been forced to leave

your mother, or allow you to come to such a conclusion. That would be a lie. I chose to leave her. It was my will, and my will only.

Vanity, I think, was a part of my determination; but it was not the only part. Yes, Robert, I was vain. I thought myself wanted. I saw myself triumphant, vanquisher of invaders. My name would be hurrahed in the streets by the hungry. All the fears of boyhood, the awkwardness I had felt: that I never had a brother, that I spoke with a crippling stammer, that my father did not like me, that my masters thought me stupid, that I was not as brave as others, that I was not brave at all – these would be banished by the heroic act. Was there weakness? Without a doubt. Vainglory? Too much. But in my defense, there was also – and I wish there were another word for it – there was something akin to love.

This feeling which I have mentioned, for our people, our homeplace – I do not say that it is worthless – it is not. Cruelty must be countered, else our lives here are nothing: we are beasts, then, without the civilizing conscience, and deserve our stagger to the shambles. But it is a dangerous love for it can itself lead to disengagement, to a loyalty to abstractions rather than flesh and blood. It smoked up so strong in me, so ferociously strong, that I felt compelled to relegate private happiness to the subservient position. I could not do my duty to the poor of my nation while remaining a prisoner, in the farthest nowhere of the world, of the crown that had watched them starve. So many had died, Robert. Millions had died. I yearned to do nothing; I could not.

There was a time, which lasted years, when I would tell myself that your mother understood, even sympathized with this impulse that I must stand for what I felt was right. But how could she have done? How could any spouse, thus bereft? My leaving her was the worst thing I ever did. She begged me not to go and I went.

I rode away from our cottage, down the lanes by the lake; past the house where you now live with your guardians. I can see that road yet, every yard and swaying tree: many times in dreams have I seen it. There was one last moment. The man who had arranged my escape – a brave man, a patriot, we were once tight as brothers – asked if I was sure that I could proceed. It was not too late. I could never come back. Had I fathomed the full import, the consequence of my decision? I stepped into the boat and we rowed away from Hobart; and I never saw your mother again.

Robert, on my life, and on any honor I ever had, I did not know that your mother was with child when I left her. Had I known that you were growing inside her, I could never have left. Never on my immortal soul. Nor – again I swear to you – was it ever my plan that our separation, so bitter, would be permanent. My deepest hope, somehow, was to have her brought to me in America. But by the time I arrived here, it was too late.

On that journey, Robert, terrible things happened. I had to be brave – as I ask you now to be. It was not in any part of my nature to be brave but I must defeat my nature; for I did not want to die, alone. At night, on the island, which I have mentioned to you previously, it was so completely dark, as though the whole world was dying, and no flint had your stupefied father to make any fire or light. Sounds could be heard from the invisible sea. The whale-song could be eerie, and the birds. At such moments I would close my eyes and think of the astounding vastness of the world, and of my relative smallness in it, my nothingness, really. Strange to say, but this thought afforded a consolation. This, and the thought of your mother. That ever I had been loved by such a person as she; that I was loved, still – that I might somehow be again: these thoughts, I believe, were my only shelter. Without them I would have burned to the cinders.

You must forgive Uncle Boland for what you perceive to be his evasiveness regarding the final matter you raise. He would wish to be loyal to me; that is all. But yes, Robert; I have to tell you, it is true what you have heard in the town: I am married to a different lady now. She and I have been married for a number of years. I am sincerely apologetic that I did not inform you previously, for my failure to do so has caused you to be anxious. I can only tell you the truth – that the time never seemed quite correct to write of it. One had hoped to have been able to tell you face to face.

She is a very kindly person, of many talents and accomplishments, admired by all who know her. As well, she is the most intellectually gifted person I have known, and will one day, before too long, be your new mother. When that better time comes, and with God's help it will come soon, you and I and she shall be a happy little family together. This I vow to you faithfully, with all my heart. So please, never succumb to thoughts that you are alone. You will never be alone while I breathe.

It is not however the case that I have any child but you. Any such tattle you have heard is quite mischievous. In truth, I may tell you,

Robert, and this is a painful matter to several people, that privately I have never felt mentally or spiritually able to be a father again, while our situation, yours and mine, remained so excruciatingly unresolved, and I had not done justice to you and had you by me.

You ask as to why I am yet here in America, when you are so far away; and you wish to know when, at last, we shall know one another. Believe me, Robert, nothing would bring greater joy. To have a son on whom one has never laid one's eyes, to have never lofted him in one's arms, or heard his voice – this is a burden of extraordinary painfulness. When you yourself become a father, you will know better what I mean.

The want you feel for me, this I feel for you. There is never an hour when I do not think of you. But, were I to come to you now, we could not be united. Those who rule that land in the name of the despot would clap your father into jail, and then give him a worse fate; and I know that, being a good stout fellow, you would not wish that to happen. But I make you the promise that I will never rest a night, nor feel happy in my heart, nor take an easy breath in my life, until you and I have clasped hands at the long long last, and I have amended, or tried to, for all that was lost to us, and I can show you to my friends and be proud of you publicly, as any father should be of such a boy. That hour will come, Robert; it surely will. I am sorry to have hurt you. I ask your forgiveness. I do not deserve it to be given – but I dare ask it.

I have a plan in mind now, by which you and I shall be together before too long. I cannot commit it all to paper, for some of its smaller particulars remain to be managed. But you should prepare yourself, Robert, for a lengthy voyage. Friends of mine will be in contact with Uncle Boland relatively soon. Do everything you are told. Ask no question whatever. Queer things will happen, things you will not understand, but do not be afraid, only trust your companions. You will be taken to a certain port, and from there to another, and thence to Marseilles, thence to Paris. I shall be waiting for you there. It is my plan to purchase a house in that city. I have resolved, in short, to leave these United States, and go home to old Europe, where I should never have left. The air out here is too clean for my lungs and I wheeze for the smuts of home.

In the meantime, when you are lonesome, say in your mind: 'I am not alone. I have a father that loves me.' These long sad days will soon be changed to the longer and happier years. Until then, never let an adversary know he has hurt you. Make your face a globe of steel. Let all you meet be reflected. Yours is the blood of remarkable people and you are the finest son any man ever had.

Convey my best respects to your Uncle and Aunt and remember me to old Knowles the blacksmith, if he is still with us. I enclose one of our American bills for you to have a belated gift for your birthday. If Uncle Boland takes it to the bank at Hobart, it should translate to a shilling or two – at least I hope so.

I kiss this paper. Kiss it when it comes to you. I hold you in the harbor of my heart.

Be a brave and good fellow, and remain assured, dearest Robert, that you are ever in the thoughts of that fortunate man who is honored to remain the only good thing he has ever been:

Your father, who loves you –

Con†

∇

† Letter mailed in Fort Stornaway in the early afternoon of New Year's Day, 1867. Robert Emmet O'Keeffe, known to many as Robert Boland, had drowned four months previously while swimming alone in Lake Comfrey. The inscription on his tombstone at St Anthony's Church, Hobart, reads: 'Robert Emmet O'Keeffe. Only son of James and Catherine. Gone home to his mother and sister. Pray for them.'

CHAPTER 75

THE 10 'COMMANMENTS' OF JOHNNY THUNDERS

Gun is the law
Fear non other
Its a son of a bitch that cusses his mother
No liquor on sabbath
Feed y kin
Murderin hypocrits aint no sin
Keep a lock on y lust
Steal when y needy
Lie if y must
But never git greedy
These commanments I graved wit my bullet on stone.
Remember me sinner – after Im gone.

MK1025: February 66†

∇

† Graffito found during renovations of a cantina in Suarez, New Mexico, 1887.
Author unknown. Not McLaurenson. Much effort has been expended on
analysing his marque. Some have read 'MK1025' as standing for 'Men Killed:
1025', the number of Union soldiers he claimed his gang had killed during the
War. Others have seen the figures as a biblical reference. Mark, Chapter 10,
verse 25 reads: 'It is easier for a camel to go through the eye of a needle, than
for a rich man to enter into the kingdom of God.'

CHAPTER 76

NARRATIVE OF THE HOURS
BEFORE THE DISASTER

WILLIAM FAIRFAX, DOCTOR

Sighting at noon. Then 4.30 p.m — 6.15 p.m.

I thank the Tribunal for conveying me permission to testify in this manner and not appear before it in person, for my health is not good. I am a member of the Religious Society of Friends, and as such, I resile from the taking of oaths; but I write the following affidavit having affirmed its truthfulness before a magistrate:

I SAY THAT my name is William Barton Fairfax, medical doctor, retired, ordinarily resident at St Louis, Missouri. I was born at Cambridge, England, but came to the United States in 1860. On January the 1st, 1867, I was in the town of Fort Stornaway, the Mountain Territory, where myself and my wife, who has since passed away, were contemplating establishing our home.

I SAY THAT at around noon that day, I happened to look out of the window of our hotel, which was Smith's Temperance Hotel, near where the main street rises quite sharply, overlooking a sort of lea to the north; and I saw a party of riders enter the town from the south-western road. I should say the assembly comprised a dozen or fourteen riders. I know this occurred at noon precisely, because I heard the chapel bell tolling twelve.

As they drew closer, a maidservant who was at her work in our room recognized the man at the head of the posse to be Brigadier General James O'Keeffe, Acting Governor of the Territory. I must say that he was indeed an imposing figure. The gray dust of the road loaned him a curious look: that of a statue come to life.

I SAY THAT about four hours later, I was on the hospital ship *John Gould* near the southern bank of the Missouri at 16th Street, a quarter in which the preponderance is of saloons, very poor dwellings, and houses of ill repute. I am told that the quarter is known as 'the bloodiest block in the west'; but the west can be rather flaunting of such vivid designations, as the east plumes itself for cathedrals.

The *Gould* was one of several dozen steamships tied up for the winter at Fort Stornaway. Three other vessels, smaller, in want of refitting, had been pressed into the service of governance and commerce, and one was the floating office of a gold assayer.

My wife and I were delivering a child to an immigrant girl, in point of fact a prostitute, whose labor had been not without difficulty for she was aged only fifteen years. A colored boy came in and asked if I was the surgeon, adding that an important personage had been taken ill in the town but that he, the boy, had been ordered on pain of a drubbing not to reveal the patient's identity. I could not leave the girl but immediately the infant was delivered and the mother had been attended to the best of my ability, I took up my bag and allowed myself to be led by my emissary to the steamer *General Ulysses S. Grant*. That vessel was docked for repairs about one hundred and twenty paces downriver from us. My late wife, being exhausted, did not accompany me to the *Grant* but returned to the hotel alone. This would have been at about 18th Street, I am almost certain. On board, in a stateroom, I was startled to find the aforementioned General O'Keeffe, in a condition of considerable distress.

Delicacy dissuades me from fuller candor, but let me say that the General's garments, especially his lower, were heavily soiled with fecal matter. There was a sour odor in the stateroom, the origin of which was evident. Two of his subordinates, both Irishmen, were attempting to undress and clean him. His wife, also, was trying to assist, as was a gentleman I was told was a cartographer from the States, come into the Territory on Federal Government business. I cannot swear to his name. I believe he was a captain. He spoke with a Bostonian accent.

I SAY THAT the General was in substantial pain, was clutching at his abdomen and lower chest. A remarkably heavy sweat was visible on his face, which was reddened and contorted; and he had bitten quite into his upper lip, which was bleeding profusely as a result. He was at first, indeed, unable to speak at all, but presently he complained to me, vehemently enough, that he had felt what he called 'a rupturing of the gut'.

With the assistance of his wife, who had nursed in the War, I persuaded him to loosen his remaining clothing and commenced an examination of the abdominal area. There was no internal injury, at least none I could discern, but the suffering being endured by the patient made a satisfactory investigation difficult. The General, I may say, was not speaking entirely coherently, but was accusing unnamed persons of having 'murdered' or 'poisoned' him. He was also – I hesitate to write it, but I have been asked to be completely truthful – swearing that he would be avenged and would himself do murder. I have searched my memory thoroughly on this latter point. The precise words he employed were: 'I will strangle the son-of-a-bitch.'

I am not in a position to state definitely that he had not been poisoned, but such was not my opinion at the time. His tongue was a normal color; so were the whites of his eyes. There was no paralysis or trembling of the limbs. Often, in cases of poisoning, there is foaming at the mouth, or rectal bleeding, or both. Neither of these symptoms was present here. His ears and nasal passages were clear of blood.

Cholera, obviously, must be suspected in such cases, but my conclusion, on balance, was that it was not anything as necessarily grave. My feeling was that the General was suffering an especially bad case of what is euphemistically known as 'saddle fever' – in essence, dysentery and severe diarrhea, worsened by prolonged exposure to the sun. It is believed, quite erroneously, that this is exclusively a summer condition, but sun-scorch in winter can be every degree as dangerous – more so, indeed, since snow and especially ice will intensify its deleterious effects. Alas, this family of fevers has been far from unknown in the Territory, and indeed, I would imagine, is still a feature of life there now. The immoderate climate in westerly parts, the astonishing ubiquity of foul miasmic air in the towns, the poorness of standards of cleanliness generally – all these conspire to give our brave western settlers frequent reason to run, as it were. There is disagreement among my colleagues as to the causes of this dysentery, if that is what it is. My own view is that the refusal to wash one's hands, in especial after having visited a necessary place, has killed more of our intrepid if odorous frontiersmen than have all the Indians in America.

I SAY THAT I gave him syrup of ipecac to induce vomiting, and presently the desired purging was achieved. I had a bottle of blackberry brandy in my kit, which it was my practice to employ as a physic in the case of tooth extractions. I administered one fluid oz. of this, diluted, to the General, for one of its other effects is to subdue disorders of the stomach. After a while the pain decreased in intensity, though remaining. The patient managed to sit upward and to take a little boiled water. He suffered me to stitch his lip, a difficult enough task but manageable. My handiwork did not look too pretty but the bleeding was stanched. The General was running a very high fever but that is not uncommon in such cases. He told me that he was tired, was no longer in such distress but wanted badly to sleep. I forbade sleep for thirty minutes, during which we made him drink a quart of cooled water, which he did not want to do, but I was concerned for his hydration, so I fear I made rather a nuisance of myself on the point, and, as a result, heard some Anglo-Saxonisms not encountered in Webster's. But I have been among soldiers, so they did not at all bother me. They can often help a patient, in their way.

Consulting my notes, I see that he urinated at 18 minutes past five, and again, more copiously, at 2 minutes to six. This eased my concerns, at least somewhat. I then left him with the promise that I would return in the early morning. The cartographer and Mrs O'Keeffe were in the stateroom as I left.

I hesitate to mention it; but it struck me as strange that the cartographer offered to pay my account. I said this would be quite unnecessary; I had been happy to assist the General. But he insisted on giving me three Union dollars. I felt badly about accepting them – but he prevailed upon me to do so and seemed reluctant to permit me to debark until I had written him a receipt for the monies. In the end, I never spent them, but gave them to two beggar-women on the wharf. His act disconcerted me somehow.

BRIDGET WHITE, MAIDSERVANT
Approximately 7.15 p.m.

I was called up to the *Grant* about quarter after seven. Himself was inside in the bunk at the time and seemed right enough in himself. His wife was there. I did not like her at once. She had plenty of airs and went to ordering me here and about. I would be uneasy taking orders from one of that type, but says I, better hold my hour.

He asked me where I was from. I told him Dublin, Thomas Street. Then he started addressing me in the Gaelic tongue but I told him I had none of it, as did no one ever belonging to me, nor seed nor breed of us, nor I hoped ever would, for what use is a language not a body remembers but a few oul gawms sucking praties in a shanty and a few proddy flutes with the leisure for guilt. I have no graw for Fenians nor troublemakers, I told him, and no time for the rawmashe they do never stop spouting, for liberty don't butter no bread that I knows of, nor freedom don't grease no skillet. Well, he laughed at that, for he thought I was joking him. I was not joking him, but it does not matter, for a man always laughs and an honest woman talking to him and he don't understand what she is saying.

[*The witness was requested to answer the questions more directly.*]

No, I cannot say I saw anything unusual about him. He seemed an ordinary enough sort, for all the great talk of him. But bone and horn idle. That was my opinion anyways. There was nothing wrong with that Jacobin, saving your presence, that a hard day's work wouldn't cure.

He went to walking around the stateroom, cleaning a pistol, which I then saw him load and aim out of the porthole. He shot it at something – a curlew, I think. The sound of it going off put the heart backards across me, for which he said he was sorry. He came in and out a few times. Sometimes there was a man with him. I did not know the man.

I cleaned the sty of a room after him and made him up a settle, for he told me the bunk was too hard. He fell asleep after a while and I went on with whatever I was at. Herself jaunced back in and she looking around. 'There is a terrible lot of dirt in here, Maid,' says she. 'Faith, and I didn't bring any of it in with me, Ma'am,' says I. And she told me right and plain to get out.

I was on the deck talking to a man I know. I heard them quarreling, or no – more bickering. No, I can not remember the actual words that was spoke. It was only a quarrel between man and wife. I think she wanted him to lie down for himself on the bunk, not the settle, but he wanted to walk around in the God's good air. I felt sorry for herself then. He seemed a contumelious oul get. But after all he was ailing and wanted peace.

When she came out, I could see she was afterbeen crying. The man I was with – John Doran, the pilot – went over. But she did not say anything. She was silent with John Doran. She went away below. And I went home.

JOHN DORAN, RIVERBOAT PILOT
8.07 p.m. to approximately midnight

It was one of my duties to make a note of the time of First Watch, and this I did, at seven minutes past eight. You can see it in the log. Yes, sir, I went in to the General. He was sitting at a desk, writing I think. I do not know what he was writing, sir. I did not see it.

The General spoke to me in a friendly style, I think because I had assisted his wife in small ways on her passage into the Territory in the summer of eighteen and sixty-five. Yes, I was on the ship brought her in that time. I have somewhere a letter he wrote me about that subject. It was mighty courteous so I kept it. I recall that we spoke for a while about the War and suchlike. Oh, it was soldiering talk mainly, nothing of consequence. I think we talked about Fredericksburg.

He told me his wife was after retiring to rest a while and he had a fancy on him to see a little of the town. Would I be his companion for a little gallavaunt? Yes, those were his words, to the best of my recollection. I said that I had rather we do that another night, that more sport could be had of it when he was feeling better in himself. At this, he only laughed and leapt up from his seat. 'We shall be a long time dead, Johnny Doran,' he said. He took up his pistol, checked that it was loaded, and then nothing would do him only to take a saunter on the dock.

We walked down the front to where there is a row of oul cabins, mostly framed. Folks in the town would know them and what they are about. Since what happened that night I am reconciled to the Bible and church-going. I know I am on my oath now, so I must tell the truth and say that some of them was used for the entertainment of gentlemen. There was faro tables and Spanish monte and a game of poker now and again and there would be girls going in and out of them sheds.

Into one such we went and there was a company there. An oul colored boy, he used to be a slave in Kentucky, was there with the rest. His name is Nate. He is a good, reliable sort. It was his employment to sweep a little and keep the place right and he sold tobacco sweepings and beer and such. And I think he used to pick up pecans in season someplace. I remember the General asking Nate about some ear-rings he had on him. They was like a gypsy's, I guess.

The General got in a conversation with a cowboy-looking feller. I think he was out of Kanzas. It was Fenian talk I think. I did not understand much of it. I heard the queen of England being cried down, so that was

424

fine by me, but it was only in fun, it was nothing. Some of the boys started into singing songs and larking. The General gave out a poem, or maybe the words of a national Irish ballad. It was the usual oul flim-flam. People liked it fine. No, I have nothing agin the English people. I have people belonging to me in England.

There wasn't no trouble, it just was liquor talking and mockery, the kind of thing goes on when men gets into company.

I won't lie, there was girls there. I cannot remember their names and that is the truth so help me. They were not personally known to me, only one of them, Bridget Shine. Anyway it was only talking and passing the time, I would want Mrs O'Keeffe to know that. The General went out two or three times to avail of the bushes, but would not be accompanied, thinking it unmanly if he were.

Not long after midnight I accompanied him back to the *Grant*. I cannot lie, he was a little merry in himself by now, and singing, and talking, and going on with oul nonsense I did not pay much of a mind to. I did not think it any harm, or not much at any rate. He said we'd have another scoop or two again we got to the *Grant* but I was only humoring him along. He seemed to be in lighter humor than earlier. I put him into the settle bed – a kind of a shakedown it was – for he would not go in the bunk, I don't know why.

'Our day will come, Johnny Doran,' says he. 'Deed and it will, sir. Certain sure,' says I. And I left him, then, and went to my girl's house up the back road. I did not know what was going to happen.

IGNATIUS GILCHRIST,
ACTING MARSHAL, FORT STORNAWAY
Approximately 12.45 a.m.

E: You were in the army with James O'Keeffe, were you not?
W: I have had the honor of serving my country, if that's what you mean.
E: Your country being?
W: My country is the Republic of which I am a naturalized citizen, where I have resided thirty years, where my children were born, where my taxes are paid, which I serve by profession, and for which I have spilled my blood, I hope with valor.
E: I meant only –
W: I know what you meant, sir. Your question insults me.

E: You were born in another country, in Ireland is what I meant.

W: You question my patriotism one more time, you'll remember all about it for a while.

E: I am sorry that you are offended. It was not my intention.

W: As a friend of the Governor for north of ten years, I wish to say me a word before I commence about the nature of this here assembly.

E: There will be no personal statements. The Presiding Judge has made that clear.

W: Yes there will, sir. There will be mine. Or I quit this room in short order.

E: Do I understand that you threaten contempt for this Tribunal and its proceedings?

W: I 'threaten' you nothing, you milksop little shit-ass. Contempt aint strong enough, what I got for the likes of you.

E: Do you dare . . .

W: Do YOU dare, you braided puppy never held a gun but your cock. I'm a freeman citizen of the United States, I will say what I like, and *when*, boy. You Westpoint little yapper. Look at me when I speak to you! I am fifty-three years old, son, which makes me old enough to tell you what a ignorant little whipper you are. Shut your mouth about the judge! I aint interested in no judge. I'ma see to him, too, if he like. Ever been you in battle? Ever seen you an enemy? Ever had to trust men? Do you know what that is? I served with Con O'Keeffe from Bull Run to Chancellorsville. Went through Fredericksburg. Went through Marye's Heights. Some thanks to sit here now, listen to lies being spoken by fools. Slanders on a hero. Lies about his wife. Well, me, I'd put my life in the hands of Con O'Keeffe and my friends before I'd spit on a miserable little bomb-dodger like yourself.

Presiding Judge: That is enough, sir. Do not abuse the Tribunal again.

Witness: To the fuck with the lot of you. Good bye.

[*The witness departed the room. There was a motion for his arrest. After some consideration, it was denied. A friend of the witness, a United States corporal, prevailed on him to return to the Tribunal. He did, but refused to be questioned by the Examiner, insisting he would respond only to the Presiding Judge. Owing to a stenographer's error, the Judge's questions went unrecorded. The witness's answer were as follows:*]

No.

No.

No, sir.

I think so.

It isn't exactly unusual to hear shots at night from the town.

When I heard the first shots, I sat up in my bed, and I said to my wife
'That is coming from the river.' She told me it was nothing, but I
knew this wasn't right. I believe she did not want me to go away. Our
grandchild was only a month old at that time, sir, and was with us in
the house, for his mother was sick. Anyway my wife had no liking for
me quitting the house after dark. There could be danger in the town
at night.

By the time I left my house, which is on Water Street, near the stables,
I had heard me some more shots from over the direction of the river.
It might have been three shots. I don't know how many. I went up to
my deputy's house, which is on Tremont, but he was not there. I do
not know where he was. The house was empty. I took down his rifle,
which was hanging on a peg near the stoop, and I wrote him a note
to get to the river.

The rain was coming up the road. It was blinding, yes. I don't mind
saying I was afraid.

NATHANIEL FIELD, NIGHT-WATCHMAN

1 a.m.

My name is Nathaniel Field. Folks in the town call me Nate. I was born
near Cynthiana, Kentucky, and was a slave until the War come. I come
up to this Territory after the War with my wife. General O'Keeffe give
me a concession for ferrying on the river at Stornaway. Man need to
be strong to do that work. Yes, sir, I liked it fine. I like the air and the
water life.

I saw Missus Mears and her daughter Edith go by. They was two old
ladies used to go up and down the waterfront selling gooseberries and
currants and other stuffs like such, that they would pick along the banks,
and ribbands for the girls back home. They wasn't strictly supposed to do
it, but the sailors would like to see them. They was motherly ladies. Jane
was, anyways. Edith was how would you say it, not correct in her mind,
sir. She wasn't deliver right when she come in the world. But a real nice
person. No badness in her at all. Never did a harm to nobody, just she
had the ways of a child. I didn't say good-night to them, I don't know why.

I sure enough wished I had. Or run them along home. I didn't know what was coming. It's horrible to think of it. They never done a harm to nobody.

∇

NOTE FOUND IN A BOTTLE AT THE ABANDONED MINE

➤◆◆◆◆➤

SENSATIONAL LETTER! SHOCKING REVELATIONS

➤◆◆

THEIR LOVE-CHILD, THE STOLEN GOLD, & THEIR WICKED PLAN!

➤◆

THE CONFESSION OF J. COLE McLAURENSON & ELIZA MOONEY: TO MRS O'KEEFFE, THE GOVERNOR'S WIFE

➤◆

EXCLUSIVELY OBTAINED BY OUR REPORTER!

madam:

by the time you reads this paper yr husband will be in the next world an we that makes its letters shal be far from this terittory.

you hate us an we own it by the time you reads this paper. we deserves to have your damnation for we are after widowin you an christ forgiue us for it. i am puttin down this letters so you know why it had to occur an you can see it was not all our doin but that yr husband owns the great deal of it.

my name is eliza duane mooney of baton rouge lousiana. I was born in red hook brooklyn. my hvsband is john cole mclaurenson out of clarksuille tennessee. they calls john cole mclaurenson a outlaw an a bandit. to me he is the ony friend i euer got.

i am sister to jeddo mooney who you knows already. i am 18 yrs of age. i got no mother nor a father only jeddo in the world. i aint complainin none but only tellin you.

it was me an cole mc laurenson took the child from redemtion city an the traitor patrick vinson helped us do it. jeddo mooney is my ony liuin blood. i swore my mother i take care of him. i took jeddo to the place we was liuin near stornaway. he gut sick from bad air so i thought he would die but i nursed him an he come around.

a goverment man name winnerton come up here near chrismas. he told us gnrl okeeffe and yr self was fixin to take my brother out of this country and we would want to watch out for he was comin.

he was a wellspoke man of edvcation an books. he sayed he was our friend an want euery thing to come out safe an well. he sayed if we wd trust him he wold see to it.

i agreed with this winnerton that he shold go to gnrl okeeffe for to put my case for me. i wrote the gnrl a long letter for this winnerton to take along wid him. i wrote the child was my brother an the only kin i got in the world an i walked all the way from lousiana for to get him. this winnerton sayed he would take it to the gnrl and put him my case. he swore me he would fix it.

cole mclaurenson rode with this winnerton to the redemption county line and hid out in stacklin forest for a while. but near dawn winnerton come back and said it werent no good for the gnrl was determin he should take my brother and go into another country. you can see I cold not allow it. not after comin all the road from lousiana for to find him. no one cold allow it. you could not yrself. there was ony the one thing would stop my brother been took to another country. that was for the gnrl to lose his life.

i said i did not wish it for i had a respect for gnrl okeeffe an my mother had a respect for him always. this winneron said it was nearabout the only way for the gnrl wold hunt us down the rest of our liues an neuer rest until he gotten the child back and kill us.

cole mclaurenson said he wold ride in to redemption and murder gnrl okeeffe that night. this winnerton said he should not do for he had marshals in plenty. it was me agreed it with winnerton that he shold lure the gnrl up here north and what would haue to happen wold happen an on our souls be the blame for it. for a booty this winnerton ast a great share of moneys taken by cole mclaurenson from the goverment boat in august 1866. first he wanted the half of it. by the close he wanted all of it whatever we had and euery other cent we got in the world. i did not trust this winnerton then but cole said it was all right. but I did not think it was all right.

we done what we done but your husband brung this upon his own self. if he wold haue listen to the letters we sent with winnerton none of it need to haue happen. we are sure sorry for your loss but it had to come that way. all we want was for to be left alone with the child. we got us a whole mountain of judgment on cole mclaurenson and me and i have a baby i am expectin to think of. if they catch us we will get hanged him and me the both. well it is as it is. i had to do it an i am not sorry ony for your pain.

faithfvlly,

e. mclavrenson (nee mooney)

∇

E: Would you please state your full name for the record?

W: Lucia-Cruz Rodríguez Y Ortega McLelland-O'Keeffe.

E: May I know your age, if that is not . . .?

W: Thirty-three.

E: You have heard the contents of the document that I have just now read into the record.

W: Yes

E: It was addressed to you by the child's sister, and left at the abandoned mine.

W: Yes.

E: You will know that it has been published in many western newspapers.

W: So I am informed.

E: Were you at the gubernatorial house at Redemption Falls during the early hours of Christmas morning, 1866?

W: Yes, I was.

E: Were you present at approximately three o'clock in the morning when there was an interview between your husband and Captain Allen Winterton?

W: I was in the room every minute that Captain Winterton was with my husband.

E: And what did Captain Winterton say, in essence?

W: He told us that the outlaws had the child in their custody and planned to murder him in a few days. He also said that they had ill-used him. That he had suffered very greatly. That he had begged for my husband to rescue him.

E: He made no mention of any letter from Eliza Mooney?

W: None.

E: Of the boy having a sister?

W: No mention whatever.

E: Mrs O'Keeffe; there is unfortunately a certain question I must put to you now.

W: Yes.

E: It is not disputed that at one time you enjoyed a friendship with Captain Allen Winterton, whom you met at St Mary's Hospital when you nursed in the War.

W: That is correct.

E: And your acquaintance became a closer one over the course of some months.

W: Yes.

E: Did you go, in April 1865, to an establishment frequented by soldiers and a certain sort of girl, with the purpose of meeting with Captain Winterton?

W: Yes.

E: Why did you do that?

W: I am sure you can imagine.

E: For an adulterous purpose.

W: I suppose that is the phrase, yes.

E: There was no other place to meet privately and so on.

W: That is correct.

E: Did an adultery occur, or anything improper?

W: Certain familiarities occurred but not the act I think you mean.

E: Of what nature were these familiarities?

W: That is not the business of this Tribunal.

PRESIDING JUDGE: Do you mean – if I may assist – that Captain Winterton took an advantage of the fact that a fondness, an affection had grown up between you?

W: He took no advantage whatever. I met him freely, as an equal.

E: An equal? Surely not? A married woman of your station?

W: I met him as an equal. And then I ended the friendship. The rest is a private matter.

E: You have heard Allen Winterton described as a fortune-hunter?

W: Yes.

E: A man who would prey on a woman from a wealthy family?

W: I knew what he was.

E: You knew?

W: I suspected, yes.

E: Then why would you have permitted yourself to be alone with him in such a place?

W: It is a private matter whom I choose to be alone with, and where, and why.

E: Between July of 1863, when you met at St Mary's Hospital in New York, and April 1865, when you departed for the Mountain Territory, were you and Captain Allen Winterton passionate lovers?

W: No.

E: You are on oath.

W: I am aware of it.

E: And you were not lovers.

W: That is correct.

E: But you desired him as a lover? It was your marital situation that stayed you?

W: My desires, as you term them, are not the business of this Tribunal.

E: With great respect, Mrs O'Keeffe, it is not a matter of –

W: It is a matter of my telling you what I have just told you in plain words.

E: Apart from the occasion to which we have alluded, have physical intimacies taken place between yourself and Captain Allen Winterton?

W: There was an occasion on which I permitted Captain Winterton to kiss me on the mouth. I suppose that is a physical intimacy.

E: Have fuller relations occurred between yourself and Captain Winterton?

W: Lieutenant, I believe I have answered your questions quite adequately, short of drawing for you an explanatory diagram.

E: At the time of the events we are purposed to investigate, what was the condition of your marriage?

W: We had experienced certain difficulties. We had hoped to reconcile.

E: There was a child in Australia. Your husband has not been candid about his past life.

Presiding Judge: Mrs O'Keeffe, if you would like a glass of water. Or we can adjourn if you are upset.

[*The witness asked a moment to compose her thoughts. She requested to borrow a handkerchief, which was given her by a private soldier.*]

SOLDIER: God bless you, Mrs General. I love him as much as I ever. He will never be dead in any Irish heart.

[*The Soldier was ordered to be silent.*]

E: Mrs O'Keeffe; I ask your indulgence for the final question I am about to put to you. I did not wish to put it, and here I register my objection for the record; but others have thought it germane to the work of this Tribunal. You will understand that I must do my duty.

W: You may ask it.

E: Very well. Is the father of the child you are carrying and will bear in a month, Captain Allen Michael Winterton of the United States Corps of Cartography?

W: No.

E: Thank you, Mrs O'Keeffe. If there are no further questions?

[*The Presiding Judge expressed the sympathy of the Tribunal to Mrs O'Keeffe, who by now was beyond all comfort. The witness was excused and in distress left the room, accompanied by her sister, Miss Estafanía Maria McLelland. Their brothers, Rodrigo and Alejandro McLelland, were waiting on the steps of the courthouse.*

A large party of the town's poor people had assembled by the stagecoach, with an honor guard formed by a handful of the Acting Governor's former soldiers. But other citizens jeered as Mrs O'Keeffe and her family departed Redemption Falls. Some spat, or turned their backs.]

∇

CHAPTER 77

THE RIVER

The facts of his death – From the Commission's report

At approximately one o'clock in the morning, Acting Governor James O'Keeffe was asleep in a stateroom on the Federal Steamship *Grant*, having consumed a quantity of liquor. The watchman, Nathaniel Field, was patrolling the deck when he observed, by moonlight, what appeared to be a native canoe approaching with striking haste from upriver. It contained two masked figures. He challenged them to give the password. They made no reply but continued coming on. Field rang the alarm bell on the maindeck.

James O'Keeffe emerged from the stateroom in a condition of bewildered undress. Others of his posse soon appeared. By now, a second canoe had been sighted near the north bank. The Acting Governor called a warning that he would give the order to fire. A shot came from the second canoe, striking him through the abdomen. His men opened fire on both vessels.

The Acting Governor conducted himself with no small courage, loosing eight or ten shots from where he lay wounded. He struck at least one member of the outlaw band but the element of surprise was enjoyed by his attackers. He and his men were targeted ruthlessly. John Creed, farmer, was first to die, then Patrick Edward Hannigan and Michael Francis English. Two innocent women, Mrs Jane Mears and her daughter, were struck as they tried to flee. Both died. Governor O'Keeffe was still firing, although close to losing consciousness. Francis Dwyer was next to fall.

A shot burst a lamp on the hospital ship *John Gould*, causing the wheelhouse to catch fire with ferocious rapidity. Terrible scenes ensued as the unfortunate patients were trapped below collapsing decks. Falling booms and burning spars made rescue impossible, though those manning the hose wagons acted with commendable valor and are hereby exonerated from blame. The fire, alas, illuminated the *Grant*, making its occupants yet a clearer target for the outlaws.

By now Governor O'Keeffe had been dragged toward the stateroom by two of his men, Daniel Neyland Moody and Denis Arkins, both of whom would die from their wounds. His wife, understandably terrified, nevertheless was attempting to come to him but he waved her back below decks.

There was a lull in the shooting. O'Keeffe managed to haul himself partially upright, by dint of gripping onto the railing. He had lost a great deal of blood and was, by some accounts, weeping. It was at this point that a boy, later identified as Jeremiah Mooney, made his way up the ladder to the maindeck. He was bearing a long-blade knife and a Colt repeater. His clothing was drenched with blood. The watchman has testified that O'Keeffe begged the boy for help, but the child raged that the Governor was a murderer. Five other witnesses heard Jeremiah Mooney speak. Reports that he is a mute are incorrect.

'Assist me, son,' were the Governor's actual words. His dying plea was rejected.

'Yon soul you murdered was Liza-Jane, my sister,' cried Mooney. 'She is murdered in the river. Look!'

The girl's body was indeed now floating near the *Grant*. She had been shot through the chest and head.

The Governor, close to death, murmured that he did not understand. The boy ranted of a terrible journey she had endured in order to find him. He had had a fever at the hideout. She had tended and healed him. They had planned to go into Canada. She was his 'only living blood'. Marshals were shouting for the child to surrender, saying no quarter would be given did he refuse. O'Keeffe beckoned them to hold fire, even as the youth menaced him. Indeed, he protected the child from their sightlines.

'Murdering bastard and traitor!' screamed the boy. The watchman, Field, was imploring him to lay down his weapon. The child said: 'I will send him to Hellfire.'

'Christ's mercy, then,' prayed James O'Keeffe. These, we believe, were his last words.

The youth fired on the Acting Governor who stumbled through the guard-rail, falling into the water. Lawmen on the verge fetched a rowboat and flung out guy-ropes, but it was too late to save the Governor's life. Fatally wounded, he was torn downriver by the current, which was flowing at more than twenty miles per hour that night. Two witnesses would see him attempting to cling to a floating tree-trunk before disappearing beneath the surface near Liberty Falls.

The boy, Jeremiah Mooney, was arrested without resistance and taken to Strathspeigh County Jail. He has been pronounced lunatic by physicians and frequently attempts to harm himself. He refuses to speak, yet is sometimes heard 'keening' the name of his sister and 'Mamo'. As to what should be done with him, it is beyond the remit of this Commission to suggest. There is currently no asylum in the Territory.

Twenty-nine citizens died at Fort Stornaway that night, including John Cole McLaurenson, a prostitute Eliza Mooney, two simple-minded associates who had attached themselves to the gang, all but three men of the Governor's purpose, and thirteen patients on the *Gould*. Four others later died of wounds sustained in the attack. One man was blinded by the fire.

The Acting Governor's remains have not been recovered, despite searches, which have continued for many months, of a ninety-mile stretch of the Missouri River, its islands, banks and depths. It is proposed that the effort be now abandoned. God have mercy on his soul.

∇∇∇

LA FANCIULLA
DEL WEST

In the lonesome Gulf of Mexico, some say his bones are drifting,
Amid the gloomy shoals below, where Lorelei are shifting.
Now seaweeds kiss the lipless mouth of freedom's slaughtered suitor.
As now he is, so shall we all – written on the water.
Oh sorry deed, and wicked seed, oh night of shame and woe,
When Mooney murdered James O'Keeffe, all on the banks below.
And some they calls him Satan's son or Savage Jedda Wild.
What wrongs we wrought, what sins we taught,
To raise a devil's child.

From 'The Ballad of James O'Keeffe and the Devilboy Jedda Mooney'.
Collected Baton Rouge, Louisiana, 1889

The real war will never get in the books.

Walt Whitman

CODA

From the notes of a collector – His reflections upon a remarkable woman – His interest in the written word & in the compilation of archives – His belief in the revolutionary future

Professor J. Daniel McLelland
Winter, 1937

I

It is a curious fact – so it seems to an old man – that so many fictions about war are love stories. Forgiveness returns. Johnny finds his girl. The brothers, who fought in opposing armies, clasp hands and limp homeward to the meadow. Aura-Lee was not raped. The meadow is not a cemetery. Johnny does not scream in the night.

Perhaps unease is so great, and memory so harrowed, and the truths of the war so intensely disturbing, that we need to find a method of framing the story that will allow for the triumph of hope. So love conquers all. Redemption is possible. The peaceable kingdom is restored. War, in a story, is only an interruption, a fleeting deviation from the order we have made, and it is quickly atoned for, as though it had never happened. Because it did not happen. It only seemed to.

All one's life one has admired them: these fairytales of war, with their well-deserved happy or not unhappy endings, where the good are rewarded, or, at least, die young, and the agonies are rendered so discreetly. Billy is brave. Screeches become prayers. Scenes conclude early, before the amputation has begun. Words such as 'odor' are tactfully employed for what happens when Billy is destroyed. Thus the love story is a way of forgetting what has happened. As such, it is one of the reasons why wars become possible, for it says that a war can come to an end, when it cannot, except by provoking another one. Water becomes steam; ice melts to water; and a war only shape-shifts, like a witch.

II

My wife is obsessed by a puny Austrian thug whom she sees in the newsreels at the movie theater on 23rd. She says he hates millions, hates even his own citizens: Jews, Communists, trade unionists, intellectuals. Since my wife is a Jew, and since I have certain affiliations, she worries incessantly about *mein kleiner Schickelgruber*; claims to hear his saw-like shriek in her dreams. I love her, but she is the kind of woman who agonizes about these hate-filled nobodies. She has too much time to think.

What if he invades these United States? His forces are growing. How should we defeat him? I advise her not to fret. I speak slowly, loudly. The workers of Europe will tear him down by next month – we can always trust the workers, history shows us this – Europe detests a tyranny, history shows us this, too – and the newsreels will feature some other pathetic shrieker soon, and the world will spin on through space.

III

Decrepits of our age, my wife's and mine, are admitted to the movie theater at reduced cost in the afternoons. It is America's equivalent of the Inuit practice of putting the aged into the wilderness to die. I do not care to go; it makes me feel old as a mummy, and I am uneasy being in darkness, especially during the daylight hours, so few of which can remain to me now. I have always preferred daylight to dusk or dawn. I could never have been like my aunt, a poet.

Lenin predicted that the cinema would be the paramount art of our century, but on this the Comrade seer was uncharacteristically myopic. The fug of cigarette smoke floating over the stalls, purpling in the light-beam, shifting, re-forming, is more remarkable than anything depicted on the screen, and, in its way, more beautiful and true. Foolishness, sentimentality, the commodification of violence. Blacked-up eye-rollers banjoing Mammy. For this carnival of barbarisms, I am invited to pay? Vladimir, what were you thinking?

My wife weeps quietly at the melodramas of love. But I do not weep. I think weeping unmanly. I make use of her absences – her afternoons with Al – to travel down other roads.

IV

We are fortunate, my wife and I, to have been bequeathed a fine house and an income more than adequate to forestall its dilapidation. The resources of Croesus could not prevent our own dilapidation, but still, as I tell her, we fight the fight. We have servants, nurses, valets, laundresses, grooms, maids, physicians, bottle-washers. The more help we have, the dirtier the house. I do not know why that should be so. But it is.

Some years ago, the Head Cook took on the duty of hiring the staff; but either she has no idea of what she is doing, or else – my wife chides me that my theory is mean – she wishes to employ every one of her block-headed cousins. There are days when I see Irish people lurching up and down the staircase and have not the faintest inkling who they are. Ghosts? Tradesmen? The Tuatha de Dannan? They glare at me as though I do not belong beneath this roof. They ask me who *I* am!

On days like that, especially when my wife is out at her movies, I come up here to my roost, to the loft-room I call my study. It is hidden behind a bookshelf with an ingenious hinge. One is safe in here from all Celtic invaders. I like the compactness; I find small rooms comforting. A man can have too much breathing space.

I look at my documents. I think about our children. I am not religious, obviously, but I have my thoughts. Atheism itself is a kind of faith. I find it a profound consolation.

I stare out of the little window at the streetcars and taxicabs; at the messenger-boys and misfits and the policemen sweating into their tunics. And – yes – guilty, Officer – the pretty girls, too. Man does not live by bread alone!

I imagine the avenue as it must have looked in the past – a pasture, then a hunting track, then an undulating road – Manhattan was once hilly, but no one remembers that. Why would anyone have cause to? Wilderness. Field. Lane. Highway. Then the long, splendid boulevard, the ribbon of macadam, along which the young of our city marched away to the War. As they will, I suppose, in the future.

V

When I open up my boxes, a smell of the long-ago arises. Fungal. Old parchments. A suggestion of sealing wax. The past breaks in the air like an exploding spore. It fills my waning eyes. I breathe it into my lungs. I fancy that I can sense it puff through my blood. Vlad, you old impaler, I think of it as my opiate. As the movies are to my wife.

My pastime, I suppose. A rich man needs a diversion – otherwise he grows idle and dies. Some millionaires amass paintings, others rare furniture, antiques. Odd, what we shore against the inevitable. My pursuit has been to collect as much as I can nose up of James O'Keeffe and the boy Jeddo Mooney, those long-forgotten actors from America's Civil War, who somehow contain in themselves, so it seems to their collector, everything larger of war.

I have articles, memorabilia, broadsides, maps, etchings, sketches, balladry, photographs. I believe I own a copy of every text that ever mentioned them in the public prints of the United States. And I have other materials, too, of a more private nature. Journals. Personal writings. Correspondence and so forth. Even highly secret papers, classified documents. Every door can be opened, provided, of course, that one is willing to pay the price of admission. The trick, as with all quests, is finding the door. Usually it is just where you thought it would be.

I am ridiculous? Fixated? My wife has found an ally! Is it any more preposterous than collecting butterflies or beer steins or the heads of shot quadrupeds or – Heaven help us – stamps? My wife insists it is. She thinks me morbid, obsessive. *Et tu*, respected Reader: what do you collect? Books, do you tell me? My wife likes those. But I do not share her enthusiasm for the invented story; its neatness, its pretenses, its want of contradictory grain. Twain, the great contriver, put it remarkably well. Little wonder the truth is stranger than fiction: Fiction has to make sense.

I catalog my papers. It gives me pleasure to look at them. (Viennese explanations are possible, no doubt.) Yes, the inks have faded now; many of the binding-ribbons are frayed. It grows stiflingly hot in my cubbyhole in a Manhattan summer. Humidity is not good for old-fashioned paper, which often was made of cotton-rag and sometimes hemp; beaten, mashed to pulp, and then molded into quoins. Paper, alas, is a living material. Like all living things, it will die.

VI

My collection includes forgeries – I suppose that is inevitable – but only a couple and even those are not entirely without interest. There is always a little dishonesty when money is offered for old things. It should not bother us too much. It speaks to human enterprise. And I am glad to have his medals, most of which have been certified genuine, though many are so verdigrised as to be almost illegible now. Sometimes – I blush – I have pinned them to my dressing-robe and saluted myself a moment in the pier glass.

I rummage these withered foolscaps – they are like an octogenarian's skin – foxed, mottled, stippled with age. I have compared them to my own skin as a matter of fact. There are days when their contents seem sharp as wounds, and others when their meanings retreat. Those days are hard. One feels somehow alone. It is as though they treat of people who never existed: a runaway boy and those who tried to love him. O'Keeffe, I think, would have found them a fascination, would have pored over every nuance, for he was greatly attuned to language. He loved the arrangement, the deployment of words, the things they can suggest without ever directly stating. He was a man who knew well how a character is constructed. It is a pity he never completed his book.

Look at these packets of nothings. Stooks of decaying paper. Often my wife implores me to consign them to the trash. They have caused more quarrels between us; she grows testy when I mention them. Better you should have married a library, she says. Better you should have married a *junkshop*. But women rarely make good collectors, in truth. They do not appear to experience that need.

'The past is a far riverbank,' Lucia once wrote. 'We know it is there, for we can see it, and are close to it. But the water makes it always unreachable.' For me, that is not so. My papers are the stepping-stones. A precarious traverse – but possible.

At the end of a session of study, I box them. Soon I will be boxed, too, and stored away. The attic will be empty, except for the spider-webs. I will gather the dust that I am. My regret, before the silence, is that I never walked the squares of that faraway capital to which I have long yearned to make a pilgrimage. But by the time my wife acceded, already we were too old. The journey would have been dangerous that winter. In any case, once there, I would have found it difficult to return. I thought of it as my elephant's graveyard. I do not believe the reactionary newspapers, though friends tell me I should. But I cannot, so sometimes we quarrel. To have ever breathed the air of man's future made flesh, the Union of Soviet Socialist Republics – ah, beloved, I tarried too long. But to know you are there and will always be there has consoled my faithless dotage.

VII

As for Winterton's fate, I wish I could tell you more of it. Ernest Dean was the name of the border guard on the Canada side who noticed a miner crossing stealthily with a pack mule. The beast was weighted heavily with rough canvas sacks. Gold, said the miner. He had struck lucky. Prospectors did not commonly have a fine Bostonian accent. This one was acting suspiciously. When challenged, he overcame the guard, tied him up ('apologizing as he did so') and walked calmly into the Canadian night. The fugitive's face was described by hapless Dean as showing the marks of numerous burns.

It was revealed some years ago that he had been married at least twice: legally, in Cuba, as Peter John Williamson, then bigamously in Chicago, as William Paul Harris. A cartographer trained in the British Army, he had managed to flee Scotland when about to be arrested for the poisoning of a woman in Glasgow. The wounds he bore were not sustained during the American Civil War, at least not in any battle with southerners. On the infamous night of July 13th, 1863, he was attacked by a mob of New York-Irish immigrants. Angered by the proposed draft, by which they were disproportionately affected, they had burned a Negro orphanage and committed many other horrific crimes. Union soldiers and black New Yorkers were savaged by the rioters. They had been lynching an elderly porter when Winterton intervened to stop them, in his uniform but alone and unarmed. They kicked him unconscious before setting him alight. The riot would not be the last time in the American story when those who felt powerless turned their hatred on the weakest and the innocent would be murdered in the streets. One of the most shameful atrocities in the history of Irish-America, it does not feature, to my knowledge, in Irish balladry.

Elizabeth Longstreet remained in the Territory almost seven more years, working mainly as a laundress in Edwardstown. In 1872, she married Prospero Leavensworth, a freed slave of Texas who had been a soldier in the War. For some years she had been completely blind, so that she had never seen Prospero Leavensworth, a fact she would often make jokes about. He was a kindly and quiet man, and their marriage was happy. They migrated to Liberia, on the west coast of Africa, where Leavensworth established a small enterprise exporting palm oil. Their son, Theobald Wolfe Leavensworth, was born and raised in Monrovia, at the age of twenty-six becoming a doctor in the city, then a member of the Liberian Government. His mother, an elder of the Presbyterian Church, was given a lay-chaplaincy among women patients at Monrovia Asylum, a position that cannot have been easy but which she described as 'the deepest blessing', and in which she did remarkable things. She died in November 1928. In the year of her death she had been interviewed by a Reverend William L.R. Trees, who possessed the only Edison recording machine in Liberia. The transcript abounds with the *yassuhs* and *laud-hab-murcies* that are not unusual in such documents when the speakers are black. Most of these I have taken the liberty of silently retranslating, leaving only a few examples of the original transcriber's work – more as an illustration of how such transcripts were constructed than of how standard Southern-American English was ever spoken. I have a photograph of her above my desk, and one brief letter. It is signed: 'Free at last: Elizabeth.'

Jeddo Mooney remained in the Fort Stornaway jailhouse for almost eighteen months after the night he shot his protector James O'Keeffe. His hands were shackled; the lawmen gagged him with a leather strap. Some whipped him when there was nothing else to do. Twice he was half-hanged from the roofbeams of the jail. The three men responsible were later disciplined.

Every couple of weeks they would trolley him to the home of a minister of religion in the town. He refused to have the boy in his church, though the collection plate would have been heavied by such an appearance. The Reverend would read from the Bible as the boy lay on the carpet; his wife would vamp hymns on the pianoforte. Their redemptive effect was limited, but the boy enjoyed listening to the stories, many of which were about warfare and cruelty and murder, and were thus the kind of narratives to which boys liked to listen in those distant, more literate days.

He became – how to term it? – a sort of amusement to the intrepid of the Territory, who would bribe the more corruptible of the guards to be allowed to see him. A dime bought you two minutes, a quarter twenty.

Had you paid them ten dollars, they would have allowed you to skin him alive. His very name became a byword for wickedness in the locale. The phrase 'As bad as Jeddo' appeared in local speech and fiction. 'Crazy as Jailhouse Mooney' was a variant.

Sundays, especially, were popular for visits. The devil-boy drew a good house on the Sabbath. He would toss his evil head and flash his angry eyes; this would be greeted as that moment in the zoo when the crocodile suddenly blinks from the mud. It was still a few decades before America had the movies. Frontiersmen had to make their own fun.

Somewhere among my collection I have a daguerreotype of the boy, made by unknown persons during his imprisonment. He has been stripped and hooded and is kneeling in a latrine. There are worse picturings, too, but I do not like to think of them. Some I have destroyed. I love my country. In any nation founded on civil war, monstrous things become possible. We have only to look at Ireland to know it. Kill your brother and there are few deaths unimaginable.

VIII

I have wondered what would have happened had the Confederacy triumphed. I suppose that this whole land-mass would be a South America now – Washington a São Paulo, Pennsylvania a Buenos Aires – which a handful of *familias* would rule as a fiefdom while the masses grubbed the sewers for their leftovers. The slums and *favelas* would be vast, I would have thought; would stretch from the Everglades to Alaska. American soldiers, often the children of immigrants, have done brutal and terrifying and unforgivable acts. Others have done great and courageous acts. I am humbled by those who fought with honor, often knowing their death was a certainty. Had they not, my country's emblems would be the bullwhip and the branding iron, and the giantess standing sentry over the Verrazanno Narrows would be known as the Statue of Tyranny.

IX

Mother Russia. Britannia. Cathleen ni Houlihan. Strange, how our nations are embodied as women, when our women suffer so much of cruelty. An atonement, perhaps. Or a further cruelty. Yet the emblem of our better angels is a woman. Walking roads she does not know, out of nothing but loyalty. Seeking out the child she yearns to be here, but all the time knowing he is lost. There will never be a statue of Eliza Duane Mooney. A sculptor cannot represent blood.

X

It was Marshal Ignatius Gilchrist who saved the boy from hanging. ('Sixguns Iggy,' he was called in the War, a nickname he would loathe to the end of his life, once suing a newspaperman who had printed it.) He testified on oath that O'Keeffe was already close to death when the child had fired on him that night. Nor was it provable that the boy had discharged the shot which punctured the Governor's abdomen. It could not have been provable, for the boy had not done it. O'Keeffe was fatally shot by Cole John McLaurenson, who died less than sixty seconds later, with the last of his comrades. Many songs would be sung about his deeds in the west. Some of them seem ten feet long.

Attorneys came from St Louis with portmanteaux full of law books. Doctors, professors, magistrates, reformers. Justice Carney himself wrote a passionate treatise on the boy's case: *The Speechless Child of War*. The autographed MS is in my collection, of course. One notary journeyed all the way from Boston to the Territory. He was a plump-faced, jolly, slightly malodorous man, who grew ever more jocular as he drifted further out of his depth. Sadly, as he made his way back home to the east, he was murdered during a stagecoach robbery for which no one was ever indicted.

It is doubtful, in any case, that he could have helped the boy much. There might have been an acquittal to charges, had they ever been laid. But it was made clear to the child often, and for reasons he understood, that he would never live to see adulthood. The law might not know how to deal with his crime. But there were other modes of justice on the frontier.

XI

Eliza Duane Mooney was buried at Judas's Field, a pit used by slaughtermen for the dumping of knackered horses. No priest was available, or none would come to such a verminous outskirt. Neither was there a headstone to mark her place of rest, nor even a few dollars' worth

447

of government coffin. She was wrapped in the rags of a Confederate banner, which one of the lawmen had recently confiscated from a miner; then thrown in the trench, and burned. These obsequies her only brother was forced at gunpoint to watch, and then he was returned to his cell.

That night, the boy had a dream of his mother and Louisiana, of the black metal porticoes of the French Quarter in New Orleans. It seemed that he saw her on a Mardi Gras morning, tossing handfuls of confetti, in a nimbus of streamers, when she was young and hopeful for her American life. But since he never saw her that way, he knew it was a dream. He was never in New Orleans with his mother, or anyone else. It was always the city in the distance.

XII

A hard history. A tale of war. Then came the act that ennobles this bleak tale, shading it, perhaps, to a love story.

On a hot June morning in 1868, the boy was informed in his cell that a gentleman had come forward to take him for legal adoption. A Yankee industrialist, he had been advised not to involve himself; indeed had been so advised by everyone he had asked. But he had disregarded his counselors. He was a stubborn sort of man. The rich can afford to be obstinate.

The party left Fort Stornaway at midnight, the boy and five guards, each marshal armed like a gladiator. To restrain the dangerous prisoner, they used a chain made for runaway slaves. It choked you if you attempted to move. His ankles were manacled. He wore handcuffs and a hood. He was shackled by his waist to three cannonballs. He was incapable of speech, but they gagged him anyway, and often stubbed their cheroots on his face.

They traveled by night, always by night, as Americans slept, unknowing. There was a fear of rioting, if people saw the identity of the passenger. Reconstruction was not a happy time for our country.

He was delivered to an attorney's office in Utica, New York, and there met the representatives of his protector. He was taken into a prosperous household at New York City, where he lived for a time with the stable-grooms. A bout of scarlet fever brought about his removal. The doctors said his death was a certainty. He awoke to the gaze of two people to whom he had never spoken a word but who had nursed him back from death. Estafanía McLelland and her father, Peter. Difficult individuals the both, in numerous ways. But they would not see a child die in a stable.

Lucia was in Spain when the boy almost died. On her return, she agreed that he remain in the house, where he worked for some years in the kitchens or the cellars, rarely being permitted upstairs. Sometimes he saw Lucia through the rails of a gate. He was told not to address her if he did. He blacked her shoes. He groomed her horses. He slept under the protection of her father. You do not believe this, I know; the boy did not either. Nevertheless, it happened. There were stranger acts of compassion in our country in those years. Not forgiveness, perhaps. But mercy, perhaps. A sense of responsibility, clothed often in silence; but no less real for that.

Habited in adequate clothes, fed three times a day, given a bed in which to sleep, shelter from the elements, he presently regained the power of speech and became, if not happy, more controlled. Maurice Hall, a Scotsman, a butler who attended libraries, took him under his wing and the child proved a quick-witted student. But when that kindly man died, the boy took it hard and some of his old ways returned. Peter McLelland insisted a tutor be found for him. None lasted long. Their charge was too mercurial, given to fits of raging insolence or tearfulness. No scholarly gentleman saw any hope for his betterment. It was Lucia who accepted the role.

Every weekday they worked in her private library, at books and parchments, old musical scores. Always they were alone, at Lucia's insistence. She would have no helpmate, not even her father. Her brothers were not permitted to enter. Slowly he learned, this boy who had caused her great pain. Patiently, resolvedly, she helped him. That room in Manhattan saw remarkable solidarities as the seasons gave way to years. Did she forgive? We must suppose so. She did not speak of her feelings. Nor ever, so far as I know, and I have studied all her surviving papers, did she commit her private motivations to paper. These are complicated questions. Perhaps she wanted forgiveness herself. Those from whom we seek mercy are sometimes not the ones who can give it, but since they are present in our lives, we ask them. An onerous burden. We see ghosts in one another. But when I picture her guiding that boy from the darkness he inhabited, I believe that human life is worthwhile.

For music Jeddo Mooney showed a particular facility, and also, perhaps curiously, for languages. By the time he was eighteen he had French enough to make a way, could read a children's psalter in Spanish, conjugate simpler verbs in Latin. Gradually he lost the drawl and whaang of Louisiana; his vowels became flatter, and he came to speak like a princeling. He still could be eccentric, although, as with many perceived eccentricities, Jeddo Mooney's, if considered, spoke volumes. Somewhere along his path, he began to refer to various members of his adoptive establishment by fondly familial designations. Peter McLelland became 'Uncle', his widowed sister 'Aunt Winfield', their aged mother '*Abuela*', the Spanish term for a grandmother; though I imagine she must have been uneasy with such an induction. That formidable old lady disliked what she termed 'the primitive tongues' and would grin rather bleakly when subjected to them. But the boy's curious habit was to name everyone in the household a relation, and, by all accounts, nobody objected. The cook and the housemaid shared titular aunthood with practically every female who remained more than an hour on the premises, while the groomsman, a Michael Sweeney, of the County Roscommon, was named affectionately 'Uncle Mikey' or 'Mickser'. Sweeney, for his part, referred to the youth as 'Little Cuz'. A genealogist visiting the house would have been perplexed.

Some notoriety about events in the Territory still persisted; there was talk of a disreputable journalist writing a muck-raking book about them. It was put to the boy by a concerned Peter McLelland that he might consider changing his name. He adopted, with gratitude, the surname of his protector, and with it went out into the world. In time he would graduate from a college overseas, would marry and have three children, whom Peter McLelland idolized. I have been told that that strict old gentleman, who spoke rarely of his affections, had come to regard his ward almost as a son.

As for Lucia-Cruz McLelland, certain readers will know her history. The loss of her and O'Keeffe's child – she died at five months, María-Elena – brought an anguish from which I think she never quite recovered. But other griefs she overcame with the dauntless love of life that everyone who knew her was touched by. She was among the first women to receive a doctorate from Harvard University, and became one of the *stellae minorae* of American poetry: initially under the pseudonym Charles Gimenez Carroll, and later, as a translator, under her own pre-marital name, the revelation of which she was often to regret, for she truly had no craving to be recognized. She published two capable novels

– Gramercy Park and *The Rivers* (a third, *Ricardo Connolly*, she rewrote many times before ultimately destroying as unsalvageable) but poetry brought her the kind of small celebrity then available in American letters. Her translations of the lyrics of that great Nicaraguan, Félix Rubén García Sarmiento, known to aficionados of literature as Rubén Darío, became the standard texts in English. Her method of dealing with praise was to ridicule it utterly. It was her habit to read every sentence of a commendatory review mentally inserting the word 'not'. I think she felt admiration to be a dangerous drug; especially when dispensed to a writer. But that may have been something of a pose, of course. Perhaps marriage had taught her self-protectiveness. A sketchy biographical monograph of her was published in 1910. As its author, I do not especially recommend it.

Men always loved her, and she adored them, too. There were affairs that would have made Floria Tosca seem a model of prudence. She received many proposals, one from Darío himself, who, though many years her junior, stormed her with polysyllabic declarations of ardor. ('As he did with almost every woman he knew,' she often said. 'Especially after his marriage.') She married again, briefly; the relationship was not happy. For private reasons, I do not wish to give an account of it here. O'Keeffe was the husband she was meant to have, she came to feel, and as she aged she became rather Latina and old-fashioned about such matters. Strange to say, perhaps; but in many ways I think of Lucia as the most intensely traditional Roman Catholic I have known.

In her later years she had a close companion with whom she would go walking or attend recitals. A widower, he had been a cavalry officer in the War. I believe it was an intimate and tender friendship, but when it became clear that he, too, entertained wishes for legalization, he was gently but purposefully dismissed. He was the Lieutenant who had questioned her at the Fort Stornaway Tribunal. Lucia used to call him *El Interrogador*.

She died, eleven years ago, at Wexford, Ireland, a city she visited three times, and whose people loved her dearly. Her last thoughts were of James O'Keeffe, that most elusive man. She felt he was in the house. She seemed happy. She requested to be lifted to a window-seat he had often mentioned – from where, in childhood, he had watched the American grain-ships in the harbor – and it was there that she passed away, tranquilly, without much pain, in the November of her ninety-third year.

XIII

There are very few veterans of O'Keeffe's brigade living now, but there are some still among us, and they should never be forgotten. They congregate every year on the Fourth of July and march down Fifth Avenue to Washington Square Park. There a blessing is given and Drum-Taps is played. There are speeches, of course. An aged cannon is fired. Former Confederates sometimes attend, old Irishmen in grays and drabs, clutching sandwich-bags and rosaries; uneasy in this northern city. I have heard the rebel yell in Washington Square Park as the enemies grit false teeth and shake hands.

When the official ceremony is over, those Con O'Keeffes who feel able – a surprisingly considerable number, given their age and ill health – gather again into formation. They process down the Broadway to Battery Park, a tortuous walk in a Manhattan July. Past dime stores and shoe-shines and tattoo parlors and barrooms, through the dirty grit of high summer. Past those vertebrate turrets that are the glory of our architects – and of all of us, for they speak of indomitable New York. Passers-by stare. Some of the storekeepers offer water, but I have rarely seen a marcher break step to accept it. They are old, but they walk, and some are in wheelchairs. Many are amputees; others are blind. The young sometimes go with them – great-grandchildren, I suppose – leading the old by the hems of their uniforms. At the time of the War, these frail men were children. Now they seem childlike again.

By the walls of the Battery, a silent prayer is offered. It is always silent, I do not know why. A wreath of lilies is blessed and thrown into the harbor, from where so many of their hungry forefathers first set foot on America. They sing the martial written for them in the American Civil War, reputedly by Lucia, but really, I think, by O'Keeffe:

> *We are marching for the Union in the blue and in the green;*
> *All are sworn to loft in gallant hand the sword of honor keen,*

Etcetera.

The last time I witnessed these rites, in July last year, a hurrah was given out for a small brotherhood of Americans who had gone the previous winter to fight Fascism in Europe. Some Irish were among them; others would join them, at Jarama, at Zaragoza, at Madrid and Valencia. Heroes to some, villains to others, they were sometimes called

Communists in the press. They organized under the banner of an assassinated revolutionary. The Abraham Lincoln Brigade.

XIV

Strange stories continued to adhere to the memory of O'Keeffe. In 1902, at Wichita, Kansas, a dying Alabaman thief made a confession to a preacher that he had pulled the wounded Governor from the Missouri still alive, but had strangled him an hour later when he realized who he was, and buried him in a mound of stones. This baroque was said to have occurred four miles downriver of Fort Stornaway, in a narrow rocky inlet where the Alabaman had been prospecting for silver. Federal marshals were summoned to the fading hobo's bedside, but he recovered unexpectedly and withdrew his declaration, insisting he had been in the grip of a delirium when he made it and had no recollection of ever having seen the Missouri. Troopers were sent anyway, to reconnoiter the site he had mentioned. No body was found, and no grave.

More weirdly, there is the story of the Missouri Mummy. In 1904, two sweethearts were keeping company near the northern bank of the river at Fort Meade, when the boy lost his footing, slipped down a bank, and happened upon a gruesome find. What appeared to be a human body wrapped entirely in muddied bandages was lying in a leaf-filled hollow at the foot of an undercliff. A post-mortem revealed that the corpse was that of a middle-aged man, five feet ten in height, 'with a prominent chin', but there was no way of knowing how long he had lain there, nor how he had met his demise. The remains had been eviscerated before being swathed in the cloths, a practice believed common among certain native peoples. The story ripped around the territory that O'Keeffe had been found at last, that the initials 'JCO'K' were still discernible on a laundry tag, but there was absolutely no proof of anything so cinematic. One detects the seasoning touch of some western newspaperman. The Mummy was stolen from the hospital where it had been examined by the coroner and was later said to have turned up in a traveling carnival of gypsies. They exhibited it, reportedly, at twenty cents a time (a buck was the cost of being photographed with it sitting on your lap) before eventually, when the flies and the road-life took effect, dumping it in the Ohio River. That is a shame. I should have liked to buy it for my collection. But it might have been a purchase too far for my wife.

¿Quién Sabe? as Lucia's least unknown poem is entitled. And I will leave you with a strange story of my own.

A good many years ago, I will not say how many, I was in the little town of San Juan del Sur, Nicaragua, for a purpose I prefer not to disclose.

San Juan is a tiny but not unattractive pueblo, on a horseshoe-shaped cove near the *frontera* with Costa Rica. In my memory there is a volcano on the northern horizon, stark, black, still smoking after two hundred years, but perhaps I am confused – I have no notes by my hand. The night is very late as I write.

There are fincas and coffee fields and the huts of campesinos, and there is a priest's house that is said to be haunted. Nearby rise the headwaters of a mighty river that flows hundreds of miles eastward, into the Lago de Nicaragua (*Mar dulce*, the locals call it – 'the sweet sea') then on through treacherous jungle, through mangrove swamps never mapped, all the way east to the Costa Atlantica, the region of that nation where the people are black and speak English with a vaguely cockney inflection. Not Mestizos or Indians, they are the descendants of Caribbean slaves. Bluefields is the name of their town.

From that Mosquito Elysium, so the San Juan people told me, once a year would come a boat bearing a strange old 'Caudillo' – their word for a knight or an owner of lands, although it can also mean a strong man, a ruler. He was old as Adam's father, in their colorful parlance. His face bore a million lines. His spectacles were much remarked upon, for their lenses were the blackish purple of deadly nightshade – they appeared to have been fashioned from the bottoms of wine bottles. He would be carried through the town in the arms of his servant, to the cantina of a moneylender on the Calle Masaya in the smugglers' quarter. There he would pawn a purseful of gemstones. Uncut Missouri sapphires.

Every year it was the same. A clutch of Yogo sapphires. He seemed to have an inexhaustible supply. He was not paid their worth – the moneylender always swindled him – but every year without fail he returned. He signed no paper, requested no receipt, never once haggled, always accepted the offered robbery. Indeed, he did not speak at all to the pawnbroker or his wife, leaving all verbal intercourse to the *sirviente*. This done, he would be carried to the whitewashed church and rest in its coolness an hour. No one ever saw him kneel; he would sit upright as a tombstone, crumpled sombreiro in his lap. A couple of notes from his billfold he would give to the servant, who would hand them to the Padre or place them in the poorbox. *Para los niños y las mujeres que tienen hambre*, the box was marked. For the children and women who are hungry. And once – so it was told me by a person who knew – the servant asked a nun who was placing malinche flowers on the altar could he beg a cup of water for his elderly master, who was greatly distressed by the heat. The good woman found a pitcher and gave it to the servant, who blessed her, and no more was said. That night, as she was sweeping the aisles of the church, she found a handkerchief that had been left on the offertory table. It had been carefully folded, placed under a prayerbook. It contained fifteen one-hundred-dollar bills.

He and his man were 'como *Quijote y Sancho Panza*'. Ancient and slow and comical in their seriousness. He wore a dress-sword in a rusting and shabbily tasseled scabbard; the black lace gloves of a Don. Even the beggars stared as he was borne through the hot dust, perspiring in his ebon-black broadcloth. Dogs and yapping children would attend the curious progress, back to the jetty and the panga-boat. He would be propped by the servant on its bowed old bench, sword across his knees, black lenses on his face; then both men would take up the heavy oaken oars and wordlessly push for the east.

The people could never understand why he came all this way. The voyage was so dangerous. The jungle could kill you. Why not send a messenger, some little *chacho* from Bluefields, who would happily do this errand for a few cordobas and a carouse? His answer to that question was the only instance anyone could remember where he had uttered a sentence in the town.

'*Un hombre con acento cockney no es de fiar con el dinero.*' A man with a cockney accent is not to be trusted with money.

He would be due in a month or so, so the cantina-keeper told me; for usually he arrived in July, before the rains came on. Perhaps I should wait, if I wanted to meet him? *Un mes. Dos meses. No más, hombre*. I considered it seriously. But I did not wait. It would probably not have been him. I would have been disappointed.

I prefer to imagine him among the shanties of Bluefields, gazing out on the Atlantic, dreaming of Dulcinea. Tilting at the beacons with his unholy stare, getting drunk on Los Flores rum. A fancy, I know. Rhetoric, nothing more. There is little doubt that he died in the Missouri.

The ballad of War does honor to the departed. This has been a story of some who endured. Lucia-Cruz McLelland, who is buried in Ireland;

Elizabeth Longstreet, who is buried in Africa; and silent Jeddo Mooney, a boy who changed his surname, whose silence is broken by having been your narrator:

Jeremiah Daniel McLelland,
Professor Emeritus, Columbia.
1, the Fifth Avenue, New York.
Christmas Eve, 1937

ACKNOWLEDGEMENTS

I thank my beloved Anne-Marie Casey, my editor Geoff Mulligan, my book agent Carole Blake and screenwriting agent Conrad Williams, both at Blake Friedmann Literary Agency in London, and Jewerl Ross at Silent R Management, Los Angeles. In 2005/06 I was a Fellow at the New York Public Library's Dorothy and Lewis B. Cullman Center for Scholars and Writers; I thank the staff, the librarians and my colleagues for endless kindnesses, and Gary Forney, Jon Axline, Lenore Puhek and staff at the Montana Historical Archive for their hospitality during a research trip I made to Montana in December 2005. That state is an infinitely more welcoming and beautiful place than the fictional and somewhat differently located Territory described in this novel. I thank Patricia Normanly for sending me unpublished letters of an Irish soldier who died at Gettysburg, Rachid Diallo for his booklet *Time Travellers: the American Civil War,* James Kincaid (Univ of Southern California), Declan Kiberd and Anthony Roche (Univ College Dublin), staff of UCD Library, John M. Hearne, Ruan O'Donnell (Univ of Limerick), and Justin Furlong (National Library of Ireland). For translation assistance: Julia Carty, Miryam Delgado, Anthony Glavin, Eanna O'Lochlainn, Dr Seán Ó Riain, Hugo Hamilton and Kevin Holohan. I am greatly indebted to my father Seán O'Connor, Monica Casey, Eimear O'Connor, Judy Finnegan, Richard Madely, Amanda Ross, Natalie Fox, Beth Humphries, Madeleine Keane, Briony Everroad and Rosa Bruno, and to Peter Ward, who designed this book with such skill and care. 'Cochise and Johnny Thunders' is a rewriting of 'Morrissey and the Russian Sailor', recorded by Connemara *Sean-Nós* singer Seosamh O'hÉanaí (Joe Heaney) and others. 'Western Thunders Blues' is influenced by Huddie Ledbetter's 'Out on the Western Plain' (exquisitely recorded by the late Rory Gallagher). Derek Warfield and David Kincaid have recorded Irish ballads of the Civil War. The Works Progress Administration recorded interviews with former slaves in the 1930s; *The Emergence of Black English: text and commentary,* eds. Bailey, Maynor, Cukor-Avila, includes transcripts and discussions of the many questions they raise. Some orthographic elements of the transcripts appear in the recollections of Elizabeth Longstreet.

Unless otherwise indicated, photographs are on glass, wet collodion, from the Library of Congress collection 'Selected Civil War Photographs, 1861-1865' (call-numbers below), mostly created 'under the supervision of Mathew Brady'. I thank Kathryn Blackwell at the Reference Section. The Library of Congress advises that there are no known restrictions on publication. Page 1: 'Petersburg, Va. Row of stacked Federal rifles; houses beyond', April 3, 1865. LC-B811-3229. P. 17: Originally titled 'Candidates for the Board of Education Opposed to Reading the Bible in Schools'. Viewable at www.assumption.edu/acad, credited as *Harper's Weekly*, '1850s'. P. 61: 'Chattanooga, Tenn., vicinity. Tripod signal erected by Capts. Dorr and Donn of U.S. Coast Survey at Pulpit Rock on Lookout Mountain', 1864? LC-B811-3661. P. 103: 'Petersburg, Va. Confederate fortifications with chevaux-de-frise beyond', 1865. LC-B811- 3302. P. 118: 'Unknown location. Embalming surgeon at work on soldier's body', between 1860 and 1865. LC-B811-2531. P. 159: 'White Oak Swamp, Va. View', between May and August 1862. LC-B811-2601. P. 191: Photograph of drawing of slave punishment apparatus. LC-USZ62-31864. P. 233: 'James River, Va. Butler's

dredge-boat, sunk by a Confederate shell on Thanksgiving Day, 1864', LC-B811-2550.
P. 283: 'Erin Go Bray', print, published by William Holland, London, March 1799.
P. 379: 'Portrait of Boy Soldier.' Morris Gallery of the Cumberland, Nashville,
Tennessee, between 1860 and 1865, re-photographed 1961, Elsie G. Redman, LC-B8184-
10573. **P. 408**: 'Nashville, Tenn. Fortified railroad bridge across Cumberland River' by
George N. Barnard, 1864. LC-B811- 2642. **P. 437**: 'Portrait of a soldier group', between
1860 and 1865, re-photographed 1961. Copy of undated photo made by LC of tintype.
G.K. Holmes, Cornwall Bridge, Conn. Photographic print. LC-B8184-10694.

Any Civil War source-list must include Shelby Foote's masterpiece *The Civil War: A
Narrative*, and Ken Burns' magnificent PBS documentary on the conflict. A chronol-
ogy, by Don Harvey, of all the war's engagements, is at http://users.aol.com/dlharvey.
Redemption Falls is a work of fiction, taking license with historical and geographical
fact, and making no claim to textbook reliability. More than a hundred thousand
Irish immigrants participated in the war, but the Irish Brigade of these pages is not
the famous 69th New York and Jeddo Mooney's contingent is not based on any one
real battalion. Students of Irish history will have noted that elements of James
O'Keeffe's curriculum vitae have echoes in that of Thomas F. Meagher (see the
latter's *Memoirs, Comprising the Leading Events of his Career Chronologically
Arranged, With Selections From his Speeches, Lectures and Miscellaneous Writings*,
1892), but O'Keeffe is as fictional as everyone else in this novel and is not a
camouflaged version of any real person. Well-researched works on TFM and his
friends include Gary Forney's *Thomas Francis Meagher*, John M. Hearne and Rory T.
Cornish, eds., *Thomas Francis Meagher, The Making of an Irish American*, Thomas
Keneally's *American Scoundrel*, William H. Lamers' *The Thunder Maker*, Kirk
Mitchell's *Fredericksburg*, Lenore Puhek's *The River's Edge*, Reg Watson's *The Life
and Times of Thomas Francis Meagher* and Richard S. Wheeler's *The Exile*. Other
works on Irish combatants include Susan Provost Beller, *Never Were Men So Brave:
The Irish Brigade During The Civil War*, Frank A. Boyle, *A Party of Mad Fellows: The
Story of the Irish Regiments in the Army of the Potomac*; William J.K. Beaudot, ed., *An
Irishman in the Iron Brigade: The Civil War Memoirs of James P. Sullivan, Sergt.,
Company K, 6th Wisconsin Volunteers*; Joseph G. Bilby, *The Irish Brigade in the Civil
War: The 69th New York and Other Irish Regiments of the Army of the Potomac*;
William Corby, *Memoirs of Chaplain Life: Three Years With the Irish Brigade in the
Army of the Potomac*; James P. Gannon, *Irish Rebels, Confederate Tigers: The 6th
Louisiana Volunteers, 1861-1865*; Ed Gleeson, *Rebel Sons of Erin: A Civil War Unit
History of the Tenth Tennessee Infantry Regiment (Irish) Confederate States Volunteers*;
*Commanding Boston's Irish Ninth: The Civil War Letters of Colonel Patrick R. Guiney,
Ninth Massachusetts Volunteer Infantry*; Lawrence Frederick Kohl, ed., *Irish Green
and Union Blue: The Civil War Letters of Peter Welsh, Color Sergeant 28th
Massachusetts Volunteers*; Daniel George Macnamara, ed., *The History of the Ninth
Regiment: Massachusetts Volunteer Infantry, June 1861–June 1864*; John Mahon, *New
York's Fighting Sixty-Ninth: A Regimental History of Service in the Civil War's Irish
Brigade & the Great War's Rainbow Division*; Kelly J. O'Grady, *Clear the Confederate
Way!: The Irish in the Army of Northern Virginia*; J. Vincent Noonan, *Forty Rounds :
An Irish Regiment in the Civil War*; Philip T. Tucker, *The Confederate Irish*.

Deepest thanks to my beloved sons, James (7) and Marcus (3), for tolerating their
father's absences during the writing of this novel, and for providing him with
frequent demonstrations of the rebel yell. To them, the last hooraw.